WHERE THE WATER RAGES

JACQUELYN SILL

What readers are saying about *Where the Water Rages*

Where the Water Rages will keep you reading beyond where you thought you would stop. In her own personal, passionate language, Jacquelyn Sill combines a universal spirituality with gritty realism. In the end, triumphant heroism will win your heart.

-Bruce Gevirtzman
Professor, California State University, Fullerton, California
Author, *An Intimate Understanding of Teenagers—Shaking Hands with Aliens, Straight Talk to Teachers,* and *Audacious Cures for America's Ailing Schools*

Where the Water Rages is a beautifully written novel, taking the reader through the full spectrum of emotions. Each main character pulls you in like a magnet. You are immediately immersed in the mind of the child and her plight, begging for her to be rescued, feeling all that she feels. There are moments of high suspense, where you find yourself reading at lightning speed to see what will unfold, and moments where your heart feels strangled for all that is lost. There are moments of hope, miracles, and restoration as well as unexpected humor where you need it most to cut through thick tension. It is an honor to read and recommend this novel to readers.

-Christina Armentrout
Children's Director & Educator, Central Christian Church, Lancaster, California

From the very first pages, I was drawn into the stories of Noi, Kimly, and Dak. *Where the Water Rages* has that "can't put it down" quality that marks every great book. From the romance and adventure to the eye opening and real look into the thriving sex trade in Southeast Asia, Jacquelyn Sill manages to provide deep insight to a relevant issue plaguing our world today, all the while speaking deep biblical truth about God's unrelenting pursuit of each one of us.

-Charlene Heydorn
Redeeming Love Founder and CEO. Redeeming Love provides a home and resources for survivors of sex trafficking in the U.S.

Where the Water Rages is both entertaining and thought-provoking. Jacquelyn Sill does an amazing job of weaving together a story that keeps you wanting more while at the same time opening the eyes of her readers to the tragedy of human-trafficking around the world. It is a story of hope, courage, and redemption. Whether held captive by a literal slave trader or the painful memory of a past mistake, there is freedom for those who have courage to face their captors head-on.

-Jennifer Aufrecht
Staff Member at Christ's Church of the Valley, San Dimas, California

Jacquelyn Sill is a bright new talent who peers deeply into the human soul. Her work brings to life a dark corner of existence and deepens our understanding of the horrors of human trafficking. She does not shy away from the nuances of attraction, love and grief and her complex characters are drawn with profound depth, understanding and compassion. *Where the Water Rages* is a universal story that renders exquisitely all of the moments and decisions that make up our quest as we figure out who we are and where we are going.

-Tehila Lieberman
Editor, THL Final Copy
Author, *Venus in the Afternoon,* Winner of the Katherine Anne Porter Prize in Short Fiction

Published by KHARIS PUBLISHING, imprint of
KHARIS MEDIA LLC

Copyright © 2016 Jacquelyn Sill

ISBN-10: 0-9971176-9-9
ISBN-13: 978-0-9971176-9-1

All KHARIS PUBLISHING products are available at special quantity
discounts for bulk purchase for sales promotions, premiums, fund-
raising, and educational needs. For details, write:

Kharis Publishing
709 SW Elmside Drive
Bentonville,
AR 72712
Tel: 1-479-903-8160
info@kharispublishing.com
www.kharispublishing.com

DEDICATION

For the children, the voiceless.

ACKNOWLEDGMENTS

I am grateful this experience arrived at the point where I can formally thank the following people for the part they each played as *The Trade* became *Kimly's Trade* and finally evolved into *Where the Water Rages, a Novel.*

Jennifer Aufrect, Carissa Renee (Gonzales) Sill & the 2012 Uganda YWAM Team: My first readers. You endured a lot of Kimly *heading* places rather than walking, hurrying or driving. You were the ones who expressed so much belief in the story despite the pages being out of order and my limited skills with basic grammar.

Tehila Lieberman and Amanda Barnett: My editors. As humbling as it was to have the character's choices challenged, I am grateful for the part you played. You not only altered Kimly's story, but your guidance helped shape me as a writer.

Charlene Heydorn and Christina Armentrout: My eagle-eyed friends. When I asked you to read the manuscript prior to publication, I had no idea that you would play such a significant part in its final edit. Thank you for saying yes to my spontaneous request and for using your giftedness to polish the rough edges.

The followers of jackiesill.com: My blog readers. You know who you are—you are the ones who were quick to remind me, with each post, that while I may have made a mistake, I wasn't a mistake. You are the ones who overlooked my immature writing style to see the potential for what God might want to use. You are the ones who said, "Keep writing."

Bruce Gevirtzman: My 9th grade English teacher. Each time you reached out and expressed admiration for something I had written, I fell backward in time. Like a fourteen-year-old girl, I reread your words and was tempted to print them out and hang them on my refrigerator. Thank you for being so attentive to ensure that I wasn't lured into a scam on my journey to publishing. You were the closest thing to being my literary agent.

My Indigogo Supporters: You kickstarted me into chasing a goal until it actually happened. Your support allowed me to acquire a professional editor. Thank you for sacrificing your cash and publically supporting my dream.

Islabug Designs: The freehand lettering for the cover was done on a whim and in one sitting. You are an upcoming artist, who nailed the artwork because of your understanding that torment can exist where waters seem peaceful.

My Cantina Laredo Family: Those who have not stood on that expo-line, in the heat of an Arizona summer, on a bustling Friday night cannot comprehend the bond we forged. Your names and faces are eternally written on my heart.

Jack and Billie McElroy: My parents. I'm grateful to you for all the times I said, "I'm bored" and you told me to read. Thank you for buying me my first favorite series, Little House in the Big Woods. Thank you for handing me George Orwell's book about…farm animals? I caught Mom's love for fiction and Dad's love for embellishing an otherwise commonplace story to make it intriguing. I love you both.

David, Emily, Austin, Adam, Josh, Ceesa, Isla and Jude: My tribe. The balance between isolation and community that is required for an author to successfully bring a manuscript to fruition is delicate. In writing this first novel, I was fortunate to be surrounded by people who understood this subtle tension and readily allowed me space or gave me their attention depending on where I was in the process. This book was a family venture, a project that facilitated healing. In the end, despite my selfishness, it was always going to be all of me, for all of you.

Above all, and in all, I thank God for allowing me multiple chances to be more like Christ.

PROLOGUE

When I was five Momma gave me flavored ice. Its brilliant color tricked my eyes, and even when it burned my tongue, I longed for more. I wanted it to become a part of me. Sinking my teeth in quickly, I learned painfully this was not the way to eat the sweet red ice. Now that I am nine, I know that ice was meant to be eaten cautiously. Before tonight, I thought the pain of that ice cold moment had become one of my lost memories. Tonight lying on the stone floor waiting for Uncle to return, my aching hip and my legs burn cold.

When Uncle returns, he will take me back to his village. He will take me away from the cold stone floor and I will sleep in the smooth dirt beneath the hut that Uncle shares with Auntie and cousin Purn and the two babies with matching faces.

But that is not the place I wish to be.

The place I wish to be is with Momma. I wish I were in the hut where I once lived with Momma. I wish I were nestled close to Momma on her mat.

Momma's mat is softer than my own because Momma's mat is filled with Momma, whose hot sickness could spin knots in my stomach, forcing me to hold my breath. Tonight, I wish I could breathe in Momma's sick smell. I wish I could feel her hot unpleasantness on my face, on my arms and legs.

"Sickness will be my freedom, Noi." Momma once said as we lay on her mat together. Life had not been kind to Momma and she said the sickness was the only way she would ever beat life. I wrapped Momma's long dark hair around my fingers and Momma whispered in my ear, "If misfortune finds you in your first life, you will spend every life after trying to avoid meeting him again." Misfortune had found Momma.

After Momma's sickness had smelled bad for many days, she

sent word to have Auntie take me to her village to live with her. Auntie was Momma's sister, and even though they were once children from the same village, Misfortune had not yet found Auntie. Auntie had the family Momma had always wanted--for herself and for me. For every nothing Momma had, Auntie had a something. Auntie had a little girl just like me and two baby boys who shared the same face. They were matching babies. Sometimes I would forget they were not the same child. The day Uncle came to fetch me, Momma told me I needed to go so that her misfortune would not become mine. I wanted to be a good girl, so I hid my tears when I asked Momma, "Who will be your family if I go?" Momma rubbed my hair off my neck with her hot hand and said, "You are my family. I am your family. That is forever."

The first few weeks living in the hills were like nothing I had ever known. I played with my cousins and did chores for Auntie. All the days I thought about Momma. I missed her softness, but my heart was full when I would roam the hills with my cousin Purn. When I was with Purn, Thailand's sun burned brighter, and it was warm on my arms. Some mornings, I would close my eyes and when the sunshine touched my arms it felt like Momma's hand.

Mornings were my favorite because that is when the birds fluttered through the trees catching bees. The colorful birds waved at me with fanning tails and sang songs in words I did not know. My favorite bird was the Blue Tailed Bee Eater. His cackling, rattling song made me giggle. Sometimes I would cackle, "kit-tik, kit-tik" and thank him for eating the stinging bees.

Uncle had three chickens and a hog. When Auntie wasn't looking, Purn and I would tease the hog. I would hold a custard apple in front of the porker to rouse him into chasing us. Everyone knows a custard apple is too delicious to give to a hog. Knowing this made us run faster. When we would tire, we would jump out of the pen, lie in the shade and enjoy the green, lumpy sugar fruit. I decided that when I returned to live with Momma, I would bring her a basket of custard apples from Auntie's tree.

The hut we all shared was made of large pieces of bamboo which had been cut, flattened and pieced together to form strong walls. How I wished Momma could see Auntie's fine house. It did not rest in the dirt, but was held above the ground by bamboo rods.

Alongside Auntie, I gathered fronds from the palm trees, so

Uncle could repair the roof. Once we had collected many fronds, we flattened them and let them dry in the sun. The rains were coming soon. Uncle said we must replace the fronds on top of the hut before we felt dampness in the air.

When the sun went down, Purn and I would crawl under the two room bamboo hut; we would cuddle close together in the smooth dirt until we fell asleep. With interlocked arms and faces nearly touching, we were almost the same person. When I would look into her eyes I would see my reflection. I had seen my reflection once in a piece of glass, but with Purn, I could see myself full-size.

Sometimes the moon slid across the sky and made horrifying shadows in the trees and bushes. I often wondered where my Blue Tailed Bee Catching friend went when the shadows came. Why was she quiet at night? Did she fly around the shadows so they could not touch her? Did she flutter to another part of the hills that didn't have horrifying moon shadows? Did she fly up to the moon and sit on a star?

I had been with Purn for many days and I had seen many nighttime shadows when Auntie told Uncle she wanted to travel the day's journey out of the hills to the small village where Momma was living. She wanted to take me along. I inched closer to the corner of the hut where they were talking.

"You may go. The girls must both stay. They must take care of the babies. Two babies, two girls."

Auntie tried to bargain, saying she would take the babies with her, too.

In a low voice, Uncle replied, "I will not stay in my home without my family. Am I not a man, that I should be dishonored in this way?"

"She is my sister, this is her only child. Soon she will…" her voice was nearly a whisper, but Auntie stopped and looked at me.

Soon she will…what? What will she? I pulled a splinter from the bamboo wall and looked back and forth between Auntie and Uncle. I wanted to leave the hut, but I wanted to know what "soon she will" meant for Momma.

Uncle looked at me, but his words were for Auntie, "If you talk of leaving me alone again, you will never go." Uncle calmly turned his eyes on Auntie, "Not tomorrow. Not ever."

Auntie continued cluck, cluck, clucking her request like one of her chickens. He had not silenced her with his threat, and her cackling wasn't doing anything to soothe Uncle's mean spirit.

I did not like the words passing between them. I pressed the bamboo splinter under my nail bed until I found a drop of blood. Cluck, cluck, cluck…Auntie continued. Finally, Uncle's thunderous voice overpowered the hut like a bolt of anger. Courage came to me. I dropped my bamboo splinter and spoke.

"I will wait to see Momma," I interrupted the lightning and the chicken.

I told them that Purn and I would stay and help Uncle with the matching babies, the chickens and the hog. Auntie looked down at her hands, and I spoke confidently, "I will make you proud." When she raised her eyes to mine, she did not smile, but looked away quickly.

The next morning, Auntie left before we even fed the chickens. Eager to make her proud; I worked hard throughout the day. When the blue sky had turned dark gray, I crawled under the hut with Purn. I was ready to fall asleep next to her warm body. After only a few moments in the soft dirt, Uncle called for me to come up into the hut.

When I came to where he was, the matching babies were nearly asleep. He told me to take the babies down to Purn, and then to come back up.

"But Uncle…" I began to protest, but he turned toward me sharply, anger distorting his face, and my words stayed hidden in my throat.

Even though I was tired from the day's chores, and I wanted to rest in the dirt with Purn, I did as I was told.

When I returned from taking the babies to Purn, Uncle told me to lie on his mat. I felt Uncle move closer. Beneath me, I could hear the babies fussing, and I wanted to go to them. No matter how I tried, I couldn't get far enough away from Uncle. He used one hand to hold my leg while he pulled my shirt off my body. Hard scratchy hands moved across my skin. He pulled himself on top of me. When he was as close as he could be, closer than anything I had ever known, I turned my head as far away as I could and I stared into a dark corner of the hut.

I didn't need the moon to slide across the sky and make horrifying shadows. I knew what was in them now. Darkness was here and it was touching me. For the first time ever I knew where the Blue Tailed Bee Catcher went when the shadows came at night. She didn't fly around the shadows; she didn't fly up to the moon and sit on a star. No, when darkness comes my Blue Tailed friend flies straight into the shadow where there is no color. She flies to the back of darkness and it was there I found her waiting. In the darkness her blue tail loses its beauty, her song loses its music and she is alone. With Uncle's Darkness on top of me, around me and a part of me, I move as close to the Blue Tailed Bee Catcher as she will allow so we can be alone together.

When Uncle was finished, he stood up and as he did he coughed.

"Go get the babies and put them in their beds. And bring me some water," He spoke calmly, and the darkness made me obey.

Uncle told me to sleep with the babies. I tried to disobey him and I tried to stay awake. Eyes open, I waited for Uncle to fall asleep. Lying on the bamboo floor next to the babies, I made plans to sneak away once I heard him snoring. I would return to Momma. Perhaps if she knew that even while living with Auntie, misfortune had found me, she would let me return home.

My body failed me and I fell asleep. In the morning, Uncle woke me and ordered me to follow him. I did as I was told. After we had walked for a long time, we reached a stream at the base of the hill. I watched the water rush across the jagged rocks, holding them prisoner. The meadow reached the edge of the water, and many rocks, which had somehow escaped from the stream, peeked out from the grass. I kept my eyes on the ground as we walked so I would not trip over the pointed rocks. Some of the boulders were as tall as the matching babies, but some were smaller and sneakier. They would lay in wait for me, and when my eyes tired from the glaring sun they would attack. The moment I let my gaze relax on the swiftly moving waters, a sharp rock would bite me on the foot. A new bird saw me walking and called out from the edge of the trees. The Red Bearded Bee Eater sang, "kit-tik, kit-tik, kit-tik" but I did not answer him.

Uncle stopped walking. We stood at the edge of a creek that was nearly a small river. It was wide and deep. Uncle stared down at me. I looked away and focused instead on the slippery rocks trapped under the cool water. I wished I could fall into a rock, break into a thousand pieces, and float down the river. I wished the stream could take me to Momma.

"Undress," he said.

I heard myself whisper, "No."

Until the word came out of my mouth, I did not know I knew the word. I didn't say "No" to Momma, because I didn't feel "No" I felt "Yes" much of the time. I wasn't trying to be a good girl. I was just being me, and I was a "Yes." Today I was a "No."

I saw a shift in Uncle's eyes, but he still glared at me. For a moment, I felt powerful. I smiled and said it again. This time I said it much louder. I said it so the water holding the rocks captive would hear me.

"No!"

Uncle's hand came up so quickly, I couldn't even flinch, and before I had a chance to relax my prideful grimace, I felt the blow against my ear. A jolt of pain rushed through my head, as if a thousand stinging bees were using me as their nest. I stepped backwards, and tears filled my eyes. He was a palm tree, I was a stick. I did not have a chance to overpower him beyond what I willed in my heart.

Grabbing my hair, he pulled me into the stream and under the water. As my face went below the surface, I breathed in the water and pain shot down my throat. Lightning filled my lungs. I coughed it out, but then instinctively, I sucked in more. It hurt worse than the Darkness of the night before. I didn't know anything could hurt worse than the Darkness. He pulled me up out of the water and threw me down on the rocky bank and told me again to undress. My crying was fierce, the coughing was painful, and I could still feel the ringing in my left ear from his blow to my head. I pulled my wet clothes off of my body.

Once I was undressed, Uncle untied the string on the waistband of his pants and lowered himself on top of me.

I lay on the rough, rocky bank and tried to disappear. This time there was no blackness to swallow me. The Red Bearded Bee Catcher no longer sang his song; the shame of what was now occurring silenced him. I wondered if I would ever hear the bee catching birds sing again. I did not want Uncle's Darkness to take my favorite memories. I tried to summon the Blue Tail's rattling song, the pleasant memory of holding Purn in the dirt, or the softness of

13

Momma's mat, but the pain in my ear rang louder, and Uncle's weight on top of me caused the jagged rocks beneath me to dig deep into my back.

The sun beat down on me with anger. What had warmly touched me before, now hated my body.

After he had finished, Uncle stood up. He reached down with hands like claws and picked me up by my shoulders. He did two things. First he kissed my lips. He kissed my lips and stole the last place for me to hide. My lips held my secrets. His claim to my lips brought more shame than I could bear.

Then, like a soiled rag, he tossed me into the river. I landed in the water and wished I could float away. Uncle told me if I told anyone what we had done he would bring me to this place and drown me.

"Drown me now," I whispered as the icy water moved across my naked body.

Uncle let out a laugh. Then, he said simply, "After I drown you, I will tell your mother how you disgraced her. I will tell her how you came down to the river and drowned yourself because you were so angry with her. I will tell her how you despised her for being sick. I will tell her how you wished to be dead rather than help your Auntie with her family. She will die knowing her daughter was her greatest disgrace."

He left me in the icy water, and the water's chill could not lie; I did despise Momma for being sick, and now, I wished I were dead. I was her biggest disgrace. Everything Uncle said he would tell my mother was the truth.

When Auntie returned home, I returned to sleeping under the hut with Purn, but it was never the same. I tried to pull her close, but my arms felt different. For months, I lived this way with the family that was slowly starting to despise me.

Many mornings Uncle would pull me out from under the hut and tell me to follow him down to the stream. I tried many ways to get him to stop bringing the darkness into me. No matter how I begged, he would always threaten me with drowning and disgrace for my Momma. I tried crying, scratching and biting, but he would become enraged and pull me under the water until my lungs burned like cold fire. When I stood firm and bravely faced him down, I would be met with another jolt to my ear and then pulled under the icy water. I was learning to hate the water, to hate the morning, and to hate myself.

I wanted to run away, but I did not know where "away" was. Plus, I knew Uncle would tell my mother I was disobedient, and she would be disgraced. Disdain was rooted in the eyes of Auntie and Purn. My cousin was jealous of the morning walks I shared with her Father.

"Papa, can I come too?" Purn asked as she crawled out from under the hut.

"Why do you harass your Papa?" his sharp answer silenced my cousin.

When Purn and I were alone, she would call me names. She told me I was uglier than the hog. My Auntie's eyes would no longer look at me and her words were only bitter.

The moisture was getting closer, but the rains had not come, so Purn and I continued to sleep under the hut. One night as I was staring into the moon's horrifying shadows, I heard the chicken and the lightning battling above us, so I turned to Purn wishing I could pull her close to me, but Purn had been slowly moving further and further away from me. Now, with so much space between us, there was no way to reach her.

The sounds above me were frightening. I heard Auntie's clucking turn to yelling. She was angry about me. My name was a nasty word, one of the words that should never be uttered. I heard the sound of things breaking, and I heard a final blow which was so familiar it made my left ear sting. The lightning struck the chicken. Misfortune had found Auntie.

The following morning, Uncle pulled me out from under the hut and told me to follow. I did as I was told and followed Uncle as he walked a path that led us away from the stream. I followed all day. I was hungry and sore, but as much as I wanted to stop, I didn't want my Uncle on top of me. I didn't want his Darkness to swallow me. So, I continued to walk without a word.

As we traveled the road beneath us changed. My feet have always walked on dirt, but the roads we walked had become hard and hot against my feet. We came to a village where the walls of the huts were made of thick, square gray stones. The large dwellings did not have palm fronds on their roofs, but were made of metal like the pot in Auntie's fire kitchen. I was curious, and I was hungry. One did

15

not outweigh the other.

Uncle stopped outside one of the gray rock huts, which was bigger than any hut I had ever seen. There he spoke to a man with evil eyes and strange purple markings on his neck. The purple-marked man held a burning stick between his fingers. When he looked at me his eyes made me feel naked. I pulled my arms around my waist and tried to disappear. The purple-marked man put his burning stick to his mouth and sucked in deep. Then, with smoke filled words, the purple marked man asked my age and told Uncle that I was bony.

"She was born about nine years ago, I think," he replied, "And, some men like the bony ones. Besides, this one is a virgin." I did not know the word he called me, but it made the purple marked man smile. Tears spilled down my cheeks and into my mouth. My tears tasted salty. I was filled with shame for the things Uncle was saying about me, but I was also thinking about food. I didn't understand who I was becoming—how could I feel this pain, be consumed with fear, and think about food at the same time?

"She belongs to me, and I don't want her. Her mother is dead," Uncle   said.

"That's a lie!" I protested, "Momma's not dead!"

Uncle's hand hit my ear, and I allowed myself to fall to the ground. I hoped that maybe the purple-marked man would have pity on me.

Uncle smirked, "She may be feisty, but you can tame her."

"Is the Mother going to come looking for the child?" the purple-marked man asked as he sucked the last bit of life out of his burning stick.

"No, she can't. She was a whore who lived a disgraceful life. Her sickness finally gave her what she deserved."

I shivered at the way he was speaking of Momma.

"You should have seen the child's mother in her prime," Uncle said as he placed his hand on his chest. "The woman was as beautiful as Buddha's Queen Mallika. Surely the child will look like her. Your profits will be sudden, and they will only increase as she grows more beautiful. I expect to be paid a fair amount for her."

"What do you call her?" the purple-marked man asked Uncle. Before Uncle could answer, the strange man turned to me, "Child, what is your name?"

"Noi," I whispered my name, and then I immediately hated myself for giving it to him. I wanted it back. I didn't want the purple-marked man to have my name.

Uncle bent down and pulled me up. He nudged me towards the stranger, and the purple marked man grabbed my arm. I tried to pull my arm back. "Uncle!" my voice was high, as panic overtook me. I used my free arm to try to peel his fingers off of me, but his dirty hand would not budge. I leaned back and away, allowing my legs to buckle beneath me. The purple marked man grabbed the hair on the top of my head and pulled me across the dirt and gravel. With both of my hands I tried to pull his fingers away from my hair and my head. My short pants slid down to my knees. I used one hand to try and pull my shorts back up while my other hand flailed about. My hip and my backside were on fire as the rocks tore into my skin.

When we were almost to the entrance of the square rock hut, another man appeared in the doorway. This man had baggy pants and long stringy hair. With two long strides he was close enough to grab me at the waist and lift me in the air. The man with stringy hair walked along the side of the square rock hut until he reached a smaller hut that was also made of flat, square rocks. He tossed me across the floor of a small room, and my head banged against the ground. He slammed a wooden door behind me.

I crawled into a corner of the room, and wrapped my arms around my legs until the thin line of light peeking out from under the door faded to black. After hours of waiting for Uncle to return, the door opened and the stringy hair man came back to the room. He set a bowl on the floor and turned to leave. I ate thick cold noodles so quickly that my stomach hurt. The pain felt good because it was the first pain I had felt in months that I had done to myself.

1

Kimly's bed sheets were damp with sweat, and she wondered if the air outside her hotel room might be cooler. Her feet hit the marble floor, and she moved towards the window, pleased she had remembered to step lightly and didn't bring her foot down on broken glass.

She lifted the window wide. Sure enough, the Chiang Mai night air was cooler than the air in the stuffy hotel room. The Thai city was wide awake. Even from eleven floors up, the buzz of the people bustling in the streets, their laughter and their music, was as unsettling as a mosquito's nest.

Wide awake, she looked at the clock on her nightstand. 10:13 p.m. *Great. Jet lag*, she scolded herself for taking a nap upon arriving in the room.

Tiptoeing across the glass-strewn floor, Kimly moved into the bathroom, where her cell phone sat charging.

Kyle, Missed Calls (2)

"Nope. Not doing that." Kimly mumbled as she reached over and turned on the shower. She decided she might as well go out for a walk; there was no sense in lying awake on the scratchy sheets.

Climbing out of the shower, Kimly wrapped her long dark hair in the towel. Cool beads of water brought down her body temperature, so she refrained from drying off completely. The mirror reflected the lean body of a half Thai and half Caucasian beauty, but after 33 years of eyeing her own reflection, Kimly no longer saw the fullness of her appearance. The hands of time had stretched and pulled on her skin, slightly changing her features and what Kimly saw was a body altered by time and childbearing. Thirteen years had passed since she had given birth to twin boys, and while losing the baby weight came fairly easy, she carried a different load on her shoulders. The pressure of parenting and the strain for significance altered what she saw reflecting back at her.

Leaning across the sink, Kimly pulled her long neck up and looked into her own eyes. She paused and then tilted her forehead until it was an inch from the mirror and gazed into dark brown eyes that strongly resembled her Mother's. She had never met her biological father, but she had once seen a picture of him. Shirtless, holding a beer can in an insulated cooler in one hand and a cigarette in the other; he was sitting under a tree at a park picnic table. Her father's image was too small for her to deem his eye color, but she assumed by his light hair and the tones of his skin, he probably had light eyes. *Blue, green...who knew?*

Her half-sister, Thao, had her mother's eyes, as well. Two sisters with the same eyes, but Thao saw the world differently. From the beginning, Kimly's Mother and her Step-Father must have known Thao would please them; they chose their daughter's name hoping it would set her on a clearly defined path. While being far from popular on the playground, Thao's name meant "respectful of parents." Thao was born to please her parents, and she had done so her whole life-- even in her marriage to a strong, Asian man. The name given to Kimly also had a meaning--Golden Lion. She never understood how anyone was supposed to live up to that name, and in her floundering, she managed to make countless decisions to disappoint.

Unlike her sister, mathematics and science didn't come easily for Kimly, but that didn't dissuade her parent's aspirations for her to become a Doctor or an Engineer. In Kimly's second year at the University of California in Los Angeles she secretly dropped the mind-numbing classes, and changed her major to journalism. Kimly's parents had solid plans for their eldest; plans that would unfold in concrete buildings with stable walls, but Kimly felt she had a different destiny. For as long as she could remember, she had regarded each morning's delivery of the Los Angeles Times as something magical. The feel of the silky paper and the smell of the print were lovelier than a scarf laced with lavender. In her youth, Kimly would slide her hand across the newsprint as she read fluid stories of real events that were happening...somewhere. Lifting her hand and looking at the darkened print residue on her fingertips instilled fantasies where she was a distinguished international reporter like Christiane Amanpour.

Kimly also willfully rebelled against her parents' conservative and traditional lifestyle in the company she kept. Choosing friends her parents despised, she constructed a community that created constant chaos between mother and daughter. Eventually, and perhaps unavoidably, Kimly drifted towards promiscuity in her dating life. By intentionally surrounding herself with people her mother disdained, she unintentionally found herself pregnant at the age of twenty.

Kimly had been seeing Kyle Denim and the night she told him she was pregnant, she fully expected him to break up with her. She was emotionally prepared for the break-up, but her biggest concern was that he might not help her pay for an abortion. The young couple sat in Kyle's parked car outside her dorm room while Kimly hemmed and hawed, attempting to tell what needed to be told.

"Do you remember when we went to Becca's thing? Last month?" Kimly looked down at her finger nails. The paint was peeling away from her left thumb. She pulled it into her palm and made a fist.

"Yeah, why? Kimly, what's...look at me. Are you crying?" Kyle reached across the small space between them and brushed Kimly's long hair away from her face.

"No, I mean...I'm fine. It's just..." she let out a sigh, and looked up. "Kyle, you didn't use anything. I mean, we didn't use anything." Kimly stuttered.

"Kimly...what are you..."

"I need to have an abortion," she looked down again at her chipped nail polish.

"Kimly, are you pregnant?"

"Well, that's usually how these things work, Kyle," she answered.

"Are you sure?"

"Yes, I'm sure. The stick turned blue. Blue means pregnant."

"Crap."

"I'm sorry," Kimly said, and she wiped her eyes with the back of her hand, but instinctively held her thumb close to her palm.

"No! I'm sorry. But why...?"

"Why? What...what do you mean why? I'm pregnant."

"No, I mean, why the abortion?"

"What...?" Kimly looked up at Kyle and made eye contact for the first time since she climbed into his car.

"Kimly, I love you." In that moment, for some reason, the fact that Kyle loved her seemed to erase an abortion as a viable solution for the unplanned pregnancy.

But as weeks passed and the pregnancy continued, Kimly felt more uneasy about their situation. Secretly, she still saw the blue stick as a something that could be aborted. The day everything changed was the day she learned there were two. It was only her second visit to the doctor, and she knew she still had time to have an abortion. On the drive over she had been considering the best way to broach the subject with her doctor. During the visit, Dr. Warren told Kimly she was measuring a little larger than expected and suggested an ultrasound. A part of her wondered if an ultrasound was a bad idea; she had seen images of the unborn, and she feared it could confuse the situation.

A few moments later she was lying on a table with warm jelly on her belly and an Ultrasound screen to her left when she saw two tiny hearts beating side by side. The blue stick had multiplied and her pregnancy had taken on an identity. The idea of discarding two blue sticks was harder for Kimly to process.

The original plan was for Kyle to drop his classes at UCLA and take on more hours at the grocery store while Kimly finished school. Within a month, Kimly's morning sickness was so intense that she dropped all but one of her classes. Carrying twins proved to be harder than Kimly imagined, and when it was time to register for the next semester, it was hardly feasible.

Eventually, Kyle's detour through the produce department shifted, and once the twins had been born and he and Kimly were on their feet, Kyle enrolled at Cal State Long Beach and earned a degree in Mathematics with an emphasis in Actuarial Science. As it turned out, Kyle was an excellent Actuary: people saw him as trustworthy, and his financial instincts were on par with a fortune teller.

In the years that followed the birth of the twins, Kimly saw the blue stick in a disparaging light, while Kyle had redefined the blue stick as a challenge. He worked harder because of the boys. He worked harder to make up for all that Kimly felt she had lost.

Now married, Kimly felt she just transferred who she was disappointing. No longer under the microscope of her Mother, Kimly was certain she disappointed her husband with her lack of interest in marriage and parenting. Their shotgun marriage at the age of 20 had resulted in twin boys, Jacob and Dylan, being born to a young woman with no desires to be a wife or a mommy. She wanted to be a journalist before she had met Kyle Denim, and pregnancy did not change her desire or her drive towards her journalistic goals.

Once the twins started school, Kimly was able to find part-time work for a local newspaper, but she never saw that blue stick as something she was able to overcome. Oftentimes, weeks would pass at the paper and she wouldn't get the chance to submit an article of substance to be considered. The paper had more people on the staff than pages in the paper, and the compelling leads were consistently given to people who were available to work late into the night. Spontaneous Happy Hour outings, last minute concerts or basketball games weren't conducive to life with two small children and each time she declined an invitation, due to parenting, it only sealed her fate as "Office Mom." The articles given to Kimly were issues regarding Working Mothers or Childcare. She slowly evolved into an expert in fields she had little interest in and she never achieved the status she had dreamed she would achieve. Her life had become as unremarkable as the stories she reported.

In the few steps between the bathroom and her suitcase on the luggage stand, a sliver of glass managed to find Kimly and assault her foot. "Aahhh!" She let out a cry as she hopped to the edge of the bed. She flipped on the light on the nightstand, and by its dim glow she was able to pull the tiny assailant from her foot; the pain eased immediately.

She looked at the shattered glass on the floor. Across the room, on a small teakwood table, sat a glass bottle like the one she knocked to the floor. Before her arrival, the tall glass bottles had been filled with the hotel's complimentary water and placed on the edge of the table for easy access. When Kimly had entered the room, she had accidentally knocked one of the bottles off the edge of the table, and it landed with a crash. Water and glass had cascaded across the marble floor. After her long flight, Kimly opted to grab a towel from the bath and throw it on top of the wet glass. Exhausted, she decided she would deal with it later.

"Later" had arrived, announcing its presence with the sliver of glass in her foot.

Removing the towel from her head, Kimly ran her fingers through her dark hair and threw on some jeans, a tank top, and a pair of sandals. She reached inside the pillowcase on her bed and pulled out her passport and her cash. She shoved them into her handbag and tiptoed around the glass and out of her room.

As she stepped into the hallway and closed the door, the sounds of the city which had climbed the outside walls and into her room through the open window were stifled. She paused for a moment because she thought she heard whispers…or was it crying? Standing completely still, her curiosity was piqued. The elevator was to the left, but the whispering was coming from the right. Her inquisitiveness moved her toward the whisper. Stepping softly along the marble floors, Kimly followed her voyeuristic spirit. She reached the end of the hallway, passing the rooms of other sleeping guests. Or, at least she presumed the rooms were occupied. For all she knew, she was the only guest on the eleventh floor. The isolating thought gave Kimly goose bumps, which turned sour when she thought of another possibility: the idea of being surrounded by rooms filled with lovers made her feel nauseated. Kimly couldn't remember the last time she had made love to Kyle in a hotel room. Now, spending an evening with him in that setting would be cheapened by his selfishness.

The light from an Emergency Exit stairwell spilled into the hallway, and she stopped and listened. Two women were whispering in what was, most likely, Thai. *Naturally, they are speaking in Thai, Kimly,* she thought, *what did you expect?*

While she knew she wouldn't be able to understand what they were saying, she moved closer to the archway. Inside the stairwell, two Thai women, each wearing a salmon pink dress with a white maid's apron, were standing close together on a landing about five steps below Kimly. The older woman had her arm around her coworker, obviously comforting her. The dark hair of the older woman was pulled into a tight bun, giving her a harsh, stern look. The woman she was comforting was younger, and she had full rosy cheeks and glossy dark hair that stopped at her chin. Her most obvious feature was her very pregnant stomach exploding beneath her traditional uniform, stretching the dress' stitches to exhaustion.

Kimly had been watching for mere seconds when the rosy-cheeked pregnant woman sensed an onlooker. She turned her head abruptly and looked up the stairwell at Kimly. Their eyes met, and Kimly pulled back quickly, pressing herself against the wall, disappearing into the dim hallway. The woman had the same familiar look in her eyes that Kimly had seen in the images which had drawn her to this side of the world. It was not a genetic feature. It was something so painful it penetrated Kimly's heart and made her uncomfortable.

Well, that was dumb. Say something, Kimly chastised herself.

Peeking back around the corner at the two women Kimly said, "Hi, umm...I have a problem in my room. I need a new towel, and I have some broken glass,"

The older woman stared at Kimly with sharp eyes. The woman's scowl reminded Kimly of an Aunt on her Step-Father's side of the family. Aunt Chao despised Kimly for being born five years before her Step-Father had met and married her Mother. There was nothing she could do to please the elderly woman. More maddening was how her own Mother overlooked Aunt Chao's contemptible behavior as if the reason for her disdain was understandable.

"A towel in my room has glass in it," Kimly tried again.

"Towel? Oh, towel..." the rosy-cheeked pregnant woman began to awkwardly move up the stairs towards Kimly. As the young woman followed Kimly into her room, she noticed a red mark on the woman's round face. Across her right eye she wore a wound. Kimly wondered if this was the result of a temper gone wild. The pregnant woman caught Kimly's eyes on her and looked away, shielding her face with her hand.

"I'm sorry," Kimly looked away, as well. She showed the woman the broken glass under the towel. The pregnant woman immediately set about cleaning the wet mess. Pulling the towel and the broken glass towards her, she handled it cautiously as she carried it out of the room. In the moments she was gone, Kimly rustled her bed into shape, quickly pulling the covers up and fluffing her pillow. The young woman left the room momentarily and returned with a straw broom. As she swept up the glass, Kimly's eyes were drawn upwards from the straw broom and landed again on the woman's swollen cheek. She reached into her backpack and pulled out a stick of gum.

"Gum?" Kimly extended her hand to the woman.

"Mai, mai," the woman was shaking her head quickly back and forth, " Khaawp khoon kha," and with those unfamiliar words, the rosy-cheeked pregnant woman finished her work and left Kimly alone with her gum. Kimly fell back onto her bed and stared at the ceiling.

"Karma," she whispered.

She was certain the universe was now settling a debt for her unfriendly attitude hours earlier. The deficit was specifically towards the woman she had been traveling next to on the 17-hour flight from Los Angeles to Bangkok.

In the beginning, Kimly had succeeded in warding off every attempt for polite conversation made by the woman seated to her right. But, somewhere over the Pacific, in the dimly lit cabin, Kimly caught the woman watching her, a slight smile lingering. She politely smiled back and then looked away.

"I'm sorry," said the round African-American woman, who was at least 30 years her senior, "I was just thinking 'bout how lovely you are with your hair, black as a raven, and 'bout the creativity of God. I'll tell you what, if I tell you nothin', God certainly has a knack for making us so different and so uniquely beautiful. It makes a daughter wonder about Him and His plans for each of his children."

Kimly wanted to burst out in laughter while simultaneously moaning in frustration. Kimly had hoped this time on the plane would be a good time for her to go over Matthew's notes before she arrived in Chiang Mai. Her abrupt departure had made it difficult for her to have an adequate meeting with Matthew, and she still had some unanswered questions regarding the assignment and the contacts.

She could only imagine what the next 10 or 11 hours would be like sitting next to a God fanatic. Kimly quickly played her options in her head:

- Option One: Smile and say nothing. Hopefully, that was the extent of the conversation.
- Option Two: Tell her that I don't believe in any "God" let alone one who "decided" I would have hair black as a raven.
- Option Three: Politely tell her that I have a headache, and close my eyes.

Kimly hesitated a moment too long and the woman continued her nonsensical talk. "I just think of the small details He works out in my life, every day, and I get a little overcome with His glory. Some people call everyday miracles "coincidences"...but I don't think so. Mmm, mmm, no." The elderly woman shook her head and pulled her face into an angry grimace. "I think God is active! He is...I tell you that much, I do." Her grimace turned upside down and softened into something peaceful, "He's a part of our lives. And, the more I seek Him, the more I seem to find Him, even in the small things—like...your beautiful hair. Dark as a mystery."

With her Thai Air seatmate droning on and on, Kimly could no longer use Option 1. She had to give the woman a verbal response. Option Two or Option Three felt incredibly harsh, but because of her hesitation, she was now going to have to hear all about God and Heaven and Hell.

Were Kimly to express her own doubts about God, she was fairly certain the woman to her right would have no problem recognizing Kimly as more of a sinner and less of a daughter lovingly anointed with raven black hair. *So much for the rest of the flight*, she thought to herself.

Kimly spoke quietly to the woman, practically whispering, as if the news she bore would cause her to be ejected from the plane midflight, "I don't ever think about God."

The woman did not miss a beat, and she smiled at Kimly as if this news didn't surprise her at all. She said gently, "I understand. I didn't used to think 'bout Him either. But, I can tell you this, He still thinks 'bout you. Even if you aren't giving Him much mind, He is thinking 'bout you constantly. And, He has a plan for you. He has a great plan."

With that, the sage woman smiled, reached up, extinguished the overhead light and closed her eyes. Kimly was stunned. She just stared at the woman for a few moments, waiting to see the end of the trick. But the woman wore a content look on her face and, within a few moments, she seemed to drift off into sleep.

The metal tube soared through the night sky, and Kimly thought of the irony in the woman's words. The gentle woman had spoken bold words, with such certainty, to a girl who was clearly never planned by anyone. And even more ironic was that while Kimly knew the truth, there was a part of her that found security in the thought of a God who may have a plan for her life.

Hours later, lying on the hard mattress in her muggy hotel room, feeling a gentle pulsing where the glass had pierced her foot, the truth Kimly had always known was fairly evident. No one had a plan for her life. Certainly, not God.

2

Kimly pushed the button for the elevator and stared blankly at the fake wood grain paneling affixed to its closed doors. After a moment, she looked up at the digital number pad over the elevator entrance. The number three remained illuminated, unchanging, so she turned from the doors and wandered over to the wide windows overlooking the city below. It was nearly midnight, but the city was wide awake. In the distance, the skyline had faded to blackness, but the sidewalks directly in front of her hotel were trimmed with golden lights from the booths of street vendors participating in the Night Bazaar.

Glancing back at the elevator's digital number pad, she rethought her satisfaction at being on the eleventh floor. The digits told her that the elevator had only moved to the fifth floor. Earlier, when Kimly first arrived at the hotel, she had noticed the elevator's doors were quick to close once she had entered. They didn't stay open long enough for more than one person to enter or exit. But, after the flight, the cab ride and checking in, she had been distracted and hadn't realized how slowly the elevator had climbed.

Five minutes passed before Kimly was finally out of the hotel and walking along the Chiang Mai sidewalk. There was a line of people coming out the door of a fast food restaurant on her left. The familiar chain seemed out of place with its iconic golden arches standing tall between two authentic family-owned Thai restaurants. It was there that Kimly located a money exchange kiosk. Banking business was being done in a room the size of a jail cell amid the crowded streets. The room was divided in half by a countertop with a thick glass barrier which extended to the ceiling. Behind the glass, two tellers sat, ready to exchange currency. However hazardous it might seem to be walking the streets and flashing cash so late into the evening, the exchange station was as busy as a traditional bank just before a holiday weekend. Kimly made the exchange, placing the Thai Baht she had received in exchange for her American Dollar deep in her purse.

On both sides of the street, as far as Kimly could see in either direction, street vendors were selling their wares. The vendors had carts and tables and each merchant's booth was nudged up to the next. Walking in the line of people, she was forced to keep moving forward on the crowded sidewalk. Noting the low prices some of the trinkets were marked with, Kimly wondered how they managed to turn a profit. Her dollar was going to go further in Thailand than she had hoped. The exchange was great, and the prices were low. She should be able to budget her cash flow without much difficulty.

At the street corner, Kimly stood for a moment watching the activity inside a nail salon. In many ways, the small business was similar to a nail salon in the west. Eight or nine tables, with a chair on each side for the client and the manicurist, were jammed close together in the center of the room. Spice rack shelving on the walls held a rainbow's assortment of nail polish. What was remarkably different was the activity taking place in the front windows of the corner store. The glass windows revealed spa size fish tanks with hundreds of tiny fish in a feeding frenzy. The oddity was what they were feeding on. Above the tanks were wooden planks, and sitting on the planks were customers, men and women, with their feet dangling in the water. The tiny fish swam furiously from one client to another nibbling dead skin from their feet all in the name of exfoliation. The sight made her think of her son Jacob's fish tank at home and she wondered if Kyle had told her sons where their Mom had gone. The thought made her wonder if Kyle would tell the boys together or individually. Kyle and Kimly's twins had hearts that beat in unison until they were born, from that day on those boys' hearts pounded with the synchronicity of a bad drum line.

Turning to examine the other three corners of the busy intersection, Kimly spotted a coffeehouse on the opposite corner. Standing on the sidewalk, eager to cross, she watched cars, scooters and motorized rickshaws pass through the busy intersection. She could have waited all night for traffic to stop, allowing her passage, and it would have never happened. Where Kimly had come from, the combination of heavy traffic, busy restaurants, and the probability of a pedestrian filing an injury lawsuit, would create enough of a concern to warrant a crosswalk, but this was not the case in Chiang Mai. She spotted other pedestrians maneuvering through the heavy traffic. Starting and stopping, their jumpy movements were reminiscent of a live-action version of the video game "Frogger." Kimly decided to try her luck at getting to the other side of the road without getting squished.

Filled with a surge of adrenaline, Kimly made the first movements in her attempt to sprint across the street, when an arm grabbed her own.

"Wait," the voiced attached to the arm said.

Looking down at the masculine hand holding her arm, she moved her eyes up and saw the handsome profile of a Thai man. He had dark olive skin, a strong jaw line and light lines around his eyes.

The man's head was turned sharply towards her, but he was looking beyond her at the street. Kimly turned her head to the right and was immediately embarrassed, as a scooter carrying two teenage boys went speeding across the space where she was just about to step off the curb. The scooter was close enough to generate a slight breeze, and she jumped back slightly.

"Umm...thank you," Kimly responded feebly.

"No problem," the man released her arm slightly, but not completely, and then said, "Now."

Without hesitation, Kimly followed the lead of the stranger. Later she would chastise herself for being so vulnerable with a man she did not know. If either of her sons had responded to a stranger so compliantly, she would've gone into lecture mode warning them of the dangers lurking on busy streets. But, in this moment the man felt incredibly safe, and she found herself drawn into his security. He appeared to be close in age to herself, and he had an air of confidence; self-assured and yet, respectful to her at the same time. She got the feeling he might be accustomed to helping people.

When they were almost to the other side of the street, the man released her arm, and Kimly slowed her pace. She felt awkward walking with him, as though they were together. She hoped he wouldn't be heading into the coffeehouse, but she hadn't even finished thinking the thought when he not only opened the door to the coffeehouse, but turned to her, smiled and said, "After you?"

"Thanks. I mean, thanks for the street and...yeah," her voice trailed off, and she felt frustrated with herself for being so flustered.

Dammit, Kimly, you are a grown woman—a Sophisticated Journalist Traveling the World Exposing the Inhumanity of Human Slave Trading and Sex Trafficking, she thought to herself, *One interaction with a stranger should not make you blush.*

"No problem," he said again. "Really...until you get used to the streets, they can be tricky. I mean, I take it you aren't from around here?"

Kimly stumbled over her words, while explaining she was an American journalist. And only after she had talked for nearly a minute about her goals in Chiang Mai, did she realize that the poor guy was probably just being polite. She couldn't remember this ever happening to her before; she was distracted by his movements, by her attraction to him. *Pull it together, Kimly!* She silently scolded herself.

Once she had stopped talking, the handsome stranger grinned at her as if he had a secret he wasn't willing to share. Kimly turned away from him, towards the barista, and ordered a decaf, thankful the girl spoke English. Against the back wall of the coffeehouse, two green overstuffed chairs had taken refuge. In one chair sat a twenty-something-year-old man with his eyes glued to his laptop. His greasy black hair was in sore need of a trim and he appeared to be in the process of growing a goatee. He seemed content, relaxing alone in the coffeehouse with his earphones sealing off the people around him. Kimly took her decaf and sat in the twin chair.

Picking up one of the newspapers sitting on the small square table near her seat, Kimly began skimming the front page when the man from the street walked up and said politely, "Hey, have a good night. And, be careful out there."

And with that, he was gone. *Well, that was humiliating,* Kimly thought to herself.

She wasn't sure what it had been about the man that had struck her nerves. Yes, he was handsome, but she had been around handsome men before. It wasn't merely his appearance. There was something different about him. *Was it his eyes?* She thought. She tried to recall, to concentrate on the color of his eyes. *Were they gunmetal gray?* Is that even possible? Something about his eyes had turned Kimly into a bit of a fluttering teen. She mentally chastised herself and focused on the reason she had made the trip: *The Article. Humans. Slavery. Sex trafficking. Focus, Kimly, you can't afford to be distracted while navigating through this darkness.*

She couldn't deny her decision to make the trip was a bit volcanic. It had been a long time coming and had erupted quite suddenly. Kimly had thought about taking a journey for years. Sometimes she would think about it while she was in her most tiresome mom moments: carpooling, dentist's appointments, fussing over homework assignments and enduring never-ending loads of laundry. Sometimes, the yearning would be triggered while wandering the aisle of the grocery store: an ingredient foreign to her, yet a staple in another culture, would peak her interest and she would daydream about foreign lands.

Over the years different causes piqued her interest. Children in different parts of the world were starving, and she was not. She knew she couldn't feed them all, but she thought that maybe bringing awareness might inspire others and alleviate the plight of some. A few years passed, and Kimly noticed that it wasn't just food the kids lacked, it was protection. Young boys were dragged from their homes in the middle of the night and forced into a militia, but her twins were not. Other people's children lost limbs to infection brought on by jiggers because they had no shoes, yet she tossed barely worn, outgrown shoes into a Salvation Army bin. The burden she felt towards the children was made worse by the easy lifestyle her own boys had.

It was a constant conundrum within her. If she left her children at home while she traveled to another part of the world, she would certainly learn more about injustice, but would her absence be understood by the twins? But, if she stayed home year after year, waiting for the right time to make the trip she had dreamed of, would life pass by without her ever having done anything of world changing and problem-solving significance?

But as the twins grew older, Kimly began to wonder if the reason she had never made the trip had less to do with being a parent and more to do with her marriage. Eventually, every discussion she had with Kyle about taking a trip ended badly. Her last conversation with Kyle about her making a journey plowed to the front of her thoughts.

"Matthew's exposé is turning out to be pretty successful...based on the emails he received, it looks like this is going to catapult his whole career," Kimly mentioned to Kyle as she washed the summer squash she was making for dinner. Their twins, Dylan and Jacob, were in their rooms, supposedly doing homework, although Kimly could hear the faint sound of Dylan strumming his guitar. Kyle was seated at their dark dining table messing with his cell phone; a habit of her husband's that she was growing to disdain.

"It's weird..." she continued, "I feel like, given the opportunity, I could've easily done what Matthew did."

"Everyone says that..."

"Well...I know. I mean, of course, everyone says those things—but, I mean...I did a third of his research for him. I'm not being naïve, I'm aware that there's more to it."

Kyle said nothing but continued to type and click on his screen.

"Hello...can you hear me now...?" Kimly mumbled.

"I'm listening." Kyle rebutted.

"Really? What did I say?" she asked.

"You said that Matthew's article was going to catapult his career, and I agreed with you. I said, 'Everyone says that'...God, Kimly, give me a break."

"You're so...ahh!" Kimly stopped herself. "Okay, you *weren't* listening, but whatever. What I am trying to say is, I did so much leg work on Matthew's story and I think I need to take things to the next level."

"Kimly..."

"Wait, hear me out..." Kimly's continued.

"Here we go..." Kyle interjected.

"I'm ready. I want to do this, Kyle. I have been life's spectator for too long."

"You're not a spectator. I hate it when you go there."

"That's just it, Kyle, I'm not going anywhere!"

Kyle rose from the table and moved across the kitchen. Kimly stepped in front of him and dropped her voice to a near whisper, "It looks like Matthew might leave the Tribune for a job at CNN. He's been talking with one of their associate producers. Things are happening for him. My point is that I keep thinking: it's time. It's *my* time!"

"Really? It's your time? Kimly, we've been through this. Dylan and Jacob have so much going on. Do you honestly think that you leaving right now would be best?" Kyle stepped around her, opened the refrigerator and pulled out a bottle of water. "Good God, Kimly…I have so much going on."

"People always have stuff going on," Kimly's voice began to rise, "but think about it…we can afford for me to go—we are in a better place financially than we've ever been in. You have a strong clientele now. Hell, they love you at that office. You have more freedom than ever to adjust your hours. You've been making a lot of time to go to the gym. It seems like you go every day now…" Her arguments were coming quickly, some of them hitting her for the first time as she shot them out.

"Oh…okay, so now I go to the gym too often? Jeez…Kimly."

"I didn't say that. Why are you being so defensive?!"

"I'm not being defensive. I'm being…damn it, I don't know, *realistic*. Kimly, we have been over this so many times. You taking off to Thailand for God knows how long leaves me here to take care of everything! Even if I gave up every hour I spend at the gym, I still wouldn't have the time or the energy to take care of the boys and give work the time it needs."

"Then come with me. Take some time off. We can leave the boys with my sister. She's always saying she wants to spend more time with them."

"Go with you? To Thailand? Now? Kimly…for God's sake, this is the worst time."

"It's always the worst time. I don't know why you aren't willing to make a small sacrifice for something that means so much to me."

"That's just it, Kimly! This isn't a small sacrifice! This is a bigger sacrifice than I have in me. I keep telling you, this isn't a little thing you are asking."

"Well, just tell me this, Kyle. Exactly how little do you need to sacrifice in order for me to do something significant?"

"Oh, I don't know, Kimly, but why don't you just tell me this…do we have to have this conversation every time a colleague of yours writes a story that gets some attention?"

The couple now stood in battle stance on opposite sides of the kitchen.

"You know what's so funny about you asking me to come with you?" Kyle asked, but then he answered his own question before Kimly could, "You don't really want me there."

"Why would I say you should come if I don't want you there?"

"Cause that's what you do, Kim…" Kyle lowered his voice, "you're the queen of manipulation—but you don't see the hole you're digging until you're in it. You invite me to go to Thailand, hoping that by doing so I will agree to you going. But then you'll put up a wall to let me know I've taken some great experience away from you. The Great Wall of Kimly that keeps people out and controls what they do."

"Why would you say that?" Kimly whispered, but she already knew. The disunity between the couple had grown strong over the years. Love making was robotic; communication was limited to what was necessary for running a household and raising two teenagers.

"If you asked me to go away with you so we could reconnect, then this would be a completely different conversation. Wouldn't it?"

Kimly stood quiet and diverted her eyes from her husband's.

"Yeah, that's what I thought." Kyle tossed his half empty water bottle across the kitchen where it landed in the sink, and he turned and left the room.

Kimly watched the activity in the cafe until she could feel herself beginning to relax. She decided to return to the hotel to try to get some sleep and adjust to the new time zone. Tossing her cup in the trash on her way out the door and heading back toward the busy intersection, Kimly was acutely aware of people who might be watching her cross, and she looked around for the gray-eyed stranger.

She stopped herself from looking for the handsome stranger and reminded herself of the freedom that came with making this trip alone. Restraints lifted, Kimly was finally doing what she wanted— for herself. Marrying young and parenting her boys, these things had taken the driver's seat for long enough. It was time for her to have a significant impact on the world.

She edged into the street and crossed without hesitation. Each step across the street transformed into a statement. Making it to the other side proved she wasn't dependent on anyone for such a simple task. Definitely not a man who left her *fluttering*.

3

When the Royal Lanna Hotel had its Grand Opening in November of 1956, the elevator would have been considered top of the line. In the decades that passed, the city had grown and with the onset of tourism, the little box had a hard time lifting its cargo. When the hotel was sold in 1992 the new owner, a businessman from Britain, updated the south wing and added a newer model. The glass box was double the size and twice as speedy. Most people missed the elevator, because it was further down the hallway from the main entrance, and somewhat secluded.

Kimly had discovered the offset elevator quite by accident when she had returned from her coffee outing the night before. Now as she rode down the secret elevator, she thought about how subdued Chaing Mai appeared. All the festivities of the previous night were gone; vanished with the rising sun. She glanced at her cell phone: 7:10 AM. "You look much different in the morning..." Kimly whispered to the city through the glass elevator wall.

Her night had been restless despite the decaf; she tried to distract herself with Matthew's notes, but her mind kept revisiting the unpleasantness she had left at home. Once the sun started to creep up, Kimly climbed out of the scratchy sheets for the second time and started her day. When she saw that her phone wasn't connecting to the hotel's wifi, Kimly booted up her laptop to see if an email from Matthew's had come through. Focusing on her investigation, following Matthew's instructions—these were the things that were going to take her mind off her marriage.

After making several unsuccessful attempts to get online Kimly realized she wasn't going to be able to get past the Royal Lanna Hotel's firewall; their security had blocked her out completely. She decided to make her way downstairs and talk to someone at the front desk about the Hotel's "FREE WIFI."

In the lobby, burnt orange cushions rested on sturdy wicker chairs, and nestled among them were ornately crafted tables with round glass tops. Hanging across the walls were pieces of solid wood. Each one had intricate jungle and mountain scenes carved into it. The hotel aspired to have a tropical theme, which seemed to work with the torrid, muggy air.

The young man standing behind the counter of the hotel's front desk smiled and did a "palm-to-palm-head-bow-thing" in greeting. Kimly mimicked his actions in response.

"I'm sorry to bother you," she could hear the pace of her words slow, but she continued in the same fashion, "I made several attempts to connect to the Internet last night, and it doesn't seem to be working."

He smiled and nodded, as if she were complimenting him on the hotel's decor and said, "Yes. Internet is down. Not working."

This was not good news. She was able to get her phone contracted for overseas Satellite service, but without wifi, she was a fish out of water in the foreign city. She had assumed that she would be able to use her laptop once she had arrived in Chiang Mai in order to connect with her contacts and move the story forward.

For the second time, Kimly began to wonder if her hasty decision to leave home earlier than planned might have been a mistake. In retrospect, maybe she could've waited, but waiting would have meant facing Kyle and talking about her travel plans, and the night Kimly decided it was time to leave, was not by coincidence the night she also decided she would no longer discuss it with Kyle. Her husband had unwittingly given her permission to ignore his voice.

For years Kyle's hours had fluctuated as he climbed the Actuary ladder; starting first as an Associate, until he passed all his exams and built a reputation. Kyle spent many evenings wooing potential clients at high-end restaurants, while Kimly and the boys ate dinner at home. Eventually, Kyle became the Senior Actuarial Analyst with Echo Partners Consulting Firm and had a strong portfolio; his need to wine and dine clients became less frequent. Kyle was genuinely relieved to have maneuvered away from the demands associated with pursuing clients. He was earning a solid reputation and the scales were shifting in his favor.

That's why it was odd when Kyle started coming home at unusual hours again. In an erratic and often spontaneous fashion,

Kyle would call and say he had a last minute dinner. Other times Kimly might get a text message telling her that he was overwhelmed at work and encouraging her not to wait up. It wasn't unusual for clients to jump ship with a changing economy, so Kimly understood his drive. What she didn't understand was Kyle's new and sudden obsession with physical fitness.

One of the perks offered in Kyle's employment package with Echo Partners was a membership to the fitness gym located on the 7th floor of the company high-rise. As far as Kimly could remember, Kyle had made no mention of using the workout facilities. Then, several months ago, just before the onset of summer, Kyle came home with a new gym bag and a new interest in getting fit. She thought Kyle's enthusiasm would wane after a few weeks, but that didn't seem to happen. Almost daily, Kyle took the gym bag with him when he left the house.

One evening as Kimly was tossing Jacob's soccer jersey in the washing machine, she heard Kyle come in, climb the stairs, and head straight for the shower. Following the sound of her husband, Kimly nearly tripped over Kyle's gym bag which he had tossed on their bedroom floor.

Kimly would later look back and see the small coincidences that had lined up to reveal the unknown. For Kyle, it was a formidable perfect storm. If Jacob hadn't left his soccer jersey in his school locker for two days, Kimly wouldn't have been doing laundry at that precise moment. If Kimly hadn't recently written an article about water conservation in the home, she wouldn't have been agitated by the small load of laundry before her. If Kyle had taken a shower before he came home, he wouldn't have left his gym bag unattended.

When Kimly opened Kyle's gym bag to remove her husband's dirty clothes, the workout attire had a fresh feel to them. It was as if they hadn't been used. Two voices immediately combated for her attention. One told her it was no big deal; the other asked why he had jumped into the shower so quickly. She probably would have listened to the first voice, if she hadn't seen what she saw next. A cell phone, less sleek than the model the firm bought for Kyle, was nestled in the bag with the unused gym clothes. It's hard to know which part of her knew what she was finding; was her head leading her heart or vise-versa? Either way, a part of her knew what she was holding.

Turning the phone on, Kimly clicked on the text messaging icon, and she saw that there was only one chain of messages. Before thinking about what she would see, she clicked on the message thread.

Hey baby, I checked in. Room 131.
Running late. I'll make it up to you.
Better hurry or I'll start without you ;)
You were awesome today. Home now. Goodnight.
Goodnight baby.

Through the tiny screen of the cheap phone, Kimly realized that infidelity had entered her world. She scrolled up and saw naked selfies of her husband's mistress. Deep green eyes peeked up from under thick auburn hair; the woman's full breasts were exposed. The phone almost bounced out of Kimly's quivering hands. Her first instinct was to open the shower stall door and scream in Kyle's face, but her mothering instincts took over and Kimly walked down the hallway and closed each of her sons' bedroom doors. *Protect the boys from the chaos,* she heard herself thinking. She walked back into their master suite and quietly closed the door. The water from the shower had stopped and in the silence she heard a question rising to the surface in her own mind: *Why are you staying? Your sons are not little.* Her inner thoughts were so clear and so loud she felt like Kyle might hear them in the adjoining bathroom.

Kimly turned off the phone and slid it back into the gym bag. She zipped it closed and left it where she had found it. A wave of nausea ran through her as she silently crawled into bed and pretended to be asleep. Her heart was pounding wildly, but it was different than any beat she had felt in the past and she tried to fight the hammering muscle by holding her breath and counting. Within a few moments, she noticed that her counts were taking on images. When she said a number, she unconsciously pictured an image associated with the number. She realized what she was doing when she reached the number sixty-two and she pictured the engraved 62 on her high school locker. She went back to the number one and challenged herself to picture the twins at the age of one, then two, then three. And so on. Once she had remembered them through their thirteen years she was calm. Lying awake with her eyes pressed closed, each time her mind would render the images of the naked redhead, Kimly would force them out with quick counts to thirteen.

As she got further into her sleepless night, she realized what she really wanted to do was escape. Kyle was harmless; he wouldn't stop her from leaving him—but was that all she wanted? No, she wanted more. Kyle had replaced her as his lover; he had replaced her as his confidant. Something inside her husband had believed he could get away with an affair without Kimly putting together any of the clues. A light bulb switched on in Kimly's head, and she finally understood why Kyle didn't hold much respect for her investigative abilities: he had been living a double life right in front of her! Kimly's pain morphed to rage, giving her the independence she needed to envision herself leaving the country without his support.

The following morning Kimly climbed out of bed before her husband and left the house without waking him. Tempted to send a text message to his gym bag phone, she resisted the urge. By letting him think he was keeping his secret, she kept the upper hand. She taped a note to the bathroom mirror instead:

"I forgot about a deadline at work. Can you take the boys to school? Don't let them leave without their jerseys (they're in the dryer) —thanks"

Once she arrived at the office Kimly emailed Matthew and a few other coworkers from the paper who could help her make contact in Thailand. She then went to the bank to open a private account and moved money from their joint savings. By lunch, Kimly had scheduled a doctor's visit to update her vaccines and purchased an airline ticket. She planned to leave in three weeks.

Everything went as planned for four days. Kimly was able to avoid eye contact with Kyle. Of course, she realized over those four days that her husband had been avoiding eye contact with her for some time. When her hammering heart would begin to beat wildly, she returned again to counting the twins at age one, and two, and three, and so on—challenging her mind to conjure new images of their changing features. Kimly didn't initiate any conversation, and when Kyle spoke she agreed to anything he said, lest starting a fight. She knew better than to fight with Kyle. The intensity of an argument could cause her to get passionate and reveal her knowledge of his affair. In the end, she was the one who would lose what she wanted. If he apologized and begged her forgiveness, it would be nearly impossible to leave. And if he learned that Kimly knew about the affair, it could be the open door for him to move out and be with the red-headed tramp, a thought which made Kimly sick to her stomach.

Plus, she wasn't entirely sure what she wanted Kyle to do anyway. Obviously she wanted him to end the affair, but then what? Did that calm the turmoil inside her? An affair is an ocean, turbulent and deadly; no one gets out without some damage around the edges. Kimly's silence was her lifeboat. Soon the waves were going to crash, and Kyle would feel the weight of his choices. Kimly wanted to be on another continent when it happened. It was the only good in it for her.

In the hours of the night separating yesterday from tomorrow, things shifted. It happened when Kyle reached for her. The hand she had always known came up under her t-shirt as she slept and her husband began to gently fondle her breast. Kimly pushed his hand away, pulling her t-shirt back down and wrapped the covers tightly around her. Something about rejecting him made her feel powerful and vulnerable at the same time, and she woke the next morning convinced that she needed to move her departure date forward.

Three days later, when Kimly left the States, she was still waiting for her contacts to come through. She dropped the twins off at school, and before calling a cab to take her to the airport, fashioned a brief, handwritten note and taped it to the bathroom mirror for her cheating husband to find.

"I know about your affair. I'm going to Chiang Mai. –Kimly"

Of course, the young man working behind the counter in lobby of the Royal Lanna knew none of these things when he sensed Kimly's frustrations about the malfunctioning internet. Using broken English he reiterated his apologies, "We are so very sorry for such inconvenient for you…"

"No, it's fine," Kimly mumbled, but inside she scolded herself for not remembering to purchase the English to Thai phrase dictionary she had been eyeing on Amazon. In her hasty departure she had successfully avoided having an unpleasant conversation with Kyle, but had she unwittingly set herself up to have limited conversation with anyone in Thailand…other than the barista at the coffeehouse?

The coffeehouse! She remembered the greasy haired young man from the night before had been using his laptop. She spun on her heel and rushed back to her room to grab her laptop.

Twenty minutes later, Kimly adjusted herself into the green overstuffed chair and was making another attempt to get through the security firewall, this time from the coffeehouse. Her failed attempts were growing in number. No matter what she tried, her computer would take her to a bright red page which read: "STOP! FIREWALL BREECH!" The fear tactics of a society consumed with viruses were alarming. Kimly was so fixated on the computer screen, she didn't hear the man attempting to speak to her.

"Well, I hope you aren't ignoring me after I saved your life," his deep voice finally caught her attention.

She looked up to see the familiar eyes of the man who had helped her cross the street the night before.

"Oh, hi, sorry. I was just trying to understand my computer. It's a like foreign language," she had gotten her bearings back, giving her the ability to verbally spar with the handsome stranger. Gone was the silly, school-girl fluttering.

"So...did you stay in the cafe all night for fear of crossing the street?" He teased.

"Oh yeah, that's exactly what happened. I looked around, and there was no one to walk me across the street so I figured...I better hang it up here."

The man flashed a relaxed smile, and he reached his hand in her direction, "Hi, I'm Dak."

"Hi. I'm Kimly."

"Kimly...that's pretty. Is it a family name?"

She smiled politely, "My father is an American, I don't really know his heritage, and my mother is Thai. My mother is really into the meaning of names. Kimly means *Golden Lion*," Kimly rolled her eyes in a pattern she had mastered over the years. "So, Dak?" she hesitated, wondering if the name was common among Thai men.

"It's short for Dakum. Dakum Kesapan."

Dak sat in the twin green chair and the two began exchanging small talk about Chiang Mai. Kimly shared observations about the strange habits of the street vendors and the abundance of people riding scooters. The conversation turned out to be a great distraction to her continued failed attempts at getting connected to the Internet, so she continued looking at Dak when he spoke, and then every few minutes returning her attention to her laptop.

Kimly answered Dak's questions about her life in the states, but she evaded anything personal. As vague as she tried to keep it, Dak finally asked her point blank, "Are you married?"

Kimly hadn't had time to think about how she wanted to answer the question if it should arise, but she knew her hesitant response, combined with her reactive deep breath, had answered Dak's question. She had given herself away.

"Um...kinda."

"Ah..." He smiled at her, sipped his coffee and smiling said, "That's *not* possible. There's no such thing as being *kinda married*. That's like being *a little pregnant*."

Even though Kimly knew it wasn't her fault, she felt awkward and ashamed when she mentioned that she was separated from her husband. Holding an expression of genuine concern, Dak's response was short, "I hope you two can work it out."

Kimly didn't have it in her to explain the reason for their separation. Saying it aloud would require putting it into a sentence that she couldn't quite construct. She was too embarrassed to add anything about her two sons at home. Logically, she knew Jacob and Dylan were fine. They weren't babies; her boys were thirteen. For some strange reason, when she looked at this man, a legitimate stranger, the memory which came spiraling forward was a conversation she had recently had with her son, Dylan.

Two days before Kimly packed her bags and left for Chiang Mai, she and the boys were in the car, waiting in line at a drive thru hamburger joint after soccer practice. Dylan was riding "shotgun" in the front seat, and Jacob was in the back seat looking down at his phone, numbly playing an NBA game.

"Is Dad having an affair?" Dylan asked.

"No!" Kimly quickly lied. "Dylan, why would you ask that?"

"Josh said that his Dad had an affair, and now his Mom and Dad are getting divorced."

"Josh is an idiot," Jacob interjected without looking up from his game.

"You're an idiot." Dylan replied.

"Shut up, fag!"

"Stop it! Both of you." Kimly adjusted her mirror and eyed Jacob, who continued playing his video game, unfazed by her warning.

"Have you ever had an affair?" Dylan questioned.

"No. Dylan, what is…"

"Good." Dylan interrupted his Mother. "Because I would rather you died, than you had an affair."

Kimly held onto the steering wheel as if it were the only thing keeping her from being thrown off the planet. Every fear she had about her marriage failing had always been centered on what it would do to her boys. She knew that thousands of children had survived divorce, but was "survival" where she wanted to set the bar? Did she want her boys to feel as if they had "survived" living in two homes? But, what did that mean she should endure? Even now…here she was carpooling the twins around town, and for all she knew Kyle was holed up in some cheap motel with *her.*

"Do you love Dad?" Dylan stared straight ahead. Kimly was pretty sure her son wouldn't be satisfied with a simple 'yes'.

"Yes," Kimly answered.

"Does he love you?" again, the thirteen-year-old didn't turn his eyes to hers.

"Gaaay…" Jacob mumbled from the backseat.

"Jacob! Stop." Kimly thought again about how important it was to answer Dylan with real answers. Before she left town she was going to have to explain some harsh realities to her sons. Simply telling him 'yes' was not going to bring comfort to the chaos brewing behind those chestnut eyes.

"Yes," Kimly answered, and she was filled with shame.

Kimly adjusted her grip on her gravitational anchor, and she and her sons rode home in silence.

Kimly looked at Dak, then back at her computer and then changed the subject by asking what his business was in Chiang Mai.

"Do you own your own business?" her eyes glanced down at his casual attire. Dak sat across from Kimly in a pair of blue jeans and a t-shirt with a surf logo.

"I'm just here to serve," he stated simply.

Kimly assumed he must be teasing, so she responded playfully, "I see…you're just here to help nearsighted tourists cross the streets."

"If that's what God wants, then sure," Dak smiled.

She started to chuckle but then realized, *He's not kidding.* A part of her was disappointed upon realizing he was serious. He had seemed so normal, now to find out he was some sort of religious wacko was disenchanting.

"I'm taking a *sabbatical* of sorts."

"A sabbatical? Are you a professor?"

"No. I'm a Pastor. I lead a small church; they supported the idea of me taking a leave. For personal reasons—time to clear my head, so to speak. "

Kimly gave a subtle nod. She had pegged him as conservative when she mentioned her separation, but he seemed too young to be a Preacher. *Too bad,* she thought. While it might have been nice to have a friend in the foreign town, Kimly was sure he wouldn't to be too thrilled to learn that she didn't share his fascination with God.

"I returned to Thailand about 2 months ago, because I felt as if there was something God wanted to show me."

"Returned?" she raised her eyebrows, but Kimly wasn't completely surprised. The Thai man's English was natural; with only a slight Thai accent. Dak sat his coffee on the table between them and scratched his face lightly before answering.

"Yes, returned," Dak took in a deep breathed, exhaled and continued, "I left Thailand when I was nineteen and moved to the states to go to college. It was my mother's dream. It was there I met my wife. We married, and I've lived in that community for about 20 years."

"Your wife...is she traveling with you?"

"No, I'm here alone. My wife passed away a little over four years ago." Dak said.

"I'm sorry...that's...well, I'm sorry."

"Thank you, yes. Thank you." Dak said.

For the next thirty minutes, Kimly and Dak chatted about travel while she attempted to break through the firewall. Frustrated, Kimly gave up. She mumbled her complaint and closed her laptop.

"Is it important that you get online?" Dak asked.

"I'm writing a story...it's an investigative piece. I'm a journalist. I need to read an email. It's not downloading on my phone and the firewall here is blocking me out."

"Well, you could always come to my place. I have a computer. You're welcome to use it."

"Umm...yeah...I don't think so," Kimly tilted her head at him.

He smiled at her and agreed, "No, you're right. You don't even know me."

There was a moment of awkwardness, and then Dak spoke again, "Or, you could come with me to a place I know of that has Internet."

Kimly smiled at him, with squinting eyes. He let out a little laugh, "Oh, yeah, I guess that isn't much different."

After a moment, Kimly said, "How about this. You give me the address of this place, and I will take a cab there. This way if I change my mind on the way, or if the place you are describing looks sketchy, I can just leave."

"Umm...no, that won't work. What if in my evil plans, I gave you the address to a dangerous place to lure you there?" Dak teased.

She couldn't help but grin at him. "Well, now I know you won't do that."

"Because...?" Dak drew out the word.

"Because you just told me."

The two left the coffeehouse, and Dak led Kimly toward several motorized rickshaws. As they approached, the drivers standing nearby began to call out, "Tuk tuk...tuk tuk!" Kimly looked at Dak with a question in her eyes. He smiled and mouthed, "Taxi," and gave her a wink.

Kimly played down her enthusiasm about riding in the three-wheeled vehicle, while Dak talked to the driver in Thai. Dak had given her the address on a piece of paper to help her to feel relaxed about following a stranger, but he was telling the driver where they were heading. She watched Dak jog across the street and climb into a forest green convertible Jeep Wrangler.

As the rickshaw traveled through the narrow streets of Chiang Mai, Kimly absorbed the sights. Simple things, like a frail woman walking with a chicken in her arms, made Kimly smile. She was glad she was alone because her fascination would have overtaken the cool demeanor she had been aiming to portray. Now, seated alone behind the driver of a motorized rickshaw, no one was watching, and she didn't have to maintain her composure.

When the rickshaw made a sharp left turn, Kimly grabbed the metal handrail to her right. This was a ride her twins would've loved, especially Jacob. Of course, he'd probably want to be driving, given the chance. The hammering in her heart began to rise, so Kimly quickly shifted her thoughts. She reminded herself again, that her boys were fine. It was Thursday evening at home; they had soccer practice and homework. If Kyle had any common sense, he was keeping things in order for their boys.

Along the roads they traveled Kimly noticed a myriad of extravagant birdhouses. In front of the businesses and residences, dollhouse-sized dwellings were perched high on pedestals. Some of the birdhouses were only large enough to house a single crow, while others could house an entire flock. Each birdhouse was unique, but they still had similar themes reflecting wealth. They were trimmed in gold and many had pillars, rather than walls, with tiny statues of Buddha in the center. Some of the houses had flowers and food sitting on the edge, resembling more of an offering than a feeding.

As much as traveling in the open-air taxi gave Kimly a raw view of the streets, it was equally disorientating to be traveling on the opposite side of the road. She wondered why such a simple navigating task was inconsistent in differing regions. It had never made any sense to Kimly why the world's population couldn't agree on which side of the road to travel. There were only two choices, after all. The rickshaw sped past a large gold and white Buddhist Temple, her eyes scanned the mint green painted exterior, trimmed in deep orange scalloped pine. Resting at the top was an enormous Buddha. Kimly mumbled, "Is there nothing on which we can agree?"

Riding in the rickshaw behind Dak's vehicle, Kimly kept one eye on the Jeep to make sure she was still following it. Several times when they had stopped at an intersection she spotted Dak's eyes in his rear view mirror. He was watching her, and his constant observance made her uneasy; imaginary headlines flashed through her thoughts: MISSING AMERICAN WOMAN LAST SEEN LEAVING COFFEEHOUSE WITH THAI MAN.

Kimly's hand clenched the metal handrail. What exactly was her plan if this man did take her someplace sketchy? How was she going to tell the driver to leave quickly? For all she knew these men already knew one another and the whole thing was a setup, including the story of him being a pastor and the dead wife. *Stop it!* She chastised herself, *Name one great reporter who investigated a story without taking a chance? The whole reason you came here was to be in the trenches. You knew there was going to be a certain amount of risk.* Kimly continued her inner dialogue as the rickshaw bounced along the highway, and while her hammering heart calmed slightly, her right hand never released its firm grip on the metal handrail.

4

The hand painted sign at the entrance read, HOUSE OF HOPE CHILDREN'S HOME. It was painted with a rainbow of child-sized handprints. The two car caravan pulled off the highway and into the dirt parking lot. Dak, Kimly, and the rickshaw driver had traveled to Doi Saket, a small city north of Chiang Mai.

"Safe enough for you?" Dak was grinning as he crossed the lot and joined her at the rickshaw.

"Yeah, I guess this is pretty safe," she playfully rolled her eyes. And then she turned and handed the driver a 1,000 Baht bill, thanking him for the ride. The driver nodded, thanked her and was about to pull away in his taxi when Dak put his hand out to stop the driver.

"Yoot," Dak called to the driver, "Khaa?"

The driver responded, "300 Baht."

Dak shook his head and held out his hand to the driver. The driver reached into his pocket and pulled out some bills, handing them to Dak.

"Khaawp Khoon Khrap," Dak nodded as he thanked the driver and handed Kimly her change. Kimly averted her eyes, too embarrassed to thank Dak for his gesture, and she slid the baht into her handbag.

The House of Hope Children's Home was not much to look at by the standards of a woman who had grown up in a prominent Southern California beach city. The main building was large and it appeared to have had many alterations and additions done without a master-plan. One of the rooms on the second level protruded six feet out from the side and had no lower level below it. It was held up with over a dozen rods of bamboo. Kimly's eyes locked on the room above. Dak followed her line of sight and laughed a little, "I know, pretty crazy, huh? But, that bamboo is stronger than it looks." He motioned to her and they began to walk across the patchy grass. The cinder block walls of the main building were unpainted, but the trim was bright blue, and the roof was painted the same. Next to the large building were two unpretentious houses, each with its own laundry line of gender appropriate clothing.

"It's unbelievable…"

"You know what else is unbelievable? This is where I grew up."

Kimly's eyes shot over at Dak, and then over her shoulder at the sign behind them. "You're an orphan?"

"No. I'm not an orphan. I mean, my mother passed away a long time ago, but she raised me here—at the orphanage with the other children. She was a caregiver."

"Really? Wow. What was that like?"

"It was pretty wonderful, actually. I mean, as a kid, there were times I loathed it. You can imagine…endless playmates, but I had to share my mom with them all."

"Did your father live here as well? Did he help run it?"

"No, no. I never knew my father. He was killed before I was born. That's how Mom ended up here. She was young, alone and pregnant, and with the political chaos happening in Bangkok in the 70's…she had to find someplace safe. Sunan Injiam is the proprietor of House of Hope. He took her in when I was a baby."

A little further in the distance, Kimly spotted a fenced-in playground, and behind the fence, she saw a couple of other neglected sheds and a white cow grazing in a field. They had traveled far enough outside of town that the sounds of traffic were minimal. It was serene, but not silent. There was a distant, mesmerizing shuffle of voices and a light tapping of piano keys. Dak's eyes were already on hers, and his smile grew when the faint shuffling voices turned to singing. Kimly held Dak's eyes, squinted her own, paused and listened. It was the voices of children singing.

Dak gave her a wink, "Follow me."

Doing as she was told, she followed as he led her toward the sound of the sweet crooning. They entered the building from an entrance on the side and were able to watch the choir singing without the children sensing they had an audience. At least thirty children, waist high at the tallest, stood in lopsided rows serenading a young man who couldn't have been more than a teenager himself, as he played the piano. A small woman in her twenties stood facing the children, moving her graceful arms in tempo and mouthing the words they sang aloud.

Kimly was taken aback at the reaction of the children when they noticed Dak standing at the edge of the large room. It started with one small boy. He was dutifully singing with the other children, his fidgeting and squirming body exposing his boredom. When he spotted Dak, his eyes grew wide and the sounds he was barely emitting suddenly flared to a roar, "DAK!" The child's voice, and the child himself, bounced across the room. The rest of the children followed his lead and before the pianist had ceased playing Dak was being smothered by the affections of about two dozen small children. Each of the children wanted to touch him. Kimly imagined Dak must confuse so many children, but his eye contact and the exuberant tones told her otherwise.

It took nearly 5 minutes for Dak to get the children to calm down. Kimly watched, awed by the beauty of their interaction. Initially, the small Thai children reminded her of her own boys when they were much younger, but the foreign language interrupted her reminiscing. As the children spoke, more than any other time she could remember, the language barrier felt like a true barricade. It was an isolating feeling to be so close to beauty, yet unable to experience its fullness. Dak was natural with the children, relaxed. He didn't mention having children. Maybe that would happen for him someday; as handsome as he was, he would surely find love again.

The children were intrigued by the stranger; they wanted to get close to Kimly, and it caught her by surprise. One little girl, dressed in a yellow sundress, grabbed Kimly's hand and began to sway and sing. Kimly wondered if Dak had known this would be the reaction of the children and if he was using their precious faces to try and win her trust. If that was his plan, it was working.

After several more minutes, the petite woman who had been leading the choir of children clapped her hands together several times and spoke to the children. Kimly had no idea what she said, but the little voices quieted, and the little ears listened. Without a moment of haste, the children seemed to forget about them entirely and raced toward a doorway on the opposite side of the room, cheering and chattering with each stride.

Dak tilted his head towards Kimly's and chuckled, "She offered them their morning snack. It seems plum mangos are more popular than we are."

She felt his hand on her arm as he leaned in and said, "Come with me, let's get you online..."

He led her out of the cafeteria and down a hallway. At the end of the hallway, the two approached a room where an older Asian gentleman sat behind a desk leaning forward with his forehead resting in one hand, while the other hand held a telephone to his ear. When Dak tapped lightly on the open door and the gentleman lifted his head from his hand, weariness lifted from the man's face and was replaced by a broad smile. The gentleman motioned for them to enter.

The room they entered was wallpapered with Polaroid photos of children. Columned rows had labels above them, suggesting their placement as some sort of filing system. The elderly man continued his conversation while Dak and Kimly soaked in the faces in front of them. Nameless children, most wearing little clothing, hung looking from their place on the wall.

The gentleman concluded his conversation and lowered the phone to the cradle; before it even met its bed, the man was on his feet and heading around the desk to greet Dak.

"Dak! I mean, Pastor Dakum! This is the best surprise!"

"Stop, it's Dak. I'll always be Dak."

"Yes, yes, Dak. You will always be Dak," the man said as the two shared a familial hug. "Oh son, I've missed you!"

"Seems like each time I come by to visit, you are off somewhere else...vacationing, I assume." Dak winked at the gentleman.

The gentleman's demeanor with Dak was so casual and familiar, it was awkward for Kimly. Their obvious affinity reminded her she didn't know this man she had met on the street.

"Sunan Injiam, I'd like you to meet Kimly..." Dak motioned out his hand toward Kimly with a lingering pause. "Demin," Kimly interjected, reaching an outstretched hand towards the gentleman, "Kimly Demin. It's nice to meet you."

After a few moments of pleasantries, the conversation slid into the proprietor's concerns with the plumbing in one of the small houses, which served as the girls' dormitory. All the while Kimly continued to look at the pint-sized faces plastered around the room. The Polaroid eyes looked back at her, reminding her of her own vulnerability. She knew nothing about this man who had led her here, well, almost nothing. It wasn't lost on Kimly that Sunan had referred to Dak as "Pastor Dakum."

Sunan Injiam had no reservations in allowing Kimly access to his computer, especially since it would free up Dak to check into the misbehaving toilet in the girls' dormitory. The two men made their way to another part of the facility leaving Kimly alone as she dug into her email, grateful for the privacy and freedom to fully concentrate her efforts.

Everything Kimly had read about Thai's slave trade described a vile and disturbing industry. Adults were lured and held captive under the guise of employment, women were seduced by smooth talking pimps, children were no more valuable than week-old produce, sold to captors who had no qualms about inflicting permanent damage on their little limbs—or even gauging out their eyes. Kimly had spent months reading news articles about exploited children, articles that would assault the senses of her new friend. In her estimation, Pastor Dakum's deep olive skin would turn a shade of pink if he were to encounter a small portion of the darkness she hoped to unearth. Yes, Kimly was fairly certain her contact was going to come through with a very reliable source to get her started, and she wasn't going to downplay it to keep from embarrassing a church boy's sensibilities.

Amid the junk mail in her inbox, Kimly found the email she had hoped for. Matthew Rawlings had worked alongside Kimly at the newspaper for three and a half years. He started as her intern and caught on quickly. Once he was brought on staff they maintained a trusting relationship. He knew she was smarter than the stories she was being assigned. That's why Matthew didn't have any problem bringing her into his circle of trust while he investigated a piece that would expose an advanced organization of sex trafficking happening in the Los Angeles Area.

Young women were being recruited through "Fantasy Websites" with a promise of an explosive online modeling career. Most of the naive women were American runaways; teenagers from small towns across the nation flocked to the metropolitan city where they were coerced into filming pornography believing that they would find fame. Three pornography sites were named as gateways for the owners to find the girls best suited for building up their sordid prostitution ring. In this city so close to the Long Beach port, prostitution wasn't new; harlotry had been around longer than the

WI IERE THE WATER RAGES

downtown skyscrapers. What struck readers was the number of girls being trafficked and their median age. Girls as young as eleven had been coerced, exploited, and sold. After the success of Matthew's twelve-week exposé, his status in the news industry had changed pretty rapidly. Matthew Rawlings had been offered a job with CNN before the final segment had even been circulated.

Matthew's immediate success had Kimly turning more than a pale shade of green. Her jealousy was tempered only by her pride in him for exposing such an atrocity. She was thankful he had been able to bring light to an area advancing such injustice and evil, but at the same time—it stirred her own feelings of insignificance. She read Matthew's series of articles like Pastor Dakum might read the Bible.

When Kimly began her plans to travel to Thailand, Matthew was among the people whom she trusted and consulted. He was more than willing to help her find contacts in the Asian city, but the last time he had spoken to Kimly, her planned departure date was still a few weeks out. An email from Matthew was the best possible scenario for her last minute change of itinerary.

```
FROM: mrawlings@cnnnews.com
TO: kdenim@tribune.com
SUBJECT: Lead in Chiang Mai

Kimly-
My apologies for being so slow in getting
back to you. I got your message saying you
headed to Thailand earlier than you had
planned. I guess my email will get to you
after you've landed. My contact in Bangkok
agreed the most authentic route for you
would be to pursue the story from the angle
of purchasing a "live-in" housekeeper. You
don't fit the profile of the other buyers.

Your stats were correct. The majority of
the people taken are forced into
prostitution. The second largest group is
used as factory workers or on fishing boats.
There are also a huge number of people who
```

are sold as in-home slaves. Makes you sick, eh?

Kimly had no house to receive the housekeeper. *I need to figure that out*, she thought to herself.

It was wise that you went to Chiang Mai, rather than Pattaya Beach. Slave trading and sex trafficking is rampant all over the country. Moving a person across the border can fetch a distributor 15,000 baht, moving high-end merchandise could fetch anywhere from 25,000 to 30,000 baht. Kimly, in that economy, that's a fortune. People get passionate about their money. ESTABLISH A COVER AND MAINTAIN IT.

Matthew went on to tell Kimly that despite common misconceptions about trafficking, the people involved in this industry did not hold a preference for children as much as they desired "unusual." A virgin could be sold one time to a customer for the equivalent of $750 American dollars, but after the first night she would be sold to multiple clients in one night for $2.50 a session.

I don't want to scare you, and I hate to sound harsh but, if you are not careful, YOU could become a target.
You are an attractive American woman alone in the middle of an Asian city. You could fetch a large sum from wealthy Nationals. If you attract the attention of the wrong people, it could be disastrous. It is difficult for distributors to get their hands on a sophisticated woman. The majority of those who are victimized in the rural land are small children or runaways who are hungry and desperate.

Kimly shuddered when she read the word "sophisticated." Matthew went on to say how important it was that the people she contacted believed she was a resident of Thailand with a slew of contacts. She cannot appear to be someone who could easily go missing without questions being raised.

"Well, did you find what you were looking for?" Paring knife in hand, Dak peeled an apple as he walked back into the small office. He sat in a chair across the desk from Kimly and waited for her answer. Her dark eyes were transfixed on the computer screen, as she ingested the information in Matthew's email. She had made notes regarding the contact from Bangkok, and she was now gathering information about the streets of Chiang Mai.

"A little over-focused, are we?" he teased her, trying again to break the invisible hook holding her captive.

"Yeah, what? Oh, sorry. My colleague came through...actually better than I had hoped." All of this was said without her gaze leaving the screen. When she finally tore her eyes away from the screen, Dak was shaking his head at her, with a sly grin as he chewed on his apple. She tilted her head at him inquiring about the joke she had missed.

"What?" She feigned a polite smile. As much as she wanted in on the joke, she was fairly certain she wasn't going to find it as humorous as he. "Oh...forget it," she waved her hand, brushing him off, and shared a minimal amount of the information from Matthew.

"My story, that is, the story I hope to write is an investigation into Thailand's slave trade," Kimly paused. Dak nodded, but said nothing.

"I was hoping to connect with abolitionists. I am interested to know how they are able to rescue people, but the contact I got is a little different than that," Kimly moved the mouse across a calendar mouse-pad. There was a large green K in the middle of the pad, and across the top it read KASIKORN BANK. "I am going to meet with someone who will connect me with people who get other people what they need." Kimly released her grip on the computer's mouse to make air-quotes at the last part. "I'll present myself under the guise of an American who just relocated to Thailand, I will fit a certain profile," she kept her voice low.

"I don't...know you, and I don't mean to intrude," Dak paused and swallowed the small piece of apple he had been chewing, "but, this sounds pretty intense."

Kimly took a breath, smiled and answered nonchalantly while looking down at the dated mouse-pad calendar, "oh, it's fine. I just need them to trust me, to believe my story. They just need to connect me to the 'distributors' working in this area."

"And, these 'distributors', they are here, in Chiang Mai? Are you sure?" he asked. "Chiang Mai is full of families; it's not like the border cities."

Why are church people so naïve to the real problems in the world? She thought to herself.

Matthew's warning in the email was just part of the information Kimly opted to leave out when relaying information to Dak. After all, she reasoned, this isn't his journey. Most of the information Matthew had sent her, she kept to herself. What she did share with Dak was her intention to meet with the contact.

"Where?" he asked.

"That's what I was just looking at..." Kimly read the email silently.

```
Meet   the   contact   on   Sunday   night   on
Rajdunnern   Road,   in   Old   Chiang   Mai.   It   is   an
ancient   city.   The   vendor   will   be   400   meters
west   of   Tae   Pae   Gate.
```

"I need to go to a street called...Rajdunnern Road"

"Walking Street. You're meeting someone on Walking Street?"

"Walking what?" Kimly asked, "I thought Walking Street was down South at Pattaya Beach?"

"Well, every city in Thailand has their version of Walking Street, Kimly. Chiang Mai's is just more family friendly."

Kimly didn't know this man. Not really. They had shared a cup of coffee and she followed him out to an orphanage where she had watched children fawn over him, but other than today's escapades, she really didn't know him. She wanted to like him. It wasn't too annoying having him around, but she didn't know if he was someone she could trust completely. She also didn't want him getting in the way or holding her back. She lived one lifetime being held back, she hadn't flown to another continent to live like a librarian. She diverted her eyes from his and looked up at the wall. Little Polaroid eyes looked back at her.

Very calmly, almost nonchalantly she spoke to him, "Okay, well, that's where I'm meeting my contact. On this…Walking Street."

"So…this 'contact'…do you know him? I mean, I'm assuming it's a man?"

Kimly could tell she was going to have to use her words carefully if she didn't want a lecture from Daddy Warbucks and his little orphans about the dangerous people in the world.

"This contact is someone who can help me get the information I need about how people who come to visit Thailand, or come to live here for that matter, manage to get slave labor. Or sex slaves."

Dak looked down at the knife he had been using to cut the apple.

"What time is the meeting?" he stared intently at the tip of the paring knife.

"Well…I just need to make my way 400 meters up …Rajdunnern Road…sometime between 8 and 11 PM."

"Okay. That will work," Dak responded flatly.

"Wait, what?" Kimly stared at him, dumbfounded.

"The time will work. I know Walking Street, and it's fairly crowded, but we will just stay together and it will be fine."

As charming as Dak was, there was no way Kimly was going to allow him to tag along and get in the way with her first contact. It had taken her a lifetime of internal battles, culminating with the discovery that she was married to a cheater, to get her to make this journey. She wasn't going to throw it away because of one man's misogynic fears.

"Dak, thank you so much for everything. Seriously. You have made this a great day…with the kids and helping me get online…but honestly, I came here knowing I would be doing this alone. I am not expecting you to hold my hand, or be my driver as I navigate—"

Dak interrupted Kimly, "Rum mai dee tod pee tod glong."

"Excuse me?" Kimly raised her eyebrows.

"It's an ancient Thai proverb, 'Those who can't dance blame it on the flute and the drum.' In other words, the bad worker blames the tools."

"Okay…meaning what? How am I a bad tool?" Kimly responded, unsure if he was trying to be overly condescending, or if his cocky attitude was imaginatively inflated by the way he wielded the paring knife.

"Don't get defensive, Kimly. I just think you should consider it might not be wise for you to go alone to an unfamiliar place and meet with someone who may not speak English. You don't have the tools to do what you are trying to do."

"You're assuming I don't know whether or not my contact speaks English." She shot back.

"Well, do you?"

"No. But, you were still assuming."

Dak smiled at her, "And you're assuming if you can lure me into a small debate, I'll forget the bigger issue."

Kimly had to choose her words carefully. She wasn't going to admit he was right about it being dangerous, because she wasn't convinced it was dangerous. She hadn't come this far to start behaving as if she were in the middle a made-for-TV movie, where danger lurked around every corner.

Handsome or not, gentlemanly or not...she had come here with a purpose, and she wasn't going to let him get in the way. She sat for a moment and stared once again at the Polaroid faces around the room.

Finally, Kimly spoke, "Ok, well. I am meeting the contact at Walking Street on Monday night. So, since you insist on coming, you can come to my hotel and pick me up at eight. On Monday. Does that sound okay?"

Dak looked at her, but said nothing. It made her a little nervous because she thought perhaps he had seen through her lie, but she held her gaze into his stunning eyes. Her stomach was doing somersaults, but she held it together. He stared back without flinching. Then he gave her the slightest smile, causing her heart to start hammering. She lifted her chin and looked away.

Finally, Dak replied, "That sounds just great, Kimly."

5

The Chiang Mai Kimly had found herself in was quite large, but at the city's inception, the town had been smaller and surrounded by a towering block wall and a moat. Once called the Rose of the North, the original town, renowned for its beauty, rested at the base of rolling mountains surrounded by flourishing green countryside. This "Walled Township" had maintained a fascination from much of the world due to its seclusion. Until the 1920's Chiang Mai could only be reached by way of boat or elephant, its romantic isolation evoking mystery.

As Chiang Mai expanded, the walls remained, and the original township became a historical site and a tourist attraction. The ancient walls now surrounded a myriad of hotels, two colleges, and a Buddhist temple. The area which had once been the town square served as an arena for the town's festivals. And the main street, Rajdunnern Road, which ran the 3000-foot length of the city, evolved into the city's famed Sunday night "Walking Street."

Walking Street was similar to the Night Bazaar Kimly had encountered on the streets near her hotel. Some of the vendor's wares being handmade, while others had come off an assembly line, there were t-shirts, purses, knives and jewelry and just about every third booth had items fashioned from Thai silk. Each booth ran right up to the next. As tourists entered the shopping arena they were greeted by the assortment of treasures. Merchants were eager to make sales, practically accosting them to make purchases early on the walkway, before the shopper realized the same trinkets were available in abundance further down.

The entrance to the walled city was Tae Pae Gate, and that is where Kimly arrived by taxi on Sunday night, a full day before she had told Dak they would meet and go together. With Dak's light eyes penetrating her own, she felt lying to him would satisfy his fears, but still keep her free to meet her first contact without the companionship of an overprotective outsider. When Dak arrived at her hotel, ready to take her to Walking Street on Monday night, Kimly would simply explain she had decided "at the last minute" to go the night before.

Kimly made her way down the street, amazed at the amount of people moving through the small area. She had calculated how many steps she would need to walk to travel 400 meters, and concentrated on counting while she moved through the crowds. About half way down Walking Street she would make contact with a man named Thaksin. Matthew's initial email had been a little vague about Thaksin, and she had needed clarification if he would be aware of her true identity, or be under the impression he was setting a real transaction into place. She had sent a follow-up email to Matthew asking him to clarity. She didn't know if she would be able to breach the firewall at the Royal Lanna, so she asked Matthew to use text messaging rather than email. When she woke on Sunday morning she had received a text from Matthew.

Thaksin is safe. Don't break your cover with him.

The message was a little more cryptic than she had hoped. The safe part was good, but it didn't really answer her question. For all she knew, Thaksin would assume Kimly was a Thai-American woman who was seeking a live-in housekeeper at a reasonable cost. It seemed too simple to believe anyone would buy the story, but Matthew was adamant they would. A little voice in the back of Kimly's mind questioned how a stranger making inquiries into purchasing another human being could get access so easily, but she squelched those thoughts. She hadn't questioned her luck when the stick turned blue, why should she question it now if it was finally spinning in her favor.

Watching the people around her, the street vendors making their living and the crowds of tourists, nothing she saw gave her intuitive flares or uneasy feelings. Dak's concerns had given her a tiny bit of a shiver, but now she was certain, it was all unwarranted. Perhaps, tomorrow night when she met up with him and told him she had been able to move through the evening streets unscathed, and even make a successful contact, he would relax.

She noticed a large Buddhist temple on her left. For some reason, the lavish ornamental design made her shudder. Kimly wasn't sure why. She had never had any aversions to Eastern religions.

The booth Kimly was to approach would be selling wooden bowls and carved wall hangings. She had calculated 400 meters to be just over 1300 feet. The plan was to count her footsteps, while keeping a long stride. What Kimly didn't take into account was the amount of people who would be walking or the number of times she would have to stop short. When her step count was at 1290, uneasiness rose in her chest. Craning her neck to see over the people in front of her, she tried to locate the described goods ahead. She continued in this fashion until she was at 1322. That was the number of steps she had taken when she saw a booth ahead selling the most intricate and beautiful carved wood. Each wall hanging had a theme-- elephants, mountains, monkeys, peacocks. And within each carved wall hanging the seamless grain of the wood flowed, giving it a unique signature. Kimly couldn't help but be drawn to the raw beauty of the smooth wall hangings.

As she approached the booth, Kimly heard someone whisper, **NEAR.**

It was loud and present, and she jumped slightly and turned with a full expectation of seeing Dak standing beside her. There was no one. She looked at the collection of wooden bowls, jewelry boxes, and carved candles. In the booth, behind an eight-foot table, a small framed man was wrapping a large wall hanging in newspaper. Behind the man there sat a smaller table with an assortment of wood polishes and a bag full of rags. Next to the table was a small footstool, which Kimly assumed was used for a seat. It was hardly what Kimly had imagined when she pictured a slave trader. The small framed man finished the transaction he was making, handing the wrapped wall hanging to a woman with a wide jaw line. He turned his attention to Kimly.

"You want? 500." The small framed man motioned to a set of three wooden bowls which descended in size.

Kimly could feel her pulse rising. She stayed calm, and spoke nonchalantly, "Umm...no. That's not what I am looking for."

In the shower that morning, Kimly had rehearsed the exact wording Matthew's email had told her to use, changing the inflection each time.

"I'm in need of Special Assistance from Thaksin. I have a special purchase I need to make from Thaksin--to bring back to my home. I need something special IMPORTED."

Kimly looked away from the man almost as soon as she had said the words. She was fairly certain she had said the word "special" one or two more times than the email had instructed, and she was also pretty sure the color in her face was either a glaring red or a pale white. The man sat down on his footstool and looked up at her for nearly a full minute. She didn't move. She didn't make eye contact again.

Her heart was pounding, and she caught her breath in her throat. She needed to get her breathing under control. The rest of the shoppers on Walking Street were suddenly too close and too far away at the same time. She swallowed hard and held her gaze down at a wooden box sitting on the table. The grain of the wood moved like muddy water flowing across the two engraved elephants. Each elephant faced the other, but a tree stood between them. The wood grain gave the appearance of movement, but the elephants would never connect. The box looked magnificent on the bright red table cloth.

Finally, the man stood, walked to the table and bent down to the ground. He worked under the table for a moment. Certain she must have made a mistake, she tried to decide what she should say. The man stood, walked over and handed her a small box. A butterfly was carved into the lid, and the box was small enough to fit into the palm of her hand.

"1400 baht," he said without an ounce of emotion.

Her first instinct was to protest--to barter, but she refrained. Reaching into her handbag and pulling out two 1000 baht bills, she murmured, "Thank you."

Dropping the small box into her bag, Kimly turned to make her way back through the crowds. She wanted to look inside the box, but she was shaking so badly she was afraid she might drop the lid attempting to open it. Maneuvering her way toward the large Temple she had seen, Kimly vaguely remembered seeing a sign for restrooms in its vicinity. She wanted to be alone, even if it was in the small disgusting cubicle that held a toilet.

As Kimly made her way around to the back of the building where the restroom sign pointed, she heard the voice she had heard earlier.

NEAR.

Once again, the loud voice caused her to turn. Looking over her shoulder, she noticed a face making her uneasy because while it was familiar, she couldn't place where she had seen the man before. She stopped walking and held her eyes on the man. He looked towards her but then looked away.

The women's restroom wasn't the filthy mess she had anticipated. The plastered walls were painted off-white and a row of baby blue tile ran around the perimeter of the room. Pale blue flowers danced on cotton curtains which served as doors in front of the stalls. Positioned above each of the free standing sinks was a mirror. Someone had carved a word into the mirror directly in front of Kimly. She had no way to know if it was profanity, or simply a person's name. As Kimly surveyed the room, the scratched mirror revealed the familiar-faced man walking into the restroom. Kimly inhaled deeply.

The familiar-faced man appeared to be in his early 30's. The distinguishing feature Kimly had obviously noted subconsciously was the dark dominating neck tattoo. The primitive design was a combination of swirls, scallops, and fingers crawling up from his chest and around his thick throat. It gave her the chills. His head was shaved, and he wasn't much taller than she. What the purple marked man lacked vertically was redistributed horizontally. He was broad-shouldered, scarred and inked, and standing in the doorway Kimly had just entered. Kimly turned to see if there was another exit.

Relief would have rushed through Kimly when she spotted another door across the restroom, but no sooner had it registered and her brain sent the signal telling her to move than she saw a smaller and younger man wearing a blue track suit making his entrance. He paused when he stepped through the doorway, and just stood nodding his head.

The man with the neck tattoo walked up to Kimly until he stood just a few feet away.

"Hello, how you doing tonight?" His words seemed abnormally calm in comparison to Kimly's racing heartbeat.

Kimly sucked the thick air into her lungs and replied, "Fine, thank you," as she attempted to pass him.

He reached out his massive arm, grabbing Kimly's bicep under his thick fingers and said, "Whoa....wait a second. I'm not done talking to you."

It was at that moment Kimly heard the most welcoming sound she had heard since landing in Thailand.

"Hey, Kimly, you in here?" Dak's voice entered the room, and a millisecond later the man she was suddenly grateful to see followed.

The tension was colossal, with the strange man holding Kimly's arm, but Dak didn't pause for a beat, "Seriously, I have been looking everywhere for you. Are you ready? Let's go."

All four players stood completely still. Kimly looked at Dak and then back at the man holding her arm. The tattooed man was staring at Dak, but his grip on Kimly didn't lessen.

The definitive standoff lasted just a few moments, but the seconds moved stubbornly and with deliberation. Dak lowered his voice, locked eyes with the stranger and said, "Let her go."

Despite the confidence in Dak's voice, Tattoo Man did not release his grip on Kimly's arm, nor did he pull his dark eyes away from Dak. "Or?" Tattoo Man challenged.

"No," Dak shot back quickly. "There is no 'or'. We're not doing this. Let her go."

Dak's voice was calm but commanding. If Tattoo Man were able to emit fear from his fingertips, Kimly could feel it. Like a spider the fear crawled along her bare arm and up her shoulders. His grip on her arm was terrifying; his evil penetrated her skin.

Tattooed Man released Kimly's arm.

"Out," was all he said, and the two men both turned and walked out of the women's restroom. Kimly looked at Dak, Tattoo Man's single syllable threat hanging between them. The men were gone, and she was grateful, but the tension remained in the restroom. It was thick, and neither Kimly nor Dak spoke for nearly a full minute.

"Are you okay?" Dak finally broke the silence.

Before Kimly could answer, two older Asian women shuffled into the restroom. They stopped short at the sight of Dak, obviously uncomfortable. Dak turned and Kimly followed as they headed for the door.

"I'm sorry...Ummm, please excuse us. This is...um, I'm sorry..." Kimly offered apologies to the older women, but her profuse rambling was pointless, and the uninterested women gave them a blank stare.

Walking Street was still in full swing, only now the crowds looked much more threatening to Kimly. As the couple began to move into the line of people making their way along the souvenir adorned path, the crowd became so dense that soon they were walking in a single file with Kimly in front of Dak. Kimly couldn't help but keep turning her head and looking over her shoulder to ensure that Dak was right behind her.

"You're fine. Just keep going straight ahead," Dak whispered just loud enough for her to hear. His calm confidence was appreciated; the bathroom altercation had knocked the wind out of her sails.

As they crossed through Tae Pae Gate, Dak took hold of Kimly's arm at the elbow and led her to the right, "Come this way. We're almost there," his tone gentle, but strong.

"I'm so lucky you were here, Dak. And, that you happened to see me in there. I just don't—"

"It's not luck, Kimly. I knew you were here. I was waiting for you. I was watching you the entire time," Dak opened the passenger's door of the Jeep.

"Wait, what? But, how?" she pulled the door closed, and the door's cracked plastic handle scraped the inside of her forearm.

Dak walked around the front of the convertible, and she could see him shaking his head as he formed his thoughts. He began speaking before he opened the driver's side door. "Kimly, I know you thought you were fooling me, but, Walking Street only happens on Sunday Nights. If you are going to lie to me, you might want to get your facts straight first."

He winked at her with the last thought. But, behind the wink and the mask of sarcasm, she sensed anger. She had lied to him, and he was disappointed in her. And, to top it all off...he had been right about her safety. She didn't want to look at him, so she focused instead on the light scratch her arm had received from the door handle. Dak revved the ignition of the Jeep, "I understand you came here alone, and I'm sure you believed it was going to be fine. And I hope it will be. But, I cannot let you walk head first into disaster and not try to stop you."

As Dak backed out of the parking space a clunky roll of gray duct tape rolled along the floorboard and slammed into Kimly's foot causing her to jump.

"Kimly, you are not in a safe place. It may look safe, but it isn't. And, with the fascination you have for your story..."

"I understand," Kimly stopped him midsentence. "I do. I get what you are saying. I'm sorry I lied."

"It's not about your lying to me," Dak stopped her. "I don't expect anything from you. I just don't want to see you get hurt. I wouldn't want any woman to be doing the things you are talking about doing, especially alone. The people who do these things are dangerous. You are opening yourself up to a frightening world with the story you are writing."

"Okay...slow down. What just happened in the ladies room had nothing to do with the story I'm writing. I literally just bought a box and then headed to the restroom. Those men just noticed I was alone. They were creeps, but we have no reason to believe the two incidents were connected. And, honestly...even if you hadn't come in—"

"What? If I hadn't come in...what? What do you think would have happened? You are so naive, Kimly."

Dak put the car in gear and made his way into the line of cars moving toward the traffic lanes. Night had fallen completely over the city of Chiang Mai. Nighttime belonged to the city and the people of Thailand. Inhibitions were lost. Cars, scooters and pedestrians crowded the small roads. Kimly stared out the window and tried to calm her nerves. She was still shaking from the thwarted assault, and now she was also irritated with the man who had come to her rescue. She stared blankly out the front windshield and wondered why this was so difficult for him to grasp. Did he push himself into her situation only to serve as an obstacle? It was very male of him, and it reinforced Kimly's resolve to be a woman who did something significant. This trip—this story—was a necessary step in her breaking free from the men around her.

There was no conversation on the ride back to the hotel, but the Jeep was far from quiet. It wasn't the sounds of the city as they drove the topless Jeep through the nighttime activities that pierced the silence. Nor was it the honking from the variety of taxicabs and rickshaws. The tension between Kimly and Dak was earsplitting. The roaring silence was practically painful. When Dak pulled under the expansive awning of the Royal Lanna's carport, Kimly surprised herself by not jumping out immediately and slamming the door behind her.

"Look," her words came out more gentle than she had actually felt, "I'm so thankful I met you. Especially after tonight. And, I'm really grateful for everything you have done to help me so far. But...the thing is."

Stopping herself, Kimly felt the reverberations of her heartbeat. The muscle was once again pounding hard inside her chest. She looked toward Dak, curious if he could hear it as well. Dak said nothing. Was he waiting for her to let him off the hook? He wasn't stopping her, and anyone with the slightest social skills would know where she was heading with the opening to her speech.

"It's not an accident that I am in Thailand alone. I planned to be here alone. I planned to do this on my own. I appreciate your friendship so far, but this was never supposed to be a team effort."

Dak took a deep breath in and without making eye contact, he responded, "Open the box. What's inside? I'm guessing the vendor was your contact, right?"

Raising her eyebrows, Kimly looked across the car at him. He raised his eyes to hers and the two were transformed into Samurais wielding their swords, each demanding submission. The standoff didn't last long. She was a curious soul, and that inquisitiveness was a chink in her armor.

Kimly shoved a hand into her bag and retrieved the small wooden box. Lifting the lid, she found a slip of paper which was folded until it was the size of a nickel.

7000 baht - Nawarat Bridge - Thursday 2 AM

Dak sighed, and then he said simply, "I'll be here tomorrow at nine. We can get some coffee and talk about what's next. Try to get a good night's sleep, and don't unlock your door once you are in your room. Come on, I'll ride up with you in the elevator." Before she could respond, he opened his door and made his way around the Jeep.

Kimly was stunned by his confident and direct style; she didn't even know how to respond. She simply climbed out of the Jeep and did as she was told. It wasn't until the door to her room was locked, and she was filling her bathtub with hot water that she ran through the events of the night and realized she now had a partner.

JACQUELYN SILL

6

When the light beneath the door returns, I know the night is over. I crawl from the place where I was sleeping because the ground is wet with my pee. I shift my body so that I am no longer lying down, but sitting against the flat stone wall. The door opens and the stringy hair man returns. He has one of the fire sticks in his mouth. He stands in front of me and looks at a place where I peed. He tilts his head, sucks on his fire stick and then tosses the white hot stick in my pee.

"Stand up." He grunts, while his fire stick makes a going out sound.

When I stand up my hip yells at me because it hurts from where the rocks bit me. The stringy hair man grabs my shoulders and turns me so I am backwards to him. I do not like his hands on me. I do not want him to bring Darkness to me. I pull away, but he grabs my hair and pulls me back. The stringy hair man's hands are too big. They are too strong. He holds both of my hands in his one. I can feel that he is tying my hands together with hard string. The twine scratches my skin like the foot of a rooster. I pull and twist, but the stringy hair man is too strong.

He pulls me outside and toward a motorcar. I saw a motorcar one time in the village where I lived with Momma. One of the villagers had a hot sickness. The motorcar brought a man to the village. He wore pieces of glass on his nose, and the glass made his eyes look big. This is a motorcar, but it is not that motorcar.

The stringy hair man pushes me into the back of the motorcar and closes the door. In the front of the motorcar the man with the purple marks on his neck sits holding one of his fire sticks. Smoke lingers from his mouth. I do not want to be in here. I do not understand why Uncle has not returned to take me back to the hut in his village.

When the motorcar begins to move, I am tossed around the seat and my face falls hard against the door. Red blood begins to come out of my nose. I rub my shoulder up and wipe it on my shirt. The stringy hair man spins a large ring and the motorcar turns so fast that I fall again. This time I roll off the rubber seat and onto the floor of the motorcar. I curl up into a ball. I ride in the motorcar for so long that my red blood turns hard.

When the motorcar stops, the stringy hair man opens the door and pulls me from the floor of the car. I turn my head to bite his hand, but my eyes stop me. My eyes are busy seeing a strange village. I have now seen three villages. This one is unlike any of them. Lights cast shadows from windows covered by glass out of giant huts made of stone. In the shadows I see small patches of grass growing in tiny meadows. Poles, like trees, hold lights in the sky above the road. His rough hands untie the twine around my wrists and free me. The piercing pain in my nose and the rooster scratches on my wrists are overshadowed by my fascination with this village. We stand in front of a door the color of the evening sky. The baggy pants man pounds many times; when the door opens I can hear music, and I can smell food. My stomach yells its demands making me cry. I am hungry. I am just very hungry.

The man with rough hands pushes me through the doorway. He says something to a woman in a shiny red dress; she yells something back at him. I do not understand the words they are using; their words are not my words. I stare up at the face of the woman in the red dress; she has a different kind of face than the people I have seen before. Her face is flatter, and her eyes are hiding. The eyes of this woman are further apart than mine, and they lay flat against her face. I wonder if she was born this way or if someone did this to her. I am hopeful that she will have pity on me; perhaps she will give me food and help me find Momma.

She comes to me and takes my arm, and I notice her strange fingernails. The tips of her fingers stick out further than I have ever seen and they match her shiny red dress. She begins to pinch my arm with her long sharp claws. As I pull away, she shoves the red claws in deeper. We walk into a warm room with several pots over flames. Food. She is going to give me food. I do not care that she is pinching my arm because the pain in my stomach hurts more than the pain from the red claws.

She opens a lid and shows me the food in the first pot. Beneath the steam of the boiling water I catch the smell of chicken. I lean in towards the pot. Looking up at the flat faced skinny lady, I smile and nod my head, and I say, "Chicken."

Laughing, she says something to me which I do not understand, and then she slams the lid on the pot. Drops of boiling chicken water spray in my face. Wincing, I yank my free arm up to my eyes.

Pinching my arm, she pulls me out of the food room and down a dark hallway. She shoves me through a doorway and releases my arm. The floor is made of flat square stones and is cool beneath my feet. In the middle of the room sits a wooden barrel, nearly as tall as me. On the side of the barrel someone has painted a picture of a fish the color of the sun. The barrel is filled with water. Slamming the door behind us, she speaks her words at me, but I do not understand. She steps close to me and speaks her words again and this time she motions to the barrel of water. My eyes follow hers as she looks at the barrel, and then I look back at her again.

Pinching my arm, she yells her strange words at me again, "Peluxng pha!"

Her flat face speaking words I cannot understand is scarier to me than the man with rough hands. I begin to cry harder. She slaps my face and pulls at my clothes.

"No!" I scream, and my surge of energy seems to have taken her off guard. Her claws release me, and I am faster than a hog as I rush away from her to the other side of the sunfish barrel.

She rushes after me, but I move quickly. A wasp-like anger rises in her, and I will surely be stung if I am caught. She reaches across the barrel and her strange claws grasp a clump of my hair. She tries to hold me in place, but I swing my hands and splash the water in the barrel. Slapping the water away from me, I manage to drench the flat faced lady with barrel water. She releases my hair, and I run to a corner of the room.

Standing with her arms wide and glaring at me, the flat face lady looks down at her wet dress. She brushes her claws across herself and then pulls them through her long hair. The water must have ignited a fury, because she screams as though the water burns. This I understand.

She turns her head and looks to the side of the room. Her eyes fix on a long broom wedged against the wall, holding another door closed. She reaches for the broom and pulls it to her chest. At that moment, the door from the hallway opens, and a round lady with hair the color of the barrel's sunfish waddles into the room. I have never seen anyone with sunfish-colored hair. She is holding a bowl and smiling. The smell catches my attention. Staring at her bowl, I stand completely still. A moment later the skinny lady slaps me across the face. Her claws scrape my cheek, and I pull my hand up to my face, but I am too hungry to care. My eyes stay on the round woman with sunfish-colored hair. She scowls at the wet skinny lady and lowers the bowl.

"Would you like some curry soup?" she speaks softly to me. The fish colored hair lady knows my words. I nod, very slight. But, yes.

"Here, you can have some soup. And after you eat the soup, you will take a bath. Okay?" she walks towards me. I nod, again very slight. But, yes.

She hands me the soup, and I begin to drink it by tipping my face into the bowl, then I tilt my head back and pour the soup into me. I eat quickly in case the flat faced lady tries to take it away. I use my fingers to push pieces of chicken into my mouth. The chicken and carrots burn my tongue as they make their way to my throat.

I am still hungry. I ask the round woman, "More?"

"You take a bath and then you can have more." She turns to walk out of the room. When she reaches the door, she stops and says something to the flat faced lady. The flat faced lady with the wet dress yells at her and on the way out the sunfish-colored hair lady slams the door. I pull my clothes off, and I begin to carefully climb into the barrel. I want more soup.

Next to the barrel there is a wooden crate. I climb up on the crate being careful not to step where the wood is splintered and sharp. I pull one of my legs up to the top of the barrel and twist my torso while tightening my grip on the edge of the large water trough. The flat faced lady is speaking her strange words. I do not know what she is saying, but she pushes me from behind, and I fall face first into the cold water. She throws a bar of soap into the barrel, and when I come up for air, the soap hits me in the eye. She is laughing. I rub my eye and splash more water in her flat face. She becomes angry and she reaches into the barrel, pressing my head under the water.

I am fighting her, as I am desperate for air. I cannot grab air while I am underwater. If I breathe in the water, it will burn my lungs and make me cough and cough, until the soup I ate comes back up. Uncle is coming to life in the flat faced lady. I press my hands and feet against the side of the barrel and push myself down deeper into the water where she cannot reach me. I look up through the barrel water. Once I see that her hand is gone, I come up fast and I do not stop until I am climbing out of the barrel. She is angry, and when I am out of the barrel, she grabs my hair and slaps my face.

With her red claws pinching my arm, she drags me towards the doorway. I will not go with her. I try to pull away. She grabs my hair and pulls my squirming wet body out of the barrel room, down a narrow hallway, through a doorway and into another room.

The walls in this room are the color of the sky at dawn. There is a light at the top of the room, and there is a large table with soft blankets on it. The blankets make me think of the tiny blooms that grew on the hills where I once lived with Purn. In the wall there is a glass window like the ones in the buildings on the street, but this one is covered with color. The soft blue on the wall is also on the window. I cannot see out the window to the strange street with lighted tree poles.

The flat faced lady turns me around and begins to pull a comb through my hair. I pull away and move to the other side of the room quickly. Enraged, she opens the door, yells, slams the door, and glares at me. I glare back.

A moment later the sunfish-colored hair lady comes in, but she is not smiling, "You little brat. I gave you something to eat, now do as you are told." The cold chill I feel standing wet on the stone cold floor does not compare to the icy stare she gives me.

I am certain no one has told me to do a thing. "Let Xuan comb and braid your hair," her head nods toward the flat faced lady, "and then sit on the bed." She motions to the large table with the soft blankets. I stare at her, but I do not move. "If you do not do as you are told, you will not eat. And later, I will take you into the barrel room and drown you." She turns and walks out of the room, slamming the door behind her.

Xuan comes around the 'bed' and reaches for me. I decide this is a fair trade. I will allow her to comb my hair for a bowl of curry soup. She works quickly and then she pushes me away and says something I do not understand. But, I remember the sunfish colored hair lady had told me to sit on the soft blanket table-bed, so I climb up. I pull one of the soft blankets around my naked body. As soon as I am on the table-bed, Xuan leaves the room. I am pleased to be alone. I would like to leave and find my way to Momma, but I do not know the way out, and I do not know the way to Momma.

The door opens, and in walks a man. He does not look like Uncle; he does not look like any man I have ever seen. His sweaty skin is pale, and his hair has left his head. I want him to go away. He reaches up and pulls a slim metal bar across the top of the door. Now, my eyes are fixed on the slim piece of metal. The metal bar means I cannot open the door. I do not think the metal bar is good.

The pale man begins to take off his clothes. He may not look like Uncle, but he is like Uncle. I pull the soft blanket tighter around me. I wish the blanket was a wall. I wish the blanket was a wall of rocks. Each rock would cut him if he tried to touch me. The rock would cut him like the rocks cut the water in the stream. I bury my head in the soft blanket rock wall. I feel the man pulling the soft blanket off me. The chicken in my stomach is sick. I pull away, and he pulls me closer. He laughs and touches my face. His face is on me, and it is scratchy. His breath is hot, and it burns away more of my good memories. I do not open my eyes; I do not look at him. I do not want a memory of this.

His Darkness finds me.

He pushes me aside. I am pleased to move away from him. He begins to pull blankets from the bed and throw them to the floor. He is looking for something on the bed. I am scared, so I jump off the bed and run to the corner. As he pulls on his pants he yells at me. I do not know his words. He tries to open the door. The door will not open because of the metal bar. He reaches to the top of the door and slides the metal bar. He yanks the door open and yells something. I hold my breath and close my eyes.

A moment later the fish-colored hair lady comes into the room with a man that I remember. It is the man with the purple markings on his neck. Everyone is yelling. The purple-marked man yells, "Noi, Noi!" and I wish Momma had never given me a name.

The fish colored hair lady grabs my arm, "Noi, up on the bed!"

I shake my head. No.

"Noi, get up on the bed, now!" She tries to pull me onto the bed, but I am fighting her. Then, she slaps my face. It stings, but only for a moment, and not nearly as badly as the sting of Darkness. I kick, and I scream, and I fall to the floor in my flailing. The purple-marked man comes over to me, and he lifts me off the floor by my hair. He throws me on the bed. He grabs my right arm and my right leg. On the other side of the bed, another man, one who I have never seen before, appears. The man is wearing pieces of glass in front of his eyes. His clothing is different; it is shiny. He grabs my left leg and my left arm. I cannot move. I scream, and I cry, but I am trapped.

I wish for death, but death doesn't come to save me. Even death despises me.

A moment later everyone is yelling. The pale man is angry. The purple-marked man slaps my face. As soon as their hands are off me, I scurry to the floor and under a blanket. The yelling leaves the room with all the people. The door slams, but only for a moment, and then the fish-colored hair lady comes back in. She pulls the blanket off me, and I resist. She is holding a bowl of soup. I look her in the eyes and knock the soup from her hands. The bowl falls to the floor, and the soup falls on her feet. I do not want her soup. This was not a fair trade.

"Fine, you little whore. Don't eat. But, do not think that means you are going to rest." She pulls the blankets up off the floor and puts them back on the table-bed. "You can thank your Uncle, if he really was your Uncle. He sold you as a virgin. A virgin! If you're a virgin, then so am I." She grabs my arm and pulls me up off the floor. "Now, come on, you need a bath, and you need to pee. I don't need any diseases or fevers." She drags me out of the room.

In the barrel room she tells me to get in the fish barrel. I shake my head. "Noi, get in the barrel, now." She stands with her hands on her hips. I pull my hands to my hips and shake my head. Her hand comes down hard against my ear. It hurts like Uncle.

When I have washed and peed, she leads me back into the room with the bed, turns and leaves, slamming the door behind her. I grab a blanket off the table-bed, wrap it around my naked body, and fall into the corner of the room.

The door opens, and in walks a man with white whiskers on his face and very little hair on his head. He reaches up and pulls the slim metal bar across the top of the door.

7

"It's mace." Dak said simply as he reached across the round table in the coffeehouse and handed Kimly the palm-sized vial. "Keep it with you all the time. Heck, it wouldn't be a bad idea if you even held onto it while you slept."

"Really?" Kimly looked down at the black and red tube in her hand. "You think I need this, even though I have my own personal bodyguard?" She grinned at him trying to season his serious tone with her own lightly salted humor.

"Well, if you have it your way, you won't always have me around on this journey," Dak returned her grin. "So, yes, I think you need it. After last night, I just think it's wise to plan for the worst."

"Plan for the worst?" Kimly twirled the small tube between her fingers. "I guess that's warranted, given the tough guys who followed me in the bathroom last night. I just don't want to start living in fear."

"I agree. Don't live in fear," Dak replied calmly, "live in hope. Plan for the worst and hope for the best." He winked at her.

"I'm noticing something about you, Dak." Kimly circled her fingers around the edge of the plastic lid on her cup.

"Oh yeah?" Dak lifted his coffee cup up to his lips, but not before Kimly saw the slight smile on his face.

"You're a fairly optimistic guy…except when you're not."

"Thanks?"

"It seems like you are always waiting for something to go wrong. It's like you want to believe the world is good, but you aren't completely certain."

"No…I know there's good. I've seen it. I've felt it."

"But?" Kimly asked.

"There's no *but*—I know there's good." Dak took a final drink from his cup and shifted in his chair. "Okay, not to change the subject, but I have a surprise for you. Let's get out of here."

They left the coffeehouse and crossed the street to Dak's topless Jeep. Closing the passenger's door, Kimly scratched her arm once again on the cracked plastic of the inside door handle. "This thing is out to get me," she said as she looked down at her forearm.

"I'm sorry." Dak reached for her arm to look at the scratch.

"It's not too bad," Kimly said as she rubbed the small abrasion with her fingers, "where did you get this..." she looked around the battered interior of the worn down Jeep, "...amazing automobile?"

"Hey, I paid 50,000 baht for this amazing automobile!" he announced.

Kimly's mouth dropped a little and she was quickly trying to do a math calculation to see how badly he had overspent.

Through his smile, he continued, "This is my Bargain Baby! Fifty thousand baht is only fifteen-hundred dollars! Quite the steal, right?" Dak reached up and gripped the roll bar on the top of the convertible.

"Quite." Kimly winked at him. "Does it have a top?"

"It does, but it's falling apart. It's held together primarily with duct tape," he laughed.

As they drove, Kimly questioned Dak on the plethora of bird houses. "Thai people really loves their birds, eh?" she said as she nodded to a large, flamboyant structure in front of a small hardware store.

"Those aren't for the birds," he followed her eyes to the ornate structure. "Those are Spirit Houses. The people place them in front of their business or homes so the bad spirits will have a place to live and leave them alone."

Kimly looked over at Dak, but his eyes were on the traffic in front of him. She thought it sounded like something a child might believe, but not an entire nation.

It wasn't too long before the Jeep pulled into a small dirt parking lot. The building they approached was surrounded by a chain link fence and tall trees covered in clusters of white flowers. The bright red sign at the entrance from the street read, "Tiger Kingdom" and it had the profile of a tiger face carved and painted into its glossy wood.

"Is this the surprise?" Kimly tilted her head sideways and smiled up at Dak, "Tigers?"

"Well, I considered taking you to an Elephant Farm, but I remembered something you said the day we met, and I thought this might be more appropriate."

"Something I said? Did we talk about tigers?" she laughed and her eyes shifted upward, her mind trying to recall their conversation.

"You told me your name means Golden Lion. I figured you must like wild cats."

"Hmm..." she was surprised he remembered her mentioning the meaning of her name, but she had thrown out the name's meaning with little thought. It was a lackadaisical habit she had developed over the years.

"You're not excited to see the tigers? They have a lion here, too."

"No, I am! It's great!" her enthusiasm compensated for her stalled response. "It's just that, I don't really think about the meaning of my name...I mean, I've heard the meaning my whole life, but, it doesn't make sense to me," her voice was flat and unemotional.

"Really?" Dak grinned. "Wait a second," he closed his eyes and put his hand to his forehead. Then, he spun towards the center of the cab and reached between the bucket seats into the backseat of the Jeep. His right hand came back holding a leather bound book. Kimly watched as he turned to the back of the book and then began flipping to the front. She recognized the book as a Bible. *Who carries a Bible in their car?* She wondered, with a hint of judgment.

"The wicked flee though no one pursues, but the righteous are bold as a lion," Dak looked up from his Bible and smiled.

"Okay..." Kimly didn't know if she was missing something, or even what the expected response was supposed to be. She had never heard someone read from the Bible so matter-of-factly.

"It's from Proverbs. That's a very old book in the Bible, and it's one of the greatest treasures we have. One of the greatest resources for wisdom," he closed the book, reached back and set it on the floorboard behind her seat.

"Okay. So, what I hear you saying is that one of the oldest books in the world says my name means I'm bold," she shrugged her shoulders.

He tilted his head, slightly, "And righteous! Don't forget righteous, my friend," he winked and climbed out of the Jeep. She followed his lead, the word *righteous* prowling around her mind.

8

Motionless flags lined the Nawarat Bridge, the air hanging just as still over the water as it had throughout Chiang Mai's bustling streets. Kimly and Dak had opted to walk to the bridge.

In his usual manner, Dak was giving her a history lesson as they walked to their destination. Kimly welcomed the distraction. Dak's voice was soothing, deep and full.

"For hundreds of years, the Nawarat Bridge stood over the Ping River, and served as the main thoroughfare to the center of Chiang Mai," Dak told Kimly. The simplicity of the bridge wasn't much to look at, but thinking about the many ancient travelers who had walked it filled her with a slight sense of awe. Now the bridge was taking her into the world she had come here to explore and hopefully toward some crucial information.

Although she had fought Dak's involvement, Kimly was relieved that she wasn't approaching the bridge alone. The quest which she had imagined might lead her to independence and self-sufficiency was, in reality, proving to be a frightening trek. She had pretended to be unaffected by the confrontation in the restroom on Walking Street, but the truth was, she was terrified. Terrified she might fail to make contact and go home empty handed, terrified she might have success at making contact and unleash more than she had bargained for.

If she were to actually identify the people at the core of an organized slave trade, what would happen after? What would she do with the information she was unearthing? What would she do if she were able to actually purchase another human being? Could she reveal a secret so well hidden that it may be happening in plain sight? And, in the end, if she did gather all the information she needed, what made her so confident she would be able to leave Thailand without anyone trying to stop her? The associate editor at the

Tribune had agreed to her leave of absence, but she never disclosed her plans to write an investigative story to anyone other than Matthew. And Kyle. In many ways, she was on her own, even with Dak by her side.

Each concrete post on the bridge sported two flags. The first was bright yellow with an orange insignia in the center, and according to Dak, it was the Royal Family's Flag. Citizens of Thailand apparently placed a Royal flag at the entrance to the markets and sometimes even on their homes to communicate respect to their King and his family. The second flag, the National flag of Thailand, bore five stripes; a thick blue stripe with two red and two white stripes on either side.

"There's meaning behind those colors, you know?" Kimly was certain Dak was trying to ease her nerves.

"Meaning behind the red, white and blue? Do tell," she winked at him.

"Well, the meaning is different for the people of Thailand than for Americans, but there really is a history of the colors. According to my sources..." he raised his eyebrows and waited for her smile, "The three colors stand for 'Nation, Religion, King,' which is the unofficial motto of the Thai people."

"Which is which?"

"See, I knew you would be intrigued. Red is for the people, the land. White is for Buddha. And, blue was the favorite color of King Rama the Sixth," Dak finished his sentence with the panache of a parade commentator.

"My mother was quite knowledgeable when it came to Thai history," He shrugged his shoulders and reached out and took her by the elbow. He led her to the side of the road where they approached a vacant kiosk. The square booth stood just to the edge of the bridge, and as Kimly stepped up into it, she could see down into the water below and across the bridge as well. The booth was painted white to match the rest of the bridge; across the top was ornamental black Thai lettering. She didn't know what the lettering said, but she imagined it was a warning: BEWARE OF STRANGERS ON A BRIDGE!

"There..." With his eyes, Dak motioned Kimly to look across the street to the south side of the bridge, "I think the men on the other side are watching us."

Across the street and further down the bridge, Kimly saw two men leaning against the three-foot concrete wall. One smoked a cigarette and looked down into the water. The other looked away when Kimly glanced over.

The man who had looked away began to walk toward them. Without thinking, Kimly took hold of Dak's arm. Her heart was beginning to race, which irritated her. She felt Dak place his hand on her back and heard him whisper, "You don't have to do any of this, Kimly."

"No." she pulled her hand away from him. If she showed any fear, he would respond as a protector. She didn't need protection. She was in control. If he began to draw out her fear she would lack confidence, and this would never work. She might need him, but how she needed him would be determined by her, not by him.

The man stopped at the edge of the booth, and he spoke slowly and deliberately in Thai. Kimly looked to Dak who was already responding, "Paa-saa-ang-grit tua pbai."

When the man answered he looked at Kimly, and this time he spoke in English with a very thick accent, "Do you have something for me?"

Kimly did have something for him. She had 7,000 baht, the equivalent being less than three hundred American dollars. Kimly knew half a dozen people who would spend more than that on a shopping spree in one afternoon. Realizing such an insignificant amount could purchase a slave filled her with disgust.

Kimly had given Dak the baht before leaving the hotel. He was a part of this now. His presence made her story more believable: A financially successful couple, who had relocated to Thailand for employment purposes. Her role as a housewife looking for some live-in help at a reasonable cost would be more believable than the story of a single woman making this type of a purchase. It was disturbing to imagine there were actual demographics for the type of people who purchase other people.

Dak spoke, his voice completely calm, "We have something for you. I don't see what it is we are purchasing."

"What you are purchasing will be delivered. This is a deposit." His hands were in the pockets of his baggy pants. The young man discussed selling another human being with ease. On another continent, in another time zone, Dak and the young man could have been bartering over the price of a used car.

"You meet us tomorrow. Another 7000 baht. You give address where you will keep our merchandise. We deliver product."

"Wait, *your* merchandise? I was told I was buying...this....her...it" Kimly had spoken up quickly, and halfway through her thought, she realized how disgusting her words were. She knew her words were not sincere, but she hoped she sounded believable. It was conflicting, this acting. Her acting skills were weak, and this was a rotten time to make that discovery.

"You not buy. It still ours. We let you use. And, you pay us."

"We pay you. How exactly do we pay you?" Dak was a natural.

"No question for now. For now, you have something for me?"

Dak reached out and handed the wad of bills to the young Asian. It wasn't a thick wad of bills. Bahts were readily available in the thousands. The man flipped quickly through the bills and then spoke definitively, "Each month, we come to your home, and you pay 4000 baht. Wait here." He turned and walked away, and toward a man who stood between two lanterns on the South side of the bridge.

Obviously, the man who stood watching and waiting between two of the tall lanterns was the one making the decisions. The flags of faith, land and royalty lightly unfurled and snapped in a strong wind that had risen. Kimly wished she could have gotten a better glimpse of the man on the South side of the bridge, but she knew he had strategically chosen the spot for its shadows.

The baggy clothed man sauntered back to Kimly and Dak; his stride sending a simple message: Be afraid. Without thinking, Kimly grabbed Dak's hand. She wondered if Dak was concocting a plan. He was the one who had told her before to plan for the worst. She wondered if Dak expected her to use her mace. She had shoved the mace in her purse at the coffeehouse days earlier and not given it much thought.

"Four O'clock. Bhuping Palace. SuSuk will find you."

With that, the young man turned and sauntered away. Kimly clung to Dak's hand and, without speaking, they began walking. The couple moved through the crowded streets in the direction of the hotel, and Kimly was thankful for the presence of Chiang Mai's Night Bazaar. Unlike the Walking Street, which only happened once a week, these vendors rested their wares on the curbs every single night. At first it had struck her as an oddity, now it was a comfort.

Each step away from the deserted bridge took her closer to the crowds. It was a flimsy protection, but she clung to it anyway.

The further they got from the water of Ping River the more the heat returned to its nearly unbearable intensity. An elderly woman selling silk placemats from a rickety table on the side of the street nodded at Kimly. The woman was missing one of her front teeth, but her smile and her confidence were unaffected. Kimly returned the nod, pleased to have made it back and pleased to be nearly home.

Home. The word that had once evoked love and family was now a source of confusion. Kyle had contorted the word into something that cut through her. He had twisted the word into a knife—no, not a knife, a mistress. A mistress is far worse than a knife. At least a knife serves a greater good.

Home had become a barren hotel room with marble floors and stiff white sheets. Everything was contorted. Even this trip was out of balance. How much of this journey had she manipulated to benefit herself? With nothing to gain, would she even care? If she had nothing to prove would she be taking the risk? She became aware, suddenly, that she was still holding Dak's hand and let go of it.

"You alright?" He didn't look at her when he asked, just continued to lead at a fast pace.

"Yeah, I'm fine," Kimly lied.

9

The wind whipped through Kimly's dark hair as the Jeep twisted up the main highway of Doi Suthep Mountain. Along the sides of the road, various trees competed with clusters of bamboo stalks reaching for the sky. Temples and Spirit Houses littered the otherwise untouched landscape, and each man-made object was calling passersby to seek something spiritual amid the natural. Kimly struggled to relax and embrace the rolling green scenery as Dak steered them up the highway. She still hadn't become accustomed to traveling on the left, or the "wrong" side, of the road. As the Jeep curved to the right, each turn felt too wide. A blue sedan traveling in the opposite direction turned the bend at the same time as the Jeep and she was certain the cars were about to collide. Instinctively, Kimly reached a hand out towards Dak—stopping her hand in mid-air. Dak reached up and took her hand in his, pulling it back down to her leg where he set it and then released it.

"You're okay," he said. Dak's voice reminded her of how quiet he had been. Fear had been growing inside her chest since he had picked her up at the hotel. Dak, who was usually talkative—sharing the history of temples, roads or gardens, was silent.

They had been traveling for about thirty minutes when he made a left off the highway and into a scenic stop. He shifted the gear into park, and then he said, "I want to show you where you are—"

"Okay." Kimly interrupted and reached for the door handle when Dak placed his hand on her arm and continued.

"...and, I want to pray with you," he didn't move his hand from her arm.

"Yeah...um...okay," she stammered. "But, I don't know how."

Sitting in his Jeep and staring out the front windshield at the thick bamboo trees on the edge of the mountain, Kimly had conflicting feelings. She wasn't interested in talking about God, but she also wasn't so sure Dak was completely wrong. Closing her hotel room door the night before, she had found herself preoccupied with the make-shift lock and the cheap wobbly handle. The trip to the bridge had left her shaken. Standing on the marble floor, she had pulled the vial of mace out of her purse and decided it wouldn't hurt to sleep with the palm-sized vial under her pillow. She thought of Kyle, she thought of her sons, she thought of the marriage that was ending and all she felt was fear. Kimly had stared at her reflection in the bathroom mirror, and she saw the truth in her eyes. She was rooting for Dak to be right about the existence of God. She thought about the woman on the airplane. As she turned off the bathroom light and the darkness swallowed her ever-changing features, Kimly wished the woman's "God with a plan" were real.

"Praying isn't something someone knows or doesn't know how to do," Dak said. "It's just talking. Prayer is simply talking to God and telling Him what's going on."

"Doesn't He already know?" She hoped she didn't sound sarcastic, because inasmuch as she would have asked the question cynically a few days ago, she was genuinely trying to understand.

"He knows what is going on, yes. But, He wants us to share with Him how we see what is going on," Dak was able to relay this so simply to Kimly. "And then He wants us to tell Him what we want, and he wants to hear how we feel about it all." It was obvious he had told others before her. She wondered again about the Preacher thing.

"Can I just listen to you pray?" Her question didn't seem to surprise Dak, and he responded with a smile, "That would be outstanding. But, first, let's go look at where you are, my friend."

The scenic lookout point was about the size of a basketball court, and as they approached the entrance, they were greeted by vendors selling snacks and disposable cameras. Add a few popular trademarks, and she would have felt like she was back in the states. The only difference being, amid the potato chips and bottles of Coca-Cola, these vendors were also selling Baht-on-a-Stick. Her eyes were drawn to the strange sight of the 10 baht and 50 baht bills attached to long sticks which were decorated with small colorful pieces of thin tissue paper. It reminded her of a Fourth of July firework. Dak explained how the worshippers of Buddha would purchase the sticks and then burn them at the temple which was just up the mountain.

"There's another temple up the mountain," Kimly questioned,

but it was less of a question than a statement. "They build them everywhere. How do they decide where to put them?"

It was the perfect question for Dak to fall into his storytelling mode. He told her how this particular temple had been chosen by an elephant.

"An elephant?" Once again, the man had her attention. Dak went on to tell her the legend behind Wat Phra That Doi Suthep Temple. Hundreds of years ago, a monk had an ancient relic, and he claimed the artifact was a piece of Buddha's shoulder bone. He believed the bone had magical powers. The king believed in the bone's powers as well. The king and the monk decided to place the relic on the back of a white elephant, send the elephant into the jungle, and let the animal decide where to build the temple. The elephant walked through the jungle until he reached the spot where the temple sits today. The giant animal trumpeted three times and claimed the spot.

"Some stories say he sat down; others claim the animal died," Dak told the story with awe, and she understood why the Thai people were drawn to the enormous mammal. "This particular temple is now considered the 'King's Temple' because it is so close to the palace and it is an obvious choice for him to come here when he is visiting Chiang Mai."

"So, will the king be at the palace?" Kimly teased as the two headed over to the lookout point. "I have been hoping to meet him."

"Naw, he's not around. When he is around, the palace is closed to the public."

"Just like a king. Worship me, work for me, but leave me alone." There wasn't a lot of thought behind her words; she was just making conversation. If she allowed the silence to come, she would remember the severity of the darkness into which they were heading.

"Not every king," Dak responded. "There is a King, not from Thailand, mind you, who wants us to worship Him and serve Him. But, ultimately what He wants more than anything else is a relationship. That's a different kind of King, don't you think?"

Kimly assumed he was talking about God. He had the familiar, enraptured tone to his voice that arose when he mentioned God. But as far as she could see, his logic made no sense. Why was he so persistent in hearing what she thought about God if he had the answers himself?

The edge of the lookout was guarded by a sturdy iron railing. It had been painted green at one time, but now the paint was chipping away to reveal rusted, weathered metal beneath. People took turns standing against the paint chipped rails, while they were captured in a photograph with the expansive sky and cityscape as the backdrop.

"Kimly Denim, may I present, Chiang Mai. New City," Dak motioned one arm before him, formally introducing Kimly to the city she had been in for almost two weeks. "It was named New City by King Mengrai in the late 1200's...and, you'll like this..." she could tell he was thriving on the attention he was drawing from the other tourists. Coming alive as he performed, like a peacock spreading his tail feathers, his handsome jaw line and dark gray eyes were intoxicating not only to Kimly but to the onlookers as well. Two dark haired women, younger than Kimly, smiled flirtatiously at Dak and whispered to each other. Dak lowered his voice an octave and projected, "King Mengrai was head of the Lanna Kingdom." He smiled and leaned in closer to Kimly, whispering the last part of his presentation, "Does the Lanna Kingdom sound familiar to anything?"

"My hotel?" Kimly rolled her eyes playfully. "So, Mr. Tour Guide, I'm in a city which was proclaimed new eight-hundred years ago. I'm staying in a hotel named for its pioneering king, who worships at a temple that was planted by an elephant. Good to know." She turned her gaze to the modern kingdom below her. Like a child's room strewn with colorful plastic Legos, the large township spilled out across the land; she moved her thumb in front of her face and a building over twenty stories high disappeared.

"It is good to know, Kimly." Dak spoke with the same self-assured tone he had used the first day he stopped her on the street, "It's good to know where you are and to wonder about your purpose. These are things people don't ask themselves often enough. There is a reason you came to Thailand--to Chiang Mai. God has a plan." And with the last sentence, Kimly's head spun around to look at Dak.

"Yeah, I've heard that before," she answered. Dak simply smiled.

Dak and Kimly made their way back to the Jeep, and once inside Dak asked if he could pray for what they were about to do. Even though she had told him praying would be okay, when he actually started, Kimly decided it was the most awkward thing she had ever done with anyone. She was confused and couldn't determine why she found it so uncomfortable. She didn't even know if she believed there was a God. And if there wasn't a God, how was praying with Dak any different than having a conversation with him over a plate of noodles or Pak Boon Fai Dang? She felt vulnerable and exposed.

"Heavenly father, Kimly and I come to you this morning because You are wonderful. Your care for us reaches beyond the city of Chiang Mai and higher than these mountains."

He sounds so normal. Kimly thought to herself. When Dak finished telling God things he adored, he began to release pleas in his prayer, saying things Kimly had never heard anyone say.

"Thank You for how You have been protecting both Kimly and I. Please forgive me for the times I doubt what You can do; forgive me for the times I am overcome with fear." Dak continued.

The oddity to Kimly was that the crimes in which he sought forgiveness hardly even seemed like offenses. *Forgive him for being fearful? How could we do this without being afraid? Is being afraid wrong? And, doesn't everyone doubt?* Kimly's mind raced.

Then Dak began to thank God. He thanked God for so many things, from the beauty of the land to their new-found friendship. Dak thanked God for Kimly's life. She had never heard anyone say they were thankful for her life. As Dak prayed, he thanked God for the ways He had provided protection for them on Nawarat Bridge. Finally, he prayed for the place they were headed.

"Father, please keep Kimly safe in the palace. Guard each step she takes. Please allow me to be filled with wisdom and discernment. And, Father, above all else I pray that you will move in the hearts of the people involved and change them from the inside out."

Even though Kimly didn't think Dak would get what he asked for, she was moved to hear him ask for it. She imagined if there were a God, He would really like Dak's prayer. When Dak was finished praying, although Kimly couldn't explain why, her eyes were filled with tears. She had never heard anyone talk like he had. She wasn't sure what she was supposed to do, and she felt awkward at the intimacy they had just shared, so she looked away. She focused again on the thick brown and green bamboo trees out the front windshield.

It was just about time to head to the king's castle where they would meet the men on the palace grounds. Something in Kimly spoke without thinking and she said, "We're going to the palace with the true King on our side, right?"

The smile on Dak's face surfaced from deep within, "Yes, my friend, we are."

10

Dak parked the Jeep outside the gate of Bhuping Palace forty-five minutes before the time they had been summoned to meet SuSuk, telling Kimly he would feel better if they could survey the grounds prior to the meeting.

At the small ticket booth, Dak paid the 100 baht for the two of them to gain entrance. A large picture, the size of a common highway billboard, hung at the base of a paved road leading into the palace. The face of Bhumibol Adulyadej, also known as King Rama the IV, looked down with monstrous eyes into Kimly's own. King Rama looked nothing like her stepfather, and yet something about the King reminded her of the man who had been by her Mother's side for nearly as long as Kimly herself. Even though Kimly's stepfather had left Thailand as an infant, she imagined the billboard of an enormous king would send her stepfather's heart soaring.

Walking through the gates of the palace grounds and up its paved road, Kimly was struck at how different things appeared within the palace walls. Sizable buildings surrounded the walkway, painted white and trimmed in shades of orange and rust, and the scalloped edge of each building was accented in thin strokes of golden paint. The dirt in the beds of exotic flowers was a dark mixture of fertilizer, and the green grass was well trimmed. But, just outside the gate, the couple had parked in a paved lot overlooking a meager township. In front of a row of stores, roosters clawed their way around small cages, a wall was lined with trash which had fallen out of the overflowing cans and a handful of shoeless children were gathered around an upside down milk crate picking rice out of a Tupperware container.

The open front stores outside the castle were constructed of concrete and covered in gray plaster. They had rusty metal roofs to withstand the winter storms, but it was more than just the seasoned and tired construction materials Kimly noticed. It was the goods they sold. The tables were overflowing with items for tourists: T-shirts, hats, souvenir flags and handmade jewelry--small trinkets which would garnish menial profits. She wondered how many baseball caps, bearing the insignia of King Rama the IV, a merchant would need to sell to meet the needs of his family.

Coming from a place where wealth was displayed in outward appearance in houses, cars and vacations, Kimly realized she might have a limited view of what much of the world was like. Where she had come from, a person's value could be gauged by the logos on clothing, sunglasses, and handbags. "Image is the most important asset a woman has," Kimly's mother had told her on more than one occasion. Kimly's sister believed it, and Thao lived in a manner which reflected every pay increase her husband had ever made.

In this world, the land of the Thai, occupying one's thoughts with one's self-image was futile. A survival instinct took precedence, one which disregarded any concern for image. She was surrounded by people who were focused on survival above presentation.

As they approached the first small building, Kimly paused and looked at the wood framed house. Just outside the front window a remarkable tree stood welcoming its visitors. Hanging from the branches of the tree were dozens of large white trumpet-like flowers. Each flower was the size of a loaf of bread, and pointed down to the ground as if bowing. It was stunning, and she had seen nothing like it elsewhere in Chiang Mai. Knowing the kings of Thailand were famous for bringing new plants to their homeland when they returned from their travels, Kimly was curious if there might be a story behind the palace's trumpet flower tree.

The consistently talkative and pleasant man who spun tales of kings and elephants was a different creature within the palace walls. His eyes were rapidly surveying the grounds as the two moved slowly up the pathway. She wanted to ask him if he was alright, but there was no point. He was obviously as nervous as she. Perhaps he was even a bit angry with her. Their situation couldn't be typical for a Preacher.

The best thing to do would be to follow his lead, get the information from this 'SuSuk,' and then get out off the palace grounds. On the good side, the palace had guards. Kimly hadn't thought about that possibility when they had been driving up the mountain. As soon as she had seen the first one at the gate, it sent a wave of relief through her. Surely, the presence of guards would keep the meeting free from danger. Of course, the men on the bridge knew there were guards when they chose this location. She would be foolish to assume the guards made it safe. Her best guess was that this 'SuSuk' was merely here to pass along information about the required baht and how the drop-off would take place. Kimly still needed to secure a location for the drop off; it was occurring to her that Dak may be able to help her with that.

"Listen," Dak stopped, took hold of her arm and pulled her closer, "we need a plan. We should have done this in the car, but, give me your cell phone," he said as he held out his hand. Kimly pulled her cell phone out of her back pocket. Dak entered numbers into her phone and handed it back to her, "I put my number in your phone. If we get separated for any reason, call me." His eyes were intent. Kimly looked away quickly. She didn't think straight when he looked at her like that. "Got it?" he asked.

"Got it," she repeated, pushing her phone into the back pocket of her jeans.

Dak and Kimly continued up the road toward the palace, where they intended to wait for SuSuk and his men. As they passed another small set of buildings, the paved road veered to the left and shot up about 50 feet and into a deciduous forest. The palace grounds wore its fertile evergreens like a crown, and the hill strewn with overgrown ferns was reminiscent of a lost, ancient kingdom on a tropical island. It blocked their view to what lay around the bend, and Kimly's eyes wandered to a group of bungalows on her right. She presumed the dormitory-style buildings were used to house staff. Her eyes moved across the lavish grass and the brick walkways adorning each building when she felt Dak's hand on her arm once again. Kimly turned her head to the left to smile and reassure him, but he wasn't looking at her. His eyes were fixed away from her and straight ahead on a man standing about twenty feet in front of them. It was the young man they had first met at the bridge and he was smoking a cigarette and watching them walk. Kimly placed her hand on top of Dak's and gave it a slight squeeze, then pulled it away and continued walking forward. Dak was in step with her, staying close by her side. They stopped in front of the young man, and Dak was the first to speak.

"Good afternoon." Dak said.

"You," the young man looked at Kimly, "go up. He stays here."

His words were infused with smoke as he exhaled and tilted his head to the side, motioning to a series of steps leading up into one of the palace's expansive gardens. The greenery and trees swallowed the stairs. With each step, a person could disappear into the ferns in their climb to the top.

"Nope," Dak answered him. "That's not going to happen. We stay together."

"You stay together, you leave together. No deal. No merchandise," his eyes still fixed on Kimly.

"Fine, we'll leave," Dak turned to go. Kimly stood still.

"Kimly, no—" Dak's voice was a fierce whisper.

"Dak, it's okay," she didn't look away from the stranger before her. Her dark eyes held his and she felt a peaceful calm she hadn't felt since the night she had read Kyle's text messages to his mistress. "It will be okay," she assured.

"No. I am not going to let you go up there alone—" Dak protested, but, before he could finish, Kimly turned and looked into his eyes and stated flatly, "It will be okay, it will." She reached her hand behind her and placed it on the phone in her back pocket.

They stood face to face, and neither spoke. He was shaking his head, and she just held his gaze. Then, she looked at the baggy clothed man and said, "Fine," as she headed up the stone steps and into the overgrown plants.

Her surroundings were mesmerizing. The ferns were enormous and the trees had thick vines falling to the ground. Some of the vines had fallen, landing onto another tree, and the two had grafted together. The walkway narrowed in places and the ferns brushed softly against her arm.

After climbing about thirty steps, Kimly saw a man waiting for her. Kimly opened her mouth to speak, but nothing emerged. His neck. The tattoos. It was him, the man from the bathroom at Walking Street.

Just as she turned to rush back down the steps, she heard the deep voice of the man from the restroom issue a command, "Stop."

She didn't have to obey, did she? She stopped. As she gazed straight ahead, the most brilliant bush of purple asters caught her attention. The sharp pointed petals pierced the green fern it neighbored. The fern submitted to the radiant beauty of the aster. She looked back at the man with the tattoos, pulled her chin up and held his gaze.

Tattoo Man nodded his head up towards the stairs, clearly indicating she should continue climbing the steps. *Is he going to follow me?* She turned and moved upward, the sound of her heart pounding growing louder with each step. She had taken about seven steps when she turned and glanced over her shoulder. Tattoo Man hadn't moved to follow her. *So, you're not him?* She continued her climb.

Reality snapped into focus. She knew there would be many people, many men, involved in this underground business. She reminded herself that to these men--this was just a business. Just like any large corporation, there are underlings and there is a CEO. *Am I meeting the CEO, or is this SuSuk below someone else?*

A small opening in the trees appeared, and in the alcove there sat a stone bench overlooking the palace grounds. Sitting on the bench, with his back to Kimly, was a man smoking a cigarette. Kimly approached, practicing her lines in her head, when the man spoke, "Come, have a seat."

Taking a deep breath, Kimly moved forward to the edge of the bench. The man was wearing a gray suit and a black and gray striped tie. The suit jacket was unbuttoned, and his shirt had a reflective luster. He sat, one leg crossed over the other, and dangled his foot. When he pulled his cigarette up to his lips, she noticed the gold cufflinks attached to his pale pink shirt. He wore rimless glasses with a gold bridge. His oily complexion was smooth, and his thin eyebrows pointed down towards his eyelids. He had almost nailed the appearance of the wealthy and successful Asian businessman, one who would be holding a meeting with clients in a Bangkok sky rise. Everything was almost perfect. Almost. His black dress shoes were unpolished and slightly scuffed, and they didn't blend with the image he was trying to portray.

She wasn't sure how she should greet him. Her heart was pounding. If this man was to believe she was just another client she couldn't act fearful, she needed to appear desensitized to their arrangement. As she got closer, she cleared her throat to speak.

"Come and sit. We have to discuss a few things," he motioned her to the edge of the stone bench.

Kimly drew in a deep breath and moved closer to the bench.

"Go ahead. How does this work," being near him was repulsive, so she decided whatever he said at this point, she would simply agree.

If he asked for more money, she would agree and then leave with her life.

"How did you find me?" he took a drag from his cigarette.

"Your men were waiting when we came up the path."

"No," he did not turn to look at her. "How did you find me?" He gazed across the grounds of the palace.

"You told us to come here. Early this morning, on the bridge," she was confused.

"No. How did you find me?"

Kimly turned her head away and looked out across the palace grounds. In the distance, she saw an expansive building resembling a ski lodge. The white building sported a twenty-foot orange tile roof which shot at an 80-degree angle toward the sky. There were several pillars across the front of the building protecting the ample porch. Was that the palace? She expected it to look more "palace-y." Perhaps her notions of royalty were completely off. Did corrupt underworld figures have access to influence in the Royal Family?

"I bought a box from a vendor on Walking Street. It contained the name of the bridge," Kimly tried again to answer the business man's question.

The strangely dignified man, who Kimly determined was, in fact, SuSuk, inhaled long on his cigarette. He still hadn't turned to look at her. He exhaled. She waited. She had moved her boat into his port, given him the answers he sought; it was up to him to navigate the waters.

"I once tried to own a dog," SuSuk looked at his cigarette, but still not once at Kimly, "I find him outside my house, so I decide I will feed him." He took a long drag from his cigarette and then flicked it forward. It flew over the ridge and disappeared in the greenery. A ring on his hand sparkled in the sun, which was just above eye level.

"I feed him every day for many days. Then one day, I went out into my yard to have a picnic. This is what you Americans like to do...to have a picnic. I was in my yard eating the leg of chicken. I was sitting under my tree, eating my leg of chicken and when I turn my head, the dog grabbed my chicken from my hand. He took what was mine. I had fed him, and I had planned to keep feeding him. But, he took what was mine."

Kimly swallowed hard and then breathed deeply.

"I could have killed him, but what would he learn?" He didn't continue. He sat staring straight ahead. *Is he waiting for me to answer?* Kimly's mind swam trying to think up proper responses to his question.

"Nothing. He would have learned nothing if I killed him. So, I cut off his front leg. A leg for a leg, right?" Kimly's eyes were going to betray her. She could feel the lump building in her chest. His voice dropped to a near-whisper, "You're not looking for a housekeeper, are you?"

"No...I mean, yes, I am. Whatever you think I am...No, I'm not. I just want a housekeeper who won't cheat me and won't steal—" she was trying her best to be convincing.

"Stop," he interrupted her performance. "Answer my question. How did you find me? How did you know to buy the box? Who told you to go to Walking Street?"

Kimly's mind was spinning. *How could I have been so stupid?* Answers were a million miles away. This should have been a simple answer, and she couldn't conjure up anything in response.

"You know what I think? I think you are looking for more than you should be looking for. I think you are trying to steal something from me. I don't like it when someone steals from me. What's mine is mine," and with that said, SuSuk turned and looked for the first time into Kimly's brown eyes.

She looked away, "I don't know what you are talking about. I was told by a friend you could assist me in getting the help I needed. But, if this is not what you do, that's fine."

Kimly stood, and SuSuk grabbed her wrist. "I'm not finished." He stood and began to lead her back toward the path. Dak couldn't help her from the bottom of the steps. If he came running up the steps he would meet the tattooed underling half way up...then what? The thought of Dak getting hurt kept her from reaching into her pocket for her phone. She needed to get away.

When SuSuk reached the path, he pulled her along the steps down a different route. She looked around wildly for a clue as to what she could do. She grabbed a vine, holding it tightly; she attempted to stop them both. "Stop, please," she insisted. "Where are you taking me?"

SuSuk's strength was greater than hers. Kimly held tight to the hanging vine and it dug into her palm until she released it and continued stumbling through the mock jungle with him. He pulled her around the corner of a small white cinder block building and pushed her against the wall. With his right hand, he tightened his grip on her wrist. She pulled away from him trying to maneuver her body and gain control, but he used the forearm from his left arm to push her neck against the blocks. His gold cufflink cut into her jaw line.

Moving his face close to hers, he stood in front of her and Kimly could smell the burnt tobacco on his breath. "You will not steal from me. You will not make a fool of me. Do you think you are worth more than a dog that I fed?"

NEAR.

She heard it. She had heard this voice before, and she had not recognized it, but this time she knew. It was God. It was the God with a plan, Dak's God. When Dak had prayed in the Jeep it was more than just hopeful words, God had heard Dak's prayers and He had come with them to the palace grounds.

She closed her eyes and tried to think of the words to plead with the God with a plan to help her. "Open your eyes, you stupid woman. Look at me." Kimly didn't raise her eyes to his. She was afraid the evil would overcome any bit of confidence she might muster. She continued to search for the words a person might use to plead with God for protection. She didn't know how to pray, so she simply began a silent uttering of phrases she remembered Dak praying in the Jeep. *Forgive me for doubting. Surround me. Change the hearts. Please move…please.* She could only remember pieces of what she had heard Dak pray, so she just kept repeating them.

Suddenly, a man and a woman walked around the corner and joined them on the path. The man was carrying a small baby wearing a bright pink hat, and the woman held the hand of a skinny boy with knobby knees and a baseball cap. SuSuk turned his head. It was only for a moment, but it was the moment Kimly needed. Kimly pulled her right knee straight up into her assailant. When she felt her knee make contact, she forced herself to keep driving it upward. SuSuk fell forward, pulling his hands to his stomach and lower groin, but not releasing her wrist. Kimly pulled her wrist upward and grabbed hold of his fingers with her teeth. She bit down until the blood from his finger mixed with the spit in her mouth, and she felt him release his grip. Kimly took off running down the unfamiliar path behind the family, barreling into the young father as she passed.

Both feet flying down the path, she didn't turn to look back. If he was following her, all the more reason to run and not look. When she exited the fern garden, she was completely disoriented. She didn't know where on the palace grounds she was. Wherever she had ended up, it was deserted. Her instincts told her to run towards a large pink and gray building she could see off in the distance.

NEAR.

Kimly stopped. "I don't know what that means, God. Lead me. Please." She whispered.

Turning abruptly, Kimly ran in the opposite direction. She was now heading away from the pink and gray building and down a path lined with colossal bamboo and flowering trees. She ran about twenty feet when two trees which had grown so close together they had formed their own small alcove caught her eye. She climbed into the natural hideaway. She pushed her back into the tree and tried to calm her breathing. Her heart was pounding in her ears, and her breathing was so intense, she knew she wouldn't be able to speak, but she reached into her pocket and pulled out her cell phone.

With shaking hands, Kimly held the phone close to her ear. The phone on the other end rang one time and then, "Hi, this is Dak Kesapan. I'm not able to get to my..." *Are you kidding me?* She hit END hoping that his voicemail was an indication that he didn't have cell reception and not something far worse. Pressing herself deeper into her tree kiosk, she held still and silently repeated the same prayer over and over. *Please protect Dak. Please protect.*

11

Watching the sliver of sky deepen and not knowing if her self-indulgent and egotistical drive had caused an innocent man to suffer was making Kimly's stomach churn.

There had been guards at the entrance. Kimly decided if she could safely get to the front gate, the guards could notify the police and help Dak. Her information might be limited, but she could give detailed descriptions to give them a lead in finding Dak.

The air was cooling down with the setting sun, and the palace grounds would be closing soon. Kimly couldn't stay hidden much longer; she needed to get to the entrance while there were still people around. Both of her feet stung when she wedged her way out of the small opening. Pins and needles weakened her attempts to maneuver gracefully. Bearing down against the pain in both feet, she tried to run the path in the direction she hoped was leading to the entrance. As she turned each corner Kimly would pull herself into the nearest tree or fern to peek around the bend. When she had made it far enough down the path that she could no longer see the hideaway or the pink and gray building she was encouraged, until she remember she had no idea if she were heading in the direction of the entrance, or deeper into the palace grounds.

"GA RU NAH." A loud voice came blaring from overhead.

Kimly jumped and spun around. Looking upward she spotted a speaker, attached to a palm tree, blasting out a male voice she could not understand. It was a monotone announcement, and the unfamiliarity of the language exasperated her. She placed her hands on her face and pressed them hard against her eyes. She leaned back into several bamboo trees and took a deep breath, holding it in.

Two strong hands came down on Kimly's shoulders and pulled her forward. She pulled her hands away from her face and down against the threat. She instinctively let out a cry, a scream.

"It's okay...it's me," Dak's voice was a loud whisper. "Let's get out of here!"

Holding Kimly's hand, Dak led the way as the two continued down the path Kimly had been heading. They moved as quickly as possible, and finally the path merged into a paved road. Soon they rounded a bend, and Kimly saw the small building with the white trumpet flower tree. They were almost out! Passing the guards, Kimly slowed to a stop.

"We've got to tell them," she nodded her head towards two guards in a small booth.

"Tell them what, Kimly?" he pulled on her hand and led her through the gated entrance and past the ticket booth. Without another word, Kimly and Dak ran toward the Jeep.

Hearts racing, tires spinning, they were soon speeding down the mountain, away from the spectacular palace grounds.

"Where are we going?" Kimly was becoming familiar with the roads, and this was not the road they typically traveled en route to the hotel.

"We're going to my house. You're coming to stay the night with me," he responded.

"No. No, I'm not. Take me to my hotel," she argued.

"Stop being ridiculous. I'm not taking you back there. You're staying with me," his voice grew deeper and more intense.

Kimly shot back, "I'm not being ridiculous. I want to go back to the hotel. Take me to the hotel."

"You're kidding me! Why? There is no reason for you to go back, and it's impossible to know if you are safe there," Dak glanced at her, but then quickly looked back at the road.

"I'm safe there. Everything I have is there. Plus, I am not going to stay with you," Kimly knew the last part sounded harsh, but she wasn't trying to be offensive. The man was a distraction to her; she could feel her attraction to him growing stronger. In her whole life Kimly had only ever been intimate with one man—her husband, and now that her marriage was falling apart she wasn't sure she was thinking straight or that she could trust herself if she were alone with Dak in his home. Waiting for Dak in her palace tree hideaway had been the most terrifying part of the day. She didn't understand how it was possible, but her affections for him were growing deep. This was never part of the plan.

"Kimly, listen to me. You are in over your head. Do you understand?" he wasn't yelling. It was worse. Each word came out of his mouth a slow intentionality as if he were speaking to a child.

"Dak, listen to me. I'm not staying with you." She pulled her long hair into her palm and wrapped a ponytail holder around her locks. She turned her head away from him and watched as trees buzzed by on the side of the road. The darkness had swallowed any space between the trees and the mountainside was now a blur of shadows.

"Why are you so stubborn?"

Arms folded, Kimly didn't answer. She waited almost a full minute and then she replied, "If you refuse to take me to the hotel I can always walk from your house, or call a cab. Or a tuk-tuk."

"You're not walking." He drove for a few minutes in silence and then finally slammed his fist against the steering wheel.

"The hotel is safe" Kimly's voice was softer.

"Why are you so convinced of that?" Dak challenged.

"Because I honestly don't think he knows where I am staying!"

"Really? You understand the mind of a madman? Kimly, he's not merely a criminal, he's a *crime boss*."

"Think about it, Dak, if he knew where I was staying—" her voice was rising, and she gained confidence as she spoke. Her theory coming to her as she said it, "why would he go to such elaborate measures to draw me up the hill, to the top of a fern garden in the middle of the palace grounds, if he knew where to find me?" She lowered her voice, "There is no logic in it. The man could have just showed up at my hotel room six hours ago and thrown me against a wall. Right?"

The Jeep sped along in roaring silence until they approached the busy street of the Royal Lanna Hotel, where they were greeted by the brightly lit golden arches of the worldwide fast food chain standing next to the hotel. The restaurant had been a part of her childhood, and later its Happy Meals were part of her sons' adolescence. Tonight the big yellow M was a herald reminding her she wasn't as far from home as she felt. Kimly broke the silence, "Can we get a Big Mac?" she let her head fall back against the headrest. "I'm starving."

He shook his head and didn't look at her. He didn't answer her either. She didn't want to try to guess what he was thinking. Certainly every choice she had made thus far had opposed his better judgment.

It wasn't until they had pulled under the carport of the Royal Lanna Hotel that Dak spoke.

"Yes, Kimly, I will get you a Big Mac."

12

Inside the water barrel room there is a smaller room; the sunfish-colored hair lady, Pakpao, calls the room a "closet." Pakpao uses a broom to wedge the closet door closed when she locks me in the small space. Being locked in the closet began the night they brought another little girl into the Darkness room.

Pakpao ushered me into the barrel room and I first saw her little head peeking over the side of the barrel as Xuan washed her short hair. Pakpao pushed me into the closet and told me to stay quiet. I did as I was told, mostly because I had many questions about the little girl I had just seen in the water barrel.

It was not long before I heard cries through the wall. The little girl did not scream when the man came to her room, instead she whimpered like an injured kitten. He did not leave her alone for many hours, and her soft bleating hurt my heart.

For a day and a day, I waited in the closet, listening through the wall while men brought Darkness to the crying kitten.

While I waited in the closet, I imagined Xuan coming to fetch me, and me pulling her into the barrel of water until she couldn't breathe, but when the door was finally opened I was so weak and hungry, I just crawled back to the room with the table-bed. I found the little girl curled into a ball in the corner. Her nose was bleeding, and she had welts on her tiny body. I wrapped myself around her, but she did not wake up. I thought she might be dead. I decided if she was dead, I wouldn't tell anyone. It would be better to hold her body and let her death drift into me.

Pakpao entered the room, sat a bowl on the floor, and told me to share with Lawan. This is how I knew the little one had a name. "Lawan," I whispered, "wake up." When the little girl woke, she opened her eyes only for an instant; she dropped her chin deep down onto her chest, leaned close to me, and whispered, "Mommy?" I let her call me Mommy, and decided I would take care of her.

Now, Lawan is crying from the barrel room. She has been all day in the barrel room behind the closet door with the broom, and I have been in the room all day and into the night, while Darkness comes to visit. I have given up trying to remember life before Misfortune and Darkness found me and stole so many of my good memories. Like the rocks trapped in the stream, I am trapped inside the room with Darkness. I am a rock in a stream, a prisoner to Darkness. Rocks cannot escape. I close my eyes and let the Darkness wash over my body.

After the last man leaves my room, I lie under the blanket and listen to Lawan crying on the other side of the wall. I cannot get to where she is because the door to my room has a metal lock across the top on the inside, but it also locks on the outside. I knock against the wall and tell her I will be with her soon, "Mommy is here, Lawan, do not be afraid..." I stand and walk over to the door to the room. I pull on the handle, but the door will not open. I begin to bang on the door and scream.

When the flat faced lady, Xuan, opens my door, her glassy-eyes are filled with rage. She yells at me, but I do not understand her screaming. I point at the wall, and yell, "Lawan! Lawan!" She slams the door. I wait for her to return with Lawan. She doesn't come back. I bang again on the door. Finally Xuan comes back. I hate her. I yell again, "Lawan!" She rolls her eyes at me. I reach up and grab her long hair, wrapping the matted strands around my wrist, again and again, she is pulling away from me, but the more she does the more it makes her scream. I pull her hard towards the barrel room, through the doorway and to the closet where Lawan is trapped.

While I am kicking the broom which holds the closet door closed, Xuan is able to knock me to the floor. Xuan and I are both kicking and screaming when Pakpao comes in the room. In a fit of rage, Pakpao chooses sides and begins kicking me as well. Her foot slams into my face. I use my hands to shield my eyes. A moment later, she kicks me in the stomach. I scream and pull myself into a ball. She is still kicking. She stops and looks at Xuan. The two women begin to yell at one another. I move to the wall closer to the door with the broom holding it closed. I pull myself up and then I begin to kick the broom. Over and over I kick it. When it falls to the floor, the door pops open. Lawan crawls out and grabs me. I hold her.

Pakpao looks at the two of us, and then she looks hard at Xuan. She raises her hand and strikes Xuan across the cheek. She raises her hand again, but stops and shakes her head. Using Xuan's unfamiliar words she shames the girl, and then she turns and leaves. Xuan grabs me by the hair and leads me back to the room I hate. Lawan is attached to my side.

When we are back in the room, Lawan races to the corner and curls into a ball, where she begins to shake and weep. Xuan releases me, pushing me to the ground. When I look at Xuan she isn't looking at me, but at Lawan. Although her dark eyes are not pitched against me, I can see the hatred pouring out of her.

The blacks of her eyes remind me of the seeds in Auntie's Custard Apples. Can it be possible that she is sweet like the sugar fruit? Good fruit does go bad. I have tasted many custard apples, some of them were ripe and fresh, making my tongue want to sing songs; some of them were flimsy and wilted, but even fruit which has gone bad was at one time sweet. I think eyes with so much hate could only come from an evil seed.

Xuan walks over to Lawan and begins to kick her. I push myself up off the ground. I will not let her hurt Lawan, but she stops and turns. Her evil seed eyes glare at my weak body. Smirking, she leaves. I gather Lawan's small body in my arms. After a few moments I whisper soft sounds in her ears and coax her up into the bed. I close my arms around her body and hold her heart close to my own.

I lay as still as a rock until the sun pokes me in the eye. I cannot understand how I can feel it through the painted window, but I feel its rays burning my face. It is so hot, I am certain I must be outside, but when I open my eyes, I am on the bed. The room is still and dim, but I feel the burn across my cheek. I reach up to the hot spot on my face. I remember the fight. I roll over and sleeping next to me is Lawan. She is swollen across the lips. When she wakes she will hurt even more, so I let her sleep.

I climb down from the bed and walk over to the window dark as dusk on the wall. In the night, the window becomes the wall. But right now, in the morning, the sun finds places to peek into our room. Tiny crumbs of light sneak through, giving me a taste of sunshine, reminding me I am still alive. Using my fingernail, I pick at the paint and make some of the specks larger. One scratched speck is almost as big as my thumb. I look through the hole and see the street.

I do not see anyone by the window, but every day I will look. Maybe one day I will see Momma. Maybe she will come looking for me, and she will see my eye. Momma would know my eye.

13

Kimly stood with her back pressed against the tree and held her breath. Something was moving behind her. She wanted to look around the tree and see who or what it was, but it was too risky. She needed to stay perfectly still. She felt a branch move near her head. Whatever it was, it was getting closer. She raised her hand to pull the branch away from her face but her arm was trapped by another limb of the tree.

It was a tiger, and Kimly could see its silhouette moving closer. She felt its claws pulling against her neck and...ripping her shirt. She couldn't breathe. She couldn't scream. Pain shot through her, the tiger was on top of her. She brought her free hand up to shield her face from the teeth of the tiger. Kimly's hand was not a hand, but the golden paw of a lion.

He slapped her across the face. She opened her eyes. A man was on top of her. Kimly tried to understand what was happening. Her mind raced to catch up to whatever she had missed while sleeping. The hard mattress beneath her and the scratchy sheets sent messages flaring.

SuSuk was on top of her. Kimly let out a scream, and tried to use her arm to resist, but SuSuk's knee was on top of her hand holding it straight against her left side. Pushing him away from her with her right hand, SuSuk thwarted her movements by pulling her hand down trying to wedge it beneath his other knee. Kimly fought to pull her arm toward her face, toward herself.

He grabbed her right arm and pulled it over her head; pulling his own head backward he brought his head down quickly, making contact with hers. All of her muscles failed her for a moment, and SuSuk was able to get her right arm by her side and under his knee. He pulled his hand up and placed it around her neck. With the other hand he unfastened his belt and attempted to lower his pants.

"You are a fool. You are a crazy, stupid fool," SuSuk's whisper was hot against her face. "You are in Chiang Mai alone. Did you think I wasn't following you?

I see your plans to steal what is mine. I am the one who will take." Kimly pulled her arms trying to free them from under his knees.

SuSuk tore Kimly's shirt wide open. His hands on her chest felt as if they would tear through her skin. "My men will find ways to enjoy you on a nightly basis. It is going to excite them to have a woman for a change, instead of a child." SuSuk held his hand on her breast. "And an American woman is even better."

SuSuk began fondling her breast, and Kimly was filled with a rush of angry adrenaline. Pushing down against the scratchy sheets, Kimly twisted her hand and was able to gain a little bit of space between her hand and SuSuk's knee. She began to push her fingernails through his thin pant leg into this skin.

"You are of no use to me in Thailand, but I can use you in Laos," SuSuk's laughter was almost as frightening as his touch. "You think you are so smart. You are not smarter than me. The men in Laos will line up to pay for an American. They will appreciate the curves of a woman for a change." SuSuk ran his hand down her side and lifted the elastic waistline of her shorts.

Kimly dug her fingernails deeper into his knee as if she were digging a spoon into a tub of frozen ice cream. She didn't think she could go any deeper. SuSuk shifted his knee slightly, and it was enough for Kimly to pull her hand free. She moved it straight up and under her pillow. SuSuk adjusted his weight on Kimly as he pulled her shorts down.

Bringing the palm size tube right in front of her own face, Kimly tightly squeezed her own eyes closed, and pressed the button. The mace shot directly into SuSuk's eyes.

SuSuk pulled back and instinctively grabbed at his eyes. His lifted his knee in his reactive movements and Kimly's other hand was freed. She pushed him away, but he gripped her arm trying to hold her in submission. She reached her arm around and shot him again. This time, she held down on the vial until he was no longer on top of her.

Stumbling over one of Kimly's shoes on the floor, SuSuk's arms flailed about in an attempt to find his bearings. His hand hit a clear glass water bottle on the edge of the table, and it tumbled down and fell hard onto the marble floor. The crashing sound broke through the room like thunder chasing lightning through a stormy sky.

Kimly jumped off the bed and threw herself against the wall. Every nightmare she ever dreamed was coming true. She watched him stumbling towards the bathroom. She had to get out. Reaching down, she pulled her shorts up with one hand and with the other grabbed her laptop. Kimly made her way toward the door staying close to the wall when her bare foot came down on a piece of glass. She screamed and tried to keep moving. The man spun around. With one hand on his eyes, he reached towards her with the other. Kimly raised her laptop above her and brought it down against the side of SuSuk's head.

He jolted back but immediately came back swinging. He made contact with Kimly, and she fell back against the table and landed in the broken glass. Tiny jolts of pain shot through her and she screamed. And then, as if someone else were in the room assisting her back to her feet, Kimly pushed herself up, still gripping her laptop.

SuSuk's breathing was getting more labored, and in the dark shadows Kimly had no problem hearing where he was. Kimly moved closer and pulled her laptop up over her head. She brought her laptop down as hard as she could against the top of his head. He reached the doorway leading to the bathroom; SuSuk had one hand on the door jam and the other was feeling for the sink when Kimly hit him again. And then again. She had hit him four times in the side of the head when he finally dropped to the bathroom floor.

Kimly dropped the laptop, grabbed her phone off the bathroom counter, and bolted out the door of her room. She didn't know how long she had until SuSuk woke up.

She ran down the corridor and around the corner to the faster elevator. Hopefully, SuSuk was alone, and hopefully, he wouldn't know about the hidden elevator. She pressed the button and pulled herself flat against the wall while she waited, instinctively trying to cover her exposed breasts with her torn shirt. Her hands were shaking so badly, she didn't know if she would be able to push the buttons on her phone to get help.

The door to the elevator opened, and she jumped in and pressed the button marked "L" over and over. *Come on! Really? Close!* She was beginning to panic. *Please!* Finally, the doors closed and the elevator began to descend slowly. Kimly's mind raced. Her mouth was bleeding, or maybe it was her eye. *What if there are others in the lobby? How did he get in? Did the desk clerk give him a key?* During the short journey down the eleven floors, Kimly decided she needed to get into a crowd of people. Looking out the glass walls of the elevator and seeing the mass of people on the street, she was grateful she was lodged in a city that thrived by appealing to the materialism of its tourists. Greed and the desire to acquire were working in her favor as the streets were overflowing with both merchants and clientele. She was barely dressed and what little she wore was splattered with blood. She was sure to draw attention, but given the situation, a slew of onlookers might keep her safe.

Before the doors were completely open Kimly was squeezing between them and running full force out of the lobby and into the street of the Night Bazaar. The golden arches of her childhood called to her and she moved swiftly across the sidewalk. It was far from being an embassy, but it was brightly lit and full of people. Kimly slid through the restaurant's glass doors. A petite woman standing in line with a man and two teenage girls looked up at Kimly and let out a soft gasp. Kimly heard the woman say, "Oh no..." and their eyes met.

Kimly quickly turned to a hallway on her left where she saw the sign for the restrooms. As soon as she stepped into the restroom, Kimly locked herself in one of the stalls and called the only person she knew in Thailand.

"Kimly?" Dak answered after two rings.

"A man. He was in my room..." Kimly started to talk, but tears were coming with her words.

"Where are you?! I'm on my way."

For the second time since landing in Thailand, Kimly heard the sound of Dak's voice reverberating on the tile walls of a public restroom. Kimly's breathing intensified. Her pulse, which was already rapidly beating, skyrocketed. She opened the stall door when she heard him, and Dak's eyes revealed that he was as frightened as she. He had tried to warn her, but she had been so stubborn. He didn't say a word; he just grabbed her by the shoulders and led her out of the restaurant. Neither of them spoke as he led her through the crowds, passing a street artist and a vendor selling crispy baked apples. Arriving at the Jeep, Dak opened Kimly's door, and she climbed in. He moved quickly around to the driver's side and climbed in without looking at her. He just sat there for a minute and stared straight ahead. From where he was parked, the Jeep faced the entrance to the hotel.

Dak's eyes were locked on the doors of the Royal Lanna. "Sorry," he mumbled as he reached into the back seat and pulled up a sweatshirt, "you're probably freezing."

She wasn't sure if she was freezing or not. Kimly's mind was spinning, like a video on an endless loop she replayed the assault over and over in her head. She hadn't realized she was shaking, and she wasn't sure a bulky sweatshirt would stop what was happening. Nevertheless, she was barely clothed. Pulling his sweatshirt over her head and covering her near nakedness did make her feel better. Kimly pulled her legs up under it as well and wrapped her arms around her quivering self.

Kimly's mind was racing, *What if they are still watching?* She tried to push the thought out of her head and gain control of the fears beginning to erupt. She didn't want to fall apart in front of him.

"My passport," she whispered.

"Not tonight," he answered and turned the key in the ignition, his voice was nearly as coarse as the sounds from the engine. As Dak drove, he looked over his shoulder to change lanes, and Kimly watched his eyes. The familiar gray kindness was missing, and something had replaced it. Anger? She could only imagine his anger towards her.

Dak had been driving for about ten minutes before Kimly spoke again, "All my money is at the hotel."

His words came out less harsh this time, "You don't need it. We'll figure it out in the morning."

14

Dak turned off the main highway and into a residential area. Most of the homes were dark, and the absence of street lights limited visibility to the shrubs and cars spotlighted by the Jeep's headlamps. Not that illumination would have made a difference to Kimly; her eyes were glazed over and latched onto the dashboard of the Jeep, as she replayed the last hour in her mind. Finally, Dak slowed the Jeep and turned into a narrow driveway. The house was set deep into the yard, and Dak and Kimly were greeted by three scraggly dogs.

"Yours?" Kimly asked Dak while eyeing the hospitable hounds.

"Naw, they don't belong to anyone. I just feed them," Dak mumbled as he climbed out of the Jeep and slammed the door. Kimly turned toward the passenger door and was trying to locate its handle, without scratching her arm on it yet again, when it opened suddenly. Dak stood waiting. Lowering one bare leg onto the gravel driveway, while its twin followed meekly, Kimly climbed out of the Jeep and stood in Dak's driveway feeling very exposed. In her bolt from the hotel, Kimly didn't think about how much clothing she wasn't wearing. Now, standing in Dak's yard, she wished she were dressed in more than a pair of clover-leaf boxers and a bulky sweatshirt.

"Come on, let's get you inside," he barely looked at her, and she was certain he must be furious. She didn't blame him. He had tried to warn her, but now because of her stubbornness, he had to come to her rescue. The gravel was sharp beneath her feet. She winced but didn't cry out. She wondered if there was glass in her foot and immediately remembered her first night in Chiang Mai.

Dak walked ahead of her and unlocked the door. Taking a deep breath Kimly tried to move faster across the rocks, but the pain was nearly unbearable. Suddenly, Dak came towards her, reached down and placed one arm around her back and lifted her into his arms and carried her across the gravel and through the front door.

The bungalow was no more than ninety square feet. A navy blue plush recliner sat in one corner next to a small table. On the table sat a lamp whose shade was too big, making the lamp appear unstable. On the table next to the deformed lamp sat a pile of books. On the floor next to the table were several uneven piles of books.

There was no wall between the reading room and a tiny kitchen, which consisted of a sink and a stove with about two feet of counter space. A square wooden table with three chairs sat off to the right. Two of the chairs were alike while the third was an oddball. Behind the table there stood a small refrigerator with a faux wood finish. On the other side of the reading area were two French doors, which were open wide against the walls of the living room. Through the doorway, Dak's queen sized bed was disheveled, likely from when he'd answered her frantic call and dashed out. Dak began to gather a few dirty dishes from around the room, as if Kimly would care.

"Um...you probably just saved my life. You really don't have to clean up."

Dak didn't respond, but just continued toward the kitchen.

"Dak, I'm really sorry you had to come. I didn't know," Kimly's voice cracked, but she took a breath and reigned in her emotions, "I mean, I didn't think. I don't know...anyway...I'm really sorry, and I understand if you're mad because you got dragged into this."

"Oh, for crying out loud, Kimly," Dak had stopped moving about the room and faced her, "you think I'm mad because I *got dragged into this?*"

They both stood still, and she shifted her eyes down to the hardwood floor. Overwhelmed with all she had already been through, the sound of Dak's raised voice was unbearable. Kimly's pulse was no longer clanging wildly, but there was a painful sensation building behind her left eye. Plus, strange emotions were rising, as SuSuk's dark voice echoed in her head. The plans he had for her and the memory of his hot breath chilled her blood and made her shiver. As hard as she tried, Kimly couldn't hold in the tears any longer. Dak's arms reached out, and she was suddenly encompassed in his warmth. He pulled Kimly close and she could feel his strong, warm arms and body enveloping her. She could hear his heart pounding, and its firm beat was comforting. One of his hands came up and rested against the back of her head. More tears were rising, but she pushed them down.

Once Kimly knew she had managed to control her tears, she pulled her head back a little. She looked up into Dak's gray eyes and whispered, "Thank you."

"I'm sorry, Kimly," he immediately released her; "you have been through so much. I shouldn't have yelled. Let me show you where the bath is. Maybe you'll feel better if you shower or something..."

Dak's voice trailed off as he headed through the bedroom and an adjoining door. Kimly knew she was supposed to follow, but she was too nervous to move. His kindness was going to break down every defense she had. She could feel intense emotions rising again, and she didn't want him to witness them.

A moment later he returned and told her he had placed a towel in the bathroom. The way he avoided eye contact told her how uncomfortable this situation was for him. Kimly could only imagine that among the rules he had to obey as a Preacher, there must be one about not bringing a strange woman to his house and then telling her she could shower.

If there were any doubts about the danger she had encountered in the hotel room, the bathroom mirror was brutally honest with Kimly. When she looked at her reflection, tears she had been holding in came falling down her dirty face. Her left eye was in the beginning stages of swelling, and she had a nasty cut on the top of the right side of her lip. She remembered SuSuk had hit her, and she remembered falling and landing against a table. But, during the attack, it felt so minor. It almost seemed as if he hadn't made full contact. Now, looking at the damage he had done, she was amazed she had been able to bring him down. It was almost as if someone else had been helping her. Kimly knew she had faced SuSuk alone, but when she remembered the incident, she felt another presence, as well.

Hot water ran down Kimly's body, and different body parts shouted out in stinging pain. It wasn't enough to bring her to tears, but the tears came regardless. Apart from the physical pain, she felt an emotional anguish such as she'd never felt. She knew the sound of the shower would drown out her crying, so Kimly allowed herself to succumb to emotions. She leaned against the tile wall and for the first time since she had arrived began to see the danger of her obsessive drive. *Why am I doing this?* For the first time, it was hard to see a reason to continue. *For accolades? For attention?* What was the motivation behind the insane choices she was making? *Stop and go home.* But as soon as she heard herself thinking those thoughts, she felt a different wave of shame. *What would I be going home to? A failing marriage. A life with no purpose.*

Kimly wrapped the towel around her head when she noticed that along with the towel, Dak had left a clean t-shirt for her to wear. She looked at the torn shirt she had been wearing and saw it was speckled with traces of blood. She pulled the black t-shirt over her head and stepped back into her clover-leaf boxer shorts. She let her hair fall from the towel, found a comb and pulled it through her mane. Dak had been right about her feeling better after a shower.

When Kimly limped out of the bathroom, the French doors separating the living room from the bedroom were now closed. There was no curtain on the door's glass windows, but Dak had moved the recliner so the back of his chair faced the bedroom. She approached the doors, opened one and peeked around the chair. Dak sat reading. She recognized the book as the same leather-bound Bible he had reached for in his Jeep.

"You take the bed," Dak smiled up at her.

"Are you sure?" she asked, but she already knew what he would say. His superhero nature would never allow her to sleep on the floor or in a chair. It was a silly question to ask, but she still had to say it.

"I like my chair. And no one ever lets me sleep in it," he winked.

Settled in against his downy pillows, Kimly watched the back of Dak's head through the glass doors for some time. He was perfectly still. Kimly couldn't imagine what the Bible could possibly be telling him that was relevant to what they had been through, but every part of her was curious.

15

Breaking through the blinds of the bedroom window, the sun's rays attacked the room. The white sheets soaked up the sunbeams, making the cotton bedding warm to the touch. Rolling over in Dak's bed, Kimly was disoriented. Her head was pounding, and there was a ringing in her ears. Something was pressing down on her left eye. As Kimly lifted her hand toward her face, her muscles responded to the slight movement by sending waves of pain throughout her biceps and shoulders.

Pressing down on the thick bedding, Kimly could see the glass doors without lifting her head. Everything on the other side of the glass barrier was still. The dark brown drapes on the far wall were drawn, giving the room on the opposite side of the glass the appearance of night. It was as if the house were divided into two separate regions. The room on the opposing side of the glass was dark and dismal while the room where Kimly lay was bright. It was two conflicting worlds in the same house. Despite the pounding in her head, Kimly lay still and marveled at what the light was accomplishing. What struck her as odd was that she was sure she belonged on the other side of the glass.

Crawling out of the bed, Kimly took a step and was reminded of the cut on the bottom of her foot. She made her way to the bathroom, bracing herself for the image in the mirror, but what she saw was worse than she had feared. The swelling and cuts and bruises on her face brought clarity to the extent of her failure. Dak had obviously been right. She had gotten in way over her head.

When she exited the bath, she noticed that the dark room on the other side of the glass was now alive with light. The drapes had been drawn open, and sunshine was illuminating the entire house. As she made her way toward the living area, she could hear faint rustling sounds. The stiffness in her joints and raw wounds made her move slowly. But, the worst feeling was the humiliation she felt in anticipation of seeing Dak.

She pulled Dak's sweatshirt over her head and wished she could either crawl back under the stark white sheets or crawl out the front door and vanish. She opened the glass doors between the two rooms and ventured into the living area of the house. Dak was in the small kitchenette pulling things out of a brown paper bag. As she approached she was wary about making eye contact with him. Last night had been so tense, and she was apprehensive of the lecture Dak might give.

"Good morning...how are you feeling?" His voice was gentle.

"I'm okay. Thank you, by the way." She cleared her throat at the end, looked up at him and then quickly back down at her own hands, noticing a cut on her right palm which she hadn't seen.

"Kimly, you don't have to thank me. I'm really sorry you went through what you went through"

"Yeah, me too. But, thank you for the mace. If I hadn't had it, I don't know what he...I mean...I only had it because you gave it to me. And, that's what..." Kimly's voice cracked, stopping her midsentence. Familiar pressure began building just below the surface.

"Then, praise God you had it. Now, how about I make us some breakfast? I can't vouch for my eggs...but I make a mean cup of joe."

"Coffee would be great. But, you don't have to make eggs for me...you have already done so—" "Coffee and eggs, coming up!" Dak interrupted, "And, I know I don't have to...I want to."

The heat rising from the coffee mug was painful against Kimly's lip, but the effort was worth the reward. She sipped it slowly and let out a sigh. It tasted better than any coffee she'd had in the two weeks she had been in the foreign city.

Raising her hand to her swollen eye, Kimly was embarrassed by her appearance. She hadn't realized how much of her confidence was derived from vanity.

"We have to go back to the hotel," Kimly's voice was meek.

"And...why...do we have to go back to the hotel?" Wire whisk spinning in the bowl, Dak didn't have the classic bodyguard tone to his voice. The two were not playing the game they had mastered over the last two weeks. They were just Kimly and Dak, discussing the situation without any fireworks.

"I don't have any of my things. My clothes, my laptop...I dropped it. I mean, after...well, I dropped it, and I don't even have my passport. All my money, too," her voice cracked again.

"I already went," using his wire whisk he motioned toward the front door. She moved her head, perhaps too quickly, because a lurching pain shot down her neck. And, there it sat, perfectly contained. Her suitcase.

"You went back?! Why would you do that?! I mean, you went *alone*. He might have still been there. How did you get in? They could've been watching you, and he could have followed you."

"Calm down," Dak pleaded. But Kimly didn't, she stood up from the oddball chair and headed to the front window of the bungalow.

"Kimly, no one followed me. Trust me."

"Why? I mean, how do you know?" She was standing next to the window frame, peeking around its edge, looking out the glass. Kimly noticed there were bungalows like this one on both sides and another series of them across the street. They were charming, more charming than she had realized when she climbed out of his Jeep at 3 AM. The rooftops were covered in palm fronds; she could even see some of the sprays peeking down at her over the edge of Dak's porch. The walls were covered with wood paneling and trimmed in flattened bamboo. Kimly pulled her head back in and looked around the room. The interior walls and ceiling were drywall, painted some shade of beige. The tropical bungalow theme only existed on the exterior.

"I know because I went back as soon as you were asleep. I waited outside until I saw him leave," Dak paused, and Kimly turned her head away from the window and looked at him. He clenched his jaw tight. After a few beats, Dak continued, "and then I went in. Fortunately, he didn't close the door to your room on his way out, so I gathered your things and packed them in your suitcase." Dak was pouring the egg mixture into an iron skillet. Kimly could already tell he was going to burn the eggs; the fire was too high, making his skillet too hot. "Then, when I left the hotel, I stopped by the front desk, paid your debt and checked you out. Afterward, I drove through the mountains for about an hour. If they were following, I think I would have noticed," Dak began to move a wooden spoon quickly around the pan; trying to stop the damage he was doing to the poor eggs.

With a heavy sigh she let out a small, "Thank you." Kimly grabbed her suitcase and tipped it to the side and began to unzip the bag.

"Darn it. They're burned," Dak was legitimately surprised.

"Crap," Kimly's words were almost on top of his.

"It's okay, I have a whole dozen."

"My passport. It's still there. It's in my pillowcase," Kimly's eyes were pleading with him to respond, hoping he had seen it and had grabbed it.

"It's what?" Dak's eyes darted from Kimly to her suitcase. "I grabbed everything I saw. It's where?"

"No, you wouldn't have known. I read somewhere that tourists sometimes keep their passports inside their pillowcases while sleeping as a safety measure," Kimly was getting flustered, "I didn't think to...I don't know, I was trying to get out—"

Dak interrupted her, "Kimly, you didn't do anything wrong. It's okay. I will just go back and get it."

"Well, fine. But, I'm going with you."

"Kimly, there's no reason—"

"Dak. Seriously. I'm going with you."

"Can you just tell me why you aren't willing to—"

"Dak, I don't want to stay here..."

"Oh come on, Kimly..." Dak interrupted.

"...alone." She continued, "I don't want to stay here alone. I'm scared, okay?! I'm going with you."

"I can imagine you are scared. I promise, you're safe here."

"Dak!" she interrupted him, "Arguing with you hurts my lip, but if that's what needs to happen before we go back *together*, then fine...let's argue," she turned her back to him and looked out the window.

Dak dropped the bowl and wire whisk in the sink where it clattered.

"And, by the way," Kimly continued, "your skillet's too hot."

Twenty minutes later, Kimly could hear the shower running, so she figured she had a few minutes to quickly change her clothes. With Dak on the other side of the bathroom door, Kimly decided to grab some clothes out of her suitcase and do a quick change in the kitchenette. Opening the suitcase, Kimly was slightly embarrassed at the thought of Dak gathering her things and placing them in her bag. She grabbed her bra which was on top of the pile and rummaged around until she found a clean shirt and some jeans.

Her cell phone charger was wrapped in a knotted mess. As she pulled on the wire to untangle the cord, she decided she should probably charge her phone. She zipped up her jeans and went in search of her phone. She had no idea where she might have set it. Looking around the room, her eyes spied the device through the glass doors sitting on Dak's nightstand.

As she slid through the door and into his bedroom, she stepped lightly on the foot with the cut. When she grabbed the phone, she noticed she had a missed call. Slowly lowering herself onto the bed, Kimly stared at the notification.

Kyle, Missed Call

How did I miss your call? She stared at the clock on her phone and tried to remember the time difference. *Eleven and half hours. Backwards or forwards?* Either way, it was late morning for her, which meant it was late in the evening back home.

After the incident the night before, Kimly would be lying if she said she didn't want to hear Kyle's voice. It seemed strange to not call him after the violent assault. But, she wondered what she would say, *"Hi, how are you? Oh, I'm fine; I was almost raped last night, so I left the hotel and slept in the bed of a handsome stranger. How are the boys? So, are you still seeing your mistress?"* Returning the missed call was a legitimate reason to call. One Kyle wouldn't question. Kimly was rehearsing her opening line in her head when Dak walked out of the bathroom and into his bedroom.

"Oh, hey, I'm sorry—" he stopped short. Dak stood shirtless in the warm, sun-filled room, wearing a pair of 501 jeans and holding his white towel. His masculine chest was light bronze, and Kimly caught herself lowering her eyes from his face to his broad shoulders. There had been so much tension between them as they forced down Dak's second, and slightly less burned, scrambled eggs. But, this current tension had a different vibration.

"No!" Kimly's voice was almost a shout, "You're fine, I'm leaving...I'm sorry...I just...I came for my phone." She moved across the patterned rug and through the glass doors, fumbling over her words as she crossed the living room without turning back, reached for the front door and walked out onto Dak's porch.

The smallest of the scraggly stray dogs was eager for company and came to Kimly's side. She looked around the yard with its overgrown plants. Another dog lay chewing on something in the shade of the

Jeep. She noticed the Jeep was now wearing its hardtop shell which was battered and worn, and she noted that Dak hadn't been exaggerating about the duct tape repairs.

Sitting on the steps of the bungalow, Kimly dialed the number to her husband's cell phone. Each ring made her pulse race faster. Conflicted, she hoped Kyle wouldn't answer while she also wondered why he wasn't. *Where are you?* "You've reached the cell phone of Kyle Denim. I can't take your call. Leave a message after the beep." Kyle's voice was so calm. Her heart hammered, her eyes brimmed with tears--she was a battered mess, but the only man she had ever loved, the man to whom she had been married for two decades was thousands of miles away, with a calm voice.

"Hi, it's me. I'm fine. I'm just calling returning your call. I mean, I saw you called but I didn't hear my phone because of the shower, not my shower, I mean...anyway, I just wanted to see if the boys were okay. And to tell you I'm fine. Really, I am. Talk to you later."

Kimly stared down at her phone. Why was leaving a voicemail so intimidating? The call timer on her phone read one minute and twelve seconds. Kimly stared at the timer and decided that very well may have been the longest conversation the couple had had in the last year, that hadn't ended in a fight.

16

When Dak and Kimly approached the hotel's front desk, the young man working looked up at them and did a double take, after which, his face was nearly expressionless. It gave her suspicions that he was working with SuSuk or at least aware of SuSuk's presence in her room the night before. Perhaps when the desk clerk saw Kimly had checked out of her room, he assumed SuSuk relocated her.

What if he does work for SuSuk? It was unnerving to Kimly, and she could feel her pulse rising, but she could feel Dak's eyes on her, so she put on her best poker face and pushed the fear down. After all the looks Dak had thrown at her throughout the morning, she wasn't going to reward him with any inkling that his concerns were justified. She maintained her composure.

"Sorry, no passport turned in," the clerk looked at Dak when he answered. It was obvious the clerk was having a difficult time looking at her. This man had guilt.

"Well, can we go up and check the room? Just to make sure it isn't there," Dak's nonchalant tone kept the conversation pleasant.

"It won't be there, the room was cleaned," the clerk busied himself with some papers on the counter. Kimly wondered if his abrupt tone had to do with fears for his own safety.

"Okay, but seeing that her passport wasn't turned in, and she doesn't have it, we'd like to check the room." Dak said in a sharp tone, but the clerk simply diverted his eyes to the papers in front of him.

Finally, Dak leaned and spoke to the clerk in hushed tones, "Bpit torng   lang   pra..."
The young man's expression was clearly conflicted. He looked at Dak with hard eyes, and then he said in a lowered voice, "Wait here." The desk clerk retreated behind a thick mahogany door.

"What did you say to him? Should we leave?" Kimly heard herself speak without thinking that Dak may respond in the affirmative, but Dak was consumed with his thoughts. There was a small squint around his eyes as he looked at her.

"You're fine. We're here. Let's just see what he says," Dak said as he reached behind Kimly and patted her back. She took in a deep breath and asked, "What did you say, though?"

"It's an old saying I picked up from my mother, 'put a gold leaf on the back of a Buddha,' it means 'do a good deed without seeking attention.' I thought it was worth a shot."

The desk clerk returned and reached his hand across the counter, "I hope you find what you are looking for," he said as he handed the key to Dak, but his altered, and now confident, gaze was set on Kimly.

Dak turned and took steps in the direction of the elevator, but Kimly was paralyzed by the desk clerk's eyes. She was stupefied by the change of tone from the once hesitant clerk.

"Kimly?" Dak stopped and called for her. She followed his voice without fully taking her eyes off the man behind the counter. She was fixated on the possibility of what may have been right in front of her the whole time. Replaying every interaction she could recall, Kimly didn't notice when Dak led them to the older elevator. Kimly stood distracted in the lobby waiting three minutes for the elevator doors to open.

As they climbed into the small cab, Kimly awoke from autopilot, "Why are we using this one? I mean, the other is faster—"

Dak shrugged, "I don't know...I just went this way."

The elevator doors closed, Dak pushed the button marked 11, and the two stood waiting for the elevator to respond. It didn't. The elevator waited a full minute and when it finally decided to make the journey upward, it did so with a jerk and a scream.

At the ninth floor, the elevator doors opened, and standing outside them was the rosy cheeked pregnant woman Kimly had encountered on her first night in the hotel

"Hello," rolled naturally off Kimly's tongue and she might not have given the incident too much thought, except for the response of the rosy cheeked pregnant woman, "Oh, ah, khaawp khoon kha, mai..." and she began to back away from the elevator doors, all the while shaking her head. The doors closed abruptly between them.

Even after the doors had sealed them on opposing sides, Kimly called out to her, "Wait!"

Kimly lurched across the cab and slammed her hand on the button to open the doors, but the elevator ignored her request. It felt like an eternity until the jerk and scream alerted Kimly to the elevator's plan to engage, all the while, she was pressing the buttons marked 9 and 10 over and over. A few moments later the elevator stopped at the tenth floor. When the doors opened, Kimly bolted out of the cab.

"Wait, Kimly," Dak was rushing right behind her. "What are you doing?"

"It's her, the pregnant girl...she was the one who was cleaning my room! I've got to find her!" Kimly hollered over her shoulder as she made confident strides down the hallway.

"Let's just take the elevator back down! She couldn't have gotten very far!" Dak stopped outside of the cab with one hand bracing the doors open.

"No...This is better—" Kimly wasn't slowing, "come on!"

At the end of the hallway they reached the stairwell Kimly had discovered the first night in the hotel. Racing down the steps, they reached the ninth floor in a matter of seconds. Kimly turned and headed back down the hallway towards the elevator.

"Kimly, stop!" he called out to her, but she didn't pause. "Kimly...she didn't want to talk to you! She's not going to be at the elevator waiting. She probably headed down the stairs to get away!" With Dak's words hanging in the air, Kimly skidded to a stop.

Her breathing was labored, "You're right! We've got to go down. But, we have to cut her off...come on!" And Kimly started to run again, giving Dak no choice but to follow.

Kimly reached the hidden elevator a few seconds before Dak, and pounded on the button relentlessly until the doors opened in front of them. She pushed the button marked "L" and the elevator responded quickly. "Let's take this down to the ground floor. We can get down faster and meet her at the bottom of the stairwell....right?"

"Unless she used a service elevator..." Dak suggested.

The doors were closing as Kimly whipped her head up and looked at Dak. She drew her hand up to her lips and bit down on her index fingernail.

"Don't worry. She couldn't have gotten too far..." He reassured.

The elevator doors opened, and Kimly was running again. This time Dak was right by her side. They crossed the hotel lobby, maneuvering around an elderly couple and their luggage. They came to a stop in the middle of the lobby and stood looking around the perimeter of the hotel. There was nothing that indicated the direction of the stairs. There had to be access in case of a fire, but neither of them could see how to get to the stairwell.

Finally Dak whispered, "There…"

She followed his line of sight and she saw a hallway that must extend behind the front desk. They walked briskly down the hallway, passing the restrooms until they came to the end and were greeted by two doors, one bearing a sign that read: STAIRS, and the other unmarked.

Kimly pushed the heavy door open to what was, presumably, an employee break room. The wall on her left was lined with lockers. The individual metal cabinets were dented and the silver paint was peeling away, revealing a darker shade beneath. On the other side of the room a dirty rice cooker and a pile of newspapers sat on a rectangle table which was pushed up against the wall. There were two doors in the room. On the wall with the lockers there was a door painted white, and across from it there was a door was made of sturdy wood, with a deadbolt and a palm-sized window at eye level. Kimly moved near the white door and placed her hand on doorknob. She stopped when Dak put his hand on her arm and whispered,

"No—"

"It's okay…" she whispered back, but when she looked over at him, his eyes were fixed on something outside of the small window on the door with the deadbolt.

"She's right there," he whispered again and pointed through the window.

Kimly turned and was reaching for the handle, when Dak took her arm again, "Wait, Kimly, don't go barreling after her. She's obviously frightened. Slow down."

Kimly nodded and she opened the door slowly, peeking around the corner. She exited the hotel into a narrow alleyway. The space was paltry, only a few feet between the hotel and a tall concrete wall. One end of the alley led out to the street where the vendors would soon begin setting up for another Night Bazaar, and the other end led to the parking lot where the Jeep was parked near the hotel's back entrance. The alley was lined with trash cans, boxes and crates. Someone was attempting to grow a garden in a large wooden barrel with a picture of a yellow fish painted on the side. The weathered barrel was filled with dirt and an assortment of flowering plants. None of the plants were thriving, and there were a few cigarette butts shoved into the dirt. The rosy cheeked pregnant woman was sitting on a plastic milk crate. She had one arm wrapped around her middle, resting gently on her expanding belly and she held a cell phone close to her ear.

"Hi..." Kimly spoke as softly as she could. "Do you remember me?" She moved closer to the pregnant woman. The woman whispered in the phone and then quickly hung up.

"My passport...it was in my room. I was hoping you had found it."

The woman responded, "Mai, mai....khaaw tho..." while she scampered back into the hotel. Kimly followed her back into the break room, but the woman disappeared through the painted door. Dak held the painted door open, and the two of them followed her with their eyes. She turned and looked over her shoulder, then went through another door. Repeating over and over, "Khaaw tho, khaaw tho..."

"She's apologizing, Kimly," Dak placed his hand on Kimly's shoulder, "I don't think she is going to be able to help you."

"I don't understand? Do you think it's because of SuSuk?"

Dak and Kimly exited the break room and walked back to the lobby. The pregnant woman was gone. Kimly's adrenaline tapered and she began to feel the throbbing effects of running on a foot with a fresh cut on its bottom. "I need some pain reliever," the words fell matter-of-factly out of her mouth, and she turned her swollen eye up and looked up into the now familiar grayness.

He smiled down at her as they continued to walk. "Yeah, I bet you do...let's go check your room for the passport."

Dak and Kimly pulled apart the bed searching for Kimly's passport, but just as the young clerk had predicted, it wasn't in the room which had been meticulously cleaned.

"I think it's going to rain." Dak stated flatly as they crossed under the hotel's carport. "Let's get back to my place and we can look up the address to the American Embassy. I believe it's in Bangkok."

"Yoot...yoot." a woman was whispering loudly from behind them. It was the rosy cheeked pregnant woman calling to them from the side of the building. With light footsteps, she came toward them from the alleyway. She had one hand across the bottom of her pregnant belly, and the other hand was extended forward, holding Kimly's passport.

"Khaawp Khoon Kharap...thank you," Dak rushed across the drive to take the passport.

Dak had the passport and the girl was quickly descending back into the alleyway, when Kimly met Dak halfway across the drive. "Thank you...thank you so much!" Kimly called out to the rosy cheeked pregnant woman.

She could feel Dak's hand on her arm holding her back.

"It's okay," she looked up at him, "I'm not going anywhere." Dak smiled, shook his head, and responded, "I can never tell anymore," and the two headed back to the Jeep.

Dak drove the jeep into the bungalow's gravel driveway just as the sky opened up above them, and rain pounded on the roof of the Jeep.

"Wow!" Kimly hadn't yet experienced Thailand's dramatic weather shifts, and as the rain held them captive in the Jeep, she leaned her head back against the headrest and watched the water coat the windshield.

"Do you like the rain?" Dak asked. He was leaning his head back against his headrest, too. But he wasn't watching the water show. Dak was watching Kimly.

"Yeah, I love it," Kimly answered, "I mean, doesn't everyone?"

Dak didn't answer, and he didn't turn to watch the rain; his gray eyes just watched her watching the drops dance across the windshield until she felt their presence. When she turned her head and looked at him, the interior of the Jeep suddenly felt much smaller. In the moment before she had looked at him, the sound of the rain beating down on the car had been deafening, but now, with those gray eyes fixed on her own, the silence was piercing. Dak looked away first, and without his eyes to immobilize her, she pulled herself free and dropped her eyes to the passport in her hands.

Looking at the insignia on the cover, she wondered aloud, "Maybe I should just go home. Maybe what I wanted to do isn't—" she stopped talking when she opened the passport and a business card adorned with a picture of a steamed shrimp, kale, and noodles fell into her lap. The card was weathered, with frayed edges and a crease down the center where it had been folded.

The Bamboo Breeze
44 Moo 7, Phaholyothin Rd.
Mae Sai, Mae Sai, Chiang Rai,
57130, Thailand
+66 53 731 118

"I think you should go home, too, Kimly." His voice was subdued, and he only turned and looked at her after he had finished talking.

"Dak, this is our next lead…it has to be." Kimly's voice rose and she handed him the business card.

When Dak looked at the card, he didn't respond as she expected, "Where did you get this?"

"It was in my passport. The pregnant lady…she must have put the card in my passport, she must be trying to help me!"

"Whoa, slow down. You're assuming so much, Kimly. This could mean nothing. You don't even know how many people touched your passport. Anyone could have put it in there, for any reason!"

"No…I could see it in her eyes! Dak, I could feel it! We have to go here," she reached over and took it out of Dak's hand, "Where is this…Bamboo Breeze?"

Dak's hand brushed against hers when he tilted the card she was now holding and looked at the address, "It's in Mai Sai, that's about as far north as you can go and still be in Thailand. It's not close, Kimly, it's a couple hours from here."

"A couple hours? Let's go. Let's go check it out. Is it a restaurant? Why would she give me a business card for a restaurant?"

"Kimly, this needs to stop. It needs to stop now. Have you already forgotten what happened to you?!" He swiveled the rearview mirror so it was facing her, "Look at you. That man could have killed you! I'm not going to help you get yourself in another situation like that!"

Kimly didn't raise her eyes to her reflection, "You have to!"

"No, actually, I don't!" Dak snapped, "*You* don't have to do this! There are already people doing this, it is not up to *you*!"

"No, you're wrong--I do! I have to do this!"

"Why?! Just tell me why…why *you*?"

"Because, I don't know…*because*! Because, I can't continue to do nothing with my life!"

"Nothing with your life? Kimly, you've already done something with your life. You're a mother, you're a wife, and you are a journalist. In being you are doing."

"That's not the same! Everyone does those things. I need to do something that *everyone* doesn't do," she pulled her hand up to her swollen lip and covered it when she finished.

"Why?" he shook his head, and she looked away.

Calmly, without any emotion, Kimly finally responded, "You don't have to go with me. I can get there on my own." Without hesitation, Dak opened the door to the Jeep, climbed out and slammed the door behind him. Kimly watched as he climbed the stairs to the front porch of the bungalow and went inside.

The rhythm of the water hitting the roof of the Jeep added drama to their confrontation. She closed her eyes and allowed her shoulders to relax when her cell phone began to vibrate. The incoming call was from Kyle.

"Hello? Kyle?" Kimly's voice betrayed her, quivering.

"Kimly, thank God. You answered."

"Is everything okay there? Are the boys okay?"

"Yes, they are fine. They are in bed."

"What time is it? I lose track..."

"It's just after 1AM."

"Oh, sorry. I didn't think of it when I called..."

"No, it's fine. I haven't been able to sleep much since you left."

Kimly shifted in her seat. She suddenly regretted answering at all.

"Ok...well. I should go." The wave of politeness had only been able to carry them for a few moments.

"No wait, how are you?"

"How am I?" Kimly moved her hand up to her neck and felt her hammering heart.

"Yeah...I mean, you said you were fine. I didn't know..."

"I'm fine. Kyle...I don't...look, how honest do you want me to be?"

"Kimly, I'm sorry. I'm a jerk. I'm stupid and selfish and I don't deserve you."

"Okay. Well, you'll not hear me arguing with any..."

"Please..."

"Please what, Kyle?"

"Come home."

"Come home? And then what?"

Before Kimly had found Kyle's phone, she would have easily argued that her husband would never, could never, cheat. Kyle was so opposite of what she understood cheaters to be.

"Who is she?"

"She's not important." Kyle whispered.

"What?"

"She's not important." He cleared his throat and almost commanded, "she doesn't matter."

"She doesn't matter? Oh, well…as long as she doesn't matter, you know, by all means, go ahead and screw her."

"Kimly."

"What?"

"You know what I meant."

"No, Kyle, I don't know what you meant. She certainly mattered enough for you to throw out the last fourteen years. Hell, she mattered enough for you to get a secret cell phone."

"You found the phone. But, how…when?"

"Jeez, Kyle, it was in your gym bag."

"You were going through my bag?"

"Are you kidding me? That's your concern? That I didn't trust you? That I violated you in some way? I'm not doing this. There's too much going on here. We have a new lead. I have to decide if I want to follow it." Kimly took a deep breath and shifted her eyes to the bungalow.

"Who's *we*?"

"What?"

"You said, 'we have a new lead.' I spoke with Matthew and he said you were in Chiang Mai alone. So, who is *we*?"

"It's no one. I met someone. He's helping me."

"What do you mean, you met someone? In Chiang Mai?"

"It's not as weird as it sounds. Look, he's helped me a lot. And, well, really I don't think" Kimly let out an exasperated sigh, "I don't think I can do it without him, anyway…so just forget it."

"Who is this guy, Kimly?!"

"He's…*not important*. Okay?"

"Ha. Ha…very funny, Kimly. Who is he? What do you even know about him?"

"Look Kyle, I gotta go. Tell the boys I called and tell them I love them, and I'll be home soon."

"Kimly, wait…"

Kimly pressed, END CALL. The phone call had been less than four minutes. Outside the rain had dulled to a light drizzle, and Kimly climbed out of the Jeep and walked toward the bungalow. She hadn't thought she would be going home so soon.

When she opened the door to the bungalow, she found Dak packing a green duffel bag. "I thought…really?" she paused, but he didn't respond. "Are you sure?" her heart began to pound. *Who is this man?*

"I can't let you go there alone," his voice was flat. He didn't look at her, but walked through the door leading into the bathroom.

"I won't go. I mean, I came to tell you I'm not going to try to go without you," Kimly walked closer and raised her voice, hoping he could hear her across the room and through the open bathroom doorway. She could hear him gathering his things in the bathroom.

He emerged from the bathroom holding a small black toiletry bag, "Okay, Kimly, I got it…thanks for trying to make me feel better about losing. Again." She thought his comment was an attempt at humor, but his voice sounded slightly wounded.

"No, I'm serious! I know I can't do this alone! I need you," the last part came off her tongue as a whisper. He stood, one hand resting on the back of his neck, staring at his bag for a long minute.

"But, I do want to go," Kimly whispered.

"I know you do. And, I want to believe you will be okay. I'm just—"

"I know! I know! But, we will be more careful this time…I'll stop fighting you…and I'll do whatever you think is best and I won't argue with you about…anything!" Kimly bounced a little at the end of each declaration.

"Ha!" Dak was laughing his words out, "Now, *that* I would like to see!"

Kimly closed the few feet between them and hugged him around the neck. Dak's arms wrapped around her only for a moment, and then he pushed her away and stepped back, "Okay, okay—" Dak held his hand up in front of her, "there's only one thing," his smile faded, "If we are going up to the border, I need to bring a gun."

"A gun?!" Kimly's eyes were wide, and her voice dropped to a whisper, "You have a gun?"

"No," Dak zipped his bag, "but, I know where to get one."

PART TWO

17

Dak wasn't crazy about driving in the rain, but he also wasn't crazy about spending another night with this woman in his bed. It would be better to get on the road and get as far as possible before dark. He had no idea how long the storm would last. Besides, the rain in Thailand fell differently than the storms that waged war on Midwestern farmland. His aversion to driving in the rain, while justified, was unmerited in this situation. There was no black ice in Thailand; the roads were not going to slide out from under him while he drove.

"Look over there, on the hill," he pointed, wanting Kimly to see the enormous temple outside the window because he knew she would get a kick out of its history. Kimly's head was burrowed into a makeshift pillow, and she was sound asleep.

Her swollen eye looked worse while she slept. *That should have never happened! Thank you for the ways you've kept her protected*, Dak silently prayed.

Dak shifted his eyes back and forth from the wet road to the woman in the passenger seat. Even with her swollen eye and lip, she was stunning. Kimly had scrapes on her arms from the attack; Dak zeroed his eyes on a bruise which was forming on her right arm. She must have put up an incredible fight. *Such a beautiful woman so far from home. What kind of man lets his wife get so far away....Stop! Don't start thinking that way.* He knew entertaining that type of thinking was a bad idea. He needed to control his thoughts. He couldn't let his mind drift...there...and he couldn't allow himself to ever forget she was married. *This woman belongs to another man.*

He pulled off the highway and into the parking lot of a roadside convenience store. The familiarity of the 7-11 Store was not lost on

Dak. Certain places were home, no matter how far he traveled. No matter how he tried to escape. To this day, if he purchased a cherry Slurpee, he was transported across the Atlantic Ocean and back in time. He was suddenly a 19-year-old foreign exchange student walking to a convenience store to see the teenage girl working behind the counter. The image of her beautiful smile when he walked through the glass doors was as strong as ever. "Hey, Dak," when she said his name it was mesmerizing, and he was a bumbling fool.

"Kimly," Dak whispered. She roused and looked around for a moment. "I have to get a coffee, I'm fighting sleep. I didn't want you to wake up and be alarmed."

"Yeah, no, go," she pulled herself into full wakefulness.

A few moments later they were back on the highway, each with a cup of almost fresh coffee, "Umm...safe to say, you make better coffee than this," Kimly set her cup in the drink holder and reached down for her bag.

"Well, thank you...that is a good to know. If I ever decide to open a roadside store, I will endorse my coffee on the signage."

"Yeah, you do that. Oh...but don't mention your eggs," she attempted to wink, and then reached her hand to swollen eye, "Ahh...ouch."

"See what happens when you mock me?" Dak winked.

"How much further do we have to go?" Kimly dug through her purse until she pulled out a pack of gum.

"About an hour, we are stopping tonight in Chiang Rai. We can stay there tonight and head up to the border tomorrow."

She offered him a piece of gum, "Is this where you are getting the gun?"

"Yeah," Dak smirked, "Have you noticed your voice drops to a whisper whenever you say the word *gun*?"

"It does not," Kimly smiled, "Does it really?"

"My sister lives south of Mae Sai..."

"Sister? So your mom remarried?"

"Oh no, she's not really my sister. She was one of the orphans. We were very close and she adored Mother. They had a bond, and Mother *unofficially* adopted her. When I went away to college, Nisa took care of Mother. Nisa and her husband have a big house, we can stay with them. Her husband, Steve, has a few firearms. And, I'm sure he'll let me take one up to Mai Sai."

"And you're okay with it? I mean, you know how to use a gun?" Kimly asked.

"Yes," he smiled. "I am more comfortable around a firearm than you seem to be…you dropped your voice again."

"Hmm…did I?" she didn't pause for him to answer. "So, that's odd, you know. I mean for you to know how to use a gun. I don't picture a vast array of guns in an orphanage or a seminary."

"Yeah, hardly, you are correct about that." Dak took the last sip of his terrible coffee. "It was my father-in-law who taught me. He insisted really. And when Frank insisted on something, he usually got it. I think he saw it as a rite of passage in order for me to marry his daughter. He wanted her to be protected."

"Okay then!" Kimly smiled, "As long as you know how to shoot."

"Well, what about you? Have you ever fired a gun?"

"I went through a gun safety course as part of an article I once wrote on firearms in the home. I don't own one, but I know how to release the safety and I can keep my arms locked. As long as the bad guy is a piece of paper attached to a hay bale, I'll be fine."

"Well, *okay then* indeed, like you said, we are good to go…" Dak smiled and for a moment, the two of them were less like strangers chasing a lead and more like friends navigating their way on the wet roads.

"Man, I love the rain. Don't you?" her question seemed rhetorical, but Dak answered anyway, "It's alright. I don't like driving in it if I don't have to."

"Oh…do you want me to drive?" her genuine concern made Dak uncomfortable.

"No, no…That's not what I meant. I'm good," he gave her a reassuring smile.

With each mile on the highway, the anxiety of what had happened in Chiang Mai was further behind them. The sun was settling down behind the hills, but the mood in the Jeep seemed to lighten a little. Kimly was asking questions about the Thailand countryside, and it occurred to Dak that up until now she hadn't seen the fullness of Thailand. Kimly had become familiar with the city of Chiang Mai, but its outlying regions were a land of rich color and culture. He watched as Kimly's head invariably whipped around when the Jeep sped past a roadside store or an intricate Spirit House. It reminded him of the time he and Tina had taken Samantha to Disney World.

Dak turned off the main highway and drove into the hills. "If you liked the mountain where the king built his palace, you are going to love where we are going tonight!" Dak was eager to arrive, and had it not been for the weather, he would have increased his speed on the two lane road.

"Well, as much as I liked the palace the whole incident has become a bit of a dark spot in my mind."

"Hey, I'm sorry, I didn't mean—" Dak said.

"No, no...I'm fine," Kimly interrupted and gave him one of her fake smiles. Dak could now discern her real smiles and her fake ones. Kimly could throw up a stone wall with a smile, and she usually put up one of the fake ones whenever the conversation drifted to her marriage.

As the road twisted up the mountain, the tree line grew dense, with layer upon layer of a variety of species of trees. Glossy green leaves waved to the travelers as the Jeep sped past. Deep in the trees, sturdy homes with electricity neighbored wooden fragile huts. Dak heard Kimly whisper, "Fascinating..." He saw her eyes locked on a hut made entirely out of bamboo and dried palm tree fronds. Sitting in its dirt driveway was a brand new full sized truck.

The paved road narrowed to a muddy path. Each bump threw Kimly slightly, and Dak instinctively reached over to brace her. Dusk was evaporating into darkness, making it more difficult to see the road. The Jeep's headlights illuminated the pathway only about six feet in front of them. The raindrops grew wide as tree leaves. Dak knew he needed to maintain speed, lest his Jeep find itself stuck in the mud.

The road narrowed again and tree branches slapped against the windows as the Jeep drudged through the soggy path. "I hope they're home," Dak joked half-heartedly, "Waiting for them in this storm might be eventful."

A moment later Dak spotted Steve's truck parked in the dirt driveway, and he tapped lightly on his horn as they pulled closer to a red house built on stilts. Two dogs stood under the white deck, taking shelter from the rain. A black lab ventured out when the Jeep came to a stop, but he only walked halfway to the car before he decided the rain was intolerable and he retreated to his deck awning.

They sat for a moment in the Jeep, Dak's hand on the door handle, and Kimly holding her bag tight across her chest.

A light on the exterior of the house came on and illuminated the porch. The front door of the red house opened, and a red headed man with a hearty mustache to match peeked out, using his hand as a shield from the rain.

"Ready?" Dak asked.

"To get soaked?" Kimly answered, "Sure."

Once inside, they were welcomed as Dak had hoped. Nisa was preparing dinner for she and her husband, and she quickly added some noodles to the pot.

"This is the best surprise! Why didn't you call and tell us you were coming?" Nisa's round face lit up when she looked at Dak.

"And miss the surprise?!" Dak crossed the kitchen and lifted the lid to one of the smaller pots; a spicy aroma filled the room. "I'm just glad you don't mind feeding us…what is this? Pak boon fy dang?"

"Ah Dak, you oughta know your sister by now," Steve spoke with a thick Midwestern accent, "if she had her druthers she'd be makin' supper for ever' one of our neighbors in the Ahka village." The storm continued outside, but there was impenetrable warmth inside within the walls. The voices and smells ignited Dak's senses.

During dinner Dak witnessed Kimly steer the conversation away from herself and her purpose for coming to Chiang Mai, all the while continually pulling her hand up to her face to shield her bruised eye.

"Steve, how long have you lived in Thailand?" Kimly asked as she took a sip of water.

"Oh dear, it's been quite a while now…going on, what?" Steve turned his gaze to his wife, "close to thirty years now?"

"You were twenty when you came, and you've been here… what, twenty-nine years? Although you'd never know it by his accent." Nisa smiled at Kimly.

"Ahh, you can put a coat of paint on a tractor, but that don't make it a racecar." Steve responded.

Steve shared the story of how the youngest son in a farming family had ended up in Thailand. Steve's family had attended a Baptist church in Southern Illinois his entire life, and one Sunday morning the pastor preached a sermon asking the congregation to give a special offering for a Missionary living in Thailand. The village where the Missionary was serving had no running water. The Pastor's message and the idea of limited water stuck with Steve the entire week.

"Ever' time I'd run the tap, I'd think 'bout them folks. My whole life, I'd heard Pa prayin' fer rain. And, sure enough, rain 'ould show up. But even when we were waitin' fer the storm, we always had water from those taps." The following week Steve asked the pastor if there was anything he could do beyond giving money.

"I just had an itch under my skin," Steve said, "I wanted to get my hands dirty, ya know?"

"Oh, I know. I understand completely." Kimly nodded at Steve.

"My pastor helped me get a passport, first one in my family, and I jumped on a plane a few months later. Poor Ma cried 'nough tears to water Pa's fields for weeks."

Dak knew Steve's story, he had heard it many times, but it sounded different this time around. His own loss gave him a new empathy for Steve's Ma and her field of tears.

"Turns out an American missionary workin' on a water project in the Thai highlands was bitin' at the bit for some help." Steve continued, "Wasn't here long when a man showed up in the village with some teenagers to help us with a water project. Took one look at that face," Steve smiled at Nisa and gave her a wink, "and knew my life weren't never gonna be the same."

Steve and Nisa had married, and Steve had taken Nisa back to the States, where she studied Nursing. After a few years working in the hospital, the couple decided to return to Thailand. They built a life using her medical skills and his expertise as a handyman to serve the people in the local villages. As Steve continued to spin tales about his first construction experiences with bamboo, Dak watched Kimly laugh and eventually lower her hand from her eye. He wasn't sure if she was consciously lowering her defenses, or if she was just tired and relaxing in the hospitable environment.

The next morning, Dak woke to the fattest cat he had ever seen trying to sit on his chest. He pushed the orange tabby to the floor and rolled over on the couch. Steve and Nisa's hospitality had refueled Dak, but he woke with a tinge of guilt. Dak knew he and Kimly had been evasive when answering questions about their trip, and he felt he owed Steve a more thorough explanation before he broached the subject of borrowing a firearm.

He lifted himself off the couch and went into the kitchen, where he was able to locate the things he needed to make coffee. He started the coffeemaker and walked softly toward the bathroom. Every thought, a prayer.

"Good morning," Steve's voice greeted Dak when he returned to the kitchen. Steve sat at the end of an oblong wooden table with an open Bible. Steve was a confident man, intimidating to most, but only until they knew his heart. His compassion and his love for the Lord was rivaled by few.

"Good morning!" Dak loved the sound of Steve's drawl, its deep intonations taking him back to experiences they had shared. When Steve first arrived in Thailand, his voice was too deep for his skinny frame, but time had eventually evened the score.

"Can I get you a cup of coffee?" Dak asked as he headed over to the countertop.

"I smelled it a-brewing. It's why I came down." Steve was naturally cheerful.

Once the men were settled with their cups of coffee, Dak was eager to tell Steve the depth of the situation in which he found himself. He shared the whole story of the last few weeks: Walking Street, Nawarat Bridge, the palace and finally the assault on Kimly in her hotel room.

"I promised Nisa I'd ask you 'bout that bruise on her eye. I'll tell you what, this girl might oughta jump on a plane and hightail it outta here?" Steve's tone was light, but the concern in his eyes told Dak he understood the seriousness of the situation.

"She won't go," Dak answered. "Trust me, I've tried."

Steve just nodded. Dak was certain Steve was praying. *Good*, thought Dak, *ask God to tell me what to do*. Dak was eager for wisdom beyond his own.

"Do you think God called her to Thailand?" Steve asked.

"Kimly doesn't like to talk about God," Dak murmured. "She's not closed off to the possibility of there being a God, but this strong willed woman is miles away from resting in the freedom God offers."

"Dakum Kesapan. What do you know about miles away? That sure as heck don't sound like the Dak I used to know."

Dak just stared across the long table. He hadn't realized he was writing Kimly off, but it was true.

"Sorry," Steve continued, "but I remember a different Dak. It sounds like you're doubtin' God's ability to meet Kimly where she is."

140

"No, you're right. Don't apologize. I hadn't even realized it, but I've been very careful with her."

"I think that's normal. I mean, given your situation," Steve stood from the table and as he did he mumbled, "More coffee?"

"Yeah, sure," Dak handed Steve his cup and continued, "no, I don't think the situation is altering my view. I see her situation, and I see her need to understand grace."

"No," Steve looked over at Dak and tilted his head and then turned back to the coffeemaker and continued pouring the coffee, "I'm talking about you--a widower for what? Five years now?"

"Coming up on it. This November," Dak responded.

"And here you are now, spending the last few weeks with a beautiful woman." Steve crossed back over to the table with Dak and sat down.

"Steve, she's married. I didn't tell you she was married?" his voice was urgent.

Steve drank from his mug. The room was quiet, and outside a dog barked. Someone was moving around upstairs; their footsteps made the ceiling creak overhead.

"No, my friend. You failed to mention that fact."

"I don't know why I forgot to mention it. But, yeah, she's separated from her husband, and I don't know why or even how long. She won't really talk about it. When I bring it up, she changes the subject."

Steve nodded.

"She told me the first day, and I really didn't plan on spending so much time with her. It just kind of snowballed."

Again, Steve nodded.

"I've just been trying to keep her safe and I have done my best to maintain a sense of integrity. Well, other than bringing her to my house to sleep. Other than that."

"Dak, does Kimly know about Tina and Samantha Jean?"

"A little. I told her that Tina had passed away. I didn't want to get into everything. I don't want her to pity me or to feel uncomfortable."

"Naw, I got it." Steve took another drink from his mug.

"Tell me," Dak looked into the light eyes of the man he had known since he was a kid.

Steve had been more than Nisa's suitor; he had been Dak's

spiritual mentor. Dak had spent countless winter afternoons waiting for Steve to arrive at the orphanage to visit Nisa, hoping the young couple would let him tag along to wherever they went. Half the time he got lucky and he was allowed to go with them into town, or up into the hills. Sometimes Dak and Nisa would go with Steve for days at a time and stay in the village with the Missionary and his family. Dak cherished those memories of following Steve through the woods hunting birds or rabbits. Steve was hugely influential in convincing Dak to become an international exchange student. It was a decision which altered Dak's life.

Steve took a deep breath, "Well, you already know the truth. I could say you shouldn't be going through such an emotionally charged situation with another man's wife. But, you already know that. I could say the line you are walking is dangerous. I could tell you it's a very thin line, and the more attached to this woman you get, the more blurry it can become. But again, you already know that."

Dak was humiliated. He hadn't intended the conversation to go this route.

"I guess I could tell you that men and women play games of the heart quite differently. When a woman bonds herself to a man, it is a significantly strong attachment. Breaking that attachment will come at a cost to her. If you care about this woman, you will be damn careful with her heart. You may have your heart in check, but what about hers? I could tell you to be careful with her emotions, but, Dak, you already know these things."

Steve took a drink of his coffee, but he never pulled his eyes away from Dak's.

"You don't waste any punches. And I didn't even know I had it coming." Dak smiled, "I can only tell you this. I have not treated this woman in a way that I wouldn't be accountable for in front of anyone. We are friends. It's a relationship based on the fact that she is stubborn, and I don't want to see her get hurt. She came here alone, which tells me she is willing to continue doing this alone. I can't let her do that."

Steve nodded. Dak could tell Steve wasn't convinced, but he wasn't going to go over it again. He had done nothing wrong.

"What I came here to ask you about, what I need...I need to borrow a gun. I think with the severity of the situation, where we are heading and what we have already seen...It would be safer for Kimly, for me, if we had a gun." Dak took a drink of his coffee and wished he had asked Steve for the gun before the awkward conversation about Kimly's marital status.

"Oh, is that all? Sure." Steve lifted his coffee cup without lowering his stern gaze.

"You're sure?" Dak was relieved.

"Yeah, no problem, take a gun, that's fine. I gotta 9 millimeter and a box of rounds you can have. Did Tina's father have a 9 millimeter?"

"Yeah, among others, and it had an easy release on the magazine." Dak answered. "It's a good gun."

"Take what you need. I'm not concerned about you and guns. Naw, I've got a different concern, and I've got a question for you. If you're certain about your feelings for Kimly, why do you think you 'forgot' to mention she was married?"

18

Steve's truck led the way down the muddy path; Dak and Kimly followed in the Jeep. Steve and Nisa had spent years forming relationships with the people in rural tribes, and the morning after the storm Steve and Nisa decided visit a church in a Tai Lue village along the banks of the Mekong River. It was a shanty town in one of the provinces of Chiang Rai. The village was north of where they were, and it was along the same route that Dak and Kimly would travel to reach Mai Sai.

For the first time in days, Kimly seemed more like her old self. The swelling around her eye had gone down significantly, and it was taking on a yellow hue. When Dak asked her if she wanted to visit the church with them, she was open to the experience.

"Hey, did you get it?" Kimly whispered.

"It?" he repeated, feigning ignorance.

"The gun?" she whispered again.

"Yes, I got IT. But, hopefully we won't need it."

"I'm sorry," the sullenness in Kimly's voice was unexpected.

"Sorry?" Dak asked as he navigated around a deep hole in the road. The storm clouds had rolled on, leaving a trail of mud where dirt had once lain.

"I know how frustrating it is to do something you don't want to, just because you want to please someone else."

"That's just part of life. We all do it. I'm sure you've done your share of sacrificing for someone else."

"Hmmh," Kimly let out an instinctive muffled laugh. "You just described my marriage."

"Kimly, every marriage has hard times."

"Yeah, I'm sure they do. But...I don't know, Kyle and I...we're just...I don't know...Whoa!" Kimly exclaimed as the Jeep bounced over a rock on the road.

They drove along in silence for a few moments, until Dak was pretty sure Kimly wasn't going to pick up where she had left off.

"I've known a lot of people, and I've seen people in some pretty hard situations. I'm fairly certain that whatever is happening in your marriage can be overcome." Dak fell easily into the Pastoral role he was accustomed to.

"No, I disagree with you," her voice was calm and matter of fact, "sometimes two people were not supposed to get married in the first place. That's not a hard time. That's a bad marriage. You can't *overcome* something that should have never happened."

"Why is it only the people who are struggling in their marriage who say that the marriage 'shouldn't have happened'? It has never made any sense to me. Have you ever considered that some of the best marriages may be the ones that 'shouldn't have happened'?"

"Oh please, that makes no sense—" Kimly responded to him, but Dak cut her off and continued.

"Perhaps it's the ones who don't belong together that fight and claw, and find themselves more alive than those who have it easy. Isn't that what matters most? To live authentically is to live life well. It's not about being happy as much as we make it about being happy," as the last few words left him he realized he sounded pretty passionate, surprising himself with his intensity.

"I'm just saying I feel bad if I've pushed someone until they do what I want. I have pushed you into being involved in something you don't believe in."

Dak had no response. On the one hand, she was correct. This wasn't his journey; he was only interested in keeping her safe. On the other hand, after so many years of turning away from something, since he had met Kimly he was moving towards something. Maybe God's hand was on this for reasons he couldn't understand. Finally, he asked, "Kimly, do you want to go home? Are you doing all of this to avoid whatever is happening at home?"

Eyes wide, Kimly turned to him, "No. I'm not saying that! I don't want to go home. I'm still going. I just feel bad because I know I need you. I can't do it alone. And, I don't want you to get hurt."

"So, let me ask you...if I said, '*That's it, no more. I'm going back to Chiang Mai!*' What would you do?"

Kimly twisted strands of her long black hair around her fingers. He had watched her make the hypnotic moves with her hair before and found himself a little intoxicated by her repetitive movements. It was like watching a kitten play with a piece of string.

"Well, after I took your gun and your Jeep..." Kimly paused, "I would find my way up to the Burmese border and figure it out from there," her tone was completely serious, and she kept her gaze straight ahead.

"You are joking, right?" Dak moved his eyes back and forth between the road and the beautiful brunette in his Jeep until Kimly finally gave him a smile.

The roads to the village improved, and the caravan was able to travel on a paved road for about 40 kilometers. Soon they turned off the main highway again, and the mud was thicker than ever. At times, it was difficult to maneuver the Jeep, one tire spinning more quickly than the others, the tires getting stuck in the mucky substance. Before too long, they happened upon a group of shanty dwellings built right up to the Mekong River. They were held high above the river with long stilts made of bamboo. It was like a row of bamboo apartments. Each one shared a wall with their neighbor, and the side of the dwelling that overlooked the river was open. The view on a clear day would be priceless, but Dak wondered how they were able to weather the storms. At the bottom of the steep ridge of the embankment, there were dozens of boats. The boats varied in color, but they were common long tail boats, tied to poles at the water's edge.

After parking, the two couples crossed the road, and made their way up a path leading away from the water's edge and into the trees. As they passed the villagers, the people waved and smiled. Dak pointed out the intricate weaving he saw hung in one of the windows and he grinned as Kimly's head spun from one site to the next, taking in each of the makeshift huts built on bamboo stilts.

Dak greeted the natives they passed, "Swateekarp," and Kimly nodded at them.

Dak was curious and wished he knew what Kimly was thinking. *What must this be like for her? Is this her first time in a church? What if it is? And her first experience will be in a Tai Lue tribal village in the hills above Chiang Rai!* He looked over and smiled. He wanted to ask if she was alright because he could sense her tension, but then he remembered Steve's words the night before, "...if you care about this woman, you will be damn careful with her heart."

The path widened, and standing in front of them was a large

church. It was reminiscent of any church Dak had seen in the states. There was a large entrance with stained glass windows over the doors. Each window was cut in the shape of a large leaf, and each leaf had intricate designs in the painted glass. The brick exterior was trimmed in a light, pale yellow.

"Well, look at that..." Dak admired.

"It's kind of weird." Kimly whispered to Dak.

"What is?" Dak asked.

"The church—it's a real building...but they're living in shacks...how did this happen?"

"Steve," Dak called out, and Steve slowed down his pace. "The church building is so modern, how did they afford the supplies to build it?"

"The natives didn't build it. A group of missionaries from China came through Thailand and built and donated the buildings," Steve smiled. "It's a different kind of church planting, and it seems to be working. Once the villagers have the building, they work hard to maintain it. Each village determines who will be their Pastor, and they spend their time focusing their energy on meeting the needs of the people."

Music wafted from inside the building, and the people mingling out front began to move indoors. Dak took Kimly by the elbow and led her inside. They walked to the back of the room, where they found two seats along the wall. Dak assumed the service would be preached in Thai, and Kimly wouldn't understand. He didn't want her feeling exposed and watched.

But, he soon realized Kimly would have had to remain in the Jeep to avoid being noticed. Eyes were drawn to her. Kimly was like a goddess among them. She had their dark eyes, their sleek black hair, and their youthful, olive complexion. But she was mysteriously taller and more slender than any of the Tai Lue women. She had long lean hands, and her lips were full and rich with color. He noticed the people watching her hands. He watched as she moved her right hand up to her face. She touched her swollen eye. He wanted to tell her not to worry because it wasn't as bad as she imagined. Again, he knew he shouldn't. Kimly must have felt his eyes on her because she turned and looked at him. A fake wall smile. She must be uncomfortable.

The song was familiar to Dak; the music drifted across through the room and filled him with peace. Everything that had happened over the last two weeks, had worked together to bring them to this place, to this church, in this moment. When the people began to sing along with the song, he realized they were not singing in Thai, but a language unfamiliar to him. He knew the song in English and would have been able to recognize some of the anticipated words in Thai, but this was a different language altogether.

"This is one of my favorite hymns," he leaned over and whispered in Kimly's ear.

She smirked at him. *She thinks I'm teasing*, he thought, and he began to whisper the words in her ear as the congregation sang them in their native tongue.

"Teach me some melodious sonnet
Sung by flaming tongues above
Praise the mount, I'm fixed upon it
Mount of Thy redeeming love," he smiled at her, pleased with himself.

She just stared at him with those wide dark eyes. Her face was right in front of his and her expression was indescribable, except the small smile growing on her lips was not fake. It was real. "Keep going..." she whispered. His mind reeled, and he tried to find his place in the song. He was nodding his head in time with the music.

"Here I raise my Ebenezer
Here by Thy great help I've come
And I hope, by Thy good pleasure
Safely to arrive at home.
Jesus sought me when a stranger
Wandering from the fold of God;
He, to rescue me from danger...interposed His precious blood..."

The singing continued, and he was trying to remember the words. Tina had always known the words to every hymn. She had the voice of a dozen angels singing in harmony; she and Samantha had been the singers in the family. Not him. He was the one with the words, but right now, the words he needed were lost to him. The singing around him continued, and Kimly raised her eyebrows, prodding him with her expression. She wanted him to continue. Finally, a part of the song he knew came,

"Prone to wander, Lord, I feel it
Prone to leave the God I love;
Here's my heart...Lord take and seal it
Seal it for Thy courts above."

She turned her head and looked away from him. He watched as she moved her hand up to her face again, but this time she touched the eye that wasn't swollen. She was dabbing her fingers to her eyes, wiping away tears. Any other time he would have whispered a playful apology for his singing, but there was something moving in and about him that told him to be still.

The Pastor walked to the front of the church and began to share a message. It was lost on Dak. The language was not Thai. It reminded Dak of Chinese, but a little different. A couple of times during the service Dak looked over at Kimly, trying to gauge her thoughts. Kimly appeared captivated. Her eyes were locked in on the energized and animated Pastor at the front of the church. In his peripheral vision, Dak noticed Kimly nodding a couple of times, and he wondered what was going through her mind. Even though Dak had no idea what the Pastor was saying, he found the man's style captivating and passionate. So much so that he felt jealousy tinge his spine. Long ago, Dak led his congregation with the same fervor. Other than Tina and Samantha Jean, nothing had given him greater joy than sharing the redemptive message of Christ.

When the Pastor reached the end of his message, the people stood and began to sing. Men and women began to move to the front of the church, and Kimly grabbed Dak's arm, "I'm going outside," she whispered. She spun away from him and moved quickly toward the doors of the church.

Instinctively Dak followed. He was concerned for her safety, and he was curious about her mental state. Kimly walked around the side of the large brick building. The nearby hill was covered in small huts, all built up on stilts. Kimly moved with a purpose, not as a sightseer in a strange land.

"Hey," Dak called from a few steps behind, "You okay?"

Kimly turned toward him, and she looked surprised. Dak realized she hadn't known he was following. Her eyes were welled up with tears, "Yeah, sorry." She turned back around and continued walking into the dense line of trees.

"Hey, Kimly, wait." Dak was genuinely confused. He didn't understand how she could be so affected by a foreign sermon.

"I'm so sorry," Kimly moved close to a group of Teak trees and lifted her hand to the gray trunk of one, "I don't know why his talk affected me like this."

"No, don't be sorry. I don't know what you are thinking...but...I can tell you, it's probably normal," Dak responded.

"It was just really weird. Everything. I mean, it was nice, the singing..." Kimly pressed her fingers into the peeling, uneven bark of the tree.

"Yeah. Even mine?" Dak winked at her, and she let out a small laugh.

Then, she began again, talking much faster, "It was different. I could feel something, and it was a different feeling than I've ever had."

He was thankful that God had been moving on Kimly's behalf and working at opening her heart, especially in a place where the message was lost on both of them.

"And then there were times when what the Preacher was saying...this is going to sound vain...but, it was like he was talking to me. And, I know he wasn't...but...I don't know, it was weird," Kimly calmed herself and took a deep breath. "You know?" She let out a long sigh, and tilted her head towards him.

Dak looked at Kimly and tried to let what she had said register in his mind. "You mean, when he was preaching just now? You mean, you felt like he was speaking to you?" Dak asked.

"I know it's stupid," Kimly let out a gentle laugh, "I told you it was vain."

"No. I'm not thinking it was vain." Dak knew it wasn't uncommon for people to feel singled out when listening to a sermon, even if that wasn't the case.

"I'm just trying to understand what..." Dak paused and looked at her sleek hand resting on the trunk of the tree, then he looked back at her, "Kimly, what did you hear the man saying?"

"What?" she looked at him and looked away, wiping her eyes with her sleeve, "All of it. What he said about living for self and about dying to self. You know, what he said about losing your life to save your life."

"Kimly..." Dak was stunned.

"When the Preacher said Jesus had followers who were telling him not to go to the cross. I was thinking about how everyone sees life and death so differently...and when he said that in trying to save our physical life from discomfort, we could lose our eternal life. If we are always trying to protect ourselves from pain, we begin to die on the inside. Life comes through pain, not through avoiding pain."

"He said all that?" Dak stammered, and Kimly rolled her eyes as him, "Dak, I'm being serious."

Dak wanted to hug her; to yell out and cheer. He was filled with an urge to express gratitude for how God was communicating. He was in awe of how God had brought Kimly to the other side of the world and into the tiny Tai Lue village so she could hear the message of Christ. Dak wanted to call the people of the village together so he could tell them the ways God had protected Kimly so she might arrive at this village on this day. He wanted to explain to Kimly that God had just worked a miracle in her life—to let her know that a deeply spiritual thing had just occurred for her to be able to hear the things God wanted her to know.

Simultaneously, Dak was filled with shame. For years Dak had lived as a believer and as a Pastor, and yet he had never realized his capacity for legalism and judgment. Since his first meeting with Kimly, Dak had devalued her ability to experience God. Rather than viewing her as a spiritual being with a heart ripe to understand God, Dak had placed her in a category: non-believer.

Dak wondered how often he had he done this with other people in his life? Standing next to this beautiful woman with whom God had chosen to have an encounter, Dak recognized his own failings and he wondered if his religious approach might have drained him from fully experiencing God. When did he begin to believe a theology that God would choose to only manifest Himself to someone after they had walked up a church aisle and prayed a sinner's prayer?

"Dak, will you explain something to me," she took in a deep breath and then looked down at the cut on her hand. "Why would God choose death...I mean, for his own son?" She held Dak's gaze waiting for his answer, like a detective trying to solve a cold case from two thousand years prior.

"Kimly, it wasn't without a great deal of planning. Trust me, God allowed death to happen to His son, because God is a God of justice. But, God always had a plan, and with Jesus, the plan included a resurrection. He chose to do it this way because God wants the Spirit of His son to live in you," Dak's words were coming out jumbled and indefinite.

"I want that," she cut him off, and Dak was thankful she had. "I want that. What you just said."

"Kimly, can I pray?" Dak's question was deeper and more to himself than to her.

Dak felt a bit dizzy and nauseated, as he only now recognized something he had long known. He had evolved into a person who treated God as an elusive and standoffish being. How long had Dak been viewing God as someone who shows up occasionally? Rather than simply being present wherever there is love.

Dak led Kimly through a prayer, and Dak found himself surprised when Kimly began to pray. Eyes closed and hands clasped, he heard Kimly admit she had been living a selfish life without regard for God or others. He heard Kimly refer to herself as a sinner.

When Kimly said, "Amen," and raised her head, her coffee brown eyes were bright with peace. Dak couldn't restrain himself; he pulled Kimly towards him and wrapped his arms around her slender body. His hand came up and rested on the back of her head as he held her tightly under the peeling Teak trees. Kimly's slight tremble eventually stopped, and he felt her relax into his arms.

In all his prayers Dak had never imagined the morning being so surreal. Dak released Kimly and they both looked away immediately. A part of him wanted to tell her what she had just experienced, but he wasn't sure if he could explain it, and he didn't know if she would believe him—he wasn't sure if he believed himself.

19

NOI

ขนาด เล็ก

I am not a good Mommy. I cannot protect Lawan, and because I cannot rescue her from the Darkness she is growing weak. My little girl has become fevered and she will not eat her soup. When I touch her, I can feel the hard, fast pounding of her heart.

"Lawan, do you want to come and watch the street for your Mommy?" I call for her to get her to get up, hoping she will feel better, "I do not know what she looks like, and she does not know my eye." Lawan does not open her eyes, she barely moves her head.

I walk to the door and pound with both fists. When Xuan comes, I try pushing myself around her screaming, "Pakpao!" Angered, Xuan's hand flies like a stinging bee through the air and towards my face. Quickly pulling my head back, I continue to yell, "Pakpao!" When the fish colored hair lady comes down the hallway, she is angry, and I back up to the wall. In her fat hand, she holds a long knife.

As she glares at me, I point at my child, "Lawan is sick." I pull my head down. I do not like Pakpao's knife.

Pakpao goes to the side of our bed, touches Lawan's forehead and says something to Xuan, who leaves the room. A few minutes later she comes back with some wet towels; Pakpao pulls the blankets off of Lawan and begins to place the wet towels all over her body. Lawan's skin has changed colors in different places. Her little body has large hand sized spots on it, and she is swollen all over.

The two of them talk in Xuan's words, and I am frightened. They are not hitting me, and they are not hitting Lawan, but the look in their eyes agitates my stomach. I move to be closer to Lawan, and Pakpao pulls me back, "No—" and then she continues speaking, but not to me.

Xuan's claws pinch my arm as she grabs my arm and leads me to the barrel room. I pull my arm from her grip. She kicks the broom away from the door to the closet room and pushes me inside.

It's not Momma's mat, and it doesn't have her smell or her softness, but I have learned that being in the closet room is the only place where I can sleep and dream. When sleep comes looking for me in the closet room, I don't hide. I sleep a sleep of dreams on the hard floor because of the tiny line of light that peeks under the door. A fierce line of light stays there to protect me. I know as long as the light is tiny and only peeking under the door, I am safe. This light is tiny, but she stands up against the Darkness. I cannot be touched when she is standing guard. When the door opens she disappears and then she cannot protect me any longer. I stare at the tiny line of light I love until my eyes hurt, and then close.

Biting pain in my arm wakes me. I shift my body. Then I notice my stomach is also hurting. I have spent many hours with the line of light shielding me. But, now I am wishing for food. I have felt this kind of pain before; I want to stay with the tiny line of light, but I want my stomach to stop hurting. I want to eat. I stare at the fierce light until my eyes hurt again.

A tall custard apple tree grows in the middle of meadow. Momma sings a willowy song while she picks the sugar fruit and her long black hair is blowing in the breeze.

"Float, float the banana leaf boat..." she sings. Her voice is strong, and her body is not sick and weak. "Float, float the banana leaf boat..." Her face is full of light, "After we float our banana boat, I invite you, my darling to dance on the Ram Wong." She drops her custard apples, grabs my hands, and spins me in a circle.

Sitting down on the hillside, she pulls me close to her so she can weave sun colored wildflowers into my hair. I nuzzle up against her side, and she lets me wrap her long dark hair around my wrist as if it is a snake. I twist strands around each finger. When I pull my neck back and look up at Momma, she is smiling at me with all of herself. Her eyes are happy with me. She kisses my forehead, and then she stands up. I start to follow her, but she holds up her hand and motions me to stay. She begins to back away from me.

"Momma?" I say. I want to follow her. She shakes her head and raises an eyebrow. I freeze. Momma's eyebrow is more powerful than stream water.

She moves away from me and she turns her head away. She opens her arms, and someone is running to her. Lawan! Lawan is running into Momma's arms. I jump to my feet and begin to run after them. No matter how fast I run I cannot reach them. A custard apple tree sprouts up in front of me. I stop quickly and then run around the tree. A few steps later, another tree bursts from the ground. I decide to throw myself through the air and fly to Lawan and Momma. I jump off the ground, and I am flying through the air! Suddenly I see custard apples coming towards me. I dodge several pieces of the fruit until one finally slams into my ear. I continue flying through the sky with one hand on my head when I feel two hands grab me from behind. The hands are hard, and they hurt me when they pull me back down from the sky. I turn around. A man is holding me down. He is angry.

I am awake. Momma and her song are gone. The meadow is gone. The custard apples are gone. The hands I dreamed are still here. I twist around and try to get away. My dream is now a nightmare, only the nightmare is alive. A man has pulled me out of the closet, and he is on top of me. He is bringing his Darkness to me. "Momma...Momma..." I call for her to come out of the dream and save me.

The man climbs off me, and I scurry to a corner in the closet. I pull myself into a ball. My hair falls in front of my face. Between the dark strands of my hair I can see the man who brought Darkness into my closet. He brushes off his shiny pants. He pulls on the sleeves of his slick, clean shirt. He adjusts the pieces of glass he wears on his face. His face is swollen and bruised; his eyes are red and swollen. He is a shiny, clean monster. He is a monsterman.

I stay in the tiny closet room huddled into the corner for a long time. The door is open so I no longer have the line of light to keep me safe. I pull myself against the wall and try to disappear in the shadows. Pakpao and the clean-clothed monsterman are going into the room where Lawan is laying being sick. I pull my head up to try to see what they are doing. They stay in the room for a long time, and I am not sure why no one has come to lock my tiny door with the broom. I stare around the room. I stare for a long time at the sunfish on the side of the barrel. I would never want to be a fish. I would hate to live in the water that stings my lungs. If I were a sunfish, I would jump out of the water and die on the land. I shift my eyes to the pee bucket. It is metal with a wire handle, and it makes the room smell. With the door open, it bothers my nose because it is full.

I hear Pakpao talking as she and the clean clothed monsterman are leaving Lawan's room. If I am going to go to her, I need to do it now. I jump up and run towards the room, I am reaching for the doorknob when the door opens and out walks Xuan. I back away. Her claws try to grab my arm, but I am faster. I run back into the barrel room. I trip over the broom on the floor and I fall on my bottom. Xuan smiles. I pick up the broom and jump to my feet. Xuan pulls herself back, and then she steps forward. I swing the broom at her evil seed eyes, and then back away. She laughs at me. I back around the barrel and swing the broom again. She keeps coming towards me. I move farther around the barrel. She starts to come quickly; I feel my foot hit the pee bucket. I drop the broom, reach down and grab the pee bucket with both hands. Using the strength of a thousand nights in Darkness, I throw the pee in her face. I leave her screaming and run to be with Lawan.

I can barely open the door with the bucket in my hands, but I am crying and shaking and do not think to put it down. Xuan is screaming, and her screaming is making me shake harder. I do not want the clean clothed monsterman to return. My pee soaked hand is finally able to grip the handle. I push the door open, fall into the room, and slam the door closed behind me. I stare at the door. I have hard and fast heart pounds in my chest and running through my whole body. Oh, that pounding hearts could keep doors closed! I look up at the metal bar across the top. The bucket! I drop the pee bucket on the ground, flip it over, and climb on top. My fingers can barely reach the metal bar. I stand as high as I can on my toes and I push the metal bar. I hear Xuan on the other side. She is screaming in her words. The metal bar hates me; it does not want to move. I push myself higher on my toes. I pull harder on the metal bar. My finger slides across the bar and the metal bites my hand. I pull and pull. The metal bar finally gives in and moves across the door.

I jump off the bucket and back away from the door. I stare at the door. I stare at the metal bar and the doorknob. I do not want any of them to move. I will them to be still. I see the handle to the door begin to shake.

Pakpao is on the other side, and she yells to me, "Noi! Noi! Open this door!" I hear her yelling at Xuan. "Noi, how did you lock the door? Open it now." She continues yelling, but her voice gets smaller as she moves away from the door and down the hallway.

It is light outside; the tiny crumbs of light are shining through the painted windows. "Lawan, Mommy is here..." She is lying on the bed and the blanket is over her head. My stomach has a sick feeling. My hand, the one with the bite from the metal bar, reaches up and pulls the blanket from her face. Her eyes are awake, but she is not. "Lawan?" I touch her face, and she is cold. She is cold like a stone floor. No! Lawan is not a stone cold floor. She is too wonderful to be a stone cold floor.

"Noi, open the door!" Pakpao is back, and the pounding on the door causes me to jump. "If you don't open this door, you will never eat again. And, hear me child, I will win this battle!"

Pakpao hits the door with something hard. The sound it makes tells me she did not hit the door with her hand. She has something hard, and she is going to bust the door down. She is going to burst through the door, and she is going to let the clean clothed monsterman bring his Darkness to me...or worse. What is the color of worse? Is it darker than Darkness?

Next to the door I see the pee bucket. I wonder if I can hit her with the pee bucket when she comes into the room. Can I make her head shatter into a thousand pieces? If I could make her head shatter into a thousand pieces, then I could throw her in the stream and watch her float away. The water would keep her captive forever and carry her far, far away. Icy water is clear, but water would not be clear with the thousand tiny crumbs of her head floating down its rocky path.

Tiny crumbs of light! I flip my head around and stare at the tiny crumbs of light peaking in the through the painted window. Grabbing the pee bucket with both hands, I charge the window. I bang, bang, bang the pee bucket against the painted window. Pee splashes on my face with each strike against the painted glass.

The monsterman is the glass. Xuan is the glass. Pakpao is the glass. Uncle is the glass. Darkness is the glass. The glass gives way, and light pours in! The bucket flies from my hands and crashes, along with the shards of glass, into the street outside. Around my feet there is more glass. I step away and grab a blanket. I use the blanket to move as much glass away as I can. I pull the other blanket off of

Lawan and throw it over the window frame. I run back to the bed and gather the pillow and all the other blankets on the bed. I toss them out the window, where they land on the glass and pee bucket. I pull myself up into the window. Some of the glass is pushing through the blanket, trying to stop me from escaping. My bloody hands, legs and arms fight with the glass. I fall from the window frame into the soft blankets and pillows below me. I grab a grass colored blanket and wrap it around me. I do not know which way to run to find Momma, but I know I have to choose quickly. I run down the small street, and I do not look back at the Darkness behind me.

20

Driving along Highway 1041 of the crowded, dirty border town gave Dak a bad feeling. The rain had lifted, and what remained was a film of mud. A sweaty faced man with greasy hair wheeled a kiosk to the edge of the street. He stopped at the gutter's edge and began to pull out supplies. Soon he would be selling his wares. The people of Mae Sai were setting up their "Night Bazaar," but it lacked the flair of the ones Dak had seen in the cities of Pattaya and Chiang Mai. Pattaya's Night Bazaar was bright with lights and crude shows, giving it the feel of a seedier Las Vegas boulevard. Chiang Mai's bazaar was a conservative and reserved "family friendly" marketplace. When Dak looked around at the set up unfolding on the main street of Mai Sai, he was curious to see what the border town bazaar would offer.

Kimly had been quieter than usual since parting with Steve and Nisa. Considering the experience in Tai Lue, Dak imagined she was exhausted and overwhelmed. "You doing okay over there?" he tried to check on her again. During their drive, he made several attempts at conversation, but Kimly would feign a polite response and eventually retreat back into her own thoughts.

"Yeah, I'm sorry. I've just been thinking...I'm sure I'm just tired, too, but I was wondering," Kimly's voice was low; "maybe when we get to this Bamboo Breeze...I mean, if it's okay..." she was struggling to ask him something.

Dak knew he needed to tell Kimly that he wasn't going to take her to the address on the business card right away, but he didn't want to interrupt her when she was finally opening up. He raised his eyebrows and playfully prodded her to continue, "Yesss?"

"I need to make a call. Sorry, that's all."

He smiled, "I don't know why you're sorry. But, sure."

"I mean, I want to do it in private...I want to talk to Kyle. I need to call my husband—"

Dak interrupted her, "Yes, of course. But, here's what we're going do. We are going to check into a hotel first."

Kimly's expression became quizzical, but Dak shook his head and continued talking, "we're going to check in, and then we will find The Bamboo Breeze..." he paused and nodded his head when he continued, "...and then we are going to do a little stake out tonight," Dak was still nodding his head at her, hoping he wasn't in for another fight.

"Why are we doing a stake out?" Kimly asked as she began to dig through her bag. He figured she was looking for her passport with the business card tucked safely inside.

"Kimly, I need to see who is coming and going from the restaurant. I'm not going to let you walk into a trap," Dak looked across the small cab; Kimly had stopped rummaging and was staring straight ahead. He watched her eyes move, and he could tell she was absorbing his words; he wasn't going to back down. He would do everything in his power to stop her if she decided to do this any other way.

"You're right," Kimly said with a light nod.

The Komgkam Hotel stood tall on Highway 1041. The entrance faced the street, and the parking was in the rear. The two rooms Dak and Kimly took were situated side by side on the sixth floor. Dak was insistent their rooms be adjoining, even though he had no intention of unlocking the shared door; the thought of Kimly in a room with an adjoining door to another room—a door he couldn't safeguard— made him uneasy.

Looking out his window and down to the left, Dak's gaze fell on the deluge of cars pouring down the divided highway. The thoroughfare was lined with shrubs meticulously trimmed into triangles; diamond shaped shrubbery pointing up to the intricate golden lamppost overhead. The lights down the center of the road were constructed to reflect the royalty of Thailand.

Turning his head to the right, Dak could see houses built on the side of the hills. Each hill slowly rolled down into the city. Some of the homes shared walls, and the variation of colors was remarkable. The yard of one home would run right up to the back wall of another and in the middle of three or four homes, there was a field full of used furniture and household appliances. One of the homes had a garden with a variety of vegetation nimbly surviving amid the chaos.

Looking from left to right, Dak noted how contradictory the two regions appeared. They were so close in proximity but sharply contrasted one another. The highway on the left was obviously designed by State officials to demonstrate order and passion for King and Country, but when Dak looked to the right, he saw the unplanned chaotic manifestation of the rural lives the people were living.

Watching the people below gave Dak a chance to pray for Kimly, and for himself. He didn't have any idea what they might encounter, but Dak treasured the thought of God leading him as he tried to lead her. An hour had passed since Dak and Kimly had checked in, and the growling in Dak's stomach was telling him it was time to go knock on her door. He went out to the hallway and knocked. The adjoining door would have been more convenient, but he didn't want to "open that door," so to speak.

He could hear Kimly shifting the lock while she called through the closed door, "Dak?"

"Yeah, it's me."

Kimly opened the door and looked up at him through her bangs which fell across her face. "Hey," she said.

Kimly's eyes were now both swollen and red. She moved her hand up and pulled a portion of her hair so it rested behind her ear.

"You okay?" Dak whispered.

Kimly nodded, but didn't speak. He waited.

"You hungry?" he tried again.

Kimly took in a deep breath and nodded, then shook her head no, and then nodded again, "Sure, I mean, if you are."

She stepped back from the door, opening it as she moved back into the room and sat on the edge of her bed. Clearly, Kimly expected Dak to follow. He entered her room, shoving his hands in his pockets, watching as she put on her shoes. It was awkward. The woman was obviously distraught, and Dak wasn't sure if he should engage her in talking about it.

Kimly took in another deep breath and let out a sigh. And then, she placed both of her hands on either side of her face.

"Did you make your call?" Dak decided he had little to lose.

Kimly let out another sigh, an attempt at a laugh; "Yeah..." she stood and moved across the room, "Yeah, I made my call."

Dak stepped out of her way and Kimly crossed to the doorway, "You coming?" she turned back to him, "Or am I going alone?" she threw him a fake wall smile.

Once Dak and Kimly had located The Bamboo Breeze, they parked the Jeep across the busy highway and about 30 yards south of the restaurant. Kimly raised a Styrofoam cup to her lips and sipped old, burnt coffee.

The Bamboo Breeze turned out to be an open-air restaurant. The awning was sturdy, with thick brick tiles that extended wider than the diameter of the concrete flooring. The only seating appeared to be outside. The rails and posts were painted brick red, and an eclectic assortment of tables and chairs were situated around the patio. From what Dak could see, the employees in the restaurant appeared youthful and harmless, like any other restaurant workers. It was not what Dak had anticipated.

"Is this what you expected?" he asked without looking away.

Sipping again on her coffee, Kimly shook her head, "No. I think I pictured something darker...something sinister."

Dak raised one eyebrow at her, "Do you think everyone who can hurt you is going to have a danger sign tattooed on their neck?" It was a little harsh, and he felt bad for using sarcasm to scare her, but if it reminded her of the real darkness she was facing, then it was worth it.

They watched the restaurant for hours. They watched until the last customer scurried away, and they watched as the young workers loaded into one minivan and left together.

"That's odd..." Dak's voice lingered, and he watched the minivan pull out of the drive and head westward down the highway. It was heading towards the Burmese border, in the same direction as the Kongkam Hotel. There was no reason not to follow.

"What's odd?" Kimly was twisting around trying to see what had seized Dak's attention, gearing him into tracking mode.

"Well, all the workers are leaving together, in the same van." He turned on his blinker and looked over his shoulder, changing lanes. Kimly looked from his eyes to the road and then back again, unimpressed, "So? The guy driving the van is the one who owns a car. Why is that weird?"

"Well, only about half the workers left. We watched them lock the doors to the kitchen and then latch the gates closed, but only four of them got in the van." Dak sped up and blew through a transitioning red light.

"Maybe we missed their leaving—"

"Kimly, I counted them. There were seven. I was watching the whole time. So were you...did you see them leave?"

"No, but, I don't know…"

"I'm telling you. Half those workers didn't leave that restaurant. I was watching," Dak said, and he continued to follow the van as it traveled west on Highway 1041. The van finally slowed and turned onto a smaller street. Dak turned on his blinker and followed the minivan off the main highway, "We'll just follow and see where the van goes."

"Well, most likely you are going to watch this guy, this designated teen chauffeur, drop his friends off, one by one, at their respective homes."

The minivan stopped abruptly in front of a wide and tall steel gate, which was attached to an 8 foot concrete wall. If the van hadn't stopped, Dak didn't think he would have even noticed the nondescript building. Dak drove past the stopped van and made a U-turn a little further up the street. On both sides of the characterless structure were modest homes, and across the street a few more homes and a small mini-market completed the neighborhood. Dak and Kimly watched as a twenty-something year old girl, with thick curls, jumped out of the van. Her chestnut curls were illuminated by the headlights of the van as she punched numbers into a keypad next to the gate. The steel gate slid open, the girl and the minivan disappeared behind the gate, which closed before Dak could get them close enough to see what it protected.

Dak turned to Kimly, "Chauffeur, huh?"

21

"Let's go back to the restaurant!" Kimly's brown eyes flickered.

"Whoa, tiger...slow down! Go back and do what?" Dak pulled the Jeep forward, lifting himself in his seat trying to see over the wall.

"Do what?! See! See what's going on back there. You think people stayed there, let's check!" Dak glanced at Kimly and then looked back at the road.

The woman was a mystery. Kimly was eager, inquisitive and energetic one moment, then isolated, somber and distant in the next. For Dak, she was frustrating and intoxicating; addictive.

He shook his head. "Kimly, are you serious? We are not going back to the restaurant and poking around in the dark. Did you think I would agree to that? Are you trying to get killed?"

Without responding, Kimly sat back in her seat and pulled her hand up to her lips. She was gently biting on the fingernail of her index finger and staring straight ahead.

"I'm sorry—" he continued, but she cut him off,

"No. It's fine. You're right. I'm just wondering..." Kimly paused.

"What? What are you wondering?"

"I'm trying to understand why a maid in Chiang Mai would send us to a restaurant in Mai Sai. One run by a bunch of kids."

"Let's get up early tomorrow and go there before they open," Dak headed back onto the main highway. "We know this place is connected and we can keep an eye on it. Heck, it's a stone's throw from the hotel. Let's find out what we are supposed to see, or *not* see."

Kimly didn't respond, but when Dak glanced over she was nodding her head. He wished he could crawl into her little head and see what she was thinking, then he realized whatever this woman was thinking may just get him riled up. *Better not to know*, he determined.

Once back at the hotel, Dak and Kimly headed back up to their rooms with barely a word between them.

"Goodnight, Dak," Kimly murmured as she reached into her bag for her room key.

"Kimly, if you want to talk, if you want to pray..." before Dak could finish he was caught off guard when Kimly came forward extended her arms, pulled herself close and gave him a hug. His arms slid effortlessly around her waist, and he held her for a moment.

"Thank you so much," Kimly whispered without letting go. "Seriously, for everything."

Dak could feel the warmth of her face, her neck, and her breath. Kimly tilted her head back slightly and looked in his eyes. Immobilized, Dak stood still until the beautiful woman released her arms from around his neck and took a slight step backward. He rested one hand on the nape of his neck and stared at the doorframe, "No, I'm glad I'm here...that I've been here," Dak stammered.

"Me too," Kimly turned away and slid her room key across the lock. "Goodnight," she said, and her silhouette moved through the wooden doorway into the dark room.

Dak dug his hand into his pocket and pulled out his room key, and it wasn't until he closed the door behind him that he realized he was holding his breath. He blew out a long breath and flipped on the light switch in the bathroom.

What the heck was that? Dak's thoughts tormented him, as he turned on the shower and looked in the bathroom mirror. His reflection wasn't going to give him a break.

"Don't you start with me," Dak scolded his mirrored image, "I know she's married—" he yanked off his shirt, adjusted the temperature of the shower, but then spun back around to argue with the mirror, "and besides, I didn't hug her...she hugged me."

Dak murmured prayers as he showered, and after the watery cool down, he adjusted the pillows in his bed, and opened his Bible to the book of Ephesians. By the time he had read to Chapter Three, he had calmed down considerably. Reminded of his own need for grace, Dak tried not to condemn himself for his attraction to Kimly. It had been a long time since he had been so drawn to a woman and felt stimulated by physical urges.

"Father God, please forgive me for thinking of Kimly in a way that might not bring honor to her or to You. Of course I find her beautiful; she was created by You and in Your image. I pray that the plans you have for her…" Dak paused, "God, the plans You have for her *and her husband* will be fulfilled in a way that brings You glory."

Dak reached over and turned off the light on his nightstand, ready to be alone in the dark with his thoughts.

The bridge looked different this time; it wasn't the bridge Dak knew. He had driven over the Clinton Lake Bridge countless times, even before the accident. He knew every bump in its pavement, and the way the rails clattered together if cars traveled too quickly. Because Dak knew the Clinton Lake Bridge, he knew that bridge wasn't supposed to have a square white kiosk on the side of the bridge, like the one where he now stood. He looked up over the kiosk and saw a sign with ornamental black Thai lettering.

Dak noticed that along the short walls of the bridge there were handprints. Actually, the entire bridge was covered in small red handprints. He stepped down from the kiosk and moved to the painted handprints. Leaning down he placed his hand on top of one of them. When Dak pulled his hand back it was covered in red paint. Except it wasn't paint, it was blood. He wiped his hand against his jeans and moved away from the handprints, back up into the kiosk. Cars were suddenly speeding by, and he urgently tried to stop them. "Slow down!" he yelled, but no sound came out of Dak's mouth. Then every car vanished. Dak looked around the water and saw snow falling softly and landing on the longboats drifting through the ravine.

He heard monster tires spinning and looked up to see a white SUV coming towards the bridge. Even though the SUV was very far away, he recognized it. It was Tina, his beautiful wife. Dak could see her and his fourteen-year-old daughter. Tina and Samantha Jean were laughing. Samantha Jean was animated, alive. She was telling one of her stories to her mother, and his beautiful bride was fully engaged. He turned and looked at the road on the bridge. It was covered in black ice.

"No, not again—" Dak spoke words which made no sound, and he moved out in front of the car, waving his arms, "Stop! Tina! Stop!" the SUV continued forward and straight at him. Even though the car was still fifty yards away, Dak could see them clearly. The interior was illuminated with hundreds of candles. White candles burned bright inside the car, just as they had burned the night of their vigil. Tina, with her golden hair and blue eyes, and Samantha Jean, with her caramel skin and silky dark hair, were both glowing. They sparkled inside the warm, candlelit SUV.

Outside the storm raged. The trees whipped around and banged against the SUV. The heavy black tires waged war with the thick deep patches of rain. As the car came across the bridge, it flew past Dak, and the force of it knocked him backwards. He fell against the bridge. Dak tried to get up and chase after them, but the small bloody hands on the bridge transformed into thick masculine hands and grabbed his jacket and held him against the wall.

He watched in horror as the family SUV hit the long patch of black ice and spun out of control. He could hear the screams of his beautiful daughter and the screeching of the tires spinning wildly on the ice. It was impossible to tell which way the car was spinning. It collided with the hand wall, and the impact threw Samantha into the windshield; her screaming was silenced. The bridge shook with vibrato, but in that moment everything was completely silent. Noiseless rain beat down on the pavement; spinning tires were mute. Dak could see Tina clearly. She was gripping the steering wheel as the car headed into the icy water below. As the SUV hit the icy water, all sound returned and the vehicle entered its grave with a raucous splash. Dak pulled himself free from the hold of the small bloody hands and stumbled to the edge of the bridge. Like a vicious animal, the water was gobbling them down.

Dak dove into the water after the SUV which had already disappeared beneath the surface. Once under the water, he didn't see the white SUV, but his green Jeep. He grabbed the back bumper and pulled himself toward the sinking vehicle. The Jeep continued to plummet, pulling him deep. Fighting every urge to return to the surface for air, Dak kicked and swam to the front of the car. The water was getting deeper, but the further below the surface they went, the brighter the water became. Dak pulled open the door, a body drifted out and its dark hair floated around the head. The body began to drift up to the surface. Pushing himself away from the car, Dak swam upward through the murky water, trying to catch up to the body above. He was able to grab the body just as he came up for air, and he pulling it with him to the muddy bank of the river's edge.

Dak fought for a decent breath, choking, coughing and spitting the water out of his lungs. He turned and looked at the body. It was not his wife or his daughter. Lying in front of him was the petite frame of a young child. The girl was tiny, fragile, and her face was breathtakingly beautiful. He placed his hand on her neck, trying to find a pulse, but he felt nothing. The young girl was dead. Suddenly, her eyes shot wide open.

Dak awoke with a start. He felt sick. Dreaming about Tina and Samantha was always disturbing, but this was different. The look in the child's eyes made Dak want to vomit. He sat up on the edge of the bed and looked around the room. He hadn't turned on the air conditioning unit before drifting to sleep, and now he was sweating like a demon at an exorcism.

Dak moved across the room and adjusted the thermostat in the dark. Moving back toward his bed, he noticed a wedge of light peeking under the door which adjoined his room to Kimly's own. *She's awake?*

Dak wondered if she had left the light on out of fear. He sat on the edge of the bed wondering if he should check on her. Then he remembered the bickering he had gone through with himself just hours beforehand. Not only did Dak not want to open himself up to temptation, but he also didn't want another lecture from the mirror, and he certainly didn't want to have to take another cold shower. He rested his head on his pillow and wondered what the woman could possibly be doing. *I should have given her my Bible to read.* He thought, and then he determined to find her a Bible as soon as possible. *Where does a person find a Bible in a town bordering Communist Burma?* Dak sat up and looked down at the floor again, at the blazing line of light.

Picking up his cell phone from the nightstand, Dak typed out a text,

You awake?

He stared at the handheld device, waiting for it to answer. A moment passed, and then:

Well, I am now. Lol
Sorry. I saw the light. Did I really wake you?
No. j/k...I was awake

Probing, Dak typed: **Can't sleep?**

No

He chastised himself for not praying with her earlier: **You okay?**

Yeah

You sure?

Just a little homesick

Of course, Dak suddenly realized--that's why she was crying earlier, with the time change she couldn't get a hold of anyone at home, this would be the best time to call: **Were you calling home now?**

Yes

He didn't know how much to ask, he stared at his phone.

I wanted to talk to my sons. I got a hold of both of them.

This was great news, Dak responded: **Awesome!**

Yeah, not so much.

Instinctively he typed: **Are they okay?**

Kimly didn't answer. He waited. He turned his head and stared at the door between the two rooms.

Dylan is more sensitive. He started crying. He just wants me to come home.

Reading her text, Dak remembered Samantha's teen angst. The wrath of a teenager rivaled the brutality of a prisoner denied parole. While Dak was still typing he received another text message.

Jacob is a little more confident. He's more aggressive. He took the phone from his brother and told Dylan he was being a baby. It was just a brotherly quarrel, but it was hard to be so far away.

Dak pushed SEND and his condolences traveled through the wall between them and landed in the palm of her sleek hand. Dak imagined opening the door and talking to Kimly face to face. This woman told stories with her eyes, and not being able to look into them while she shared was limiting. Dak knew the worst thing he could do was to encourage Kimly's attachment to himself; his intentions may be chivalrous, but Steve's thick drawl echoed in his mind, "The road to hell is paved with good intentions." Dak reminded himself there was a reason the door between them was locked. If he went to her, and deepened the bond between the two of them, it was just going to make it harder for Kimly later. And again, Dak could hear Steve scolding as he shamefully thought about the possibility of Kimly's heart becoming attached more deeply than his own.

Lost in his own thoughts, he was startled by an incoming text message. **Finally my son gave his phone to his Dad, and we just**

ended up arguing.

Dak was at a loss. He had more questions than he could imagine trying to navigate through text messaging. His phone vibrated again in his hand: **I'm sorry. About all of this.**

He typed back to Kimly: **Nothing to be sorry about**

His phone vibrated a final time: **Goodnight Dak**

Goodnight Kimly

22

At just after 5 AM the next morning, The Bamboo Breeze was lifeless, or at least that is how it initially appeared, but the longer Dak and Kimly watched from across the street, the more hidden activity they could see. No one appeared to be working in the restaurant, but there was plenty of activity happening around the patio venue.

When Dak noticed a child rummaging through the restaurant's trash the incident seemed insignificant, so he didn't point it out to Kimly. However, when a second young child arrived and began scavenging through the exact can, it caught Dak's attention. Both children had walked away from the restaurant's trash bin with an armful of food.

"They're tossing out a lot of good food," Dak said as he pointed across the street to the few trash bins peeking out from the side alley of the restaurant.

"Well, it's a restaurant…doesn't that go with the territory?" Kimly leaned forward, crossing the small space in the cab, and craned her neck around to see the activity from where Dak was sitting.

"Sure, but this food appeared to be already bagged and ready to go," his urge was to shift closer to her, and Dak realized her presence was just as alluring as it had been the night before.

"Hmm…" Kimly fell back into her own seat and just stared across the street.

A moment later Kimly touched his arm, "Here comes another child."

Across the street a little boy made his way to the side of the restaurant. Looking around wildly, the child began to dig through the trash. He stopped and turned his head toward the back of the restaurant. Standing still for only a moment, the child then moved around to the rear of the restaurant and they lost sight of him.

"Where did he go?" Kimly whispered.

"I don't know," Dak responded in the same hushed sounds. "It looked like he was talking to someone…did you see anyone?"

"No," Kimly was once again leaning across the interior of the Jeep looking through the windshield on Dak's side of the car. "Should we go check on him?"

"No…not without knowing what, or who we will find." Dak turned his head, ready to tell her to slow down. Kimly's face was only a couple inches from his own. Her eyes were intent out the window, watching The Bamboo Breeze. Dak imagined breathing her in. He moved his head back against the headrest. It was not far enough.

Dak turned and looked across the street, hoping the small child would emerge soon from the restaurant. The idea of sitting in the car while something happened to an innocent child was more than he wanted to think about. Neither Dak nor Kimly spoke. The only sound in the Jeep's cab was their slow, deliberate breathing. Dak wanted to cross the street and make sure the child was safe, but he didn't think it was wise for her to join him. He assumed he was going to have to convince her to stay in the Jeep.

"I see something," Kimly whispered. "Right there, inside...do you see? It's the little boy. He's...eating."

Dak spotted what Kimly saw. In the window of The Bamboo Breeze, Dak could see the tiny arm of a child reaching into a bowl with a spoon. The child appeared to be sitting at a table eating, and although they could only see his little arm and his spoon wielding hand, he was safe.

"Well...look at that..." Dak turned his head to look at Kimly. She was still leaning across the interior of the Jeep, only now her eyes had shifted and she was looking right at him. Their eyes locked for a moment. Kimly's dark eyes were intense. Dak's breathing came to a halt. He turned his head away and looked back across the street.

The child in the window had disappeared. The two sat staring at The Bamboo Breeze, waiting. Dak could feel Kimly inches away from him, but he kept his eyes locked on the restaurant. "We need to go over there," he surprised himself when he said it. Kimly didn't respond.

"Are you sure?" she eventually whispered.

"You don't think so?"

"Yes, I do. But, I mean, I'm scared," Kimly admitted.

"No, you're right," Dak was pleased her fear was altering her pace.

The danger was real, but doing nothing while a child was lured away was reprehensible.

Dak silently prayed for God to lead him. His eyes were fixed on the small window, hoping to see the little arms, the head or some part of the child to reveal he wasn't being harmed.

"Kimly, I know you won't want to, but I need you to wait here—"

"Okay," she cut him off. "I'll stay here."

He turned and looked at the woman, once again surprised. For all the toughness Kimly tried to muster, her fragility seeped to the surface. She was a china cup in a war zone. Could it really be God's plan to bring a heart easily affected by evil up against some of the most depraved souls this side of Hell?

Hoping he could move faster than Kimly could change her mind, Dak quickly jumped out of the Jeep. Before closing the door, Dak turned and, with one arm on the open door and the other on the door jam, leaned back in, "Keep the doors locked. If I am not back in ten minutes, or if anyone approaches the car, drive away," his voice was firm.

"I'm not leaving you here."

"Kimly, just do what I say," Dak locked and closed the door.

The patio of The Bamboo Breeze faced the street, and was enclosed behind the locked gate. Dak could see a door leading to the entrance of what, he assumed, was the restaurant's kitchen, but he was more intrigued to see what was unseen. Something, or someone, had lured that boy behind the building and away from the trash cans full of food.

Dak took cautious steps around the side of the building, which was not gated. He took a final look over his shoulder at the Jeep across the street, and then walked carefully down a narrow alley. On one side of the alley was a concrete wall blocking off the parking lot of what appeared to be an abandoned building and on the other side was the light blue wall of the restaurant.

Within the first three feet, Dak reached a white door with a window. He eased his head forward and peered through the glass. Inside he saw five stove-top burners lining the far wall. In the middle of the kitchen there was a thick, wooden table, about six feet long. The wood was aged and worn, and atop it was an assortment of bowls and knives. Near the front of the humble kitchen sat a chair next to a Formica table. This is where the child had been sitting as he ate. The boy was gone, but the bowl still sat on the table. The spoon peeked shyly over the rim of the bowl.

Turning from the window, Dak moved towards the trash cans pushed against the block wall; several of them were filled with clearly visible and easily attainable food. Apples, carrots, and bread were propped perfectly in the cans. He grabbed one of the apples and looked at it. It wasn't bruised; it was fresh. *Are they strategically targeting needy children who live on the street? Are they using their hunger to lure them in for trafficking? These aren't people, they're monsters.*

Setting the apple back in the trash can, Dak moved further into the alleyway until he reached the end of the building. The property extended twenty feet behind The Bamboo Breeze, housing two small buildings and a modest-sized garden filled with vegetation. The gun in Dak's waistband was a nudging reminder that he was on unfamiliar ground. Before taking stealthy steps across the yard and toward the buildings, Dak pulled the 9 millimeter out of his waistband, checked the rounds and turned off the safety.

Both of the buildings were plastered and painted light beige. The smaller building, which he approached first, had no door in the doorway. Peering through the narrow opening, Dak found himself in a restroom. A dozen or so flies buzzed about an in ground toilet and a plastic bucket filled with water. A garden hose was attached to a spigot near the bucket of water. On the other side of the waste hole was a small table with several rolls of toilet paper and an overflowing trash can.

Dak moved back through the doorway and towards the second building. This building was twice as wide with a door and two draped windows on the front. Dak lowered himself and moved across the dirt, making sure he was below the windows. He needed to see something that would confirm the safety of the child.

As Dak raised himself up off the ground and was peering into a corner of the window, he heard a car door slamming behind him. Deliberate footsteps rushed up the alley, towards him. Looking around the yard, Dak spotted makeshift animal cages near a bounteous grapefruit tree by the back fence. He darted to a small opening behind the tree, pulling the gun close to his chest as he leaned into the tree. Softball sized grapefruits pulled the branches low which created a tent-like barrier around him.

A man approached the house with the windows; he was moving with purpose. Dak could not see his face, only his lower half, dressed in slacks and dress shoes. He stopped for a moment, and Dak could hear the jangle of keys. The stranger unlocked the door and disappeared behind it. Dak wondered how much time he had to get across the lawn. He was weighing his options when he saw Kimly's familiar figure coming around the corner of the restaurant and into the yard.

"Kimly!" he exclaimed in a loud whisper. She turned her head and looked across the yard trying to locate him.

"Over here!" he squatted, and lowered himself so he would be visible out from under the wide leaves and large fruit.

Kimly rushed across the yard and joined him behind the tree, "Dak—"

"What are you thinking?" Dak interrupted her, "I told you to stay in the car."

"Someone's here. I saw a car pull into the parking lot. I couldn't see who got out."

He took a deep breath and leaned back into the tree. "I know. He's inside," Dak nodded at the larger of the two small buildings. "We need to get out of here, we need to—" hearing the door across the yard opening, Dak stopped suddenly and whipped his head around. Dak reached his arm around Kimly's waist and pulled her towards him. Silently, they leaned into one another under the canopy of citrus and leaves.

The small boy they had seen earlier walked from the house holding the hand of the man in the slacks and dress shoes. Behind them, another set of legs followed. It was difficult to get a good visual of the person following except to see he was wearing flip-flops and shorts. All three of them disappeared down the alley as they walked to the front of the property. Dak stood completely still with his arms wrapped around Kimly's waist.

"How long do we wait?" she whispered in his ear. Dak could feel her arm around his back and her heart pounding against his chest. His body wanted to respond to her. Embracing this beautiful, married woman was muddling his senses.

Dak heard car doors slam and an engine igniting; someone was leaving. One person, two or three--he didn't know. He stood there a moment longer, one hand resting on Kimly's back, and the other wielding the gun. When Dak was certain the sound of the car engine was fading, he took Kimly by the hand and led her out from under the tree. Kimly held tight to his hand, as Dak led her cautiously across the yard. They rounded the corner and moved up the narrow alleyway. The parking lot was empty, and the gate leading into the restaurant's patio was still locked. It appeared that all three of the people had left in the car.

"Let's get out of here," Dak shoved the 9 millimeter back into his waistband and started to jog across the street. Kimly was right with him, and they were back to the Jeep in seconds. Heart pounding, Dak looked back at the restaurant while Kimly's shaking hands fumbled with the keys. A moment later they were in the Jeep, and Dak pulled away from the curb.

Dak was driving them back to the Kongkam Hotel. He decided

they needed to debrief what they had seen. He told Kimly about the unspoiled apple placed on top of the trash.

"Wait?! Are you saying they are using the children's hunger pains to lure them behind the restaurant?"

"That's what it looks like, Kimly," he was shaking his head. "Maybe you were never supposed to find The Bamboo Breeze's business card in your passport. Maybe it was meant to land in someone else's hands."

"Maybe...Dak, where did he take the child?!" Kimly's eyes widened.

"I don't know, and I couldn't see his face. But, Kimly...I wouldn't be surprised if it was your friend SuSuk. Did you see the driver's face?"

"No, I didn't. It all happened so fast. The car pulled in and the driver was moving back to where you were so quickly," Kimly's words trembled out.

"We should go to the place with the wall and the metal gate." Kimly urged.

Dak shook his head, "Kimly, we can't see over that wall, and we are completely out of our element there.'"

"It's our only lead!" she persisted. "We can be careful. Maybe we'll see more in the daylight."

If Dak were alone, he would have had the same thoughts about returning to investigate behind the wall with the metal gate. Dak's concerns were directly related to her. He worried about not being able to protect her if they encountered SuSuk. When Kimly escaped SuSuk at the palace, the pseudo-business man responded by assaulting her and attempting to rape her. Now that she had managed to do him bodily harm, Dak assumed the monster was enraged.

"Dak, let's just drive by and see what we can see." Across the interior of the car, Kimly's eyes were free of fear. They were deep, dark brown, filled with determination, but not a hint of fear.

The small road off the main highway looked different in the daylight. The seediness they had seen in the dark hours of the night had vanished. Upon approaching the tall concrete wall and metal gate, Dak slowed the Jeep to a speed which would allow him to get a glimpse without seeming too obvious. There wasn't much he could see as they passed the gate. It was sturdy, with an electronic keypad at eye level. Dak noticed a camera at the top of the wall pointing down to the opening of the gate. The concrete wall was too high to see over. Dak drove further down the street, made a U-turn, pulled over, and shut off the engine.

"What do you think?" he asked.

"Maybe go back? Maybe try peeking through an opening in the gate?" Kimly's eyes were locked on the gate.

"No," he pointed to the top of the wall, "see the camera? I don't know who is watching the screen."

They sat for a few minutes and just watched the motionless gate. Meanwhile, just outside Dak's window there was plenty of movement. An elderly man stood in his yard, moving his limbs through a series of exercises. He raised his arms slowly over his head. Next he lifted his right leg until he stood on one foot. Balancing himself with ease, he pulled his arms downward in opposite directions. The elderly man's movements had caught Kimly's eye, and she looked beyond Dak at the Thai man practicing ancient Qigong. Dak felt Kimly looking in his direction; he turned his head toward her but saw she was looking past him. She tilted her eyes up at his and raised her eyebrows. Kimly was wearing a small grin. He hadn't seen his sullen friend's real smile since they had arrived in Mae Sai.

The intensity of their pursuit, combined with the frustrations she was facing on the home front, seemed to be taking their toll on her. He thought back to the spiritual encounter Kimly had experienced in the village church. *Why am I holding back?* Dak was ashamed that he still hadn't told Kimly about the supernatural experience she had been a part of in the Tai Lue church. There was a time when he would have been shouting about her experience from the roof tops, and his decision to keep silent now was confounding.

Following Kimly's eyes, Dak turned his head, and looked out the window at the old man, who was oblivious to the audience he entertained. His face, though aged, was calm and serene. Dak figured the man to be about the age his own parents would be if either of them was still alive. Watching the frail man move through each exercise with determination and purpose made him think of the way his mother had described her husband before his death.

Dak's paternal grandfather had been a member of King Rama's army, and when Field Marshall Thanom Kittikachon took over as Prime Minister, Dak's grandfather moved up in rank. Colonel

Kesapan took great pride in his military career and he assumed his only son, Pira, would also be a military man. Pira rejected the idea, bringing disgrace to the Colonel. Pira was disowned; shunned and rejected by his parents. At nineteen years old Pira was living on the streets of Bangkok, but through determination and perseverance, he was able to gain admittance to Thammasat University. Dak's father studied fervently while living hand to mouth. One morning, Pira eyed Dak's mother, who was working as a sorter in the college mail room. Throughout Dak's life he had heard the story of the way Pira had wooed his mother in her youth. Everyday Pira would call out to her, "Pai taan khao duai gan na khrub," inviting her to go eat with him, and every day she would shake her head no. Finally, one day Dak's mother accepted. Pira had caught her on a day when she was too hungry to refuse. Once she realized Pira had little money to buy her a meal, it made his invitation all the more meaningful. He won her heart because he was poor and she hadn't eaten breakfast.

During the 1970s Thailand's Prime Minister, Thanom Kittikachon, dissolved parliament and imposed one-man rule, and the rivalry between various military and political factions intensified. It was against this backdrop that tragedy unfolded. Students from Thammasat University massed in demonstration. Workers and the general population joined, and the number of demonstrators exceeded 200,000, making it the largest public demonstration in Thailand's history. The military responded to the growing number of people, and the situation grew violent and bloody. Students ran for their lives, some jumping into canals.

On October 14, 1973, Thailand saw The Great Day of Sorrow. During the uprising over a hundred protesters, most of whom were college students, were killed in the massacre. Months before Dak was born, Pira Kesapan died fighting for the freedom of his people. How many people could say that about their father?

"I envy him," Kimly whispered.

Dak didn't answer, so Kimly's words lingered in the small space.

The metal gate began to move, and Dak and Kimly simultaneously whipped their heads to watch. Dak instinctively started the engine of the Jeep and moved slowly down the road.

"Wait, they will see us—" Kimly warned.

"No, they won't. And I want to see what's behind the gate before it closes."

From within the walls, the burgundy minivan appeared and traveled down the street opposite of Dak and Kimly. Dak sped up and was able to pass the gate before it closed. A blue sedan sat in the driveway of a house with iron bars on the windows.

"The car!" Kimly exclaimed, identifying the blue sedan as the one she had seen earlier at the restaurant. The gate was closing quickly, and the only other thing they were able to identify was a child's play set in the middle of the grass lawn. Dak was almost certain he saw a duck waddling across the lawn.

They followed the minivan back out to the main highway. Dak assumed they were heading back to The Bamboo Breeze, and he was able to follow at an unassuming distance. When the minivan turned into the restaurant's parking lot, Dak stopped the Jeep on the opposite side of the street, leaving the ignition on.

The minivan parked in the lot, and a handful of young people disembarked and walked nonchalantly toward the entrance of the restaurant. The driver of the van unlocked the gate, and one by one the passengers followed him inside. A moment later one of the young men emerged from inside with a cardboard box. Dak watched as the man loaded the apple, along with the other fresh items from the trash into the box. He carried the box with him back behind the building.

The couple sat watching for several minutes as the passengers from the van began performing various tasks in The Bamboo Breeze. It looked like any other patio-style restaurant on the busy border town highway.

"What do you think?" Kimly asked.

"What do I think?" Dak was looking across the street, "I think you and I should come back later...for lunch."

Dak and Kimly returned to the hotel to rest up before returning to The Bamboo Breeze for lunch. They had made it through the morning on several cups of coffee, but the caffeine was wearing off, and Dak didn't want fatigue to influence his judgment when they returned to the restaurant. He really wanted to spend some time praying before they returned, as well. Carrying a gun in his waistband, crawling along the ground beneath windows and hiding in trees were not usual activities for him.

Exiting the hotel elevator, they headed to their rooms without a pause. While swiping her key card, Kimly stated plainly, "I'm glad you're my partner. You make me feel safe."

Dak nodded and searched for the proper response. She hadn't said thank you, so "you're welcome" felt off. He recognized how far she had come in lowering her pride to admit she needed help. The way the whole situation had evolved, it was evident the Lord had appointed their meeting.

He smiled slightly, and simply replied, "Good."

They each disappeared behind their own door, and Dak went straight to his knees.

23

At a quarter after one in the afternoon, Dak woke groggy from a deep dreamless nap. Pulling himself up off the bed and walking to the bathroom, he shoved his toothbrush under the faucet. While he brushed his teeth he wandered back over to his phone on the nightstand. Picking it up, he noticed a text message notification; at 12:10 PM Kimly had sent a message.

You awake?

He decided he would grab a quick shower and then go knock on her door. Text messaging was inhibiting.

Fifteen minutes later Dak stood in the hallway and knocked on the door of the room next to his own. When Kimly didn't respond he knocked a little harder. He wondered if she had fallen back to sleep, or if she was in the shower. He pulled out his phone and dialed Kimly's number. It rang several times, and then went to voicemail, "Hi, this is Kimly, leave a message or send me a text. Choose wisely." BEEP.

Dak meandered back in his room and over to the window. Looking out across the city he began to think about the events of the last few weeks. God was stretching him in ways he had never imagined. Thinking back on his initial decision to return to Thailand, he could never fully explain why he desired to return to his homeland. Nothing about Thailand reminded him of Tina and Samantha, and he knew how badly he wanted to hold onto their memory. Once he arrived, he had spent a weekend with Steve and Nisa, visited the orphanage, and made a quick trip to Bangkok to visit the memorial for the Battles of Thai Democracy. And yet these places did little to affect him or revive any passion within.

Now, Thailand had become about her; her safety and her cause. The friendship he had developed with this married woman was breaking rules he had set in place for himself over the years. Dak had set the guidelines in place because he felt God's Spirit had directed him to do so for his own protection. He believed most moral decisions were black or white, and a lot of heartache would be averted if a people simply avoided living in the gray areas.

Dak couldn't think of a time or reason that he would have ever spent the night alone with a woman who was the wife of another man. Let alone a woman who was affecting him. *Is she affecting me?* He caught the thought and held it captive. Dak shook his head, attempting to physically shift his thinking. The fire he felt was merely an ember from the intensity of their situation.

Walking to the adjoining door, Dak stood still, trying to distinguish any movement. It was completely silent. He dialed Kimly's number again. It rang several times, "Hi, this is Kimly, leave a message or..." Dak hung up. He realized he didn't hear anything on the other side of the door, he didn't hear movement or the ringing of her cell phone. *Maybe she has it on silent,* even as the thought bounced through his head, Dak knew the truth. He knew Kimly. If she had decided to head off somewhere, she would have no problem going without him. He picked up the hotel phone and dialed her room. Through the wall and through the handset, he heard the phone ringing again and again.

Dak dropped the phone into its cradle and grabbed the keys to the Jeep. He couldn't imagine she would've walked to The Bamboo Breeze; it was too far to journey by foot. *The house with the metal gate!* The house was definitely within walking distance. He could probably get to it just as quickly by foot as he could in the Jeep. He hurried out of his room and toward the elevator when he felt the vibration of his phone in his pocket.

"Hey," Kimly's voice was light, "I missed your calls. Sorry, I didn't know I had the ringer turned off."

"Where are you?" Dak interrogated.

"What's wrong?" Kimly asked.

"Are you in your room?" Dak tried to sound less aggressive, casual even.

"No."

"Where are you?" the casualness left Dak as he realized she had probably gone to the house with the metal gate.

"I'm in the lobby. I'm using one of the computers."

"Stay there. I'm coming down. And don't talk to anyone."

A few moments later Dak found Kimly sitting at a faux wood desk in the hotel lobby. A slew of papers were sitting on the desk beside a clunky computer.

"I can't believe you came down here by yourself." Dak's tone was harsh.

Kimly didn't respond. She simply looked up at him for a moment, and then back at the computer monitor.

"It's just not safe," Dak continued, "I keep telling you, and you've got to trust me on this—"

"And this is why you are in a panic right now?" Kimly interrupted.

"Well...I'm not panicked—" before Dak could say more, Kimly interrupted again.

"But, I mean, nothing happened. You just *thought* something could have happened?"

Kimly exited the program on the computer and gathered her papers.

"Kimly.—" Dak didn't get another word out before Kimly stood and walked away.

Dak followed Kimly to the elevator where she stood with arms crossed over her papers.

"Okay..." Dak started and then stopped. The elevator doors opened. "Okay, I can tell you are upset—"

"Good," Kimly cut him off, still deterring eye contact.

Dak followed her into the elevator and stared at the elevator's digital numbers. When the number six appeared and the doors opened, Kimly quickly made her way out and headed down the hallway toward their rooms.

"Do you want to tell me why?" he walked off the elevator, but stopped just outside of its doors. "I really don't understand what I did—"

"I understand your fears when they are justified, but for heaven's sake—it's daylight. I was in the hotel lobby, and I was paying attention to my surroundings. You came charging down like a worried parent." Kimly turned and walked back the short distance between them. "I don't need you to treat me like a child."

Stunned, Dak responded, "Have you forgotten you were attacked, and not just once! Kimly, my fears for you have kept you safe. "

"Yes—you are right. And you have no idea how thankful I am. But, sometimes because of that, because of what you've seen, your fears are exaggerated," Kimly stepped away from Dak and towards her door. "I want your help, but I didn't come here to waste my time. I didn't come here to write a story I could have researched from the Internet. I want to get into the trenches, and your fears could hold me back!"

Dak's mind was spinning. "Hold you back? Well, then by all means, Kimly, go do what you have to do. I certainly don't want to hold Kimly Denim back!"

"You know that's not what I meant!" Kimly said as she opened the door to her room. She paused only long enough for her dark eyes to throw him a piercing glance, and then slammed the door behind her.

Dak stood bewildered in the middle of the hallway and raised both of his hands up in the air. When he finally entered his room, Dak purposely slammed his door harder than Kimly had slammed hers.

He stomped across the room to the window overlooking the city. Dirty apartments, badly in need of paint, glared up at him. His eyes locked in on a Buddhist temple in the distance. Golden rods pointed up to the sky and cast a dark shadow over a garden below. *I can't deal with this woman much longer!* She was infiltrating his thoughts and frustrating him at every turn. *I can't protect her. I can't kiss her, and I can't kill her. Why did you allow us to meet?* He threw the question up to God, praying for wisdom. Surely, there was a reason he and Kimly had met, was it merely to lead him to frustration? If her safety was the purpose, then he was going to need God to give him an extra shot of perseverance. Taming a wild stallion to give pony rides would be less frustrating. God was going to have to open his heart to what he might be missing. Surely there was a purpose in their situation.

A moment later Dak heard a knock on the adjoining door. He turned and looked at the door between the two rooms for a moment, then he heard her voice, "Dak, I know you are in there, don't ignore me." Her voice was less aggressive than it had been in the hallway. Dak moved closer, slid open the lock, and opened the door between them. Kimly stood in front of him with one arm resting on the door jam. She pulled her free hand up and rested it on her décolleté.

"I'm sorry for getting so angry. I know you were nervous, but I wasn't in danger." Kimly said, and she held his eyes and didn't look away. Dak wanted to hug her, so he didn't.

"I'm sorry for overreacting," he replied, and in a flash he saw

Tina's face. Dak felt shame for his inability to protect the woman he had lost.

Kimly took a deep breath and let her sigh fall between them.

"Maybe we should get some lunch?" she offered a real smile. Her heartfelt expression started in her eyes and then moved across her lips.

Dak let out his own sigh, "Yeah, let's go get some lunch."

––––––––––––––––––––––––––––––

Before Dak and Kimly got out of the Jeep, Dak checked the rounds in his gun. Kimly's eyes were wide. Dak placed his hand on the door handle and looked over at her, "You ready?"

About a dozen customers were dining at tables stationed around the perimeter of the restaurant's patio. Dak led Kimly to a table which gave him a clear view of the kitchen, the entrance to the alleyway, and the parking lot. Kimly rested her elbows on the table and messed with her phone. Dak watched as she snapped pictures like any other tourist. The post argument awkwardness had dissolved, and Dak realized that dining with this woman after their argument was the closest thing to being in a romantic relationship he had experienced since Tina had died, yet he reminded himself this was abnormal, and quite possibly a life-threatening situation.

When a waitress in her early twenties approached Dak and Kimly's table, Dak recognized her as the one who had punched the combination on the keypad at the metal gate. She wasn't Thai; she had olive skin, dark brown curly locks, a round full face and green apple eyes. She had a tiny nose piercing, in it she wore a ruby red stone and when she smiled her teeth glimmered like the white sand beaches in Southern Thailand.

She greeted them, "Sawadeeka."

Dak returned with "Sawadeekop," but then trusting an instinct, he continued in English, "how are you today?"

"Well, I don't have much to complain about! Thanks for asking," the girl with the ruby red piercing replied.

They placed their lunch order, and after the waitress left the table, Dak said, "I guess we can assume she's not a native."

"Ah, yeah…there was a hint of an accent. Maybe New York?" Kimly wondered aloud.

The two sat whispering about what they had seen and tried to determine if there was anything they might have missed. Soon she returned with their soft drinks and Kimly engaged her in conversation, "You aren't originally from here, are you?"

"No, I moved here—with my family—about ten years ago." She answered quickly as she set down a couple of straws and strutted away. Dak looked around at the other customers, across the patio, and then shifted his eyes over to the entrance to the alleyway, as a blue sedan pulled into the parking lot.

"Kimly," he nodded, "over to your left, next to the Jeep, the blue sedan...is it the same one?"

Kimly glanced over her shoulder; she turned back and answered, "I think so."

Dak reached down and took his gun into his grip. He held it under the table, releasing the safety. The door to the sedan opened and a blonde woman who appeared to be in her late-forties climbed out of the car. Walking around to the trunk, she opened it up and began gathering full bags into her arms. The blonde woman walked to the gate of the restaurant, where a teenager working as a bus boy rushed over to hold it open for her. The teenager took the bags from the blonde woman and said something to her. Whatever he said made her laugh.

Dak watched as the blonde returned to the car and took another bag out of the trunk. The woman moved with an air of confidence. She came through the gate again, and at the same time the bus boy returned. Once again, the teenager took the bag from the blonde woman, and they were both laughing as they walked together into the kitchen.

About that time, Ruby Red returned with their food, and Kimly engaged her in conversation, "This place is charming...has it been here long?"

"Umm...about five or six years. Would you like another coke?" the waitress motioned to Kimly's nearly empty glass.

"Sure, thanks."

Ruby Red grabbed Kimly's glass and pranced away from the table. Tilting her head to Dak, Kimly shrugged shoulders. "I'm thirsty," she smiled.

As Ruby Red sat the Coca-Cola on the table, Kimly, who didn't miss a beat asked, "Is that woman the owner...the one who just came in?" Kimly motioned toward the kitchen with her head, but she kept her eyes trained on the girl.

"Huh?" Ruby Red looked over her shoulder at the blonde woman and smiled, "Yes, she is. Can I get you anything else?"

Kimly looked across the table at Dak, "No," he interjected, "I think we're good. But I I'm curious, are you from America?"

The waitress nodded, and Dak continued, "Where about?"

"Ah...yeah. I was born in Jersey, but when I was pretty young still, my family moved to New York."

"New York, bet that was cool, huh?" Kimly smiled at the young woman.

"Yeah, well, we lived upstate. Albany...not complaining or nothing, but it wasn't all glamorous," the young waitress looked over her shoulder at a couple approaching the patio, "if you guys don't mind..."

"Oh no...go ahead." Kimly nodded and Ruby Red greeted the arriving customers.

Next to the meal at Nisa's, the food at The Bamboo Breeze was some of the best Dak had eaten since arriving back in his homeland.

"How's the pak boon fy dang?" Dak asked.

"Good...definitely better than a Big Mac," Kimly winked.

The couple was finishing their meal when Ruby Red returned, "How's everything here?" The waitress smiled her blazing white smile.

Dak complimented the restaurant on their food and then asked, "Do you think the owner would have a minute to speak with us?"

"Yeah, hold on a sec," Ruby Red responded.

When the blonde woman approached the table, Dak noticed that the dark roots of her hair were more prominent than what he could see at a distance, and the lines around her eyes were deep, giving her a sharp, uncongenial appearance. She thanked Dak and Kimly for coming to The Bamboo Breeze, and with a half smile she said, "It's always nice to welcome new customers."

"It's a great restaurant. We enjoyed it thoroughly." Dak nodded.

"Great. So glad to hear it," the blonde woman replied.

"I was curious..." Dak continued, "Sorry if this is a hassle, but we are visiting from the United States and we were curious as to where some of the more affordable places might be to purchase fresh produce. You know just for making sandwiches and the like. Do you mind directing us to the stores you use?"

"Oh gosh, there's so many to choose from…the closest market is about 3 miles east on the Rid Alley road, just off Highway 1041, you can get all you need to make a real good sub." The woman motioned with her left hand, and Dak noticed a wedding band.

"Thank you!" Dak responded.

"Yes, thank you." Kimly added. The blond woman nodded, and Kimly continued, "Can I ask another question?"

The blonde woman nodded to Kimly, "Sure."

"Earlier this morning, we noticed several children coming here to get food. I mean…to take it from the trash cans. Is this something you plan for?"

The half smile dissolved as the blonde woman responded, "There's so much poverty along the border. People are hungry and many are homeless. So, yeah, we try and make it easy for people to find food we have no need for. It seems senseless to let good food go to waste."

Kimly nodded and looked across the table at Dak who spoke up, "That's great. Nice accent, by the way." He picked up his glass and spun the Sprite around in the bottom of his cup, "The thing is…earlier this morning… we were watching your restaurant, and we saw something unusual."

Dak paused and the woman's face tightened. "I have a question for you," the blonde woman interrupted. Dak stopped talking, and he wondered if he should have taken a different approach. "How long were you two spying on my restaurant? And what would that be for, anyhow?"

Dak looked across the table to Kimly, who spoke up, "We were watching because of a story I'm writing. My name is Kimly Denim, I'm a journalist from the United States."

The restaurant owner moved her blonde bangs away from her face; she looked at Kimly and then back again at Dak. "A story about…?" she asked.

Kimly looked at Dak.

"So, you don't want to tell me what the story's about, but you are watching my restaurant," the blonde woman glanced around at one of the closer tables where an older couple had just taken a seat, "I'll betcha dollars to doughnuts, you came to Mai Sai because of us?" Her voice was quivering.

"Well, kind of—" Kimly started.

"You people. You're relentless. I think it might be a good idea for you both to leave." She turned to walk away.

"We haven't paid for our food!" Dak called out to her.

"It's on the house. Just go on now. And leave my family alone." She called back as she walked through the doorway leading to the kitchen.

24

"That didn't make any sense..." Kimly was adjusting her seatbelt as Dak looked over his shoulder at the traffic.

"No, it didn't make any sense, at all." Dak agreed, "My mother would have said, 'jap dai kah nang kah kao'." Dak spun the steering wheel and turned the Jeep in the opposite direction.

"Meaning?" Kimly's hand had a tight grip on the broken door handle.

"Meaning—that woman was acting like someone who was caught red handed. Someone took that child somewhere."

"You know *exactly* where they took that child—" Kimly interjected.

"But why?" Dak interrupted. "I can imagine that woman selling cannolis in Little Italy, not children in Thailand."

"Well, she's hiding something...why did she tell us to leave her family alone?"

As Dak drove the Jeep behind the Kongkam Hotel, Kimly turned and looked across the interior of the car, past him. He turned to see what she was looking at. Behind a large trash bin Dak saw a makeshift fort. Someone had used a couple crates, some water damaged cardboard, and a light purple blanket to make a hideaway.

"I noticed it last night," Kimly said softly. "It makes me feel guilty. I mean, we each have our own room. Whoever is living in that fort doesn't have much."

Dak's head was twisted around and looked at the small shelter; he turned back and looked at Kimly.

"Dak, we should see who is in that fort! What if it's a child?" Kimly was out of the car and flinging the door closed behind her before he even had his seatbelt unfastened. She rushed across the park, but then slowed her pace as she approached the fort, Kimly called, "Hello?"

Kimly's hand barely touched the blanket, when the stain covered linen fell to the ground, revealing an unoccupied dirty den. She looked at Dak, disappointed.

He felt bad for her and remembered days he had gone through similar experiences. He remembered a time when he was moved to feed each homeless person he encountered. Eventually, maturity taught him that there would always be hungry people among them. Dak stood off to the right and watched as Kimly searched the parking lot. "Come on," he called to her, "maybe they'll be back."

Later that evening Kimly and Dak drove the short distance to The Bamboo Breeze and watched the activity at the restaurant. It was just as mundane as it had been the night before. Young adults served customers dining on the patio, cleaned the tables and emptied trash. This time both Dak and Kimly counted the workers, paying close attention at the end of the shift. Sure enough, one of the young men didn't leave with his coworkers they loaded into the burgundy minivan.

"Do you think he lives in that little house?" Kimly asked.

"Maybe...but it doesn't answer the bigger question." Dak started the Jeep, "Let's follow the van."

"It's going to end up at the house behind the metal gate."

"Yeah, probably..." Dak mumbled.

While the burgundy minivan did start off heading in the direction of the house with the metal gate, it had only traveled about 100 kilometers when it made a sharp left and traveled south into the hills. Dak followed, hoping he was keeping enough distance behind the van to be unnoticed.

The burgundy minivan maneuvered through small residential

roads. Planted between the houses were a few small restaurants and bars. It wasn't lost upon Dak that one or two of them might likely be brothels. The van traveled for about twenty minutes when it pulled over and parked in front of a darkened house. Dak stopped a few houses further back and turned off the lights, but he didn't extinguish the ignition. He just stared out the dirty windshield at the burgundy minivan.

"Dak, I think it's going to be okay." Kimly whispered.

"Of course you think that, Kimly. You rarely think otherwise," he gave her a wink, and turned off the ignition to the Jeep. "Let's say a quick prayer." Without closing his eyes, without taking them off of the minivan, Dak began praying. He felt Kimly grab his hand, and he glanced down for a moment but then looked back up at the van; five young adults were unloading into the street. Praying for God's protection for Kimly and himself reinforced his sense of control over a situation in which he really had little. Dak prayed for the lives being destroyed in the name of lust and power, and for the possibility that hearts might be changed.

Dak saw the five young people from the minivan form a circle in the street. He stopped praying and waited to see what would happen next. He realized he was still holding Kimly's hand, and he lessened his grip to release her, but he felt her hand tightened in response. Dak looked across the car at Kimly, but she wasn't looking his way. Kimly's gaze was on the circle in the street.

"Are you okay?" Dak asked.

"I'm just nervous. I didn't think I would be, but—" Kimly stopped and looked over at him.

"We don't have to do this," Dak repeated his all too familiar mantra. She wasn't obligated to this cause. She wasn't obligated to this story. Kimly didn't release Dak's hand, and she said something which struck him as odd, "Everything ends when I stop." Only then did she release his hand and reach for the door handle.

Dak checked the bullets in his gun and then slipped the 9 millimeter into the front pocket of his jacket. He opened the door to the Jeep and stepped out onto the unpaved road, sending up silent prayers asking for wisdom and protection.

The circle of young people had begun to move, walking up a street of modest houses. Most of the dwellings were unassuming, except that there were small gatherings of people throughout the neighborhood. People mingled, the darkness hiding much of what might be happening. The dim light of a cigarette and the screen of a cell phone acted as giveaways for people that might have otherwise faded into the blackness of the unlit street.

As Dak and Kimly followed the workers from The Bamboo Breeze, they stayed back, hoping not to be noticed. Dak noticed one or two heads turn to watch them as they passed, and he kept his hand gripped tightly to the gun.

A man walking towards them had his eyes fixed on Kimly. He was on the opposite side of the street, but even on the dimly lit street, Dak spotted his dark eyes following her. Dak tightened his grip on the 9 millimeter in his pocket. The stranger's eyes moved away as he passed by them. Dak was filled with relief, and then shame. *Am I going to be able to use this thing if I need to?* The Bamboo Breeze group rounded the corner, and a few moments later Dak and Kimly rounded it as well. Amid the darkened houses, one stood out. Scantily clad girls moved around the perimeter of the property, and flashing lights sent swaying shadows across the narrow street. It was similar to a nightclub, but something was missing.

The group stopped for a moment. Dak and Kimly stopped and stepped into the darkness of a tall tree on the edge of the street. *Something is off...what's missing?* Dak wondered.

A Thai girl approached Dak from his left and said, "Khun maa tee nee khon diew rue kha?" Dak didn't answer, but instinctively pulled Kimly close to him, wrapping one arm around her shoulders, but never releasing his grip on the gun in his pocket.

"Ah..." the girl said. She turned and headed toward the group from The Bamboo Breeze, adjusting her mini-skirt, and trying to keep her balance atop a pair of tall wedge sandals. Dak figured she couldn't have been more than fourteen, and that thought was nauseating.

Dak felt Kimly pulling herself closer to him, and he whispered, "Don't make eye contact with anyone." He slid his hand down from her shoulders and let it rest on her back, "and stay close to me."

The group from the restaurant started to move again, started to walk further up the street. Dak took Kimly by the arm and they continued to follow. They were getting closer to the house with the flashing lights, closer to what Dak assumed was a brothel. As they got closer, a man sped by on a scooter, honked his horn and yelled a vulgarity. Kimly's hand slipped into Dak's, and she pulled herself closer.

There were at least ten girls out near the street. Some of the girls wore bras and shorts; others were dressed in high heels and miniskirts. Dak watched as the group they were following approached the house, the girls called out to the young men from the restaurant. Despite the make-up and the shoes, Dak could see that these were young women—teenagers at the most.

The young people didn't stop and speak to any of the girls; they just walked along in a straight line. As they got closer to the house, Dak spotted two men sitting on the front porch that reminded him of the man he and Kimly had met on the Nawarat Bridge. It wasn't his physical appearance, it was his demeanor. Something about him gave Dak the chills. Once they were directly in front of the house, the street was more populated, and by the time they were passing directly in front of the brothel, it was easy to disappear in the crowd.

Dak kept darting his eyes between the young people they were following and the men sitting on the porch of the brothel. He didn't want to fall into a trap. A dog on the porch barked and Kimly's grip on his hand tightened again. Dak whispered, "You're okay."

The young people from the restaurant didn't speak to anyone, and they didn't stop and mull about. They just walked through the crowded street and turned at the corner. When Dak and Kimly reached the corner, Dak stopped walking.

"Let's wait a minute. Let's let them get a little further on ahead." Dak said.

Dak and Kimly slowed their pace to be far enough behind the young people from The Bamboo Breeze as they made their way around the block and back to the Jeep. They stopped and stood close together under a willow while the young people loaded in their van. The driver of the van made a U-turn and drove in their direction.

Watching the burgundy minivan pass, Kimly muttered, "Why did they come here? They didn't even talk to anyone..."

Driving back to the hotel, Kimly and Dak were both quiet. Kimly broke the silence, "My boys aren't much younger than some of these girls."

"It's sickening," Dak replied.

"Can I ask you a question?" Kimly asked.

"Of course," Dak held his eyes on the road.

"What happened to your wife? You said she died. Was she sick?" Dak said nothing.

"I'm sorry. You don't have to talk about it. I shouldn't have—"

"No, you just surprised me is all. I lost my wife and my daughter in a car accident."

"What? I'm so sorry..." she was staring at him.

"No, it's okay." Whenever Dak spoke of losing Tina—of losing Samantha Jean—he became the comforter. Listeners didn't know what level of sad they should express, how much empathy they should show. They often stumbled over their words. He knew he was partly to blame, his awkwardness sending an opposing message to the one simple truth he wished he could share: There was never a reason to be uncomfortable talking about the ones he loved most. He had been married to Tina for eighteen years. His daughter, Samantha Jean, had been in his life for fourteen years, years that he marked most treasured. When people strayed from conversations about them, it was as if those years never happened.

"She and my wife were in a car accident about four and a half years ago, and they both died."

"Oh my gosh, Dak, I'm so sorry."

"I know. Thanks."

"What happened? I mean, do you mind me asking?"

Dak relayed the story of the winter night on the Clinton Lake Bridge when Tina's SUV hit black ice, spun out of control and went head first into the icy lake. He relayed the story without too much emotion, a skill he had developed over the years. The accident on the bridge was a part of who he was: A man who had lost his wife and daughter. He could see loads of questions building behind Kimly's eyes, and he wondered how long she would be able to contain them. Dak feared Kimly putting on her kid gloves. Questions he could handle, but pity he wouldn't tolerate. Especially not from this woman.

Dak parked in their familiar spot behind the hotel, and Kimly was quiet. She sat staring down at the clunky roll of duct tape on the floorboard. She picked it up and slowly slid her small wrist through its cardboard cylinder. When she finally spoke, her words surprised him, "You must think I'm awful."

"Why on earth would I think you are awful?"

"Because I'm ridiculously selfish. And you have lost so much."

"Okay, well, I don't think you are 'ridiculously selfish.' Strong willed, maybe. Selfish? Naaa...no more than the rest of the world, anyway. But, what does that have to do with what I've lost?"

Kimly took in a deep breath, "Dak, I have two sons at home, I don't think jumping on a plane to Thailand makes me a candidate for 'Mom of the Year.'"

"Okay, I got that, but, Kimly, you aren't staying here forever," he leaned his head forward and tried to get her to make eye contact, "you're going home soon...right?"

Kimly didn't answer him. She stared down at the roll of tape and said nothing. Dak was unsure if he should push her or let her think this one out.

After a few moments, footsteps clamored into the silence as a robust man approached an economy car, which Dak had inadvertently parked a little too close to. Twisting his body so his rear entered the interior of the car first, the man squeezed into his vehicle, but not without making eye contact with Dak, and raising his eyebrows in disgust. The portly man started the ignition and backed out. Kimly looked at Dak who gave a playful, teeth bearing grimace. The headlights from the large man's small car moved through the interior of the Jeep. Kimly twisted her torso and craned her neck to look behind them at the car driving away. Suddenly she exclaimed, "Dak!"

Instinctively Dak shoved his hand in his pocket, grabbed hold of the gun, and flung his head to the left, looking over his shoulder to see what had alarmed her. Dak saw nothing but the dimly lit parking lot.

"The blanket!" Kimly's eyes were locked in on the large trash bin and cardboard-crate fort beside it. "The blanket that fell earlier—it's back up! Someone is sleeping there!"

Dak's heart was pounding, and he wanted to hit her. Well, maybe not hit her, but something close to it. He shook his head and didn't move his hand out of his pocket. Kimly Denim was going to be the death of him.

"Let's go check it out," Kimly dropped the clunky roll of tape and reached for the Jeep's handle, but Dak grabbed her arm. Kimly stopped and looked at him.

Dak waited until she was completely still and looking at him.

"Please," he paused and waited again, "please, can you wait until daylight?"

"But what if he leaves?"

"If he leaves, then he must have somewhere safe to go."

"Seriously—" Kimly started.

"Seriously," Dak interrupted. "If that is a child, and he is gone in the morning, then maybe you are not supposed to be concerned with him. Or, maybe you can leave food in the morning and he will find it when he returns."

"Okay...but I'm coming down at dawn with food."

Oh, at the crack of dawn, I'm sure, Dak thought to himself, but he just nodded at her and climbed out of the Jeep.

As they made their way around to the entrance of the hotel, Kimly kept glancing over her shoulder. Dak took her by the elbow and began to lead her along, "Can you just do me one other favor, Kimly? Can you wake me before you come down here in the morning?"

Kimly tilted her head to the side and gave him a look of exasperation.

"Just humor me," Dak continued.

"You know you can see the trash can and the cardboard fort from the windows? You can see it looking down from our rooms. You knew that, right?"

"No," he really wasn't aware.

"Yep. It's right below us. You have to stand against the glass and look down to your right. Straight down. Or, if you take the screen off you can lean out." She was talking with her hands, which he thought was rather adorable. They had reached the elevator.

Dak pushed the button, "Kimly, please tell me you didn't take the screen off your window."

Kimly smiled. Dak did not.

She tilted her head at him, "What? Is that bad?"

"Forget it," Dak raised his eyebrows and shook his head. "Anyway, I would feel better if you texted me before you came down. I'll come with you."

"I think it's silly. But, fine. You can come down if you want."

"I want," he said plainly, and the elevator doors closed them into the cab.

The exhausted couple exited the elevator and walked around the corner toward their rooms. Kimly started again, "Seriously, Dak, you don't have to follow me down there. You can just look out your window. You can see it perfectly. Well, at least I can see it from my window. Do you want to come in my room and see?"

Dak shook his head and let out a quick laugh, "No, Kimly, I don't want to come in your room and see."

"Okay, good night," she shrugged him off.

"Good night, Friend," Dak waited for Kimly's door to lock before going into his own. *Do you want to come in my room and see?* Dak knew when he got into his room he was in for another discussion with his mirror, and perhaps a cool shower.

25

Sure enough, Kimly was up at dawn. Dak's cell chirped to notify him he had a text message.

I'm going. You coming?

He typed in his answer: **Give me a minute**

Dak shifted on his pillow and wondered what her plan was. This wasn't The Bamboo Breeze; it wasn't like they had extra food lying around the hotel room. He grabbed his jeans and shoes, and within a few minutes, he opened the door. Kimly stood leaning against the wall across from his room, arms folded across her chest and her long locks falling around her shoulders.

"You don't have to come down with me," she sounded apologetic, "I'm sure that I'm fine."

"Yes, I'm sure you are, but…this is better," he contended.

The Kongkam Hotel had a morning breakfast buffet, but it wasn't open for another thirty-five minutes, and there were only a couple kitchen workers making preparations. Dak followed at a short distance as Kimly glided through the small opening from the banquet room and into the kitchen. A thin man stood chopping vegetables and placing them in a metal chafing dish.

"Excuse me, sir," Kimly spoke, but the knife wielding man barely glanced up at her. Kimly stood for a moment, said nothing and smiled at him. Finally, she continued, "How are you today?"

The kitchen worker seemed genuinely bewildered as to why a beautiful woman was interrupting him just to offer pleasantries. Dak decided rather than helping her with simple Thai phrases, he would let her find her way through this one alone. He leaned against a stainless steel table near the kitchen entrance and smiled as he watched her performance.

"I," Kimly paused, as if merely mentioning herself was supposed to give him a reason to be interested. "I," she began again, "need some food. I was wondering if you could help me." Kimly talked slowly and deliberately, "There's someone who is sick. I need some food for someone who is sick."

Dak raised his eyebrows at her from across the room. The chef looked away from her and back down at the vegetables he was chopping. Dak couldn't help but smile at Kimly's awkward attempts to communicate with the hotel worker, and he shook his head when she tilted her head back at him and shrugged her shoulders. Her vulnerability was charming, and as much as he enjoyed watching her struggle, he decided to assist her. At the same moment Dak moved closer, readying himself to translate, the thin man rested his knife on the chopping board and strutted across the room.

Moving about the kitchen, the thin man loaded a plate with three biscuits, a heaping spoonful of egg and kale casserole, and a small fruit salad of pineapple and rambutan. He brought the bounty to Kimly and handed it to her. She accepted the plate while profusely thanking him. The thin man raised his index finger and motioned her to wait where she was. He disappeared deeper into the kitchen. Kimly glowed at Dak and threw him a wink. Dak found it easy to accept her gloating, knowing she was actually startled by the kitchen worker's response.

A moment later the thin man returned with a bowl and handed it to Kimly, who thanked him profusely. Dak understood when he noticed the thin man was blushing: this woman's beauty reflected off the surface of every stainless steel chafing dish around them; her vulnerability made her more charming and made him the hero.

The cardboard-crate blanket fort hadn't changed one bit since the night before. Kimly approached slowly, holding the plate in one hand and a bowl of curry soup in the other, she lowered the food to the edge of the fort and sat them on the ground.

"Hello...sawateeka?" Kimly called out as she slowly crawled forward and pulled the blanket back.

The shuffle happened so swiftly that Dak almost missed it while he was surveying the makeshift fort. Kimly fell backwards, landing on her bottom, and the cardboard, the crate and the blanket fell forward. Dak watched as a waif of a child bounded out from under the blanket and the cardboard and ran down the alley.

"Wait!" Kimly yelled. The child's clothing was threadbare. Her tiny shoeless feet pounded against the pavement, and her long ratted hair flailed behind her. Dak and Kimly watched as the urchin ran away, rapid as a raging river.

Dak looked over at Kimly sitting on the asphalt, but when she looked back at him he quickly diverted his eyes. *She had been right; it was a child.* Suddenly, the thought of his pillow and his cushy bed upstairs repulsed him. Seemingly out of the blue, the miracle of Kimly's conversion in the tiny Tai Lue church flashed through Dak's mind, and he winced; once again, God was revealing things to Kimly while Dak sat by holding tight to his stagnated beliefs.

Without words, Dak set about putting the fort back together. Dak was able to adjust the crates and cardboard to build a sturdier fort. With one hand on the fort's cardboard wall, he nodded his head at Kimly and said, "Come here, hold onto this for a minute."

Kimly took hold of the cardboard, and Dak crossed the parking lot, where he opened the door to his Jeep and rummaged about. He returned with gray duct tape and a long piece of plastic. Dak went to work, and when he was finished, he had manufactured a sturdy and weather resistant fort for the child. Kimly shook out the lavender blanket and laid it back in the fort. She took the food and set it just inside the fort up against the wall and sighed, "I hope she comes back."

As the couple trudged back inside the hotel, Dak begged Kimly, "Please, stay in the hotel, don't go anywhere, just for a few hours. I've got to get some sleep."

"I'm wide awake," Kimly responded. "I won't leave the hotel, but I thought about something, and I want to check it out."

"You thought about something?" Dak stopped in front of the elevator and pressed the UP button.

"The woman at the restaurant—" Kimly started.

"The owner?" Dak pressed two fingers to the bridge of his nose. The stress-filled, late nights were wearing on him.

"Yes, the owner said, 'so you found out about us before you came' and at the time I was thinking about the business card. So, I thought that's what she meant, but I don't think it's what she meant at all."

The doors to the elevator opened, Dak entered, but soon realized Kimly had no intention of following him. He stood for a moment, and then stepped back off the elevator, and the doors closed behind him.

"Well," Kimly continued, "later she said, 'leave my family alone'— Dak, she thought we already knew something about her family. Like, we had found something out about her *family*, and that's why we were there. And when she said, 'you people,' I think she meant *reporters* because I had told her I was a journalist."

"I'm sorry, maybe I'm tired...I'm not following."

"No, I know, it's a lot of guessing, and I'm not sure what she meant by any of it. But, maybe I can find out whatever it was that she *thought* I already knew."

"How? How are you going to find out about her family? You don't even know her name; you don't know anything about her..."

"Never underestimate the power of a curious mind," Kimly said as she pressed the elevator UP button. "I need to get my note-book; I'll ride up with you."

"Ah gee, thanks," Dak winked.

Dak spent most of the day resting and reading. He and Kimly ate a late lunch together in the hotel lounge and Kimly filled him in on what she had discovered so far, which wasn't a whole lot. She had been able to eliminate a lot of unsuccessful leads, but she hadn't found anything that gave them new insight. They decided in the evening, after the restaurant's dinner rush, they would go back to The Bamboo Breeze and watch the young people leave again, hoping to find a pattern in their movements.

That evening as Dak and Kimly were walking through the hotel parking lot, Kimly said, "I found some good stuff this afternoon. I think I may be onto something—" she stopped short, "Dak, what is that?" Her eyes were fixed on a round bump on the pavement, near the cardboard-crate fort.

About three feet away from the fort, the bowl which had held the soup was upside down on the ground, which was wet from a storm that had passed through earlier in the day. Dak bent down and picked up the glass bowl. Drippings of the curry substance fell to the ground. He looked up at Kimly, "It looks like she dumped the soup out on the ground," he whispered.

The two tiptoed over to the fort and leaned to spy behind the wall. There was no one in the fort, but inside sat an empty plate. The couple turned and looked at each other. Kimly was beaming. Dak carried the bowl along with him, and they moved back towards the Jeep.

Once seated in the Jeep, Kimly grabbed Dak's arm, "She came back!" then leaned back and pulled on her seatbelt. With her head resting against the headrest, she smiled at Dak and said, "Okay, now we know, she doesn't like soup."

Dak and Kimly drove to The Bamboo Breeze and parked across the street. As they began their stakeout, Kimly began to share the information she had found online since they had last spoke.

"I searched several travel websites until I found one with some tourist reviews for The Bamboo Breeze. At first it seemed like another dead end, but there was one comment, here read this, I printed it out for you," Kimly handed Dak a piece of paper. "I found it on a site called TripTalks."

```
THE BAMBOO BREEZE WAS OUR OASIS ****** My
husband and I were pleasantly surprised by
the delicious entrées at The Bamboo Breeze.
We enjoyed it tremendously, and found
ourselves returning several times while
staying in Mai Sai. The Navarro family has a
knack at making people feel welcome. We
enjoyed spending time with them, and the
patio was charming and relaxing. We would
give them seven stars if we could.
```

Dak looked up at Kimly, "Navarro family."

"Exactly. And, I was thinking...how many Navarro's could be living in Mai Sai, Thailand? So I started searching, but it's much more difficult to search here than it would be in the States, because many of the websites are not translated into English."

"I can help you with that," Dak smiled.

"That's what I thought at first, too. But then I remembered the accent of the waitress and owner. They were very similar and distinct, so I started looking for anything I could find on a Navarro family in New Jersey or New York."

"You looked for news about a family with an Italian name from New Jersey? Ha! Ngom kem nai maha-samut!" Dak laughed.

"What?!" Kimly instinctively laughed, as well.

"Ngom kem nai maha-samut is a Thai proverb that means a person is diving after a needle in the ocean…" Dak explained.

"Oh, gotcha. So, kinda like looking for a needle in a haystack?" Kimly thumbed through her papers, "Well…guess who found the needle!" Kimly proclaimed.

She handed Dak another paper she had printed out as she explained, "At first, I couldn't find anything. I mean, you're right; there are a lot of Navarros on the East Coast. So, I narrowed my search to news about New York Navarros, but I added Thailand into the search engine. That's when I found *this* on a Missing Child website," she motioned to the paper Dak was holding.

"Missing children?" Dak looked down at the paper in his hands. The paper had a picture of a young girl with curly brown hair and dark honey eyes. She was wearing a yellow ribbon in her hair. Under her picture was the name, Anna Navarro.

Date Missing: August 25, 2005
Missing From: Kuala Lumpur, Malaysia

"Malaysia?" Dak looked up at Kimly.
"Keep reading…" she whispered.

DOB: May 16, 2000
Age at Disappearance: 5
Sex: Female
Race: Caucasian/Italian
Height: 3'1"
Weight: 32 lbs.
Eyes: Brown
Hair: Brown/Curly
Other: Anna has freckles and a small mole on

her right cheek.
Circumstances: Anna went missing from Kuala
Lumpur, Malaysia. She may have been moved to
another region in Asia. Investigations have
led officials to Thailand and Burma.

"Thailand...but, this was over a decade ago. She would be much older now. Wait? Do you think this little girl is the waitress we met at the restaurant?"

"At first that's exactly what I thought. But, if the owner abducted Anna, she wouldn't be using the Navarro name anymore, and when I looked for more articles about Anna Navarro, I found this." Kimly handed Dak another paper.

"You were busy..." he mumbled.

Press Release
Albany, NY October 4, 2005

SafeKids, a leader in child abduction and
abuse prevention, responds to recent news of
kidnapped child, Anna Navarro, by offering a
free seminar this Monday night, October 10
at 7:00 PM in the cafeteria of Westlake
Elementary School. SafeKids is a nonprofit
organization attempting to raise awareness
and educate parents on training children to
make safe choices.

Anna Navarro, the five-year-old daughter of
Anthony and Brianne Navarro, residents of
Albany, was abducted while the family
vacationed in Malaysia. The tragedy, which
occurred in August of this year, stunned the
community when the Navarros lost not only
one child, but two.

The Navarro family was vacationing in the
border city of Kuala Lumpur when little

Anna, the youngest of four children, wandered off and was abducted. Anthony Raymond Navarro, Jr., the oldest child of the Navarro family, saw the abduction and raced after the truck. Tragically, the 18-year-old honor student and star athlete was struck by an oncoming car and killed while in pursuit of the child abductors and his little sister.

As of today, the investigation into the disappearance of Anna has resulted in a series of dead ends.

"I think the woman we met at The Bamboo Breeze is the mother. I think she is Brianne Navarro. I think they are here because they are looking for Anna."

Dak watched Kimly talking, and then he looked through the papers again. When he looked out his window he had limited visibility due to the rain which was now pounding against the pavement. Looking at the restaurant through the lens of what he had just read changed the way he saw it. Even in the dark, wet night, its sinister appearance was altered.

The couple rehashed the information for over an hour, pulling together little clues that confirmed Kimly's discovery. "The press release said there were four children in the family. Maybe the girl we met is one of the children. Maybe she is Anna's sister." Dak said. As they continued to make guesses about the family, the rain lifted and people began to pour out onto the streets again. Dak looked across the Jeep at Kimly, but she wasn't looking at him. Her eyes were fixed outside where three Buddhist monks in orange robes were walking up the street, each one holding a peach-colored umbrella. The hems of their garments were soaked with rain and mud, darkening the base of their robes to a burnt orange. The graduated tone and the lights reflecting on the wet streets appeared artful and planned.

"But...why a restaurant?" Kimly said solemnly. "How does that lead them to Anna?"

That night the young people working at the restaurant followed a routine that was similar to the night before. After locking the gates to the restaurant's patio, they set some food near the trash cans and loaded into the burgundy van. This time Dak saw the young man who stayed behind. He walked with the others to the van, but then turned and headed away from the parking lot and down the alley.

The burgundy van did not travel in the direction they had traveled the previous two nights. This time the van headed east on Highway 1041. Dak and Kimly followed at a reasonable distance, but they never let the van get too far ahead. The van had been traveling for about thirty minutes when it slowed and turned south into a neighborhood. Dak turned the Jeep to follow. The driver of the van looped up and down the residential streets for about ten minutes before arriving again at Highway 1041. Dak followed and they were led back into Mai Sai. The van never made a stop until it arrived outside the house with the metal gate. Dak and Kimly watched as their former waitress, Ruby Red, the one they now assumed was part of the Navarro family, climbed out of the van and punched the code into the keypad. The rusty wheels rolled and the gate opened for the van to pass through.

Dak and Kimly drove across the highway and parked behind the hotel. The first thing Kimly did was walk over to the makeshift fort to see if the little girl was hiding within its walls. Dak followed. This time, the girl was there. She sat with her back against the wall and the lavender blanket pulled around her.

"Well, hello…" Kimly whispered. The little girl's eyes widened and she pulled the blanket up to her chin. "How are you doing in there?" Kimly moved in closer, and the child pushed the blanket down to the ground, jumped to her feet into a squatting position. "Wait—no, don't run." Kimly lifted her hand, "Stay here…I'll go." Kimly slowly backed away from the fort.

Dak and Kimly walked to the hotel's overhang and stood staring at the flimsy fort. The rain had done a little damage, but it was holding up better than Dak had expected.

"I keep hearing my mother's voice." Dak said.

Kimly looked over at him, "Her voice? What do you mean?"

"Mother was a romantic. She believed in causes, in children. She believed in things people can't touch. I think that's why she fell for my father." Dak took a step back and leaned against the wall near the back doors of the hotel.

Kimly followed and went to where he stood, "He was that way, too?"

"Yes, I mean, from what I've gathered. I never knew my father. From what I understand, he fought for freedom—for democracy. For the democracy Thailand knows today."

"Wow…" Kimly whispered.

"I know. Wow, right? Tonight, earlier tonight…you asked, 'why a restaurant?' and it kept ringing in my head, and I kept hearing something my mother would say."

Kimly raised her eyebrows, and tilted her head.

"Ying tee dieow dai nok sorng dtua. It's kind of like saying 'a person kills two birds with one stone.' You've heard that saying, right?" Dak asked.

"Well, yeah, of course. I mean, not in Thai." Kimly smiled.

"Kimly, what if you are correct. If this is the same Navarro family, then of course they are here looking for Anna…that would make sense. If someone had taken my daughter, I wouldn't be able to return to the life I'd once had—" Dak stopped short.

Kimly looked out at the fort and watched the rain bouncing off the small puddles surrounding it. "So, you think they are here looking for Anna…I get that, but I don't think I'm following what you mean by two birds with one stone."

"What if they came here looking for Anna, and when they saw the level of poverty and homelessness, they responded to it like you have with this little girl?" Dak motioned to the fort.

"They are luring the children in with food to *protect* them." Kimly looked from the fort back to Dak. "We have to go back. Dak, we have to talk to Brianne Navarro! Whoever placed that card in my passport wanted me to find this family!"

26

The next day, Kimly and Dak sat together in the hotel lobby, and searched the internet for more information about the Navarro family. They were able to confirm Anna Navarro's disappearance on an Interpol website, and they were able to find several news stories that had used the same facts from the Associated Press wires.

Finally in an archived article posted on an Asian Correspondence website, Kimly found the twist that must have soured Brianne Navarro with the press. "Check this out…" Kimly said to Dak who was seated next to her reading some articles they had printed. He leaned closer and looked over her shoulder.

31January2006, In an extraordinary twist, detectives now believe Anna Navarro may have been murdered by a family member and her body disposed in a nearby canal. The five-year-old disappeared while the family was on holiday in Kuala Lumpur. Anthony Navarro, Anna's brother, was killed in a traffic accident around the same time the child disappeared, and police suspect he may have been involved in Anna's disappearance. The Navarro family was not available for comment.

"The press turned on them…" Dak whispered to Kimly.

"They always do…" Kimly mumbled and continued scrolling down the page. Halfway through the story there was a picture of Anna's parents. "And, there she is," Kimly said.

There were two pictures of Anna's parents; one showed the couple with all four of their children, two boys and two girls, posing for a family portrait in a park. They were easily one of the most attractive couples Dak had ever seen. The father had dark eyes and a thick moustache and the mother was blonde with dark brown eyebrows and soft features, and each of the children was equally stunning. The second photo was a candid shot of the couple as they exited the police building. The beaming smiles from the first portrait had vanished and both the husband and the wife wore dark sunglasses in the second shot, but it was definitely the woman they had met at the restaurant. She was older now, and her features were no longer as soft, but she was just as blonde and easily recognizable.

"Well, what'd ya think?" Kimly asked.

"I think you're going to want to go back to The Bamboo Breeze."

"I think you're right!"

When they approached the patio at The Bamboo Breeze, Dak took Kimly's arm and held her back, "Let's wait for someone to greet us," he leaned in and spoke low.

Kimly nodded, and stayed by Dak's side. Reading about the family's loss reminded Dak of his own, and while he hadn't ever been under fire for Tina's accident, the guilt he felt was still strong. In the early months following the accident, Dak often fantasized about the night Tina and Samantha Jean died, and he changed the outcome. He imagined himself driving them through the storm, he imagined himself gripping the steering wheel as the SUV spun on the black ice, and he even imagined himself going off the bridge and into the icy water. Of course, in his fantasies he was always able to save the ones he loved. Even without an accuser, guilt had found him.

"So, look who's back," the voice came from behind and Dak and Kimly both turned to face the blonde woman.

"We are, but hear us out—" Kimly said, "it's not what you think."

"Really? Not what I think…let me guess, you want to do a piece on my family. A 'where are they now' story. And you're going to try to convince me that it's worth my time by manipulating me into believing that this will somehow help us find Anna."

"No, that's not it, at all—" Kimly started.

"Mrs. Navarro, can we sit down and talk?" Dak interrupted.

She didn't respond. She locked eyes with Dak for a moment. The woman was attractive, but years of exhaustion sat around her eyes.

"I told you I came to Thailand from the United States to write a story. That's true, and the story I want to write is about the slave trade. I want to write about human trafficking happening in Thailand."

The woman stood for a moment looking at them and then she said, "Come with me," and she turned and walked towards the alley.

Kimly began to follow, but Dak grabbed Kimly's arm and spoke up, "Um, if you don't mind..." Both women stopped and looked at him.

"I would prefer we talk on the patio." While Dak was compassionate about what the family had gone through, he also remembered that they had witnessed a child being taken away—and other than their own hunches, they didn't know what had happened to that child.

Brianne Navarro walked back and led the way to a table on the outer edge of the patio. Once they were seated, Dak spoke up, "I'm sorry, we aren't aiming to be difficult, it's just before we knew who you were, we were watching the restaurant and we saw something unusual in the early hours.

"What did you see?" Brianne asked.

"Well, we saw a small boy, and he was alone. We watched as he dug through the trash on the side of your building."

"I already told you, we take great pride in providing food for the people of Mai Sai. But first, go back—you said you were watching us before you knew about Anna." Brianne said. She looked back and forth between Dak and Kimly and then said, "I'd like to know why."

Dak could tell Brianne Navarro was a woman who had learned how to control an interview.

"Mrs. Navarro," Kimly said, "we were given the name of your restaurant by a hotel worker in Chiang Mai." Brianne's eyes were locked on Kimly, and Dak watched the woman's eyes become softer as she processed what Kimly had shared.

"Who? Do you know her name?" Brianne shifted in her seat and looked around the restaurant.

"No, I don't know her name. I don't know anything about her," Kimly stated flatly. "I mean, at first I wasn't even sure if I was supposed to find the business card. It was left in my passport. But, since arriving here, we have seen something—"

"Something that could be alarming," Dak interrupted.

"What did you see?" Brianne asked.

Dak lowered his voice, "We saw a small boy disappear from your restaurant, and we are concerned about what has happened to him."

"You're concerned...oh! Oh my word! You think we took him for...oh, no! No, he's fine. He's at the house!"

"I'm sorry? He's at the house? What house?" Dak ventured. He guessed the boy was at the house hidden behind the metal gate, but he hoped she would expound.

Brianne's voice lowered to a whisper, "We watch the little ones who come to get food from the trash, and we learn who they are and where they live with their families. If we discover they are living on the street, we take them to the house. We rescue them in an effort to protect them and teach them how to survive."

"The young people working here...do they all live with you? At the house?" Dak asked.

"Well not all of them. But, yes. Quite a few," Brianne replied. "But, I assure you, they are not slaves. These young people are free to leave. They are paid fairly, and they are provided for and nurtured in the same way we care for our own children."

Dak repeated what he thought he was hearing, "So, you lure the children to safety, and then you care for them in your home?"

"Well, not me alone!" Brianne quickly explained, "My husband and I, this is what we do. Together. And our kids, Aaron and Alicia."

"Can we see the house?" Kimly asked. Dak looked across the table at her, but Kimly's eyes were fixed on Brianne Navarro.

"The house? It's not much, really. It's just a house," Brianne looked around the sparse restaurant, and then placed her hand to her chin and looked back and forth between Dak and Kimly. "A maid you say? In Chiang Mai..."

Brianne took a deep breath, and then said, "You can come tonight. I'll give you the address."

Dak refrained from telling Brianne they already knew the address, the description, and had even witnessed one of her elderly neighbors going about his morning exercise routine. Instead, he just nodded when she supplied the information, and the three agreed on a time to meet later that evening.

Once Dak and Kimly were in the Jeep, Kimly asked, "Do you think it's legit?"

"I actually do." Dak answered, but his enthusiasm didn't mirror hers.

"What's wrong…" Kimly drew the second word out, and Dak wasn't sure she was really asking him a question or complaining about his lack of excitement.

"Kimly we need to talk." Dak put the Jeep in gear and pulled out onto Highway 1041, making a sharp U-turn and heading west towards the hotel. He needed to tell her about what had happened in the Tai Lue church. He realized that she still had no idea the miracle God had already worked in her life. He couldn't let her move along chasing this story without knowing that there was a dynamic story happening in her own life.

In silence, they drove to a small open air restaurant and took a table near the back of the patio. Without making much eye contact with one another or the young waiter, they each ordered a soda.

Finally, Dak whispered, "Kimly, do think you should go home? I think it's great that we found the Navarros…but, to what end? Kimly, this isn't your life." As soon as the words were out of his mouth he knew he was being a coward. He wanted to tell her what had happened in Tai Lue, but it was as if he was blocked.

Kimly took a deep breath, "I'm not ready to go home…" she paused when the waiter approached the table and set down their drinks. "But, I understand what you're saying, Dak. I do."

"I don't think you do, Kimly. You do see that you *cannot* write about the Navarros, right? These people have been through too much, and you can't draw the spotlight back to them again. If what the Navarros are doing is on the up and up, you cannot jeopardize their work for your own, I don't know…*ego*."

"Dak, it's not ego."

"No?" Dak challenged. "Kimly, your pursuit of significance is enslaving you. As long as you are driven to earn accolades and make a name for yourself, you aren't much different than those you are trying to free."

"I'm not enslaved, Dak." Kimly responded.

"Slavery comes in many forms." Dak took a drink of his soda.

"The truth is, I feel like I'm supposed to still be here. Like, I belong here."

"Kimly, how can you say you belong here?" he kept his voice low and calm, "You belong at home with your sons."

"They're not little," she quickly interjected.

"I know, Kimly," he paused. "Jacob and Dylan are thirteen. I know how old they are. I know Jacob is a great goalie, but a little too cocky for his mother's liking and I know that Dylan prefers playing his guitar to spending time with his friends. I know everything you've told me. But, I know something else, Kimly. I know they still need you."

Kimly looked down at her soda and then at her hands.

"Kimly, don't you miss being there? I mean, don't you miss something about it?"

She was either being stubborn, or she wasn't. Either way, it didn't matter. Kimly unleashed an explosion of sarcasm, "Oh sure, I miss some things. Let me think about what I miss...hmmm...how about having *no real purpose*. Yeah, that's what I miss. Oh...no. wait, I miss fighting with my soon to be *ex-husband*. That was always great fun. Dak, I belong here. If you want to leave, fine, leave. But, I belong here." She looked at him, her eyes welling with tears. She looked away and focused on the bottle of soda in front of her.

"Look at me." Dak whispered, but Kimly didn't. "Kimly, look at me. Okay, fine, don't look. But, at least hear me out. Everything you have been saying all starts with the same idea. YOU. It's all about you. It's about how you feel, about what you think and what you want. And, I'm sorry to tell you this...but this isn't *The Kimly Denim Show*. You cannot go through life screaming or whispering, 'Hey everyone! I'm Kimly Denim, and I do what I want.'"

Kimly raised her chin but still didn't make eye contact. Instead, she turned her head slightly, and gazed over his shoulder.

"Most people have adopted the same self-absorbed mentality, so I don't blame you for grabbing onto it as well. But Kimly, you're on a new path. You may not realize it, but God has already worked a miracle on your behalf," Dak was surprised how the word 'miracle' made his voice quiver.

"That's great, Dak," Kimly's voice rose, "but my decision doesn't change the entire trajectory of my life..."

"It most certainly does!" Dak interrupted. "The life you are living now is going to be different—if you allow it to be. I'm not saying what I want to say...doing the right thing is not necessarily going to be doing the easy thing."

Kimly's dark eyes shifted to the left and made contact with Dak's. Her voice was quiet, but impassioned, "You don't think I know that?" she tilted her head in and whispered. Dak raised an eyebrow and lifted his glass to his mouth.

"Seriously, Dak, you think I don't know about sacrifice? I have been unhappily married my entire adult life. I think I know how to 'do the right thing' for everyone else."

Dak couldn't help but shake his head and let out a frustrated laugh, "Kimly, that's not the same. First of all, you chose to stay married out of fear, not out of freedom. Those are two different ways to be married. And they make for two completely different marriages."

"Oh my gosh...you're not making any sense." Dak reasoned he had frustrated her, and she shook her head and responded, "It's just a matter of terminology. Fear, freedom. It's the same thing."

"No, Kimly, it's *entirely different*. You chose to stay in your marriage because you were afraid of the consequences if you left. Not because you knew there would be a rejoicing if you stayed! You chose to stay because you were fearful of being judged, despised, and unwanted, not because you believed you could find peace where you were."

"You don't know anything about why I stayed. You think because I've told you a few stories about—"

"What I think," he interrupted her, his voice starting off louder than he had intended, "is that you stayed in your marriage because you were scared to death of leaving." Dak took a breath and continued, "You didn't stay because you wanted it to *work*. You didn't stay because you wanted it to get better. You stayed because you didn't want to feel like a failure. Again."

Dak knew he had gotten her attention when she opened her mouth as if she were going to respond, then she stopped and looked away.

"What?" Dak was nearly whispering, "Kimly, say it. Please, say it...whatever it is."

"I never thought about it in those terms," Kimly said, but she still didn't look at him. When she finally raised her eyes to his, Kimly said, "I mean, I never considered the things you are saying, but they don't feel like new thoughts either. It's like I've always known what you are saying. My only reason for staying has been fear, but I don't understand..." Kimly's voice trailed off.

"What, Kimly? What don't you understand?" Dak had become accustomed to Kimly's ability to pretend she was being completely transparent, and he recognized this as her genuinely allowing herself to be seen. "Kimly, you have the freedom to leave your husband. You could do it. Would there be negative consequences? Absolutely. Would God see you through the hard times? Without a doubt. Would you experience *all the blessings* God has planned for your life? *Nope.*"

She tilted her head at him. "So, really you're still talking about fear, then?"

Dak tilted his head back and squinted at her. Kimly continued, "You know I am falling for you, Dak. I'm crazy about you. There is no way you can be oblivious to my feelings. And, you know what I think, Dak...I think you're falling for me, too. I can feel it when you look at me."

Dak held her gaze.

Kimly took in a deep breath and continued, "And, even though you tell *me* to choose the right thing out of some new freedom that I don't fully understand, you are rejecting me out of *fear*. Your fear is the fear of *losing* the blessing of God."

"No, Kimly. My fear is not *being* a blessing to God. But, freedom comes in knowing that if I aim to please him, *He* will provide the blessing."

"You're lucky, Dak. I'm fairly certain that any blessings God has planned for me aren't going to be the things I yearn for."

Dak shifted in his seat, leaning forward. "Kimly, if I followed my every yearning, those yearnings would become gods in my life. Eventually, all that pleasure, would own me."

"Slavery..."

"Yes, slavery! Exactly what I've been saying!" Dak voice rose; Kimly looked around the enclosed patio. Lowering his voice, Dak continued, "Just like people become slaves to their own fears, they become slaves to their own desires. A person may think they are free because they don't submit to God, or they 'follow their heart' and fulfill their yearnings—but if that person is dependent on those yearnings being met in order to be 'free'—how is that freedom?"

"So, what are you saying? I can't have any desires? Some of my desires run deep, Dak."

"I know. I hear you. But, have you ever considered that what you consider a deep desire may not be so *deep*?"

"Are you calling me shallow?" Kimly said, half laughing.

"No—not at all." Dak smiled. "I certainly didn't mean it that way;

I'm just saying that perhaps we aren't as cognizant to who we are and what we need as we claim to be. Perhaps when we trade our deep desires for a life lived by faith—a life where we make *everyday* choices that reflect the love of Christ—maybe that life will fulfill desires that run *even deeper* than the yearnings demanding satisfaction."

27

Hours later, when Dak and Kimly arrived at the Navarro's house and the metal gate closed behind them, they found themselves in a hidden paradise. Teak trees lined the perimeter, camouflaging the wall almost completely. Purple, yellow and orange flowers danced amid shrubs, several of which had been trimmed into animal shapes. In the back corner of the lot, behind a chain link fence, a healthy vegetable garden grew. Near the front of the house, a small fountain was perched next to a pond. The fountain's water overflowed and fell effortlessly into the murky basin. Next to the pond there was a picnic table. And, in the middle of the expansive grass yard, there was a child's play set: swings, monkey bars and a fort with a slide. Beneath the slide a grumpy looking duck was nestled in the shade.

Brianne Navarro appeared from the side of the house and greeted her guests, "Hi, I'm so glad you found it. It can be easily missed from the street."

"Thank you for having us, Mrs. Navarro. We won't take too much of your—" Kimly said.

"Call me Bri. Please," the hostess interrupted and extended her hand to Kimly.

"Thank you," Kimly replied.

"Yes, thank you for opening your home. I'm Dak. Dak Kesapan. I don't think I introduced myself at the restaurant." Dak shook Bri's hand, and he remembered how Bri had walked into the restaurant full of confidence and assurance, but upon realizing she was encountering the Press, the woman's face had grown tired and worn. Her face this evening was a blend of the two.

"I spoke with my husband, and he'll be joining us shortly. He was quick to remind me that we Navarros are not the only ones who'd like to see a world where children are no longer victimized. I hope you'll accept my apologies for my behavior when we first met."

"No apologies needed, Mrs.—uh, Bri." Kimly said, and they followed Bri into the house through the front door of what appeared to be a fairly organized orphanage. The entryway was lined with shelves which were divided into small cubbies. The cube-like shelves held sweaters, jackets and shoes.

"Let's go in here," Bri directed Dak and Kimly into what would be considered a living room in most houses, but theirs had been transformed into a library. There were four tables, each with a lamp plugged into the electrical outlets that served as the tables' centerpieces. One of the tables was lower to the ground, and it had several small chairs around it. At the end of the small table, there was a large computer monitor. The walls were lined with bookshelves;

there were several bean bag chairs in one corner. Dak noticed an unfinished wooden puzzle strewn on the floor.

"This is where we do school. Everyone has to learn English. Fortunately, each child we have rescued has been able to speak the language of another person already living in the house, but we try to get them talking in English as quickly as possible."

"So, the kids speak many different languages?" Kimly asked.

"Yes, the most common are Thai, Rvwang, and Malay. English is considered the second language of most Thai people. This is why we encourage English. Plus, it's our strong suit!" Bri laughed.

A child was crying in another part of the house, which was a little unsettling for Dak, and he turned his head in the direction from which the cries came.

"This new little guy doesn't like bath time." Bri said as she led them into the dining area and offered them something to drink, apologizing for her husband's absence. "Anthony's the hardest working man in Thailand," Bri bragged. "Probably in all of Southeast Asia," she continued.

"If you don't mind my asking, what does your husband do?" Kimly asked.

"He's a buyer and an expeditor for a large fabric company in the States. He works with the distributors and he is responsible for doing factory inspections." Bri handed Dak a glass of water. "I'm sorry! Do you want ice? I've adapted to the culture here and always forget about the ice we were so used to in the States."

Dak shook his head and took a drink of the tepid water. Bri continued talking, "It doesn't sound like a difficult job, but there is a lot of traveling involved and a lot of heartbreak."

"Heartbreak?" the word came off Kimly's lips almost slowly, and her brows furrowed.

"Well, in accordance with fair trade practices, the inspections of the factories can be random and spontaneous. For the regulation of what is considered compliant with safety and health standards, a random visit is necessary. But, sometimes Anthony comes across factories which are non-compliant."

"Noncompliant...meaning?" Kimly asked.

"Noncompliant meaning the factory is, in the worst case, using slave labor. And, when Anthony encounters a non-compliant factory, he goes—actually we both go—on an emotional rollercoaster." Bri smiled her sad smile, "we are filled with hopeful stress."

"Hopeful stress...because of Anna?" Kimly asked. Dak noticed that Anna's name fell from Kimly's tongue with tentative tenderness.

Bri smiled her sad smile again, "Yes, and I'm sorry 'bout that. When we met the other day, I must have sounded like a crazy lady. It's just that, for a while, the buzz of media around us was pretty awful, and we couldn't get any relief from it. Anna, my daughter, disappeared ten years ago, and I forget the story has died down since then. After the initial stories, the press that insisted we were lying...started reporting that my boys killed their sister and covered up her murder. It was better for tourism if we were seen as a dysfunctional family."

"I'm sorry..." Kimly offered.

"Yes, well...Anna...she is why we are here. We have never given up hope of finding her. We hope we will find her in a factory, but we have to look in the awful places, too. We have to go to the places that are far more frightening."

"We read that she was abducted in Malaysia." Dak said.

"Yes, we were in Malaysia for Anthony's job. My oldest son had just graduated from high school, so we decided to turn my husband's business trip into a family vacation. One we would all remember. We had been in Malaysia for less than a week, and someone grabbed Anna at a restaurant."

"That's awful," Kimly's eyes were locked in on the woman.

"Yes, it is. Anna was just a baby. She was five at the time."

"And your oldest...that was...Anthony Jr?" Kimly asked in a near whisper.

"Yes. My son, Tony, he and Aaron wanted to walk to a restaurant down the street from the hotel. Alicia, my other daughter, wasn't feeling well, so I told them they could go, and I decided to stay back at the hotel with the girls. Anna begged to go with her brothers. Anna was Tony's biggest fan, and his feelings for his baby sister were mutual. He promised they would be quick.

"The three of them were standing in the restaurant, waiting for take-out, when Anna walked to the front of the restaurant where there were dead chickens hanging in the window. Anna was captivated by the chickens. Tony had just looked over at his brother, Aaron, and said 'Let's go freak Anna out and pretend the chickens are talking.' Anna, meanwhile, wandered a couple steps out the front door. The boys were crouching down a few feet away, laughing when suddenly, Aaron heard Tony yell, 'He's got Anna!'

"Tony must have seen them grab her from the sidewalk, and he jumped up and went running out the door. Aaron ran outside to see what was happening, but slipped and fell. By the time he reached the sidewalk, he saw his brother running down the street chasing a black truck with a covering made of burlap, plastic, and wood. The truck made a sharp turn, and he watched his brother follow it around the corner."

Dak's eyes were locked on Bri who had paused and stared straight ahead. Kimly spoke softly, "I'm sorry, you don't have to—"

"No, sorry, I'm okay. It's the strangest thing, losing a child," Bri smiled a disarming smile, tinged with grief. "The complexity is difficult to explain. Most days I'm fine. But, every so often, seemingly out of nowhere, I'm knocked over by a wave of sadness that I can't shake." Dak's eyes dropped down to his hands.

"I can't even imagine," Kimly was quick to reply. She looked over at Dak, but Dak did not lift his eyes to meet Kimly's.

"Aaron said he watched Tony disappear around the corner, and then a few moments later there was the sound of crashing metal and screaming, and Aaron ran down the street. Tony had been hit by a truck which had sent him flying into another car…" Bri's voice cracked lightly. She stopped talking and placed her hand up to her mouth. "I'm sorry…"

"No reason to be sorry…" Dak shook his head.

Bri took a deep breath, "My son's neck broke and he was killed instantly."

Kimly leaned back in her chair and looked across the table. Dak felt Kimly's eyes on him, but he didn't dare look up. He stared intently at his calloused palms. The combination of Bri's story with his own history was too much, and Dak feared making eye contact with either of these women, at this moment, might break him.

Little feet came bounding down the hallway and stopped suddenly at the doorway. Standing before them was the small child they had seen digging through the trash days before at The Bamboo Breeze. He was wearing royal blue pajamas with a familiar red S across the chest. The boy's dark hair was wet and uncombed, and he was holding a small train engine. He looked across the room at the three adults, and then he turned abruptly and ran away hollering something indiscernible.

"It's a blessing to have others who help with the children," Bri commented as the small child's boisterous cheer echoed down the hallway. "All of the young people who live with us have jobs. The youngest ones are taught to help with household chores and gardening. The older ones work in the restaurant. Some have learned mechanical skills for working on cars and scooters. We've taught many children to sew and cook. And all of the older children help with the younger children."

A door opened behind Dak, and instinctively he shifted in his chair.

"Hey, are there any Navarros around?!" Anthony Navarro's deep voice entered the room before the man. When he finally crossed the threshold into the room, his wife came to her feet.

"Well, there's one Navarro here!" Bri greeted her broad shouldered husband with a hug and a quick kiss, and then with one arm around his waist, she introduced Anthony to Dak and Kimly.

"My wife usually only brings home children…" Anthony teased. Glancing down, Dak recognized Anthony's dress shoes and slacks from earlier that morning. It wasn't long ago Dak had been hiding under the branches of the grapefruit tree, and now after meeting Bri and hearing their story, the memory of hiding was highly embarrassing.

Dak rose and extended his hand, "Dak Kesapan, thank you for having us in your home."

"Dinner with adults? You kidding? This is a treat! Right, Bri?" Anthony gripped Dak's hand in a firm handshake. Time and grief had taken a toll on the man shaking Dak's hand; barely recognizable from the hefty man pictured with his wife and children, Anthony Navarro was thinner and the dark hair around his temples was sprinkled with gray.

"Much of our days revolve around caring for the young people we've met here in Mai Sai," Bri interjected. "It is nice to have some adult company."

Bri had made lasagna and salad, and during dinner Kimly and Dak related the details about how they had met in Chiang Mai and some of the events which had unfolded over the last couple weeks. Dak was succinct, but when Kimly shared what they had been through, she laced the story with descriptions of her emotional state at each stage. As Dak watched her sharing he realized he could listen to her talk for hours. Earlier he had been trying to convince her it was time to go home, but the thought of her taking his advice and actually leaving was a little depressing. Was he ready to return to what he had before he met her?

Eventually, the conversation drifted back to the Navarro family. Kimly had questions about the factories, and she wanted to know what happened to people when they were found in dire working conditions.

"What do you do when you realize the factory is forcing workers?" Kimly questioned.

"I'll tell you what I do, I search their faces," Anthony shared. "I look for her eyes. She had my Mama's eyes, and I know I will recognize Anna by her eyes."

"The search for Anna stalled out very quickly." Bri said, "RMP began to cover their—"

"RMP?" Kimly interrupted.

"Royal Malaysian Police." Anthony answered. "Once their leads stalled out, they looked for a scapegoat. Rather than searching for Anna, they shifted blame to my Tony. Concocted some ridiculous story of a drug deal gone bad. Tried to get our younger son, Aaron, to say that he and his brother were buying drugs when Anna was taken—have you met Aaron?" Anthony turned to his wife before they could answer, "Did they meet Aaron?"

"No, sir." Kimly spoke up.

"He's a fierce colt, my Aaron. He wasn't having any part of RMP's lies, not for himself—certainly not for Tony. We saw what was happening. The search was dead. Anna was gone, Tony was gone. We went back to the States. It was the hardest time ever, and we weren't home very long before Bri and I both knew we had to come back to Asia. We couldn't stop looking for our baby girl."

Bri interjected, "The Company offered Anthony a new position, one that wouldn't require him to travel, but Anthony declined. We didn't fit there anymore."

"My job in the garment industry is what took us to Malaysia; the company assumed I would be better off without reminders, but my job is what allows me to keep looking for Anna. At the end of the day, I go to bed knowing I have done all I can. I won't ever get my son back, and I won't ever stop looking for my daughter."

"And you are pretty certain she is a factory worker?" Kimly's asked. Anthony looked at his wife and then back at Kimly. "No, Kimly, unfortunately, I am not certain. I am hopeful, but not certain. Once we stopped working with RMP and hired a private investigator, every lead led us to Northern Thailand and pointed at sex trafficking."

The two words assaulted the dinner party. The phrase was uncomfortable enough on its own accord, but hearing it from the mouth of a father who had lost his daughter made it nearly unbearable.

"If it pointed to…to sex trafficking…why aren't you? I mean, I'm sorry—" Kimly's words came out flustered.

"We look there, too," Bri said. "It's hard to think about, but we have to. Almost every night a group of us takes a turn making contact with the girls working the streets and the brothels."

"But, if your daughter is working the streets, wouldn't she try to leave? And how do you find them? Everything I researched said prostitution was illegal."

"Kimly, there is so much deception," Bri didn't seem surprised by Kimly's questions. "Anna may not know she can leave, she may not know we are looking for her. We've rescued girls who were told they were sold to the traffickers. Some of them were, I'm sure, but some of them may have been grabbed. We can't know for certain. Many of them don't know where they are from or even how old they are."

"The officials of Thailand will tell you prostitution is illegal." Anthony said, "But the truth is…it's tolerated. Anna turned fifteen last March, if she is here, she may be out on the streets at night."

No one spoke. They each stared at their empty glasses and the leftover food on their plates.

Anthony and Bri walked their guests out to the Jeep. When Dak opened Kimly's door, a roll of duct tape rolled out and landed on the gravel. Dak swooped down and grabbed the tape, "Hey, I may still need you, get back in there," he laughed as he tossed it back onto the floorboard.

Kimly looked over at the roll of tape and then back to Bri, "Oh hey, before I forget—there's a little girl living in the dumpsters near where we are staying. I've been leaving her food, and we repaired her little fort. But, I dunno, maybe someone could come by and try to lure her out?"

"Oh, no. Poor thing…absolutely we will! Do you think she's there now?"

"It's hard to say. She disappears quite often. I have no idea where she goes."

"Quite often, the kids just keep moving. Sometimes they have multiple shelters. She may be watching you come and go, or out looking for food, or just hiding somewhere and sleeping. It's pretty rare that they stay in one place very long."

About that time the metal gate rolled open, and the burgundy minivan drove onto the property. The van stopped abruptly and several young people barreled out. A young man in his early twenties approached the two couples standing in the driveway, "Hey guys, what's up?"

"What's up?!" Anthony smiled at the young man, "What's up with you?"

"Mya and Than don't want to go tonight," the young man stood with both feet firmly planted and spun his keys around his index finger.

One of the girls was talking as she headed toward the house, "I'm tired…and my feet hurt…"

Bri called out to her, "Mya, you don't have to go, honey!"

"This is our son Aaron. Aaron leads most of the searches at night." Anthony placed his hand on his son's shoulder, a handsome man with his father's broad shoulders and thick, wavy hair.

"We're the Emancipation Troop. We work in the dark, to bring people into the Light," Aaron nodded.

"Aaron, is it tonight that you're heading over to the Golden Triangle?" Anthony asked.

"Yeah," he turned his head toward his father and pulled his shoulders back, "We're just doing a Walk By. We'll only be out for a couple hours. I gotta see who's running that new house."

"The Golden Triangle? What is that?" Kimly asked.

"It's a border town—the Eastern border. Super popular for tourism…It's only like thirty minutes away," Aaron answered.

"And what exactly will you do there?" Kimly inquired.

"We call it a Walk By. Basically, we walk the perimeter and gather information to assess who is running the brothel. Once we know who is running a brothel, we know how to proceed in making contact with the girls."

"And the boys…" stepping up behind Aaron was Ruby Red, the curly hair waitress Dak and Kimly had met days before. "Hi, I'm Alicia."

"Hi Alicia…I'm Kimly, this is Dak. The boys?"

"Yeah," Aaron nodded, "most of the people who are trafficked for sex are girls, but there are some young boys out there, too."

"So, you said something about determining who is running the brothel?" Kimly asked.

Anthony spoke up, "Before Aaron or Alicia or any of the team makes contact, they figure out who the Prostitution Lord is. They don't want to initiate contact with a girl and have her suffer because of it."

"But how do you know who is running it if you don't make contact?" Kimly asked Aaron.

"We make observations, take mental notes and when we get home, we chart it all out."

"Really? I'm intrigued," Dak said.

"Yeah, we've been at it for a while, so we look for specific things. For example, we look for smokers. Ranca, he's a Lord with three places in Mai Sai, he doesn't let his girls smoke."

One of the young men standing at the edge of their circle interrupted Aaron in broken English, "The last place we walk by had only two men on porch and big dog."

"Yes!" Aaron pointed his finger at the young man and nodded his head in agreement, "That's right, Paol!" he looked back at Dak, "A couple nights ago Paol noticed there were quite a few girls, but there were only two men watching the street and they were using a guard dog. Khun Sa likes to use guard dogs. And Khun Sa won't allow music. It's an eerie feeling to see their flashing lights on a dead silent night."

Dak remembered the eerie feeling that Aaron mentioned. He hadn't been able to place what was missing, but now that Aaron mentioned it, he could feel it, and he could still see the men and the dog that had been on the porch the night he and Kimly had followed these young people. It probably wouldn't make Anthony feel safe knowing how easily he and Kimly had been able to track his family, how easily they had be able to track his kids. *Do I tell him that they need to tighten some of their procedures up, a bit?*

Dak's thoughts were interrupted when he heard Kimly speak up,

"We'd like to join you—Dak and I would like to go with you to the Golden Triangle, if that's okay," she said.

Aaron answered with a resounding, "Really?"

"I'll come, too," Anthony added. "It's been a while, but I'm up for it."

"Okay," the younger man spun his keys again, "let's load up."

Dak stood still for a moment staring at Kimly, and even in the dimly lit driveway, he could see her eyes flash, but this time, Dak's were flashing, too.

PART THREE

28

Kimly slid into the middle seat in the minivan, grateful that she and Dak were on the same page about accompanying the Navarro family on the Walk By. At least she hoped they were on the same page. She had noticed the way he had eyed her in the driveway, but she pretended otherwise in hopes that he wouldn't speak up.

Once they had loaded into the burgundy minivan, Aaron explained that because they were only doing a Walk By they wouldn't be gone long. On the nights where the Emancipation Troop approached girls on the street, they might be out until dawn. Often they had to pay the girls and try to disappear down an alley. If a girl was out on the street, allowed to work away from the sight of her pimps, it was because the girl had bought into her pimp's lies. She now believed this was the only life she could ever have.

"The overarching mission of our troop is twofold." Aaron explained he drove east on Highway 1041. "The first is information. We want to know what is going on inside of the brothels…I want to see what I can't see—"

From the back seat of the van Alicia interrupted her older brother. "We want to see the invisible, so we are always listening for clues…something one of the girls might say that will tell us a little bit more about others who may be locked away."

"Every person is a dot on a map," Anthony interjected, "these girls hold keys to the maps of the darkest form of slavery."

"So, just so I understand…" Kimly spoke up, "you talk to the girls, the prostitutes hoping—"

"These girls aren't prostitutes…" Aaron interrupted.

"The girls working…you say they aren't prostitutes?" Kimly questioned.

"What Aaron means is that the street girls aren't prostitutes in the truest definition of the word. There's nothing in it for them." Anthony looked over to Kimly, "Sure, they perform sex acts for money, but there is no gain in it for them. Some john gives a girl 100 baht on the street, and her pimp wanted her to get a 500 baht—not only will she *not* be keeping the 100, but she's going to get worked over by the pimp."

The van fell silent, and it wasn't until they reached the outer limits of the Golden Triangle that anyone spoke. Aaron suggested that his father and Dak exchange cell phone numbers, lest they get separated during the Walk By. As Dak and Anthony exchanged numbers, Kimly thought back to the Walk By she and Dak had witnessed just a couple nights ago, and she couldn't imagine how anyone would have been separated.

The minivan stopped at the edge of an alley, and the passengers unloaded. It was getting cooler out; it was probably going to rain. Kimly commented on the humidity, and Aaron responded, "It's also cooler because we are so close to the Mekong River. Don't go falling in!" he teased.

"It's just a few blocks north of here," Dak told Kimly, "The river acts as the border between Thailand, Laos, and Myanmar. There's a place where you can see all three countries at once, and the only thing separating them is the river."

Kimly pulled her jacket around her and commented, "Well, all I know is it feels like it's going to start raining." She glanced over at Dak, "you should've brought a jacket."

"I couldn't find my sweatshirt...someone took it," he winked and nudged Kimly with his shoulder.

"I didn't take your sweatshirt!" Kimly lightly smacked Dak's arm. "It's in the backseat of the Jeep!" she shook her head and laughed.

The group moved through the alley, and when they came out on the other side, they stood before a busy street ablaze with color and activity. It was as if the whole city had turned out for the grand opening of the nightclub.

Amid the activity, were a variety of sidewalk musicians; a woman was strumming on a guitar playing folk music, and a little further along, a group of five teenagers was sitting on the curb playing drums. As they walked closer to the group of drummers Kimly noticed that each of the drummers was blind. She was shuffling through her purse trying to find some baht, when Dak reached over and touched her arm, "Don't give them money…" he whispered.

"But, they…they need" Kimly started to protest.

"They don't get to keep it," Dak whispered. "And, most likely, someone did this to them. They're being used."

Small stores along the street had pulled out chairs and silk adorned tables, which held candles and burning incense. Similar to the other townships Kimly had visited, street vendors lined the path. Scooters rolled by, their horns hollering at the mounds of people to clear the path. A frail woman sat begging on the sidewalk, with an emaciated child in her arms. The woman looked up at Kimly and smiled while extending her hand. The beggar's smile revealed coal black teeth. Kimly drew closer to Dak and kept her step in sync with his.

The conversation she had with Dak earlier in the day banged around in her head as she bumped shoulders with strangers on the crowded street. They were getting closer to what was obviously the brothel. A bright blue neon sign with Thai lettering hung over an indigo building. The building was a nightclub and the sign illuminated its entrance. The girls were "entertainers," and the brothels were Men's Clubs. Very rarely did these clubs house minors. The prostitution that reigned in these clubs thrived on the girls having fully bought into the lie that they had no other choice, resulting in a deeper, internal form of slavery.

A few yards down the street, the site of a young woman's legs caught Kimly's attention. Beautiful tan legs poured into 5-inch silver stilettos and strutted across the sidewalk. The young woman wore a short stone washed denim skirt and pink studded bra. Above the sky high shoes and beneath an abundance of thick eye liner was the face of a youthful girl; she could have easily passed as her son's classmate. It struck Kimly as odd. What might the girl's life have been like if she had been born elsewhere? It made Kimly wonder how people, people like Dak, people like the woman she had met so long ago on the plane could readily use the term 'God's plan.' Was this lost girl part of His plan?

"Coon chew alie!" the girl in the pink bra and stilettos called to Kimly. Once Kimly realized the playful, flirtatious words were being directed at her, she snapped out of her thoughts.

She must have seen Kimly looking at her legs; Kimly made eye contact but quickly looked away.

"Mai me Samong" the girl began to yell out, laughing and mocking Kimly.

Kimly felt Dak's hand on her back leading her away. "Come this way…" he whispered in her ear. With each step away, the scantily clad girl's tone grew more aggressive.

Kimly did as Dak suggested. "What's she saying?" she asked.

"She was asking your name…now she is calling you brainless, or stupid." Dak told her.

Kimly silently chided herself for drawing attention. Aaron had made it very clear that the number one rule of a Walk By was discretion. In order to know which cartel was running which brothel, the Troop had to gather as many observations as possible. Sometimes it took more than one Walk By to fully make an assessment. Kimly didn't want her carelessness to give the Troop a disadvantage.

Kimly heard yelling behind her, and knew better than to turn and look, but the belting voice sounded as if it was right in her ear. She tilted her head to the right and tried to look discretely over her shoulder without turning completely around. Dak must have sensed her anxiety because she felt him reach down and take hold of her arm at her elbow. She pulled her head back around and kept her gaze forward.

The overly crowded street had been blocked off from traffic, and it was now overrun with party goers. People lingered around the glowing nightclub and loitered in the street. Aaron moved up closer to the club than he would normally do on a typical Walk By, and two of the others followed him without hesitation. Dak led Kimly in the opposite direction, and they were now in the middle of the crowd of people in the street. She felt his hand steady on her elbow, when he stopped and turned to face her. They stood face to face in the middle of the crowd which was moving in either direction around them.

She looked up at his eyes, but he was staring past her, focused on the nightclub. She guessed he was gathering information he could later share with Aaron. This man who had befriended her in a coffeehouse on a whim looked more tired than ever, the lines around his eyes more distinct. Kimly thought back to the first day she had met him, at the bustling intersection in the middle of Chiang Mai. Dak had stopped her from crossing because it hadn't seemed safe. Now, in his attempts to keep her safe, he had stood by her side in the middle of another crowded, yet obscene, street.

Looking over Dak's shoulder, Kimly focused on the small apartments across the street from the nightclub. Two dingy, rundown buildings stood like partners with a wide alley running between them. She watched as the door to one of the buildings opened, and a man entered with a skinny woman in a skin-tight dress. Something struck her. She stared at the large door, and when Dak spoke, she jumped,

"Whoa, you okay?" Dak put his hand on her shoulder.

"Yeah," Kimly looked at Dak and smiled, "I just had a weird feeling."

Dak turned and looked in the direction Kimly had been staring. Then he turned his head back and looked over her shoulder. Kimly noticed that as close as Dak was standing to her, he wasn't actually touching her. Her eyes moved down and looked at the nearness of their bodies. Perhaps Dak's Thai proverbs were getting to her, because she suddenly remembered a saying from her own childhood. Throughout her life she had heard her step-father say, "Long absent, soon forgotten." The words rang loudly, and her husband's face flashed through her mind.

"You okay?" Dak interrupted her thoughts.

Kimly drew in a deep breath and smiled, "I'm fine."

She thought how odd it was that not only could she and Dak stand so close without touching but they were also hidden in the middle of the street. Around them strangers moved and laughed, and the two of them stood, hidden in the crowd. Both somber, observing.

Kimly's glance drifted beyond Dak's face, over his shoulder and back to the battered buildings. The twin buildings were similarly worn and unimpressive, but something struck her about the door on the building to the right. It was made of metal instead of wood and appeared to be bolted from the outside. A door designed to keep people out—or in.

And then, it happened all at once. Dak grabbed her arm at the same moment the door across the street opened.

"Kimly, don't panic," Dak's voice was a whisper, "I think one of SuSuk's men just walked out of the nightclub."

Kimly didn't answer. Dak pulled her closer, "Stay calm, and just do what I say."

"He's crossing the street." Kimly's barely audible response was not a question.

"Yes, I just saw him, I mean, I think it was one of them—"

"SuSuk," Kimly interrupted.

"No, it didn't look like the man you described as SuSuk, but it looked like the man we met on the bridge—"

"No," Kimly interrupted Dak again, "SuSuk is crossing the street".

Dak turned his head toward her, and she hoped the fear rising in her wasn't contagious. Were Dak to turn his head and follow her gaze he would have seen a broad Asian man, wearing a shiny, dark suit and frameless glasses, as he walked across the street, away from the old apartments and into the crowd. SuSuk's burnt orange tie lay perfectly straight on his silk shirt, and as he made his way through the crowd, people moved out of his way.

Dak pulled Kimly to the left while simultaneously whispering, "Kimly...look at me. Don't make eye contact with him." But, Kimly's eyes were locked on the man heading directly toward her. "Kimly." Dak tried again to get her attention. She heard him, but every part of her was locked in on the evil heading through the crowd.

Suddenly, Dak's face was directly in front of her own, and Dak's lips were on hers. She felt his arms wrap around her and she felt his soft lips brush across her own, and she knew he was kissing her, but her eyes were attempting to see around him in order to track the man coming towards them. Dak's arm moved down her back and he pulled her waist closer to his own. His other hand slid through her hair and landed on the nape of her neck. Her eyes were still wide open, but Dak's face blocked her view of SuSuk. She felt Dak pulling her to the left, and she felt his arms tighten around her. The bustling crowd and the music in the background faded away, while the tapping sound of SuSuk's shoes thundered in her ears, as the prostitution lord glided past what appeared to be two lovers caught in an embrace.

Dak pulled his head back and looked down at Kimly, whose heart was pounding with fear. "We need to go," Dak said, to which Kimly responded, "I think he saw me."

Without releasing his hold on her, the two quickly journeyed back the way they had come. Dak's arm was tight around Kimly as the couple pushed their way through the crowds and toward the minivan. When they were nearing the alley, Dak pulled out his phone and dialed Anthony's cell. "Abort. We need to abort," Dak's voice was calm. "Head to the van. Now."

Kimly leaned closer to Dak and looked over her right shoulder, back the way they had come. She saw SuSuk standing just outside the door of the bright blue building. His dark grey suit was almost shimmering and the neon red sign reflected on the fabric.

Seemingly out of nowhere, a woman stepped in front of Kimly, her face just inches from Kimly's own. It was the woman with the blackened teeth, and Kimly gagged on the stench coming from her. "Aharn? Pom hue..." she pleaded.

"Pom mai me aharn." Dak said, and he reached into his pocket and pulled out some baht and handed it to the woman. "She wants food," he whispered, while taking Kimly's hand into his own.

Dak lead Kimly down the alley they had come through to get to the nightclub. Kimly only then realized how intimidating the alley was; when she had walked through it alongside the Emancipation Troop, the darkness was illuminated by the hopefulness of the group, plus there was safety in numbers.

When a door opened on their right, Dak stopped and pulled her backwards. An elderly man exited the building, and Kimly tightened her grip around Dak's hand. The frail man lifted the lid to a trash container where he disposed a bag of waste. In the light penetrating the alley from the street behind them, Kimly could see that the man was wearing an apron. He wiped his hands on the front of it and pulled out a pack of cigarettes from the pocket. Taking a cigarette from the pack, he lit it, walked to the stoop of the doorway where he had exited, and sat down.

Dak held tight to Kimly's hand and pulled her out of the shadows. They walked past the man and Kimly diverted her eyes. She could feel the elderly gentleman watching them as they made their way through the darkness to the connecting street.

The others met them within minutes, and as soon as the van was moving, Dak relayed the information the Troop needed. There was no need for debriefing in order to determine which prostitution lord was running this brothel. And thanks to Kimly's surveillance, they also knew SuSuk had a private location, directly across the street from the nightclub. If he had any slaves, they would be in a place like the one she had seen. This was big news for Aaron and the Emancipation Troop, but for Dak and Kimly it meant something else entirely.

29

"There's nothing to talk about," Dak was packing Kimly's belongings in her bag. The couple had argued from the moment they got into the Jeep, and the conversation had turned into a circle.

In the short drive from the Navarro's home to the hotel, the rain Kimly had predicted came down forcefully on the hardtop Jeep, which further agitated Dak's mood. Dak insisted that he and Kimly head back to Chiang Mai immediately. He parked in a stall behind the hotel, and while he was verbally fighting with Kimly, he began to physically wrestle with the Jeep. The downpour of rain water had snuck into the cab of the Jeep near the top corner of the passenger side door and had formed a tiny stream on the armrest. Dak reached across the cab, over Kimly's head, and attempted to stop the leak using the gray duct tape. Kimly looked up at the holes where the two missing screws would be in the roll bar overhead. She noticed water leaking in at the front of the windshield, just over the rearview mirror, but she chose not to point out the new leak.

"I'm not driving in the rain. Or in the dark…or with you. In this mood," she climbed out of the Jeep, slammed the door and stomped inside.

They rode up the elevator in silence, and Dak caught Kimly off guard when he followed her for the first time into her room. When he closed the door, Kimly froze. When he pulled out her suitcase and started gathering her belongings and tossing them into the luggage, she came to life, moved in front of him, and commanded, "Stop!" Kimly stood in his path, but Dak simply moved around her and continued to gather her things.

It was futile for each of them. No sooner would he toss something in, than Kimly would pull it out. Finally, voice raised and arms in the air, he exclaimed, "I can't do this anymore!"

Dak's frustrated tone startled them both. He lowered his arms to his waist and stared at the open suitcase. The couple stood in silence.

Once Kimly's breathing calmed, she walked over and touched his arm. "Okay, but not like this. We will leave tomorrow, but you have to let me tell the Navarros."

Dak stared at her hand on his arm, and she continued before he could speak, "I promise. We will go, but let me ask Bri to take over feeding our little girl in the cardboard fort. Someone's gotta feed her, Dak. Someone's gotta save her."

With that plea Kimly moved across the room to the window and looked down at the makeshift fort below. Not being able to get through to the little girl broke her heart. But, who was she kidding? Perhaps the child had seen awful things. Perhaps it was going to take more than scrambled eggs to win her trust.

"Kimly, you said you thought SuSuk saw you. I'm not going to be able to sleep if I am lying on the other side of a wall imagining him..." Dak paused and then said quietly, "attacking you."

Kimly began to pick up her clothes which were now strewn about the room while she answered Dak, "Okay, well, first of all, even if SuSuk saw me, it doesn't mean he was able to find and follow us. Dak, it is one night, and if it makes you feel better, we can always sleep with the adjoining door open. It will be like we are in the same room." Kimly folded a t-shirt and tossed it into her bag. "And, I promise I'll stay in my own room," she winked at him.

Dak stared across the room at her, and she gave him a coy smile inviting his banter, but Dak remained somber. "I'm teasing..." Kimly grinned slightly, almost apologetically. Dak let out a small smile, and hers grew bigger. She missed the way he was with her before their situation had gotten so intense. She missed the teasing, the laughter, the offering up of trivial information, "Okay, *friend?*"

Dak agreed to the sleeping arrangements, and Kimly agreed to head back to Chiang Mai in the morning. When Dak pressed her to know if she would also be booking a flight back to the States, she refused to give him a straight answer. She hid behind wisecracks, deflecting the conversation and changing the subject.

The door adjoining the two rooms was now unlatched, but was only an inch away from being closed when Kimly nudged it wider and peeked in to see Dak climbing into bed.

"Hey, I want to run downstairs and give the little girl another blanket and something to eat..." Kimly said. "It's so wet out there.

234

And we didn't take her anything this afternoon."

"Right now?" Dak asked.

"She's just a little girl. And, it's dark—"

"Okay…okay," Dak pulled his feet out from under the covers, "Let me get my shoes—"

"You don't have to, I can go down."

Dak rolled his eyes at her and shook his head, but said nothing.

As he slipped into his shoes he asked, "Where are you going to get food this late?"

"We left some granola bars in the Jeep, I'll just grab a couple," Kimly mumbled as she walked into his room and took the keys to the Jeep off the nightstand, and then she returned to her room where she pulled the blanket off her bed.

Dak watched her move and finished tying his shoe, shaking his head the whole time.

On the way down in the elevator, Kimly managed to convince Dak she was capable of getting into the Jeep, grabbing a granola bar, and taking the blanket to the little girl without being attacked or abducted. "The rain is fierce, and it's my idea. Dak, there is absolutely no sense in us both getting soaked."

When Kimly looked at the fort in the downpour, she was grateful Dak had used the duct tape and plastic to give the girl a more secure, and somewhat waterproof, hideaway. Kimly shoved the Jeep's keys into the pocket of her jeans, while she used her other hand to wipe her hair away from her face, being careful not to drop the granola bars or the blanket. When she leaned down and looked behind the plastic she saw two little eyes squinting up at her. When Kimly moved the blanket inside the fort the small eyes darted about and the girl cowered further into the corner. In slow and deliberate movements Kimly gently released her grip on the blanket and placed the granola bars on top. "It's okay, sweetie…it's okay," Kimly repeated as she raised both hands palm out and slowly backed out of the hideaway.

Every maternal synapse in Kimly's brain was firing; she wanted to pull the little girl out of the cardboard hideaway, wrap her arms around her, and somehow convince her she was safe. She walked back to the overhang where Dak stood out of the rain.

"She doesn't belong out here," Kimly declared with a tremble, "She shouldn't be alone."

"No, she doesn't belong out here," Dak agreed. "This cannot be what God wanted for her."

Several hours after forfeiting the blanket to the child, Kimly woke, sweating. She had failed to gauge the tropical weather. When she had fallen asleep the temperature in her room had cooled considerably by the sudden downpour outside, but a few hours into the night her t-shirt was damp with her own sweat. She sat up and looked across the room to the window. With soft steps she moved to the window, pulled it open and took in a deep breath. The air was wet and hot, but still cooler than the air in her room. Kimly looked through the light drizzle and down below at the darkness. She couldn't see anything around the trash can, no fort, no little girl, just darkness.

Tiptoeing across the room, Kimly peered through the adjoining door into the room where Dak was sleeping. She listened to his breathing; it was steady, like him. Looking at the outline of him in his bed, under his blanket, made her wish she had the courage to go crawl up next to him. Perhaps being close to him would ease the constant clattering in her heart. Would he turn her away? Of course, he would...but, what if he didn't? Kimly steadied herself in the doorframe and imagined a scenario where Dak held her in his arms. Remembering the kiss in the middle of the street, she raised her hand to her lips. The moment had been so frightening; she hadn't been able to respond to his kiss. Thinking of it now, she imagined herself in his embrace again, but this time she imagined skin against skin. She imagined his eyes enveloping her and for a moment erasing every error of her past. Kimly continued to play it out in her head even as she crossed back to her own bed and crawled under the sheet.

The man was holding her hand, and Kimly's eyes were locked on his firm grip. The warm brown hand was wrapped around hers. She moved her hand in his grip, and he relaxed his hand slightly. She responded by squeezing tighter, and bringing her other hand around the back of his. He acknowledged her movements by tightening his clasp on her hand. It was an unspoken conversation.

Kimly turned her gaze to his face, but she couldn't see him clearly. Her feelings for him were intense, so she wanted desperately to see his face. She felt his hand moving down her back, holding her in a loving embrace. She tried again to see his face. When she couldn't, she pulled her body closer hoping she might be enveloped in his glow.

She felt a tear fall onto her forehead. He was disappointed. Had she disappointed him? Her hand came up to wipe away his tear, and she squinted at him. She needed to see his face. Being this close to him was satisfying, complete. If only he understood her need for him. The dark hand came up and rested on her cheek. Strongest of all her desires was to feel the man's grip again, but no sooner had Kimly moved her own hand to her face then the hand was gone. He was gone.

Kimly opened her eyes and pulled her hand away from her wet face. Sideways rain was sneaking through the window. The floor was wet, the bedding damp, and there was a light mist across her face. She lifted herself onto her side, resting her weight on her elbow and gazed out the window, across the tall trees in the distance. The wind and the rainstorm danced atop the grove creating a symphony. Despite the beauty of the swirling branches, something in the rain was setting her off. She wanted to talk to…Kyle?

Kimly planted her feet on the wet marble floor and remembered the wet floor from the first day she had arrived in Chiang Mai. She remembered the broken glass…the hotel maid…the busy street eleven floors below.

"Ma!" The child's protest was a loud shriek piercing its way through the storm's rumbling invoking her to action. Kimly was two steps toward the window, and her head shot down to the fort.

The front of the makeshift fort was tossed to the side of the trash can. Next to the dumpster sat a car with its passenger door wide open. The little girl kicked and screamed as she tried to pull away from the man. Kimly recognized him immediately. The man with the neck tattoos dragged the waif by her hair and tossed her weightless frame into the back of the car.

"No!" Kimly yelled.

Spinning around Kimly ran into the room where Dak was sleeping. But, Dak wasn't there. He wasn't in his bed. She looked around the room and saw the closed door to the bathroom. She crossed the room and pounded on the door before flinging it open. Into the steam filled room she hollered, "They're taking her!" Without waiting for Dak to respond, Kimly spun around where she saw Dak's pistol lying on his nightstand.

Grabbing the gun, Kimly ran back to her room and pulled on her jeans before bolting out the door and towards the elevator. She pushed the button several times before deciding she couldn't wait. Turning to her left, she ran through the door marked "STAIRS". She took the steps two and three at a time until her bare feet landed hard on the ground floor, and she bolted through the lobby, to the familiar exit and into the parking lot behind the hotel. The lot was empty, and other than the rain tapping against the plastic of what had been the child's fortress, it was silent. Lifeless and silent.

Dak. Instinctively, Kimly reached to her pocket to pull her cell phone out of her jeans. She didn't have her phone, but in her pocket she found a set of keys. *The Jeep! I have the keys!*

Tires spinning against the wet blacktop, Kimly backed out and turned the wheel tightly to the right. Dropping the gun onto the seat next to her and using both hands, she spun the tight wheel back around to the left. She raced the Jeep across the lot and made a sharp right turn onto the main thoroughfare, where she saw a large truck coming straight at her.

"What the—?!" she yelled, *I'm the wrong way!* She realized. She yanked the steering wheel to the left, driving up onto the median, and crashing through a triangle shaped shrub. The Jeep bounced around the median and landed on the other side of the road. Kimly turned the wheel and straightened the Jeep out just before plowing into a white sedan. She pressed down on the gas pedal and jolted forward.

Morning traffic was minimal, and Kimly swerved seamlessly along the highway—switching lanes, maneuvering between scooters and cars. From above, she knew the car she pursued was pale blue, and while she had seen it for only an instant she was certain she would recognize it. She sped in the direction they had traveled the night before. SuSuk's men had taken her, and Kimly knew where they were heading.

Rain beat against the windshield, and Kimly tried to determine how to turn on the windshield wipers without taking her eyes off the road. The driver's seat, which was adjusted for Dak, made it equally awkward for her to navigate. Reaching under the seat, she pulled a lever, and the seat flew forward, which caused her to momentarily lose control of the steering wheel. The Jeep whipped into another lane almost impaling an elderly man on a scooter. The driver of the scooter recovered and slowed, yelling obscenities at the Jeep as Kimly sped onward.

Traffic lights held little significance as Kimly barely slowed at the intersections. If memory served, she knew the road would soon narrow and there would be an onset of curves. She didn't want to be driving in vain, chasing a ghost of a car that may not have traveled in this direction. Her hope was to catch the vehicle before it made it to the less populated territory of the rural route.

Kimly began to pray, and the desperate pleas spilling out of her mouth became more passionate until they invoked tears. "You have to help me...I can't let them take her...this is my fault...they followed me...please lead me to her....please, God, please."

Cutting across the lanes Kimly nearly ran into a large white delivery truck, forcing her to momentarily slow down. Mud from the wet roads flew up onto the windshield, and Kimly tried again to locate the switch for windshield wipers. Again, she was unsuccessful, and it was getting harder to see. The white truck slowed which elevated Kimly's pulse. Then it changed lanes, and into Kimly's view came the pale blue car she had seen at the hotel's dumpster. She pressed down on the gas pedal and tried to get ahead of the white delivery truck. The pale blue car was moving slowly, and she noticed other cars were changing lanes to get around it.

Adrenaline shot through her veins when Kimly realized she was going to be able to catch up to the car. She moved her eyes around the line of traffic and looked for a way to get over. Slowing down, Kimly crossed the lane to her right so she was traveling in the same lane as the pale blue sedan. There were two cars between them. Kimly watched as the pale blue sedan slowed and turned left, and the two cars between them traveled straight ahead. Kimly turned the Jeep onto the small road, following the sedan up a muddy hillside road.

As the road twisted, the pale blue sedan picked up speed. Kimly increased her speed so she wouldn't lose them. When the road narrowed, Kimly heard something she hadn't heard in days, maybe weeks. It was intense; she heard it in her mind and felt it in her stomach.

NEAR.

And then the pale blue sedan skidded to a stop.

The Jeep skidded to a stop behind the car, which then began to move forward again. Just as Kimly was pressing her foot on the gas, the Jeep lurched forward in an earthquake jolt, banging Kimly forward and knocking her head against the steering wheel. When Kimly brought herself up, she saw another car in her rearview mirror. The second car was pressing the Jeep forward. Kimly used the brakes to resist, but the car behind her had momentum, and it pressed her forward along the muddy road. *It's a trap!* Yanking her foot from the brakes, Kimly shoved it down on the gas pedal.

The Jeep's thick tires gripped the mud beneath them, and the Jeep sprung forward. Kimly plowed up the hill following the pale blue car, which was only one car length ahead of her. Keeping her foot pressed hard on the gas pedal, Kimly heard the car's engine roar deeply as the Jeep pushed forward and crashed hard into the pale blue sedan. The wet road and the mud worked in Kimly's favor, and the impact caused the sedan to lurch off the side of the road and barrel into a tree. Kimly spun the wheel of the Jeep until she had made a complete U-turn. She looked over at the passenger's seat where she had set Dak's pistol, but somewhere in all the chaotic jolts, the gun had slid to the side and dropped down between the door and the passenger's seat. Her only measure of protection was out of reach.

Holding tight to the steering wheel, Kimly saw the car that had been behind her was now headed straight towards the Jeep. She pressed her foot down on the gas pedal and drove directly towards the oncoming car. The car pulled sharply to the right, and Kimly turned towards the car and pressed down harder on the gas. The Jeep impacted the driver's side of the car and sent it sliding sideways down the muddy embankment. Its tires were still spinning, but the driver had no control as the car slid down the side of the hill. And, as the car slid away, Kimly saw the frameless glasses on the distinguished businessman in the passenger's seat. SuSuk was in the car.

Kimly put the car in reverse and pulled away from the edge of the hill and drove a few feet back down the road. She stopped where the pale blue car had gone over. Slamming on her brakes, Kimly bolted out of the car and slid down the mound of mud and rocks. The driver's side of the pale blue car was wedged against a sturdy tree; inside the car two men were slumped over, unconscious. It took a few minutes for Kimly to wedge the passenger's door open, and even then she could only open it about a foot. When she pressed her body through the opening, could see the child in the back seat. The waif of a child, now unconscious, was bound with a thick nylon rope. Kimly pulled the seat forward enough to squeeze in. She was unable to loosen the nylon rope that was tied around the little girl's wrists, so she untied it where it was attached to the headrest of the backseat. Gathering the child in her arms, she squeezed out of the car, pulling the small child with her, just as the driver and his passenger were beginning to shift in their seats and wake from the stunning impact.

Arms tight around the small frame of the child, Kimly climbed the wet terrain. Sharp rocks bit the bottom of her bare feet, but she ignored the intense pain as she carried the still unconscious child up the muddy hill. The raindrops, which had decreased to a drizzle, once again increased in size. Hard drops of rain pelted her in the face blending with tears falling from her eyes.

When Kimly reached the top of the hill, she could hear the yelling of the men below her, climbing from the sedan. She pulled open the passenger's door to the Jeep and sat the little girl in the seat. Kimly attempted to pull the seatbelt across the child's waist, but the little girl started to wake up and began to squirm under Kimly's hands, fighting her efforts. Terror filled the child's eyes and movements. The child yanked until she was able to wedge one hand free from the nylon rope. Kimly had to get her somewhere safe, as quickly as possible. Trying to calm the child, Kimly repeated, "It's gonna be okay, sweetie." The child's terror filled eyes widened and shifted over Kimly's left shoulder.

Then Kimly felt it. Precise. Pointed. Paralyzing pain to the back of her head.

30

Dak woke to the roll of thunder. Opening his eyes abruptly, he acclimated himself to his surroundings. It was early, earlier than he needed to be roused. But, he felt uneasy.

Dak stood from his bed and crept to the adjoining door; moving it slightly he peeked in at Kimly, who was sleeping soundly under the sheet on her bed and appeared to be glowing. Dak leaned in to see her more clearly. Kimly's entire room was illuminated with moisture. He looked around the room and noticed her window was wide open. With no screen to block the elements, the floor beneath the window was wet from the incoming rain. Kimly's face, arms and one leg, which peeked out from under the sheet, were all damp. Her light brown skin glimmered under his gaze, and the damp sheet was translucent as it lay against the form of her body.

Dak shook his head, *Woman, what am I going to do with you?* Then he answered himself, almost audibly: *Nothing. You're not going to do a thing with her.* His feelings for her had taken on a life of their own.

Dak determined the best way to avoid temptation was to get out of the room. Soon Kimly would wake and start getting ready to leave. The idea of being an open door away while Kimly showered and dressed was more than he thought he could bear. His best bet was to shower and then meet her downstairs at the breakfast buffet once she was up and about. It would give her privacy, and it would ease the battle within him.

Dak stood in the shower and allowed the hot water to ease the soreness in his joints. A part of him looked forward to returning to the less taxing lifestyle of Chiang Mai. Of course, once they returned, he was going to have to tell Kimly the whole story about what had happened in the Tai Lue church. Maybe once she realized what she had been a part of, the lengths God was willing to go for her so that she might hear Him, maybe then he could convince her that she couldn't stay in Thailand. *This isn't her home.* Home? It was such an odd word now. When Tina died, he lost his home, for home had been Tina…wherever she was. He figured that still held true: Home was with Tina and Samantha Jean. In that way, he was homeless. But for how long? How long would he allow himself to remain homeless?

His thoughts were interrupted by a loud banging on the door, followed by Kimly yelling to him. It sounded like, *they're taking her?*

"What?!" Dak yelled back. "Kimly?!"

But, there was no answer. Dak pulled the shower curtain back and saw the bathroom door was open. "Kimly?!" he called out again.

Grabbing a towel, he wrapped it around his waist as he stepped out of the shower and called out to Kimly one last time. No answer.

Emerging from the bathroom, he looked around the edge of the doorframe. The room was silent. Silent and still. He moved across the room, his senses coming alive and his pulse rising.

Nothing seemed to be out of place, "Kimly?" he called through the adjoining door. When she didn't answer, he turned to the nightstand to pick up his gun. It wasn't there. Alarm rose in him, and he rushed into her room.

"Kimly?!" he looked around at the room, the window was still wide open, and the door leading out to the hallway was ajar. He hurried to the door, and still holding the towel around his waist, he looked out into the hallway, but there was no sign of her. Rushing back through the room, he crossed the wet floor to the open window. Looking down, he saw the disassembled fort near the waste-bin. The crates were in disarray, and the plastic was gathering small puddles as it lay flat on the pavement.

Standing at Kimly's unscreened window, Dak was replaying the last two minutes in his mind as he put together what he thought he had heard her say. *They're taking her?* Then, he saw the hardtop of his own familiar Jeep Wrangler barreling through the small stretch of lot behind the hotel and turning onto the main street.

Dak sprinted into his room, where he quickly pulled on jeans and a t-shirt. He was cursing her under his breath while he pulled on his shoes. Suddenly, he realized, he had no way to catch the Jeep. Grabbing his cell phone on the way out the door, he dialed the number for Anthony Navarro as he ran down the hallway to elevators.

Over the phone, Dak explained what he thought was happening,

Anthony responded saying he would be right over to pick Dak up at the hotel, but in those few moments of conversation Dak had already exited the hotel's lobby and crossed over the main highway, "I'm at the edge of your neighborhood...almost to your place." Dak gasped.

When Dak reached their home, the metal gate was open and Anthony was driving out in a small gray truck, "Which way?" Anthony asked as Dak jumped into the truck.

Anthony wove through traffic traveling in the direction Dak had seen the Jeep heading.

"I'm sure it was SuSuk," Dak told Anthony, "she thought maybe he saw her last night! Dammit!" Dak exclaimed as he pounded a fist into the dash of the truck.

Dak told Anthony about the fear in Kimly's eyes, and admitted his own failure for not convincing her to leave town immediately.

The two men agreed that the most logical place to begin looking was the Golden Triangle. The city sat at the border of Burma, Laos and Thailand. If SuSuk had the connections he appeared to have, SuSuk could make Kimly disappear over the border into either of the neighboring countries.

"Dak," Anthony's hands gripped the steering wheel, but he turned his head to look at his friend, "based on the wide proximity SuSuk is working...being that you two first encountered him in Chiang Mai, and now up here..."

"Yeah?" Dak waited, but Anthony's pause lingered. "Say it."

"Well, it indicates he is working a large proximity. My bet is that he's not limiting his transactions to Thailand. He is not confining where he trafficks people simply because there is a border involved. If anything, the Golden Triangle's borders may be pivotal in his operation."

"So, what you're saying is," Dak's voice didn't reveal the fear behind his words, "if SuSuk is able to get Kimly over the border, we may never see her again."

They sped through the city, searching for the Jeep. Dak was filled with anxiety as Anthony turned the corner of the street where they had seen SuSuk the night before. As badly as he hoped to see the Jeep parked in front of the worn down alley apartments, Dak dreaded what that could mean for Kimly. The street was cluttered with trash. Road blocking barriers had been removed and traffic flowed freely, but the remnants from the night before remained. The small truck passed the Nightclub and then circled the block. There was no sign of the Jeep in front of or behind the building which had glowed so brightly the previous evening. They drove down the alley and circled the double building apartment complex.

Anthony pulled to the side of the road on the small street, stopped the truck and said, "We'll find her."

"I've got to," Dak responded.

"I know." Anthony said. Dak stared out the windshield. The only sound in the car was the rhythmic squeak of the windshield wipers. The people moving about the street were doing whatever they could to stay dry.

Down the hill and beyond the street, Dak stared at the raging waves of the Mekong River. It was running high; the night's storm had raised it substantially. Cars rushed by on the street running parallel with the river.

Anthony and Dak saw the Jeep at the same time. When it rolled by on the busy street just ninety yards down the hill, the two men looked at each other and Dak yelled, "That's her!"

Anthony sped down the hill, creating a wave in his path as water spilled across the sidewalk. When the truck reached the bottom of the hill, Anthony made the wide right turn, and accelerated in the same direction as the green Jeep which had just sped by. The road was wet, and the other cars were driving cautiously, defensively. Anthony was trying unsuccessfully to change lanes in front of a beat-up black truck. In front of Anthony was a motorcycle pulled rickshaw, but no matter how close he would get to the small motorcycle-cabbie, he couldn't get close enough to pull in front of the truck. Dak was yelling, "Go around!" Anthony honked his horn and swerved toward the black truck. Finally the truck slowed down and let them over, its driver looking around to determine what could be causing all the commotion.

The green Jeep was racing down the wet, paved road. The exterior was covered in mud, which was deep in the grooves in the tires, making it apparent the Jeep had been driven off the main road since he had last seen it. He thought he could see two heads in through the back window. The one on the right appeared to be Kimly. It looked like she was struggling and fighting. She must be tied down! He couldn't imagine what must have taken place in the last forty minutes since he saw her sleeping so peacefully, so perfectly. His blood pressure increased and anger rose at the thought of her now in the car with any of those men. Then Dak noticed Kimly dipping forward in her seat. He imagined she must be hysterical, which only caused the anger within him to boil hotter until he could barely breathe.

Suddenly the car veered, changing lanes erratically. He saw movement from inside of the Jeep.

"Catch them!" Dak yelled to Anthony. Anthony changed lanes as well, trying to keep up.

The Jeep veered back to the right, slammed into a flatbed truck and then straightened out again. Then it quickly slammed into the truck again, but this time when it came left it didn't stop at the edge of the highway. It hit the railing and flew up and over the ledge of the road landing on the embankment leading down into the Mekong River.

The Jeep went down the embankment and went full speed into the water. The back tires continued to spin even as the front end of the green Wrangler sank into the river. Dak watched as brown churning water pulled the Jeep into his coldest nightmare.

Anthony pressed his foot hard down on the brakes and the truck swerved to the left, slamming into the guardrail. Dak jumped out of the truck and flew over the guardrail. Still a hundred yards away, Dak's legs couldn't move fast enough, and for the first time on this journey with this beautiful woman, he truly felt old.

He could see the top of the Jeep, but the car was being pulled under water and dragged quickly away. Only the top of the hardtop shell was visible. Each drop of rain pushed the Jeep further into the water. Within minutes, there were no visible traces of the Jeep.

Running, sliding and falling down the slope, Dak landed at the edge of the water. The water was churning as the river ran south, making him certain the current had pulled the Jeep further downstream, and Kimly was no longer in the place where he had watched the Jeep go under.

Flashes of his dead wife's face fired up in his mind. Then he saw his beautiful daughter as an infant, a young child, and a blossoming teenager—all at once, as time became fluid. Faces melded together. He saw his wife and he saw Kimly. Confusion racked him like a sledgehammer, slamming into his stomach. He was in love with this woman. There was no doubt in his mind; married or not, she had a hold on him.

Questions which had raged in his mind rose to the surface. He had lived through so many stormy nights, each one reminding him of the one that stole his family, and each time he pushed down the anger over what he had lost. His failure to protect his wife and his daughter became new all over again. But now, watching the raging water steal this woman caused buried anger to resurface. He found himself screaming out "Kimly!", but the images of the women he loved were colliding in his mind, and the fury he felt came over him like a tsunami.

Dak was shoulder deep in the water, and the current wasted no time pulling him further along, when two strong hands grabbed him from behind and began to pull him from the muddy hellhole.

"Dak, you can't get to them this way!" Anthony pulled on his friend, fighting the current with all of his might. Soon, Dak's mind became fully aware, and he began to work with Anthony to climb out of the river.

The two men were on their knees on the shore, coughing up water and staring out at the current. Dak's soul was burdened. This never should have happened! I should have been with her! The Jeep had literally vanished within minutes. Kimly was gone. Once again, God was demanding more from Dak than he was able to endure.

31

The smallest boat on the water was a four-foot long tail; the largest vessel was the Blue Horizon Banzai, a 26-meter flagship. The storm had minimized to a light drizzle, and authorities had called on volunteers to help in the search for the missing American woman, while the Mekong River Patrol monitored the chaotic activity on the waters between the neighboring countries. A piece of the Jeep Wrangler had been found miles downriver along the shoreline, but the mini-SUV was still underwater.

It had been over 24 hours since Dak had watched the Jeep go underwater, but time was rushing by in an emotional blur. His last clear memory of Kimly was vivid; he remembered the way the sheet outlined her slender form as she slept. The memory of her glowing skin now mocked him as the faces of everyone around him were covered in a light film of water. From the moment Dak watched the Mekong River swallow the Jeep, he had not been out of eyesight of the water. Both Anthony and Bri had tried to talk him into resting in the van. It was Anthony's turn to try once more to convince him to rest. Dak had just climbed off one of the River Patrol boats, and he was holding a piece of black rubber. "It's from the front windshield," Dak looked down at the piping in his hands, "...I think. It could be from the back window, though."

Anthony nodded at his friend, "Hey let's go take a seat, I want to talk to you."

"I'm fine, Anthony," Dak replied.

"Yeah, I know," Anthony had a relaxed tone to his voice. "But, I need to talk."

Dak remembered this was not the first loss the Navarro family had experienced to the slave trade. This tragedy may have opened old wounds for Anthony.

"You doing okay?" Dak asked as he sat on the back tailgate of Anthony's truck.

Anthony reluctantly sat down on the edge of the tailgate, looking sideways at Dak, "You don't want to take a seat inside the van? Less water in there." he wiped his brow with the back of his hand and shook off the accumulated water into the air.

"Naw...I don't really want less water right now."

"Dak, I get how you don't want to stop looking for her. I do. I get it completely. But, how about you just, ya know, take a break? Just close your eyes for a few minutes. There are so many boats out there now, and if anybody finds anything—"

"Not to be blunt, Anthony, but I already know how bad it will feel when they find...anything." Dak replied.

They sat in silence for a moment; finally Dak put his hand in the air, "I'm sorry. I'm tired. I can feel it throughout my whole body, but...if I close my eyes..." Dak's voice trailed off.

"What? What will happen if you close them?" Anthony asked.

"I see it over and over, all of it."

"Dak, you will always see it over and over. The sight of the Jeep hitting the river is likely burned in your memory forever, but you can't avoid sleep because of it."

"No," Dak maintained a forward gaze, "I don't just see the accident. I see everything. I see her face from the moment I met her on the street. I see every day...until the last time I saw her lying in her bed."

Anthony nodded and said nothing, and the two men became mesmerized by the dirty water moving swiftly in front of them.

"I'm going to have to get her phone...call her husband. I'm going to have to tell him what happened."

"She's married?" Anthony stared at Dak.

After a moment Dak spoke, "Yeah. She's married." Dak pulled his hand up and rested his head in his palm. "You know, now—I see all the ways I could have prevented this. I could have stopped this before it got to this point. This is my fault. My lust destroyed her."

"Whoa, Dak—" Anthony cut him off and was shaking his head. "I watched you with her. You were completely honorable."

Dak began shaking his head, but didn't speak. Finally he took in a deep breath and on the exhale, he offered, "I didn't say I wasn't battling the lust. I battled it constantly. I begged God for a clear head and pure motives. I'm saying that my ego came alive under her attention and affections."

Anthony looked away; he moved his eyes out to the river.

"Her need for me made me feel wanted. And, I allowed it. I excused my behavior with the lies I told myself: 'I'm helping her,' 'She's not really attached to me'."

"Dak, given the circumstances, you didn't have a lot of other choices" Anthony tried to encourage his friend.

"I had choices, Anthony. I had plenty of choices. And, you know what the strange thing is...deep inside, I always knew I wouldn't get away with this. I knew, eventually, we would have to face the charade we were living."

"Okay," Anthony said, "I don't disagree with you. I believe God is sovereign and somehow His hand is involved in the circumstances we don't understand. Even in this. But, Dak, your lust did not cause Kimly's car to take a nosedive into the water."

"Of course not!" Dak stood from the tailgate. "But, I led her to Mae Sai. I brought her here because I let her have her way. And, seriously, it was all selfishness. It was always about me. Everything I did for her, I was really doing for myself. I allowed her to race towards destruction because spending time with her made me feel good about myself. My need to feel wanted by this woman, who was clearly never God's plan for me, became more important than what was best for her."

Anthony didn't respond. The two men were both staring out at the fast moving current of the river. "I let her drive herself over the railing. I let her drown in her own desires. This woman was so thirsty to know she mattered, and I held the answer, but I never told her."

"What answer?" Anthony stared at Dak, who stared at the water.

Filling his lungs with a deep breath, Dak continued, "She was part of a miracle. I was there in Tai Lu, and I witnessed it, but she didn't even know it had happened. If I had told her, it might have changed everything. But, I didn't tell her…"

"Maybe it wasn't for her." Anthony responded.

"It was for her, Anthony! It was. I was there and God spoke to her in a language that only she understood! She was oblivious, but it happened!"

"I believe you." Anthony nodded his head. "But…maybe it wasn't for her."

"What are you saying?"

"Maybe it was for you as much as it was for her. Consider this, God was speaking to Kimly, telling her the things she needed to hear, but maybe God was speaking to you in His silence. Maybe God wanted you to see what He was capable of doing—even without your help. You know, Dak, everything that happens to one of us happens to all of us."

The men sat on the edge of the truck and stared straight ahead. Finally, Anthony continued, "Everything that happened to Anna isn't just happening to her. My little girl being a slave is happening to me, and it's happening to you."

"So," Dak interrupted, "we're connected in the bad and the good." Dak pressed his face into his hands and rubbed his eyes, stifling a yawn that might have given him a moment's relief.

"They found it!" Aaron was running up the embankment towards the two men, interrupting Dak's verbal pummeling. "They found the Jeep about 80 meters downstream!"

Dak's breath was stuck in his throat; he wanted to hear what exactly they had found, but he couldn't ask. He stumbled to the railing that overlooked the water. "What...what, who—" was all he got out.

"The divers reported finding the body of a male trapped inside. They are harnessing a crane and exhuming the Jeep before they remove the body."

Both Anthony and Aaron stood silently behind Dak. Kimly's body wasn't in the Jeep. Dak pulled his hands up and rested them atop his head; he turned and looked downstream, where the river raged on.

32

Kimly's head was on fire. Hot, blazing pain ripped through the back of her skull. She was moving, and each bump jolted lightning from the back of her head to the front. She opened her eyes and lifted her hand toward her face, but her movement was thwarted. Looking down Kimly saw duct tape wrapped around her wrists. Laced around the gray tape handcuffs was a nylon cord, which was bound to the door handle of the Jeep. Panic rose and Kimly took in a deep breath only to realize her mouth wouldn't move. Duct tape held her mouth closed. Kimly looked to the left and saw the man she feared most in the driver's seat. Tears filled her eyes as she looked at the cold profile of SuSuk.

Instinctively Kimly began to twist and wriggle for freedom. The rain pounded against the car, and the wipers flung violently across the windshield. As Kimly twisted in the seat she saw the little girl in the back seat. The child was lying on her side, wrapped in duct tape from the shoulders down, like a mummy. A small piece of duct tape covered her mouth and her eyes were a cave of fear.

Seeing the mummified girl made Kimly frantic, and she pulled and wrestled with the tape around her hands. Kimly tried to move her mouth, to release the tape.

SuSuk reached over and placed his hand on her leg. His hard fingers squeezed her leg, and Kimly cried out in pain. SuSuk smiled.

Through his smile he said, "Koi nun lowel."

Kimly didn't understand the words, but the implication was clear. Closing her eyes, Kimly shifted her weight and pulled her legs to the far side of seat, leaning against the door when she felt her arm rub against the hard crack on the armrest.

Kimly opened her eyes and stared at the broken armrest. Shifting her weight she pulled her arm back into her waist, leaned forward and looked over at her captor. SuSuk was driving wildly while his gaze darted back and forth from the street to the rearview mirror. Kimly pulled her elbow back and leaned forward until her hands rested against the cracked armrest. Slowly she began to rub the tape against the plastic knife-like armrest. Her attempts felt useless, nothing was catching, and she twisted her head and peered through her dark locks at the driver. SuSuk's eyes moved again to the rear mirror. Kimly sat up straight and turned to look over her shoulder. Behind her she saw the car which had tailgated her earlier in the morning. SuSuk's men were behind them. Leaning forward and pulling her elbows hard into her own stomach, Kimly tried again to tear the tape.

SuSuk reached over, placed his hand in Kimly's hair and began to rub the dark disheveled strands between his rangy fingers. *Nausea.* What would happen if she were to vomit against the duct tape blockade over her mouth? She continued pulling the edge of the tape wrapped around her wrists against the cracked armrest. When Kimly felt a small rip in the tape, she had to refrain herself from moving her arms too rapidly to lengthen the tear, lest she draw SuSuk's attention. Her heart beat faster as she felt the handcuffs ripping. She froze. The small tears in the tape were so liberating she was certain they sounded like fireworks. She looked over at the spindly hand on her hair and then to the face of its owner. SuSuk seemed oblivious to what she was doing; his eyes fluttering from road to mirror. Pulling her arm back and forth across the plastic crack Kimly sawed through the tape around her right wrist.

Kimly was able to pull her right hand out of the handmade cuff, and began to peel the gray tape from her left wrist. But the tape was adhered to itself, and refused to release her left hand from captivity. At that same moment Kimly felt SuSuk's fingers crawling across her head. This time SuSuk didn't fondle her tresses, instead he yanked, pulling her head up and against the headrest. A lightning bolt shot through her skull and into her eyes, but the duct tape suffocated her scream. SuSuk looked from Kimly's face to her hands. Lunging over her, he tried to grab her wrist. Using her free hand, Kimly pushed him away. The Jeep swerved to the right, which drew Kimly's body against his. In the back seat the little girl was tossed onto the floorboard as the Jeep slammed into a truck just on its right side. The impact knocked Kimly against the window, smashing more lightning into her eyes. She leaned against the window and pushed her free hand against the hand rest as she attempted to raise herself up, but her hand slid down the wet plastic, and she fell deeper into her seat. Her free hand was now wedged between the seat and door.

As Kimly started to pull her hand up she felt something move. She recognized the feel of it immediately. Shifting her weight and relaxing herself further down in the seat, Kimly's right hand wrapped around the handle of Dak's pistol below her seat. She adjusted her grip, and pulled it up the narrow passageway. Kimly turned her head and let her dark locks fall over her lap. She pulled the gun up and brought it in front of her left hand, which was still bound to the door with thick gray tape. Kimly released the safety, leaned back in her seat and pulled the gun tight across her chest. Pressing the handle of the gun hard against her chest, Kimly aimed the barrel at the driver and then pulled her head back removing the visual barrier between them. When SuSuk looked over and saw the barrel of the gun pointed at him he reached for the pistol, losing control of the Jeep which veered to the right. Kimly's body fell towards SuSuk. The Jeep rammed into a truck to its right. Tightening every muscle in her right arm and pulling in her abs, Kimly closed her eyes and held her breath. The sound of the gun firing across the small cab was painful, but even worse than the explosion in her ears was the pain in her jaw. Kimly's inexperience with a firearm manifested itself, and the gun's force was beyond her control. The pistol jolted upward, and the impact of it slamming into her jaw nearly knocked her unconscious. With her eyes closed she felt herself falling upward, and she could have sworn the vehicle was flying. The Jeep landed in water and the impact propelled Kimly to the top of the car. The only thing preventing her from banging her head against the Jeep's roll bar was her left arm, which was still attached to the armrest and pulling her downward.

Rocks danced below the still spinning tires as the Jeep pounded against the floor of the riverbed. The loud clanking of the Jeep pierced the silence the river required of its inhabitants. Kimly pulled herself closer to the duct tape handcuff and tore at the edge of the tape. With the aid of the water, she was able to free herself from duct tape bondage. Pushing up to the roof, she ripped the tape off her face and gulped in the air trapped in the cab. Immediately, Kimly dove back under the water, searching for the little girl. The unconscious child was bouncing around in the water. Right as she caught the child, Kimly felt pain in the back of her head. SuSuk had a grip on her hair and was pulling her back toward the front of the cab. The shock of being pulled back caused her to expel the air from her lungs. Spinning around Kimly felt strands of hair being ripped from her skull. Kimly pulled herself toward the evil man under the water. In a wild frenzy, she grabbed the madman's hand in her hair. She spun her head around and locked her teeth on his fingers, bearing down like a wild animal. SuSuk released her hair, and she bolted up for more air. Then she dove back under the water, toward the small mummified child.

Kimly found the girl's body and pulled her to the top of the cab. Air filled a small space in the tail section of the Jeep, but it was growing smaller. The water was pouring in through the front of the Jeep, and the weight of the engine pulled the front section down. Kimly yanked the tape from the face of the child. She sucked in a deep breath and covered the child's nose and mouth with her own and blew the air deeply into the child. She tried again, but the little girl didn't respond.

Floating beside the two captives was Dak's sweatshirt; Kimly pulled the little girl close to her body, grabbed the sweatshirt and wrapped it around her waist. Using the sleeves, Kimly tied the girl's small frame to her own. The way to life was to go deeper into the deadly waters. Kimly gulped in a deep breath and swam into the dark waters, moving her hands along the shell of the Jeep until she reached the back window. It was too dark to see so she tried to feel for a loose place in the battered hardtop.

She felt a small shift in the rear window of the hardtop shell. It was slight, but hopeful. Targeting the weak corner, Kimly kicked several times, and then shoved her shoulder into the glass. Pressing the child into her chest with one arm, Kimly pushed the window with the other. Suddenly, as if someone on the other side removed a barrier, the edge of the window had a slight give. Kimly pressed her feet against the seat and pushed the window with her back, when the window lifted away and Kimly and the child were pulled into the current. Instinctively, Kimly grabbed onto the rear window and drug it along with her, but then released it and began to swim upward with the child.

The river was not so deep that she lost direction under its swift current. There was brightness above, and Kimly pulled herself and the child toward the light and away from the darkness. When she reached the surface of the water her first gasp of air stung like a slap in the face, but Kimly didn't falter. She fought the strong current and headed to the embankment. Clawing her way over the sand and the rocks she pulled herself and the child onto the shore. She untied the sweatshirt and the little mummified girl fell onto the rocky shoreline.

"Come on. Help me..." Kimly cried prayers through her frantic thoughts. She began to press down on the child's chest, performing primitive CPR movements, based mostly on images acquired in movies.

The little girl vomited and then began to cough, spit and cry. Kimly pulled her tightly to her chest. "Shhh....honey. Shhh." She squeezed the child into her bosom and let her cry.

She had no idea where they were. She wasn't sure which side of the river, or in which country, they had washed ashore. The rain was beating down on her face, and it made visibility almost impossible. The broad river raged and scourged. Kimly hadn't forgotten the other car that had been following them. Looking around Kimly saw an expanse of trees across the highway.

"We have to get out of here. We aren't safe here." Kimly pulled the little girl up into her arms and carried her away from the shoreline, across the highway and back into the trees

33

The overgrowth from the trees made for a welcome shelter. The river and the highway were both within earshot, yet the freed captives were completely hidden. Kimly pulled the little girl close to her and began to remove the duct tape from her skin. It was awful to see the child's face flinch with pain. After completely removing the tape, Kimly used the sweatshirt as a towel and dried the small child's hair as best as she could. Kimly, the child, and the sweatshirt were all soaked to the core. Kimly looked at her and tilted her head, knowing they weren't going to be able to communicate.

"I'm Kimly," she said as she placed her hand on her chest; "You are safe with me. I won't hurt you." The two sets of brown eyes connected. Kimly was eager for a connection, but the girl was expressionless. "I know you can't understand, but it just feels wrong not to try…"

Kimly stood and walked over to a tree with Dak's sweatshirt in hand. She wrung as much of the water out of the sweatshirt as she could and hung it over a branch which was sheltered from the rainfall. Across the highway, the storm blew strong over the river. If she could see across the river, she might have a better indicator of their location. Nothing about what she could survey gave indication to her being in Thailand, Laos—or even Burma. She knew the three countries converged at the Golden Triangle, but she wasn't certain which way SuSuk had been traveling, or how long she had been unconscious. She watched the road for a blue Cadillac, watched for any sign of SuSuk's men. Kimly didn't know if her gunshot had even made impact. She thought she saw blood in the water, but she couldn't be certain. And, if the bullet had missed SuSuk, perhaps he had also been able to get out of the Jeep.

Kimly returned to where the little girl sat in the mud, surrounded by the tape Kimly had just removed. "Sweetie, let's get out of the mud," she put her hands out to the small child to help her up, "Come on," but the girl just looked at Kimly's hands and then back up to her face.

Kimly knelt down to her level, "It's okay," she nodded her head and feigned a fake smile. But it wasn't okay. If SuSuk's men found her, she didn't know how she could protect herself, let alone the child. She had no plan. The little girl remained still; expressionless. Kimly put her arms around the child and lifted her up off the muddy ground. She carried her further into the dense trees and sat the child under the branches and wide leaves of a towering banana tree. Kimly returned to the soggy ground where the child had been sitting and scurried about gathering the gray tape, which was splayed about in the mud. If SuSuk's men were searching for them, a small piece of duct tape at the edge of the trees could reveal their location.

Kimly walked to the banana tree where she had left the child, crawled under one of its wide leaves and leaned against the trunk. Scraping a glop of sticky fruit from the bottom of her own foot Kimly thought, *Shoes would have been a good idea.* She looked up at Dak's sweatshirt, shook her head and then leaned it back against the tree. Her head still stung where she had been struck. Reaching her hand back she could feel a large bump on her skull. She brought her hand forward and looked down at her fingers, letting out a sigh of relief when she didn't see blood. Kimly didn't know how long they were going to have to wait it out, and if she were bleeding time might make her weaker.

She replayed the morning's chase and began to chide herself; *a phone would have been an even better idea. It wouldn't work now anyway*, she argued in her defense. Had Dak been correct? Should they have left in the night? *But, the little girl…who would have saved her?* Reason and regret argued. The worst thought was what she had brought on this child. She had led SuSuk to this little girl, and she didn't want to imagine what they might have done to her.

Kimly closed her eyes and listened to the wind caressing the trees and teasing the river. Soon the combination of the traffic as it hummed along the highway and the raging water became rhythmic and lulled her into sleep.

So, it's not about you?

The voice was distinct. Kimly opened her eyes and looked down at the child. The little girl sat two feet away. Her legs were pulled into her chest, and her arms wrapped tightly around them. She wore pale yellow pants, which were several inches too short, and a stained t-shirt with stretched out neckline.

Whatever Kimly had just heard was more poignant than her own rambling thoughts. The voice was alive in the trees and the rain. Kimly closed her eyes and tried to hear it again.

Nothing. She opened her eyes and looked around. Staring at the little girl Kimly asked, "Did you hear it?" The child held Kimly's gaze, but gave no response, not even a flinch.

Kimly looked up again at the sweatshirt. It wasn't dry, but it was less wet than it had been. Pulling herself up, Kimly gathered the shirt and moved towards the child. The little girl cowered. Kimly paused and tilted her head.

"It's okay," Kimly nodded and squatted down, moving closer to the girl. The two sets of brown eyes connected again. Then Kimly lifted the sweatshirt and mimicked putting it on herself. "See?" Kimly said as she lowered the garment.

Moving closer and stretching out her arms, Kimly was able to place the sweatshirt over the girl's small frame. The child relaxed and let Dak's gray sweatshirt swallow her up.

"See?" Kimly repeated. Then Kimly returned to her spot under the tree and inhaled. Brushing leaves from her palms, Kimly folded her arms across her chest and shifted her head so as to relax against the tree. The rain tapped on the leaf overhead, and Kimly closed her eyes while she listened, hoping the rhythmic beating would be interrupted again by the voice. She wanted to hear more. Anything more.

When the rain stopped tapping the leaf, Kimly opened her eyes and saw a man was holding her hand. She looked at the firm grip; she had seen this hand before. Her eyes moved up the brown skin of his forearms. The definition of his muscular arms spoke peace to her, not fear. She moved her eyes to his face. But, his image was unclear. Lifting her hand Kimly tried to touch his face, but her hand didn't penetrate anything; it moved seamlessly through the space where his face should have been. She pulled her hand back, and her fingers were vibrant. Not glowing with light, but glowing with life. It startled her, and she released his hand.

Looking down at herself Kimly saw she was naked. She pulled her bare legs up under her and quickly wrapped her arms across her chest. The rain had stopped and the bright sun was exposing her body. She looked down only to see that her body was evolving, coming to life. In her nakedness she was changing. Shimmering diamonds unfolded from her skin with spiraling movements and draped her curves. Kimly stared in fascination as her body birthed a luminous fabric which melded perfectly to her form. The fabric flowed from her shoulders, across her breasts, down her belly and all the way to the ground. She watched as the fabric slithered down her arms and came to rest at each wrist. The white sparkling gown glimmered under the sun. Kimly swiftly raised her head and looked at the faceless form in front of her. His hand stretched out to her, and she put her hand into its safe grip. He pulled her close and wrapped his arms around her effervescent figure.

Beloved.

A sensation rose in Kimly's body when she heard his voice; being close to him was satisfying. There was no striving, no anxiousness, and no competition. She was whole. She spun in a circle and the sun's reflection bounced off her dress. Tiny lights danced on the banana trees. Kimly stepped back and looked over her shoulder, into the trees. She didn't want to leave the voice, but she was curious about the trees. There was an alluring darkness in the shadows there. Taking the tiniest of steps Kimly made a minuscule movement, and her heart swelled in the shadows. A part of her came alive in the dimly lit space. She felt powerful and that power pricked her in the most sensual ways. Everything was perfect, for less than an instant. Suddenly peace dissipated, and frustration took over.

Kimly became two people at once: she was what He saw and what she saw. She was one person and she was two people and the two were not the same one that she was. Her heart pounded as she looked down at her gown. It was not sparkling anymore. The stones had been replaced with hard broken mirrors, and the mirrors were not reflecting light. Each mirror was a different size, and each bore a jagged edge. Time had aged and corroded what was once clear and bright. In each tiny mirror Kimly saw reflections of her own selfishness in the faces of others. She looked down her right arm, and the mirrors reflected the tears of her children. But it wasn't only their faces—she could see her own heart, and it was dark and insensitive. She saw the walls she had built keeping them at a distance. Looking at her other arm, she once again saw her heart, this time it was filled with prejudice as she responded to people who had tried to befriend her. She saw jealousy and spite. Faces she barely remembered cried from her callousness. Kimly's eyes moved down the front of her gown. Over her heart she saw mirrors of anger and pride, a fabric she had woven into her marriage. Each mirror reflected her selfishness towards her husband. Kimly saw the countless times she had pushed Kyle away, leaving him sexually frustrated and ashamed. The mirror allowed her to see the depth of the pain in the heart of the man she once claimed to love. Her husband was broken and hurting.

"But he hurt me..." she pleaded with the mirrors. "You don't understand. You don't understand what he did to me!"

To himself. He did it to himself.

Kimly began to tear the dress from her body. She pulled at the mirrors on the garment, but none of them budged. Each attempt to remove the mirrored gown only sliced into her fingers. Kimly worked harder, and her heart raced until she was in a wild frenzy. Every one of her fingers was bloody, but the gown had not yielded. Enraged, she fell to the muddy floor beneath the trees, and through her tears

Kimly looked to the mirrors hoping an image might show a heart that was sorry. None of the mirrors came to her aid. Instead the mirrors laughed at her, and each jagged mirror on the gown began to shout her identity.

Unfaithful. Unworthy. Unwanted. Unlovable.

In her despair, Kimly slumped forward into the mud, but even in her submission, there was no relief; the gown held her captive. The mud smelled like regret; she breathed in the foul fragrance, when she felt his hand touch her shoulder. Looking at the strong masculine hand touching her, Kimly responded and placed her hand over his. He pulled her up to her feet, and he began to rip the gown off her. Each mirror tearing into his skin. Her selfishness tore into his flesh. Her unfaithfulness dug deep causing his blood to drip from his hands. With each mirror he ripped from her body, she felt more alive. Every mirror unleashed from her lessened her rage. But, each mirror pierced him deeply. She looked at his form, he was naked and wounded. His whole body was covered in blood and deep gashes.

She looked down at her own naked form; she had small and insignificant scars. And each scar was mocking her. Every scar was a reminder of the sinful past. It made her feel more unworthy to look at what he had sacrificed. And for what? He had made a huge sacrifice for her, and she was still damaged. Ashamed, she turned and moved toward the trees. There was pleasure hiding in the shadows. He reached out his strong hand and placed it on her shoulder. She turned her head and watched as the white sparkling gown fell from his touch and consumed her form. The beautiful gown was pure and clean, and it covered each scar on her frame.

Be. Loved.

An ache in Kimly's arm woke her, and she looked down and saw the child was lying on top of her forearm with her head resting in Kimly's lap. Without waking her, Kimly pulled her arm out from under the little girl's body, and opened and closed her hand to chase away the erupting pins and needles. She looked down at the little girl, enveloped in Dak's sweatshirt, and nuzzled up against her. The child's hands barely peeked out of the thick sleeves. Kimly traced their path and saw the girl's frail fingers were intertwined and wrapped around the long strands of Kimly's hair.

Looking out across the muddy terrain at her feet, she noticed that the rain wasn't falling between the dense trees anymore, and outside the protective shelter, the storm was beginning to ease. Bits of sky poked through breaking clouds. The edge of the tree line was dark gray. Soon it would fade into darkness. The sky would blend into the trees, and darkness would surround them. There was no way Kimly was going to be able to navigate in the night, especially not knowing which country she was in. She was without passport, and she had no idea what would happen to this little child in her lap. How could she protect someone with whom she couldn't communicate? She had to get this little girl to the Navarro's. It was the only way. She would have to stay in the trees until morning.

Her heart melted as she thought how close this child had come to suffering at the hands of these monsters. She remembered the night she had awoken to SuSuk on top of her in her hotel room, and she wondered how frightening something like that would be for a child. *Something like that*...the politeness of her own inner dialogue shamed her. What did she think sex trafficking meant? Rape was rape. Kimly wondered if she had become so consumed with getting her story that she forgot about the children who would still be living in this darkness after she left the country. "Lord, protect her. Thank you for saving her, but protect her," eyes closed Kimly whispered. "I'm so sorry I dragged her into this."

It's not about you.

Kimly's eyes shot open, and she looked around. It's not about me? Have I made this about me? Did I think it was about me?

She looked down at the little girl in her lap wearing Dak's sweatshirt. She could hear Dak's voice, *"This is the Kimly Denim show. I do what I want!"*

Her heart pounded hard in her chest. She lifted her hand and held it horizontally in front of her face. Her fingers bounced around in front of her eyes. She drew them into her palm and made a fist. It was always about me! She remembered one of the many arguments she had with her husband when she pleaded her cause for making the trip, "I want to do something worthwhile!" *I did! I did want that!* She thought about the conversations she had with Dak, "I have to do something significant..."

Every thought was about her. It was all about her. Kimly looked down at the child in her lap. In her quest to do something significant with her life, Kimly had devalued the lives of those she was aiming to protect. If she was attempting to save them because they needed saving, then it would have been beautiful. But, her attempts to change their situation were tied to her own achievements; Kimly was furthering a terrible mindset: she was furthering a belief that a person's significance is related to their accomplishments. Kimly moved the hair from the girl's face and looked at her delicate features. She wondered: *What if I hadn't been able to save you? What if I hadn't been able to stop them from taking you?* It occurred to Kimly that this child could have spent her whole life locked in a room and died without ever having been more than a sex slave. *Would living as a slave make her life less significant than mine? And, if I never accomplish anything— never create a change in the world—does my life have less meaning?*

Kimly leaned her head back against the tree and allowed tears to roll down her cheeks. The rain had subsided but there was still plenty of moisture in the air, making her entire face damp. When Kimly raised her hand to her face to wipe away her tears the child shifted in her lap. Looking down at the little body resting against her own, she thought of the mother she had failed to be to her sons. *How long have I blamed them for interrupting my life?* The blue stick which had proclaimed her pregnancy flashed through her mind. Had she ever rejoiced for what she had been given?

Something in her stomach moved, and Kimly felt sick. Between the regret, the voices in her head, and the dreams when she closed her eyes, she was in for a long night. She took in a deep breath and whispered, "Please forgive me, and please be gentle with me."

34

At sunrise, Kimly could tell there had been a significant change in the weather. The ground was no longer saturated with water. She shifted the little girl off her lap, and the child rolled her head around and watched as Kimly tried to work out the kinks in her legs and her back.

Kimly moved onto her hands and knees and began stretching before trying to stand. The child sat up and watched Kimly.

"I'm not as young as I used to be," she said to the little girl.

The child stared at her but gave no response. Finally, Kimly stood and with tender steps, she walked down the slight hill toward the tree line. Kimly's deliberate moves were a mixture of aching joints and cautiousness.

The road had only two or three cars on it, and looking across the highway, Kimly could see the river's water had calmed, but only slightly. As Kimly lifted her gaze from the river's edge, her heart leaped; it was the most hopeful sight she had ever seen. She turned to run up the small incline to get the little girl only to find that the child had followed her down to the edge of the tree line. Kimly almost knocked her over, so she leaned down and caught her in her arms.

"Sweetie! Do you see that?" she put one hand on the girl's shoulder and pointed to the river with the other, "Those boats? They are for us! We're saved!"

They varied in size, and they moved at different speeds, but the water was alive with boats. Kimly noticed that a couple of the larger boats had official seals, and some were as simple as the ones she had seen in the Tai Lue village. The boats were an assortment of colors; a river rainbow.

Grabbing the child's hand, Kimly rushed down the forest embankment toward the highway. They would need to cross the highway and climb over a short concrete barrier between the busy road and the flowing river. The little girl stayed by Kimly's side as they waited for cars to pass. When Kimly began to lead them to the other side of the road, the child stayed in step with her.

The railing on the highway was a three-foot concrete block, and Kimly lifted the child up and sat her on the edge. She moved next to her and pushed herself up on top of the barrier. But, she had no sooner adjusted herself up on the concrete barrier, when the little girl had jumped down and was running back towards the highway.

Just below Kimly was the embankment leading down to the edge of the river, on it was the barrage of boats that could take them to safety. But, the little girl was now running away from the water and across the highway. She was running back to the trees.

"What the...?" Kimly turned, jumped down, and raced after the child. Reaching the highway, the little girl never stopped. Her tiny feet shuffled across the pavement, and Kimly could hear tires screeching and the sound of her own voice yelling, "No!"

The child made it across both lanes of the highway and was heading up into the trees when Kimly was just stepping out onto the pavement. "I'm sorry...I'm sorry," she rushed passed a car that was now stopped in the middle of the road.

Running up the slight incline, Kimly's heart raced. She reached the place where the two had slept, and the child was sitting under the tree. The child looked up at Kimly, eyes wide. Her arms were wrapped around her legs.

"Sweetie..." Kimly whispered, breathless. Kimly squatted down so her eyes were even with the child's own. The two sets of eyes locked in on one another. One set was a youthful well of pain and suffering, and the other, for the first time in a long time, was beginning to see. The two stared at one another until Kimly's labored breathing returned to normal.

Kimly finally shifted her weight and sat on the ground. There was no way she could leave this child in the trees, but there was no way to communicate with her either. The little girl stood and walked over to where Kimly had left the gray duct tape. In her tender arms, the child gathered the pieces and brought them over to Kimly, dropping them in her lap. Kimly looked down at the tape, of which dirt and leaves now adhered. The little girl then pulled the sweatshirt over her head, lifted it off herself and dropped the garment to the ground. The child stared at Kimly.

"I don't understand..." Kimly was desperate, shaking her head.

The little girl lay down on the ground in front of Kimly and placed her arms by her side. Kimly moved her gaze up the small frame of the child, until it landed on the girl's face. The youthful wells of pain and suffering were locked on the overhead branches and wet with tears.

The two strangers sat this way for more than a few minutes.

A line of tears ran down either side of the little girl's face. Finally, the little girl reached over and took a piece of the dirty, barely sticky tape and tried to place it on her arms, as if to bind herself.

Kimly shook her head, "No...No, sweetie. No one is going to tie you up. Never again," she reached down and gathered the child into her arms. Kimly's eyes welled with tears, and she fought to breathe through the lump in her throat.

Kimly pulled the child away and looked down into her eyes, "Is that what you are afraid of?" Kimly stared at her and waited for the child to answer as if she could. Kimly crumpled the piece of duct tape into a small ball and mumbled, "No. No more tape."

She held the duct tape ball between two fingers and showed it to the girl, and then she threw the ball as hard as she could away from them and into the trees.

"Look, it's gone," she said.

The ball of tape hit a banana tree branch and bounced back towards the two.

"Okay...well, that didn't go very far. But, it's gone. I promise." Kimly said as she pointed at the tape ball.

The child sat up and looked at Kimly's ball, and then she turned so her legs were beneath her and she was up on her knees. She held Kimly's eyes and raised her arm in front of her and pointed down the slope of the hill towards the river, toward the turbulent waters.

Kimly looked over her shoulder and down the slope at the river, "Is that what you are afraid of? The river?"

The girl didn't answer. She just lowered her arm and stared up at

Kimly.

"Oh, baby girl...of course. You're right, that water is terrifying. You probably can't swim, can you?" Kimly shifted and moved closer to the girl. "Listen, you probably don't understand a word I am saying, but trust me...the water isn't what we should fear. I mean, I understand, the water looks like it's the enemy, but it isn't. Staying here, hiding beneath the trees, this is what we should fear. If we want to be saved, we have to go where the water rages."

As the two sat in the dirt, Kimly pulled the little girl close and began to pray, "Am I like her, God? Have I been hiding in the trees?"

Kimly began to thank God for how he had been protecting them this far. She thanked God for His plan. The plan she couldn't see and didn't fully understand. She pulled the little girl back and kissed her gently on her forehead. Kimly took in a deep breath and sat the girl in the dirt.

"Can you wait here?" Kimly asked and she pulled herself to her feet. "I'm just going to go look at the water."

Kimly walked down the incline and stopped at the edge of the tree line. The boats were moving, and it looked like they were heading closer to where she was. Some of the boats were concentrated around one area, and she could see the crane attached to one was being lowered into the water. The Jeep. They must have located Dak's Jeep. She was conflicted and frustrated. Help was within her view, but she couldn't get to it. Kimly turned and looked through the trees towards the little girl. But the girl wasn't there.

Spinning around Kimly almost knocked over the child, who now stood right beside her. Kimly tilted her head to the side and said, "Well, hey..." she looked out at the highway and then back at the child. "Do you want to try this again?" Kimly asked. The child gave Kimly no response. Kimly was turned and looking at the cars coming down the highway when she felt the child place her tiny hand inside her own. Kimly looked down at the fingers peeking around the edge of her hand. The two hands reminded her of her dream the night before. Moving her eyes from the hands to the face of the girl, Kimly saw trusting eyes watching her.

They crossed the highway and approached the barrier. Kimly needed to climb over the three-foot wall without letting go of the child. She had crossed the highway safely once, but there was no guarantee the child would be that fortunate on a second attempt.

Kimly lifted the child and held her tightly as she approached the concrete blockade. She felt the child's arms tighten around her neck. The child's pounding heart beat through her tiny chest and against Kimly's own. Pushing herself up with one arm, Kimly lifted her leg up on the block and pulled herself and the child up and over. They fell to the other side, and Kimly was certain the girl was going to release her neck and run.

Kimly sat up and tried to pull the child away so she might see her face, but the child had a grip on Kimly's neck. Kimly pushed them both up and started down the embankment toward the river. With each step Kimly took closer to the water, the little girl's grip got tighter and her heartbeat more rapid.

"Please don't be afraid...I'm not going to hurt you," Kimly whispered.

Having to hold the child so tightly was going to make it difficult to get the attention of the people out on the water. Kimly's feet started to slide out from under her. She was losing her balance, and she was certain she was going to fall face first down the embankment and into the water. The gravel dug into her toes and sharp rocks pressed against the sole of her feet. Kimly tried to keep her knees from locking to avoid sliding.

Once they were on more level ground, Kimly tried again to wedge the child's hands from her neck. It was an unsuccessful attempt. The child was paralyzed with fear. When Kimly's feet touched the river, the cool water caressed her toes. She stood and let them soak for a moment. She decided it would be easier to get the attention of the boats if she were closer to where they were searching. Walking against the current, with the girl in her arms, Kimly moved upstream. The rocks beneath them were slippery and each step was slow and deliberate.

The man in the long tail boat looked familiar to Kimly. He wasn't. In fact, she had never met him or anyone else from his tribe or village. His name was Yuda and he had come downstream from Myanmar when he heard of commotion on the river. Yuda's long tail boat was weathered and worn; the wood was discolored with deep gashes in the sides. Three ribbons were tied to the front of the small vessel. Yellow, green and red: The colors of the Burmese flag. Over the top of the center section of the boat, there was a bright red canopy, a foot above them and pulled tautly. At the back of the boat, the elderly man controlled a small motor. Kimly waved one arm and yelled for help. She didn't know if anyone could hear her over the churning water, and she didn't know if she was increasing fear in the child. But, when she saw the elderly man turning the boat in her direction, Kimly began to jump up and down on the shoreline.

Within minutes, Yuda pulled up to the shore and turned off the motor on the back of the boat. Kimly waded out in the water and was now wet up to her waist. Kimly thanked the man over and over, to which he merely nodded and smiled. When Kimly tried to lower the child into the boat she was unable to pry the girl's arms from her neck. The old man in the boat just smiled at the two of them, as if he saw this kind of thing every day. Kimly tried lifting one leg over the edge of the boat, certain the entire boat was going to flip, but the old man simply moved his oar and the boat stayed right. She fell on top of the child and into the boat. Yuda moved to the back of the boat and started the motor. Soon, they were heading into the middle of the confusion on the water.

35

The gentleman driving the boat wore a green fisherman's hat with a yellow band. His cotton pants stopped midway down his calf, and his wearied looking feet wore a pair of exhausted sandals. Kimly felt the need to keep thanking him, and each time she did, Yuda would just nod and smile. She looked across the boat at the man who had just rescued her. Revelations from the night before splashed around like river water. She was fairly certain this fisherman didn't wake this morning with hopes of doing "something significant" with his life. And yet, today and for the rest of her life, Kimly would remember how he responded to her need.

Yuda steered his tiny vessel past a large fishing boat, where poor men pulled in empty nets. The long tail didn't move with fanciful speed, but the ride was smooth. The sun was coming out from behind tired clouds, and its light danced on the water. Kimly rubbed her palm on the back of the little girl who sat in her lap. The child's arms were still tight around Kimly's neck, and her legs were wrapped equally tight around her waist. Kimly placed her hand on the girl's face and rubbed her small cheek which was now wet with mist. The little girl's clothing was saturated with the water, and her hair was as wet as a mop. Kimly reached around to pull her own hair away from her neck when she noticed the little girl had once again wrapped her tiny fingers into Kimly's locks. "You like my hair, do you?" Kimly tilted her head down and spoke to the child.

Kimly turned her head and saw the gray boat they were approaching. It was stopped fairly close to the large boat with the crane attachment. Yuda steered the long tail so as they were on the other side of the gray metal boat. It was an official looking ship, small but authoritative. Kimly wondered if it was the Border Patrol. Fear battled relief. Kimly had no passport. And she didn't want them to take the child. She took a deep breath and prayed for God's protection over the little girl. Instinctively, she pulled her hands through the girl's long dark hair and kissed her gently on her forehead.

On the opposite side of the Mekong River Patrol boat, Dak stood looking over at the crane. The divers had attached the crane to his Jeep, and the plan was to bring it up and tow it to the shoreline on the Thailand side of the river. Authorities assumed they would have

270

to tow it downstream to the fishing town outside of Chiang Rai. They would be able to get it out of the water in a place where the embankment wasn't nearly as steep. Dak wasn't planning on following the Jeep to watch them remove it from the river; he was more consumed with continuing the search for Kimly. Until her body was found, she was alive. It was the only way he would allow himself to think.

Dak heard the men behind him shuffling, and one of the crew was talking excitedly to an old fisherman in a long tail boat. The old man had brought his boat up to the River Patrol vessel asking questions. It had been happening all day yesterday and again this morning. The village people saw the commotion and came out to see what was happening. At first Dak had been hopeful one of the fishermen would have news of something they saw or of someone who had showed up in their village. But, now Dak was certain the answers would come much further downstream.

The conversation behind him began to draw in the other crew members, and Dak noticed a few of them moved to the port side of the craft. Soon he stood alone watching the crane operators at work below. Then one of the crew members came to his side, "Mr. Kesapan, sir." Dak tilted his head in the direction of the young crewman and waited for him to continue. The crewman's dark eyes merely shifted to the right. Dak turned his head and followed the crewman's eyes.

Standing on either side of her was a crewman, each holding one of her arms, and a child was latched to the front of her. He watched as the most beautiful brunette he had ever laid eyes on boarded the vessel. Kimly was slightly off balance, and she held tight to the hand of one of the sailors while she regained her footing. Then she put her arm back around the child. She raised her head and looked around the boat to get her bearings.

Dak stood completely still. His eyes were locked on her face. Kimly looked around, insecure in her surroundings. Then her eyes landed on him. Kimly's eyes met Dak's and she swallowed hard and began to move around the obstacles which stood between them. He responded and moved in the same direction.

Practically crushing the child between them, Dak and Kimly embraced. Laughter and tears enveloped them. "You're okay!" Dak took Kimly's face in both hands. "I saw you go under, but you're okay!"

Kimly couldn't speak; her voice was trapped in her chest, and she didn't know how to release it. She nodded, looked at the child, and nodded again.

Dak pulled Kimly in tight and let out a deep sigh, "I love you, Kimly," he said, and he tightened his arms around her and the child.

"I know," Kimly buried her head into Dak's chest, "I love you, back."

Kimly allowed herself to be swallowed in Dak's embrace. These arms had become familiar; his touch was safe. Resting her head on his chest, Kimly closed her eyes and breathed him in. Dak ran his hand through her matted hair, carefully pulling it away from her face. His heart was pounding wildly. She looked through the dark locks falling across her face and into his familiar gray eyes, "Dak, it's time. It's time for me to go home."

Dak gently moved a strand of hair away from Kimly's forehead, stared into her brown eyes and replied, "I know."

THE END

EPILOGUE

NOI
ขนาด เล็ก

The water in the pond doesn't frighten me. Some days I will put my feet in and let the orange fish nibble on them. The tiny fish tickle my feet, and now I know they will not hurt me. Sometimes their nibbles make laughter.

After I was saved from the water, I came to live in this house. There is no Darkness here. I sleep inside a big house on a table bed that is just my size. There is no metal bar locking me in. The windows are not painted. I am allowed to go into all the rooms, and I am allowed to go outside.

On the outside of the house, there is a wall around the house to keep me safe. When I first came here, I was very frightened. But then one day, the lady with yellow hair and sky colored eyes came into my room with a woman who spoke my words. She talked to me for many hours and stayed for the whole day.

Each day the woman returned. I told her all of the things I had seen. She listened. Some of the things I told her made her cry. I asked her if she knew my Momma. She did not. After the woman had been coming to see me for many days, she asked if I wanted to stay in the big house with the table bed just my size and the wall that protects me. I told her I did.

For many days we began to talk in new words. She taught me the words the lady with sky eyes understood. One day, I even surprised myself when I asked for flavored ice. I did not know I had learned those words, but one day they began to walk off my tongue. The lady with sky eyes gave me flavored ice on a stick. It was bright red, and I loved it. I didn't let it burn my tongue.

Now, I can talk to the people who live in the house with the wall and ask them many questions. The lady who speaks my words still comes to visit, but I do not need to use my old words as much anymore. My tongue can ask most every question living in my head. And I can ask for different kinds of food to eat.

Today, we are eating our lunch outside at the table by the fish. The sun is shining bright, and the clouds are moving slowly overhead. I am sitting with Bri, and she is telling me a story about a man who was swallowed by a fish. I do not know this man, but I feel bad for him.

My mind is making questions. I am waiting for her to give me answers, when across the yard the big metal gate begins to roll. I look over and watch a motorcar drive into the yard. A cloud colored car drives through the gate. I have not ever seen this motorcar.

Walking behind the motorcar, coming through the place where the gate once was, is a lady. She is tall, and she has hair like my own. She is wearing long white pants and a white shirt. She looks like an angel from the clouds. My heart begins to beat faster than it was before I saw her. I stop chewing my food. She stops and stands looking at me from across the grass. I do not want to stop looking at her, because I do not want her to disappear. She turns her head and looks at the man who is getting out of the small white motorcar. Then two boys also climb out of the car. The man walks across the pavement and takes her hand. They are walking across the grass, coming my way. As they get closer I see that the two boys have matching faces—but they are not little like Auntie's babies.

I get up from the table and start to run. I do not run away. I am running to the woman. She kneels down and opens her arms. She is waiting for me. I run into her arms, and she catches me, but falls backwards onto the grass, "Whoa, sweetie!"

I bury my head into her chest, and she holds me there. She is laughing, "Did she know I was coming?" she is looking over my head.

"Well let's just say," Bri answers "that she's been ready for you to get here every day."

"Noi," she pulls me away from her chest, "I guess you didn't forget me. Well, this is my husband, Kyle. And these are my boys, Dylan and Jacob."

I pull my head away slightly and look up at the man with big shoulders. He smiles and stares down at me. His thick hair is curling up around his ears, and his eyes look kind. I look away. I look down at the grass. I am sitting on the grass with the lady I love.

She places her hand under my chin, and she raises my head. My eyes look in hers. "Noi, I know Bri told you I was coming," she is nodding her head while she talks. "I want you to come live with me. I want to take you with me to another place. Do you still want to do that?"

My heart pounds are fast and hard, and I want to answer her. I want to use her words. I am afraid I will say it wrong. I look down at the grass.

"How has she been doing?" the lady's voice sounds sad. I have made her sad.

"She's been good," Bri answers her. I do not want Bri to answer her. I want to answer her, but I am afraid.

"Has she seen Dak, I mean did he..." her voice cracks.

"Dak came and said goodbye to her before he and Aaron left."

"Oh..." the lady is looking down at me, "so, Dak's not here in Mai Sai?"

"No. Dak and Aaron flew out last week. They are meeting with a grant writer in San Francisco. Dak's work with the Emancipation Troop has been unbelievable. He has certainly found his calling."

The lady is running her hand through my hair; and I can feel her hand shaking.

Bri is still talking, "It was his vision to turn the Emancipation Troop into a Non-profit, and the doors that have opened under his leadership have been astounding."

The woman's dark hair falls beyond her shoulders and her eyes are reflecting my own. Our brown eyes are connected. I see a small tear in the corner of her eye. I do not want the lady to be sad. I do not want her to leave again. I pull my hand up and wrap her hair around my wrist, gently I let it drop.

My heart is pounding because I don't want to use the wrong words. I take a deep breath, and then I tell her, "I am your family. You are my family. That is forever."

The lady with long dark hair and eyes like my own pulls me close and holds me tight. This is a good memory.

Made in the USA
San Bernardino, CA
06 January 2019